To Dream of Shadows

Inspired by a Heartbreaking True Story

Steve N Lee

Blue Zoo
England

Published by Blue Zoo, Yorkshire, England.

For those who fell. And those who rose.

Berlin, 1944

"It all started when I lost my hand." Franz Kloser leaned forward on the blue-and-white damask sofa and held up his left arm. Emerging from the sleeve of his SS uniform, a stainless-steel prosthetic hook glistened in the light shafting through the enormous windows as spring embraced Berlin.

"That must've been nasty." His mustachioed host winced in the armchair to Kloser's left, then offered a white porcelain plate from the chunky coffee table. "Cake?"

Kloser smiled. "I really shouldn't." He patted his ample stomach, and his smile broadened as he once more saw the reason for his visit: his Iron Cross gleamed on his chest. Was this a dream? He glanced around the immense room, awestruck at the grandiosity of its thirty-foot-high dark red marble walls and coffered rosewood ceiling.

A dream. It had to be.

"Treat yourself." His host winked and held the chocolate cake nearer. "You only live once."

Kloser chuckled and took a slice. "It's a good thing or we'd have a heck of a lot more work to do, wouldn't we?"

"Oh, but wouldn't that make our success doubly satisfying." He leaned back in his chair, a globe as tall as a man over his left shoulder.

His host was smaller than Kloser had imagined. And his voice... gone was the rallying vivacity for which his public speaking was renowned, replaced by a soft, almost gentle tone, which belied the stature of this giant of a man. Kloser had expected to find a nature as ferocious as the man's intellect, yet the man was proving not just cordial but positively delightful.

The man sipped tea from a porcelain cup and flicked his gaze to Kloser's hook. "I hope the scoundrel responsible paid an appropriate price."

"And then some," said Kloser. "The Box."

"The Box?" His brow knitted.

Excitement bubbled in Kloser's chest. Members of his rank rarely enjoyed such an audience, so he'd thought the opportunity to tell his tale was a wish come true. But to have the chance to display his expertise as well? If he impressed now, who knew where it might lead?

Kloser said, "The Box is a punishment I designed myself, reserved for only the most deserving of prisoners. Some personnel believe it inhumane, but I've always found it immensely satisfying."

"Intriguing." His host nodded. "Is it something we could roll out across all our camps?"

"I don't see why not."

"Excellent. I'll have your details forwarded to Heinrich for him to explore the possibilities with you."

Heinrich? The Reichsführer? Was there to be no end to the surprises today?

"It would be my pleasure," said Kloser.

Beaming, he surveyed the room again to soak up the experience to the fullest. Above the mighty fireplace, a portrait of Bismarck, the great statesman responsible for unifying Germany, gazed down. Who could have imagined that barely seventy years later, Germany was set to "unify" the world?

His host said, "Now, I've read your report, which is absolutely fascinating, but"— he arched an eyebrow —"I'd love to hear all the details you felt it improper to include."

A smirk slithered across Kloser's face. "Like I said, it all started when I lost my hand and—" He frowned. "Come to think of it, it probably started earlier. Much earlier."

His host gestured for Kloser to start over.

"Picture a transport barreling through the Polish countryside. It's crammed with filthy Jews, but there's one in particular — a scheming slut barely old enough to be called a woman." Kloser drew a breath. Slut? Maybe that language was a little too colorful for such illustrious company. He flicked his gaze to his host.

The man leaned forward, a glint in his eyes like a young boy eager to hear of the misadventures of his older brother. "Go on."

1

Inge Zaleska wiped the sweat off her face on the short sleeve of her pink-and-white striped dress. She panted, even though she was doing nothing but sitting on her suitcase with her back against the side of the cattle car. Cursing under her breath, she glared at the tiny window crisscrossed with barbed wire high in the far left corner. The thing was worse than useless with eighty-six people crammed in the car under the baking sun.

She raked her fingers through her long, greasy black hair, pulling the straggly mess away from her face. Would it ever be silky soft again?

Grimacing, she struggled to flex her left shoulder, Mrs. Karkowski having slumped against it asleep again. The unbearable stuffiness saw many of the older travelers constantly dozing. Inge circled her shoulder, fighting to relieve the ache without disturbing her friend's slumber. The pain didn't go.

"I'm sorry, Mrs. Karkowski, but I have to move." Inge eased Mrs. Karkowski's head up, but instead of the old lady waking and greeting Inge with a wrinkled smile, clouded eyes stared like frozen millponds. Inge gasped and lurched away, bumping Mama on her other side.

Mrs. Karkowski crumpled over her knees.

Mama pulled Inge closer and shielded Inge's younger sister. "Don't look, Agata."

Agata buried her face in Mama's shoulder.

Robert, Inge's stocky older brother, and a man in a blue shirt picked up the body.

Robert shouted, "Dead coming through."

The sea of people parted, squashing themselves together just enough to create a narrow aisle to the far right corner. The two men shuffled along it.

Dead coming through. What a horrible and degrading send-off for a dignified woman. The only thing worse was how such a horrendous statement had become so commonplace that it was now more likely to irritate people at the inconvenience of having to move than to bring tears to their eyes.

In the corner, the men dumped the old lady on top of the other six bodies piled there.

Glassy-eyed, Agata said, "Why are they doing this, Mama?"

Mama stroked Agata's short brown hair. "Don't wonder about the bad things that are happening, sweetheart. Wonder about all the good things we'll have when we're resettled."

"But I don't want to be resettled. I want our old home, and my old school, and my old friends."

Inge clasped Agata's hand. "It'll be fun, Aga. That nasty bully Vera Bosakova won't be in your class anymore, you won't have math with that horrible Mr. Sliz, and ice cream is half the price in the new place, isn't it, Mama?"

"That's what I heard." Mama stroked Agata's hair again and smiled at Inge. But her eyes didn't smile. Inge could tell she was fighting to make it look genuine — fighting with all her might because of her love for her family — but such sadness lay in her eyes. Sadness Inge had never seen before. As if someone had said the sun was never going to shine again, so they'd spend the rest of their lives in darkness.

Someone shouted from the far side of the car, "Toilet bucket!"

A moment later, a bespectacled man passed a metal bucket to Mama, who passed it to Inge. The contents sloshed around and the stench clogged her nostrils. Holding the bucket at arm's length, Inge screwed up her face and quickly passed it to the chubby man who'd spread into Mrs. Karkowski's space.

The bucket reached a middle-aged woman who wept as she squatted over it, screened by a bald man and a boy encircling her with their jackets.

Three days ago, Inge had cried too when she'd had to relieve herself surrounded by so many strangers. Now, despite the revulsion and embarrassment, she was almost thankful for the bucket — its stink helped mask the one coming from the corner of the dead.

Robert crouched and nodded over his shoulder. "Someone saw a road sign through one of the cracks and thinks they recognized the name — a town in Latvia."

"Latvia?" asked Mama. "Where the devil are they resettling us?"

"I don't want to go to Latvia." Agata clutched Mama.

Inge twisted and peered through the gouge between two planks in the side of the car, but only trees whipped past.

When they'd boarded, they'd thought they were unlucky to be stuck against the side. However, no one in the middle could even sit with their legs outstretched let alone lie down, so having the wall to lean against meant their spot was actually prime real estate.

Inge patted her suitcase. "Do you want to swap to have the backrest for a while?"

Robert shook his head. "Maybe later, thanks."

He gestured to his right. Mr. Klein, the rotund banker, squeezed by the Kovar family, water bucket in one hand, metal cup in the other. Having looked after many of the townsfolk's money, he'd been judged most trustworthy to ensure everybody got their share of the water.

"Thank heaven," said Inge.

Klein smiled at Inge and her family. "And how are the Zaleskas doing this fine afternoon?"

Mama wiped her brow. "All the better for seeing you and your bucket, Mr. Klein."

He dipped the cup in the water. "Who's first?"

Mama nudged Agata, so the girl reached for the cup.

Klein tipped water back into the bucket until the cup was one-quarter full – the ration per head – then handed it over.

Agata downed the liquid in one go.

Mama stroked the girl's head. "Better?"

Agata nodded.

"And what do you say to Mr. Klein?"

Agata handed the cup back. "Thank you, Mr. Klein."

"It's my pleasure, Agata." He measured more water and held the cup out.

"Inge," said Mama.

Inge drank. In their baking car, the water was warm, yet sucking on an icicle couldn't have been more refreshing. She tipped the cup over for the last few drops to drip onto her tongue.

Robert drank next. Finally, Klein offered Mama her ration. She shook her head and nudged Agata, who reached for it.

Inge grabbed Agata's hand. "Mama, you need to drink."

"I'm fine, Inge," said Mama. "Your sister needs it more than I do."

"That's what you said last time."

"And it's as true now as it was then."

Inge pushed the cup toward Mama. "Mama, you weren't well before we got on this horrible train. You have to drink."

Mama glared at her. Usually, a glare was enough to see Inge abide by Mama's decision, but this wasn't about doing the dishes or cleaning their bedroom. This was about life and death.

Inge gulped and looked at her brother. "Robert, tell her."

Robert rubbed his mouth, his gaze flashing from Inge to Mama.

Inge glowered. "Robert!"

He winced. "Inge's right, Mama."

Mama reached for the cup. "I'm sorry for all this fuss, Mr. Klein."

"No apology necessary, Mrs. Zaleska. It's a tough time for us all."

Mama sipped the water, then scowled at Inge. "Once we're off this accursed train, we're going to talk about this, young lady."

Inge would normally have quaked at the thought, but this time, she was right. And being right was more important than avoiding Mama's wrath — better to have an angry mother than a dead one.

Mama took another sip, then handed the cup to Agata. "Finish it, Agata."

Mama stared at Inge, as if daring her to say something. Agata drank and handed the cup back, and Klein moved onto the next people.

Inge let her head fall against the side of the car and closed her eyes. It was the first time she'd openly disobeyed her mother in public and won. An uneasy feeling roiling in her gut told her it wasn't going to be the last battle she'd have to fight because of this "resettlement."

She sighed. Okay, so the journey was horrendous, but hadn't she always dreamed of traveling? Wasn't that why she'd studied languages so diligently? And now, here she was traveling. Of course, she'd pictured a luxury passenger carriage, not a cattle car, but travel was travel. Maybe this "resettlement" would be a good thing. A golden opportunity to start fresh.

Yes, that was it. She smirked. This wasn't the end of her life — the way Agata imagined — but the start of it. A life filled with wonder and adventure.

So where was this adventure going to take her?

2

Rudi meandered down the cobblestone road, the blackout curtains of the small houses leaving the street illuminated solely by the moon. At his side, his dog, Bruno, gazed up, attention flicking between Rudi's eyes and the stick he carried.

A horse and cart clip-clopped by. The driver nodded, plumes of smoke billowing from his pipe. Rudi nodded back.

The traffic past, Rudi hurled the stick. Bruno shot after it. A moment later, the German shepherd trotted back and dropped the stick at Rudi's feet.

Again, Rudi flung it and Bruno tore away. But Rudi winced as the stick disappeared into a roadside bush.

Bruno nuzzled through the foliage for his prize as Rudi caught up.

He patted Bruno's shoulder. "Sorry, boy, my mistake."

Rudi scratched the flash of golden brown on Bruno's chest, the only part of the dog not black, and Bruno licked Rudi's hand.

Grabbing a bigger stick lying in the grass, Rudi said, "Let's try again, huh?"

He flung it and Bruno raced away.

The wind gusting, Rudi buttoned his tunic for the two-mile walk home. They could have stayed at the local bar to return later with the others in the truck, but Rudi wasn't a drinker, wasn't a womanizer, and wasn't one for war stories, so beer after a hard week was more a duty than an enjoyment.

He smiled as Bruno returned with his prize. This? Just him and his dog? He could almost imagine the war was a world away. This felt normal. Like home. Like... living.

"Good boy."

Bruno wagged his tail and dropped the stick.

Where the buildings petered out to flat, featureless countryside, Rudi shook the stick. "Last time, Bruno."

Ahead, the bridge over the river crawled away into the darkness. The last thing Rudi wanted was the wind casting his stick over the side and fearless Bruno diving after it. Rudi might not be as lucky as last time, and he couldn't risk Bruno being swept away and out to sea.

As Bruno bolted away once more, a distant squeal stopped Rudi dead.

Slowly turning his head, he strained to hear. It had sounded almost like...

A voice screamed. A young voice. A female voice.

Rudi spun to a dirt track running parallel to the riverside road that led to their excavation site. A shadowy barn loomed at the end.

"Bruno, side."

The dog dropped his stick and raced to Rudi's side, ears pricked, eyes scouring the darkness for a threat.

Squinting through the gloom, Rudi stalked along the track. Drenched in darkness, bushes rustled and trees groaned as the wind beat their weary bows. Rudi's heart hammered as the barn reared before him, black against the night sky. He swallowed hard and crept closer.

A muffled voice shrieked in Estonian, "No!"

A quieter voice said something Rudi didn't catch. A male voice.

The woman cried out as if she'd been hit.

A third voice laughed.

At the side of the barn, shadows moved as two large shapes scuffled with a smaller one on the ground.

Rudi clenched his fists. "Hey!"

A man cursed in Ukrainian. Rudi didn't understand much of the language, but he knew enough to grasp that the man was maligning Rudi's mother.

"Let her go." Rudi marched closer.

A tall man lurched toward Rudi, a blade glinting in the moonlight.

Rudi grabbed a spade leaning against the barn wall. At his side, Bruno snarled, baring his fangs.

The man stalked at Rudi, slashing his knife.

"Bruno"— the dog glanced up for his orders, and Rudi gestured to the man tussling with the woman on the ground —"decimate."

Bruno tore away.

The man with the knife sliced at Rudi's head. Rudi dodged and battered the knife so hard with the spade, it spun away into the night.

Rudi kicked the man in the side of the knee. His leg crunched inward.

The man wailed and crumpled onto all fours.

Beside the barn, Bruno locked his jaws around the other man's arm. The man shrieked and fought to yank free, but Bruno shook his head, savaging the limb.

Rudi glowered at Knife Man, who wore a Ukrainian uniform with a white armband identifying him as a member of the auxiliary police. Men like this were scum. They gave the uniform — any uniform — a bad name. Rudi slammed the spade into the man's head. Knife Man tumbled across the dirt and crashed into the barn. He lay motionless.

Crouching, Rudi checked the man's pockets and retrieved his identity papers, then looked to the remaining monster.

The man frantically pushed at Bruno, but the dog had latched on tight. Bruno growled, twisting and riving. The man screeched.

"Bruno, release."

The dog let go and sat back on his haunches, ears pricked for further instruction.

Cradling his bloody arm, the would-be rapist cursed and scrambled to get up, but Rudi kicked him in the side of the head. The man slumped sideways, unconscious. Rudi took his papers, too.

Finally, he turned to the woman. Except it wasn't a woman; it was a girl, maybe only twelve or thirteen. What kind of animal did that to a child?

Her arms crossed over her chest and her knees drawn up, she stared at him with eyes like saucers.

"Friend," he said in Estonian, patting his chest. "Friend."

Standing over her, he reached to help her up.

She shrank back and whimpered, gaze flicking from him to Bruno, then back again.

After witnessing such violence, the poor child had to be wondering if she'd been dragged out of the proverbial frying pan only to be thrown into the fire.

Rudi said, "Bruno, roll over."

Immediately, Bruno rolled across the ground and sprang back up.

"Roll over."

Bruno rolled again.

In broken Estonian, he said, "You say 'roll over.'"

He didn't know the Estonian for "roll over," but neither did Bruno, so it didn't matter.

The fear in her eyes turned to puzzlement.

"Please, say 'roll over.'"

Her voice weak and trembling, she said, "Roll over."

Bruno rolled over.

The tiniest of smiles flickered over her face.

Rudi patted Bruno. "Friend." He then patted his chest. "Friend."

When he held out his hand again, she clasped it, and he heaved her up.

He could find backup to have these monsters hauled away, but he had their papers, so he could deal with them at his leisure. Right now, the most important thing was the girl.

He pointed toward the town. "You live?"

She nodded.

"Good." He beckoned her.

She glanced around, as if debating whether to trust him or run. "Bruno..."

Ears pricked, Bruno looked to him.

He gestured to the girl. "Protect."

Bruno scampered to the girl and pressed against her right leg. She jumped, but when she saw Bruno was being friendly, she tentatively reached out. As if she were testing if a surface was hot, she touched Bruno's head, then yanked her hand away. When nothing bad happened, she touched him again.

She smiled and stroked his head.

Again, Rudi beckoned. "Come."

The three of them ambled back to the road, where Rudi gestured left, then right. She pointed back toward town.

Heading out of town, a motorbike and sidecar approached, headlight illuminating the road through a narrow slit. It stopped beside them. A squat dark-haired German officer got off, leaving one of the town's good-time girls in the sidecar.

Rudi stood while the rescued girl crouched and petted Bruno.

The officer clicked his heels together. "Herr Oberscharführer, can I be of assistance?"

14

"I've got it," said Rudi. "Go enjoy the rest of your night, Gruber."

Gruber eyed the girl up and down. "I could take her to the camp and throw her in the barracks?"

"And why would we do that?"

"She doesn't look very Aryan, so maybe we should play safe."

Rudi sighed. "Gruber, you don't look very Aryan. Should we throw you in the barracks to play safe?"

"Only trying to help, Herr Oberscharführer."

"Noted. Dismissed."

Gruber saluted. "Heil Hitler."

Rudi saluted. With the girl and Bruno, he continued past the darkened buildings.

Ahead, chatter and laughter oozed through the windows of one of the local bars. A balding man and small woman scurried nearby, the man holding a lantern, most of its light shrouded to leave only a small beam illuminating the immediate area.

The woman shouted, "Darja! Darja!"

"Mama!" The girl raced toward the couple, Bruno accompanying her.

They dashed over, arms wide.

"Bruno, hold." The last thing Rudi needed was for Bruno to attack what appeared to be her parents in order to protect the girl. Bruno pulled up and sat on his haunches, awaiting instruction.

The family met, the woman flinging her arms around the girl and the man cocooning both of them.

Rudi meandered closer with Bruno.

While her mother smothered her with kisses, the girl talked far too quickly for Rudi to keep up, but he could guess what she was saying. She confirmed this by pointing at him and Bruno.

Her parents gazed at him open-mouthed, then the father strode over, hands together as if in prayer. "Thank you, sir. Thank you so much for saving our little girl." His German was vastly better than Rudi's Estonian.

Rudi clicked his heels. "SS-Oberscharführer Heinz Rudolf Kruse, only too pleased to help." He hated the name Heinz, so he used it only when formality demanded.

"Kaspar Tilga." He held out his right hand, and he and Rudi shook. "Please, Herr Oberscharführer, you must let us to thank you. Do you like vodka?" Kaspar gestured to a gloomy side street near the bar.

"What fool doesn't?" Rudi hated the stuff but didn't want to cause offense when the whole of Eastern Europe seemed to believe it the nectar of the gods.

Kaspar chuckled. "Then have I treat for you. Come."

Rudi followed, Bruno at his side.

The man pointed at Bruno. "You have a wonderfully obedient dog."

"Thank you. I trained him myself."

"A working dog?"

"A spoiled dog."

Kaspar laughed. "I have working dogs. Sled dogs — very useful in our winters."

"I can imagine."

They walked down a short track beside a compound enclosed by wire mesh. Inside, a dozen huskies ran to the fence, barking and barking at Bruno. He remained at Rudi's side and didn't even glance at them.

Kaspar pointed to the girl. "Darja say men grab her when she came to feed the dogs earlier. Maybe they been in the bar." He shook his head. "Thank heaven you there." He clapped once. "Now, please to wait one moment."

He scurried into the house.

The girl's mother held out her hand to shake. "Thank you, Herr Oberscharführer. If ever you need anything — anything — you ask Kaspar."

He couldn't imagine ever wanting anything, but they seemed like good people. Rudi shook her hand. "I will. Thank you."

Darja stood before him, back straight, chin up, and with a thick accent said in German, "Thank you."

He smiled. "You're welcome."

She stroked Bruno one last time, then scampered inside as Kaspar returned.

He offered Rudi a liter bottle of clear fluid.

Rudi read the handwritten label. "Tilga '37."

"Tilga." Kaspar patted his chest, grinning. "Is I." He tapped the bottle. "This family recipe. You've never drunk vodka until you've drunk Tilga vodka. And this '37" — he kissed his fingertips with a smacking sound — "is best year ever. Is vintage."

"I look forward to tasting it."

16

Kaspar wagged a finger. "Never more than one glass if you have the work next day."

Rudi smiled. "Then it's good I have big glasses."

He chuckled. "No, no, no." He placed three fingers on the bottle. "This. No more. Or is bye-bye work."

Rudi laughed. "Okay."

"Now." Kaspar clapped again. "Anything I can for you do, anywhere, anytime, you ask and is done. Okay?"

"There's really no need, I—"

Kaspar gripped Rudi's arm and stared with an unnerving seriousness. "If not for you, maybe I now no longer father be. I owe you more than I can ever pay, so anything — anything — you ask."

"Thank you."

Kaspar nodded.

They said goodbye and Rudi left. Walking back toward the camp, he eyed the bottle. Three fingers? Three sips would be more than enough so he could honestly say he'd tasted it if he ever met Kaspar again, though that was unlikely. However, it would make a good trade. Especially if it was as strong as Kaspar claimed.

Nearing the bridge, he considered going down to the barn to see if the men were still there, but there was little point — he had their papers, so they couldn't escape their fate.

3

Inge covered her ears as the train rumbled on. The elderly couple to her left were praying — again — while a small boy nearby whimpered constantly. And somewhere in the middle of the crush of bodies, a baby wailed and wailed.

She groaned. She'd tried to sleep in an attempt to pass a few hours oblivious to the horrors, but ceaseless noise and discomfort made it impossible.

Her stomach growled. By the light of the odd candle here and there, she peered around the car, hoping for a distraction from the gnawing pain of three days without food. She found only more torment as a man in a suit nibbled a cooked sausage. Inge licked her lips. If only—

"Are we slowing down?" asked Robert.

"Not again." Inge hung her head. Wherever they were heading, the journey was taking forever, not least because the train kept stopping for hours for no discernible reason.

The Germans had allowed them one suitcase of up to 120 pounds, so she'd packed only her most precious things to ensure their new place felt like home — gilt-framed photographs, cosmetics, her favorite books, her best dresses and shoes, Grandma's silver candelabra... she'd only managed to cram in sixty-one pounds, but it was sixty-one pounds of "precious" things without which life would be unbearable.

Except it wasn't.

She'd packed sixty-one pounds of junk, when she could have packed sixty-one pounds of food and water. Maybe even a cushion. The Germans were so cruel not to warn them of the rigors of the journey.

The train clunked and clanged and finally stopped.

Inge prayed they'd arrived. She ached to breathe fresh air, to bathe until her skin puckered, to drink water until she couldn't drink any more. Such mundane things, yet now, they were more precious than everything she owned. Especially water. She pictured sitting in her kitchen and running her finger through the condensation on a glass of—

No, she couldn't think of drinking. It only made her longing worse. She strained to swallow, her mouth so dry.

Inge said, "Mama, do you think we're there?"

Mama kept her gaze fixed on the door. Occasionally when they stopped, the door opened and Germans bawled for someone to empty the toilet bucket and refill the bucket for drinking water.

But the door didn't budge. And instead of a bawling German voice, a whispered foreign accent drifted in. A man. "Water?"

Anxious gazes shot among the travelers.

The voice came louder. "Want water?"

A man with sidelocks craned to the barbed window high on the wall. "Yes, water! Please!"

People squashed closer to the window.

The voice said, "Gold? Money? Jewels?"

Sidelocks frowned. "Gold? *For water?*"

"Gold? Money? Jewels?" A hand snaked in between the haphazard web of barbed wire.

A chubby woman nudged Sidelocks. "Just pay him, Josef."

Josef dug into his jacket and passed something to the waiting hand.

"I need water, too." A woman handed a bracelet that glittered in the half-light to the man beside her.

The man dropped the jewelry into the grasping hand. "And some bread. Fruit. Anything. Just food."

The hand disappeared and then reappeared, empty. "Food, yes."

Other people contributed, then the hand once more disappeared. Everyone stared at the window, waiting for the hand to return and bestow them with life-giving bounty.

They waited. And waited.

"Hello?" called Josef. "Where's my water?"

And waited.

Inge stared at the crowd. She glanced at Robert and shook her head, then looked back at the waiting people.

An hour later, they were still waiting, still gazing at the window, still praying for someone to help them.

Were they incapable of seeing the truth? Or was denial the only way they could cope with the horror of their situation?

How gullible some people were. She studied those who'd let themselves be so easily conned to be sure that when the train reached its destination, her family stayed as far away as possible from such fools so as not to be dragged into easily avoidable misfortune.

Inge closed her eyes, resting her head against the wall.

"Toilet bucket!" shouted a man from the far side.

A woman near Inge heaved the pail to the boy beside her, the contents sloshing. Person by person, they passed it toward the man. Halfway across, a bald man lifted it with shaking arms and maneuvered it around his white-haired partner so she wouldn't have to touch the filthy thing, but he stumbled.

The bucket clattered onto someone's feet. The contents spewed out, splattering everyone nearby.

People shrieked and leaped away.

A teenage boy fell over an old woman struggling to push off the floor; a man pulling his wife away tripped over another who cursed; one woman backed into another, knocking her over her suitcase to smack into the wall. All around, people pushed, trampled, squashed, and crushed to get away from the revolting accident.

As the wave of panic surged toward Inge's family, she jumped in front of Mama and Agata, spun to face the wall, and pressed her palms into the wood to form a protective shield around them. Someone slammed into her back, buffeting her, but she held firm — her family was all she had left, so she had to protect them at all costs.

A beefy man fell against Inge and knocked her sideways. Her face crunched into the wood, and she cried out.

Robert scrambled up. He heaved the beefy man away to free his mother and sisters.

Everywhere, the chaos continued — shoving, screaming, vomiting, cursing.

And all the while, the baby wailed and wailed and wailed.

4

In the sun-dappled woodland, Rudi threw a stick for Bruno. The dog bolted away, then raced back, mission accomplished. Rudi once more hurled the impromptu toy, only for a machine-gun-like tapping on wood to draw his gaze. He scanned the upper trunks, flipping open the clasp on a leather pouch on his belt and removing his binoculars.

Adjusting the focus, he panned across the trees. Where was it? Where was it?

There!

He grinned. A black-and-white bird, eight inches long, hammered its beak into a trunk. A Eurasian three-toed woodpecker.

Rudi crept sideways for a better angle.

Was he going to be lucky?

Yes!

The bird had a yellow crown. A male.

Rudi admired the creature for a few minutes, then noted the location in a small black book, which he popped into the pouch with his binoculars. Tomorrow, they'd walk this way first so if the bird was around, he'd have more time to study it, maybe even sketch it.

After a few minutes, they emerged from the forest where Watchtower 03 rose from the corner of a double barbed wire fence. He nodded to the guard and strode on, giving the perimeter a wide berth — the inner fence electrified, he didn't want Bruno to smell something interesting and investigate only to have an accident. In this insane world, Bruno was the only thing that kept him tethered to reality.

From habit, Rudi scanned both sides of the fence for depressions that would suggest a tunnel. As usual, there were none. Not surprising. Statistically, women were less likely to dig tunnels than men.

In the compound, four squat wooden barracks sat in parallel: three empty at this time of day, one bursting around the clock. He couldn't remember the last time a single one of the infirmary's beds was empty. In fact, he couldn't recall the last time most sick prisoners weren't head-to-toe.

He passed Kommandant Kloser's house, surprised the chubby man and his equally chubby wife weren't having a hectic day sunning themselves on the veranda, then moseyed on by the guards' accommodation block, the only stone building in camp because it also housed the kitchen and secure storage areas.

At the front of the compound, Rudi entered the one-story administration block.

Three uniformed men at wooden desks saluted. Rudi reciprocated, then sat at his desk. All around, shelving and cabinets contained files and books, while a large portrait of the Führer hung over a fireplace.

He lifted the file of the previous day's roll call statistics to check and sign off on but set the document back down. Maybe it was best to get the more frustrating job out of the way, so it wasn't niggling him for the rest of the day. Rudi picked up his black phone and dialed the SS headquarters for camp fulfillment.

Within seconds of being transferred to the correct person in the correct department, Rudi wished he was back in the woods with Bruno. He drummed his fingers on the desk. "Please, check again. I submitted the paperwork myself."

How was it possible that the Reich had conquered almost the whole of Europe when ordering the most basic of supplies was such a trial?

On the other end, a man with a nasal whine said, "Early May?"

"The fifth. Do you want the requisition number?"

Nothing.

"Hello?"

No answer.

Nearby, Krebs, a baby-faced man, smirked.

Pointing to the receiver, Rudi rolled his eyes. "Hello?"

Nasal Whine said, "Ah, here we go. May fifth — six hundred pairs of winter boots and greatcoats."

"That's the one." He mouthed "Hallelujah" to Krebs.

"It's still awaiting authorization."

"Still?"

"Still."

22

"Is there any way to speed things up, please?"

"Why do you need winter coats in September? It was seventeen Celsius yesterday."

Rudi rolled his eyes. "It's warm now, yes, but autumn has a nasty habit of changing into winter, and before you know it, it's *minus* seventeen."

"Let me talk to my superior."

"Thank you."

Rudi doodled on a scrap of paper.

After a few moments, Nasal Whine said, "Hello?"

"I'm here."

"I'm sorry, we can't speed this up. As you'll appreciate, supplying the Front is our top priority, so you'll get it when you get it."

"Okay, thanks for your help." Rudi slung his pen down and hung up.

He'd figured ordering winter wear in spring would give plenty of time for delivery, and yet he was getting nowhere. Of course the Front needed priority, but if the millions of forced laborers serving the Reich didn't have the tools to maintain output, their front lines might be pushed farther and farther back. It was only logical – if the small cogs in the great Nazi war machine stopped turning, sooner or later, so would the big ones.

Krebs stood before Rudi's desk, holding a manila folder. "I don't know why you're bothering. If the prisoners freeze, they freeze. It's not like we're going to run out of them."

Between criminals, political detainees, religious prisoners, POWs, and a host of other undesirables, yes, they were unlikely to run out of forced labor.

"Productivity dips every time we get a new batch until they're trained up. Why not keep the good workers going for as long as we can?"

Krebs shrugged and handed Rudi the file. "The sickness statistics."

Rudi brandished the file. "Another reason – less illness, more work."

Krebs shrugged again. "Maybe. Anything else, Herr Oberscharführer?"

Rudi handed him the papers of the men who'd attacked the girl. "Find out where these Ukrainians are stationed and get me contact details for their commanding officer."

Undermanned in the Baltic States, the Reich had been forced to employ auxiliary police. Some were decent men looking to do a decent day's work, but too many were scoundrels looking for opportunities.

Krebs frowned. "Is there a problem?"

"A big one for those two. If I get my way, they'll be posted to the Eastern Front within the week."

5

Robert made his way back to Inge, stepping over people's legs, feet, hands, and bags as if negotiating an obstacle course. He crouched before Mama, who cradled a sleeping Agata, and gestured Inge closer, so she leaned in.

It had taken an hour for the chaos in the car to subside and for people to resign themselves to sitting amid urine and excrement. Now, the car was even noisier than before: children cried, the sick moaned, the dirty whined, and even more people took to praying.

Robert whispered, nodding toward the far window, "Next time we slow to go uphill, they're making a break for it."

Inge peered at the young men huddled near the window. "Those men?"

"And me."

Mama shook her head. "No."

He clasped Mama's hand. "Mama, if I get out, I can find somewhere safe for us all and then come and find you."

She gripped Robert's hand. "No, Robert. That was Papa's plan, and where is he now?"

Months ago, Papa had gone to Hungary to find a safe home for his family. They'd never heard from him again. Desperate, they'd run to Uncle Tomas's, but unfortunately, they hadn't run far enough.

"Mama, we have to do something." Robert gestured to the car. "Look at what they're doing to us. They're treating us worse than animals."

"It will be better where we're going, you'll see," said Mama. "Resettlement is going to be what we make of it. If we fail, we'll have only ourselves to blame."

Robert grimaced. "Mama, how can we believe in this 'resettlement' when they haven't even told us where or what it is?"

"So your solution is to break the law? What if the sentries see you?"

When boarding, Inge had seen sentry boxes at the back of some of the cars. Each extended a couple of feet above the roof to give the occupant a view of the full train.

"We have to do something." Robert heaved a breath and looked at Inge. "Inge?"

She didn't want to be disrespectful to her mother so soon again, but... she stared at the squalor. "Mama, maybe Robert has a—"

"You'll stop right there, my girl." Mama's eyes narrowed and she shook her head. "And as for you, Robert, you'll sit here and go nowhere near those troublemakers. That's my final word on the matter. Just thank your stars Papa isn't here to listen to this nonsense."

Robert kissed Mama on the cheek. "I love you, Mama. Just remember I'm doing this for all of us."

He turned for the men.

Mama yanked him back by his hand. "No! I've lost Papa. I won't lose you, too."

"I'm sorry, Mama." He ripped his hand free and, stepping over obstacles, headed toward the window.

In a loud whisper, Mama called, "Robert... Robert... Robert!"

He didn't look back.

Mama's chin quivered.

Inge took her hand. "It'll be okay, Mama. Robert's not stupid, so if it looks too dangerous, he won't risk it."

Mama sniffled, clutched Inge's arm, and clung to Agata. Clung and clung. As if worried that if she let go, her family might vanish before her eyes.

Inge watched Robert stepping over people. He was right. They had no idea where the devil they were being taken or what was awaiting them. Someone had to do something.

But what if this was the last time she ever saw him?

No, she couldn't think like that. She had to be positive.

Positive? In a hellhole like this?

Inge closed her eyes, fighting to block out the stench, the heat, the unrest, the noise...

At least the baby had stopped wailing, thank heaven. There was no worse sound than an infant screeching, so that was one godsend.

The mother shrieked, clutching the bundle to her chest, "Nooo! Nooo!"

26

A bearded man touched the mother's shoulder. "Can I help?"

The mother rocked back and forth. Clinging to her child, she sobbed like the world had ended. "Nooo! God, please, no!"

Bewildered, the man gazed about for assistance, but none came.

Tears trickled down Inge's cheeks. The baby hadn't given up on crying, it had given up on life. That poor, poor woman. Inge couldn't imagine her pain. And although Inge's family had never been devout, she couldn't help whispering a prayer for the woman, the baby, and those still imprisoned in the car.

As if some celestial being heard her, the train clanked and jolted, then crawled slower and slower as it hauled more and more cars uphill.

Mama grabbed Inge's hand so hard her nails dug into Inge's flesh. Inge drilled her gaze into the gang of men crowded below the window.

A hefty man heaved a scrawny one onto his shoulders. Using some sort of implement that she couldn't see, the scrawny guy filed a piece of the barbed wire over the window.

Inge gulped. She ached to run to Robert and drag him away. Drag him back to safety, to his family, to his future. But would dragging him away be doing that, or – if this journey was any indication – would it be condemning him to a life of suffering?

One of the strands of barbed wire broke.

Some of the men grinned, others pumped the air with their fists.

Inge's heart pounded. She clutched her chest, excitement and fear battling inside her. Maybe the men were actually going to be able to do it. Maybe Robert would escape and find a safe place for them to hideaway until the Soviets or the Allies routed the Nazis.

Scrawny Guy scraped at another strand, his hand a blur.

Mama squeezed Inge's hand, trembling. "Stop him, Inge. Please."

Inge didn't move. She didn't want to disobey her mother, but in this instance, Mama was wrong. If Papa were here, he'd fight back, too.

Inge tried to swallow, but her mouth was too dry. "It'll be okay, Mama. Robert can do this. He can save us. You'll see."

A loud crunch came from the car in front of theirs, as if a huge piece of wood had been smashed.

Inge gasped.

The men beneath the window froze.

All eyes stared at their front wall.

A German shouted from farther away, probably the small sentry box on the back of the car three along.

Another crunch, and the neighboring car's door rumbled open. Inge's eyes widened. Next door was escaping.

More shouting in German came from somewhere behind their car.

Agape, Inge cupped her mouth and, with everyone else, stared at the dividing wall. So escape was possible. There was hope for them yet.

Machine-gun fire shredded the night.

Inge jumped, jerking back so violently, she banged her head on the wall.

More automatic fire tore through the darkness.

As women wailed, Robert and the other men froze.

Another thunderous round of fire.

Scrambling to escape the danger, Scrawny Guy lurched to jump down. With everybody crowded together, the hefty man supporting him stumbled and fell backward, dragging another man with them.

They crashed over. On top of Robert.

Robert screamed.

"Robert!" Inge barged through the jostling bodies and grabbed his hand as the hefty man rolled off him. She pulled to heave him up, but he shrieked.

Agata and Mama dashed over. Between them, they hauled Robert to their spot as the train's brakes squealed and they stopped.

Outside the next car, the air seethed with cursing and shouted German.

Machine-gun fire erupted again, and their neighbors screamed. The car door slammed shut.

Inge and her family cowered, hugging each other in a tight ball, gazes nailed to the door. Their terrifying door.

What if the Germans saw the damaged barbed wire at their window? Would they turn their machine guns on them, too?

6

Outside the administration block, countless feet crunched on the gravel road announcing the return of the work details. Rudi glanced up from his desk. Over the next forty minutes, parties of women trooped into the camp and formed columns of ten grouped by barracks in the roll call area, each prisoner an arm's length apart.

Krebs handed Rudi a ledger. "The figures you wanted on the income from the work details, Herr Oberscharführer."

"Any luck on tracing those Ukrainians?"

"I'm expecting a call back tomorrow, Herr Oberscharführer."

Rudi nodded and opened the ledger, but a beady-eyed, barrel-chested man with chubby jowls appeared in the main doorway: Kloser.

Rudi jumped up, clicking his heels. "Herr Kommandant."

"Roll call?"

"You're joining us this evening?" asked Rudi. Kloser usually attended every other day or so.

Kloser nodded. "I've a meeting with Söllner tomorrow, which is a pity because Six is roasting a chicken tonight. Have you tasted her chicken?"

"I don't believe I have."

"Mmm..." Kloser kissed his fingertips. "I swear, there are chefs in Berlin who'd slaughter their firstborn for her chicken. So..." He gestured to the door.

Outside, Rudi and Kloser strode down the track toward a nine-foot-tall gate. Barbed wire stretched across its wooden frame, and a sentry stood on either side.

"Any problems I should know about?" Kloser placed a cigarette from a gold case in his mouth. He didn't light it.

"I'm still having trouble with the winter wear we requisitioned." Rudi fished his lighter from his pocket and offered a light. He didn't smoke but traded his cigarette ration for whatever treats the men could find for Bruno.

"I mean here." Kloser lit his cigarette, took a drag, then jabbed the lit end toward the women standing to attention inside the compound, each dirty and wearing tattered clothing. A mixture of male and female military personnel stood guard, many Estonian Auxiliary Police.

Rudi said, "Weekly death rates are still steady, we've made it two months without an escape attempt, and believe it or not, sickness is down for once."

Kloser nodded.

"About that requisition," said Rudi. "I was wondering if you could pull any strings."

"What requisition?"

A sentry swung open the right-hand gate.

Rudi said, "All the winter wear we ordered."

"It's summer." Kloser frowned, sauntering to the front of the roll call area.

"Everyone will be requesting winter wear once the weather starts turning, so we decided it was best to get in early, if you recall."

"And we need it because…"

"Because the cold caused so much sickness and death last winter that productivity went down the toilet. And we don't want that again, do we? Unless you've given up on getting a more prestigious posting."

Kloser stroked his chin. "Hmmm. Let me think about that."

Unterscharführer Gruber saluted, standing before the massed women.

Kloser said, "Carry on."

Gruber shouted, "Barracks One."

Magda, a middle-aged woman with greasy hair, stepped forward, a white armband identifying her as a block leader, one of the camp functionaries. Her gaze fixed on the ground, she said, "Barracks One ready, Herr Unterscharführer."

Counting, Magda scurried along the columns of prisoners with her pointy-nosed block scribe scuttling after her and making notes. As Magda approached the eighth column, a tall woman dropped a rag and crouched to pick it up.

"You!" Magda darted over and hit the woman on the arm with a short wooden bat. "Stand still!"

The woman cried out and grabbed her arm.

Magda hit her again. "I said *still!*"

Shaking, the woman stood still, tears streaking her grubby cheeks.

Magda resumed counting. At the end of the row, she stood to attention. "The count is 179, Herr Unterscharführer. One-seven-nine."

Gruber checked his notes, then ambled along the rows to verify the count himself. Satisfied, he shouted, "Barracks Two."

"Barracks Two ready, Herr Unterscharführer," said Lena, the scar-faced block leader. At her shoulder stood a block scribe with straggly hair.

Kloser checked his watch.

Rudi said, "If you'd like to go, Herr Kommandant, I've got this."

Kloser shook his head. "I need to see how things are ticking over for myself every few days."

Lena and the scribe shuffled along, counting the women. At the end, Lena said, "The count is 186, Herr Unterscharführer. One-eight-six."

Rudi winced. There were supposed to be 187 women in Barracks 02.

Without a word, Gruber pointed at the first woman in the first column. Lena dashed back and started a recount.

Kloser shook his head. "If that chicken is dry because of these vermin, someone's going to swing for it."

Rudi bit his lip. While the majority of people used the phrase "someone's going to swing for it" figuratively, whenever Kloser used it, someone was invariably dangling by a noose come sunset.

There was a huge difference between being a good German and being a good Nazi. Though an SS officer, Rudi often struggled with that differentiation. Yes, the Jews were a problem. Not least in how they'd betrayed the Fatherland to bring about its defeat during the Great War. But if he had a rash on his neck, he'd dab ointment on the affected area, not rush to find the nearest guillotine.

Unfortunately, most SS personnel didn't feel the same, and because Jews seemed incapable of fighting back, some experimented to see how much suffering they could inflict. It was as if they saw brutality not as a test of their moral code but a test of their mettle, their inventiveness, their commitment to the Reich.

Lena stood in front of the last column again. "The count is 186, Herr Unterscharführer. One-eight-six."

Kloser cursed under his breath.

Rudi cringed. If the count was repeatedly off, the only way to find who was missing was to go through the prisoners' numbers one by one, which wasted an inordinate amount of time.

Gruber referenced his file, then shouted, "Twenty-six."

A woman in the back row raised her arm. "Here, Herr Unterscharführer."

Lena and the scribe darted over and noted the number sewn onto the woman's shirt. "Twenty-six, Herr Unterscharführer," called Lena.

Gruber made a note. "Twenty-nine."

Another hand shot up. "Here, Herr Unterscharführer."

Near to twenty-nine, a woman with sunken eyes scanned over each shoulder.

Kloser yelled, "You!"

He stormed over, pointing. "You!"

Rudi followed, Gruber and Lena trailing behind.

Trembling, the woman stared at her feet. The nearer Kloser got, the more hunched the woman became, as if trying to shrink into the ground.

Kloser waved the prisoners aside, and those surrounding the woman scattered. She cowered.

Kloser said, "Do you know who's missing?"

The woman stared down to avoid eye contact. "I'm sorry, Herr Kommandant, but I think it's my younger sister. She's so sick that she went to lie down while I used the latrine, and now I can't see her."

"Sick or lazy?"

Her voice faltered. "She was b-badly beaten yesterday, and now sh-she can barely walk?"

"Beaten for being lazy?"

"She's a good w-worker, Herr Kommandant. A strong worker."

"Are you suggesting we beat prisoners for no reason?"

Shaking, the woman said, "No, Herr Kommandant, you only b-beat us w-when we deserve it."

"Therefore, your sister deserved the beating she received, so she has no excuse for missing roll call."

"But—"

"Did I ask you a question?" Kloser jerked closer to her.

The woman hunched into an even tighter ball. "No, Herr Kommandant."

Kloser reached behind him and snapped his fingers. Gruber put his whip in Kloser's hand.

Without another word, Kloser hit the woman across the back. She staggered forward. He clobbered her again and again until she crumpled into the dirt.

"What's the rule about roll call?" Kloser kicked the balled figure, and she yelped.

Speaking through winces, she said, "Unless they're in the infirmary"— gasp —"everyone"— gasp —"must attend roll call, Herr Kommandant."

Rudi moved closer and whispered, "Herr Kommandant, don't let this miserable piece of scum ruin your special chicken. Allow me to handle this."

"I appreciate your concern, Rudi, but to be honest, you're one of the causes of this insubordination — you're too darn soft with this vermin. Now watch, and you might learn something." He cracked the woman one last time, then turned to Lena. "Give me that bat."

Lena handed him her wooden bat.

"Now, where's this sister?" he asked.

Lena led Kloser, Rudi, and Gruber into a gloomy barracks with bare wood walls and a dirt floor. Rudi grimaced, the stench of stale sweat and excrement like a punch in the nose.

They strode down a narrow aisle with three-tier bunk beds on either side, cut through a gap where a brick stove stood, and continued down the second aisle between more bunks. Ahead in a middle bunk, a woman lay beneath a grimy gray blanket, filthy feet sticking out of the bottom.

Without a word, Kloser cracked the woman's body with the bat.

She shrieked, instinctively curling up.

He beat her again. She screeched.

Again and again, he pounded her as if she were the Devil incarnate and he alone could protect all of humanity. Pounded, pounded, pounded...

The woman stopped writhing and stopped squealing, but Kloser continued battering her anyway. Finally, he slung the bat down and stood, panting.

Rudi touched his arm. "Let me finish things now. If you stay in here too long, this stink is going to ruin your sense of taste for your meal."

Sweat beading on his brow, Kloser nodded. "I think I've made my point." He swaggered away.

Rudi looked to Lena. "Take her to the infirmary. Tell Baumann to do whatever he can."

"Yes, Herr Oberscharführer."

Rudi trudged away, head bowed. Yes, there was a huge difference between being a good German and being a good Nazi. Which one was he?

7

The train jolted, brakes squealing, as dawn bled through the gaps in the car's planks. As usual, everyone looked to the door. Inge included. Except this time, part of her didn't want it to open – would they be given water or be sprayed with bullets?

Ever since the failed escape attempt, Mr. and Mrs. Klein had been knelt in prayer, the Kovar children had barely stopped whimpering, and a white-haired woman had shrieked gibberish as if she'd lost her mind. They couldn't take much more.

Inge turned to Mama. "Do you think—"

With eyes half-closed, Mama's head lolled to one side and her breath came in short pants.

"Mama!" Inge shook Mama's shoulder.

Her mother's eyes flickered wider and turned fractionally toward Inge. Whenever the water bucket had made its way to them, Mama had insisted Agata take her share. But the last time they'd seen that bucket was two days ago, which meant Mama had barely drunk for five days.

Inge shouted, "Water? Has anyone any water?"

No one answered.

"Please!"

A man nearby snickered. Okay, so thinking that someone in this situation could be hoarding water instead of drinking it was crazy, but there was a chance. There was *always* a chance.

"Please!"

Trembling with the effort, Mama tapped Inge's arm. Her voice barely a whisper, she said, "Don't worry"– gasp –"I'll be okay."

Inge peered through the hole between the two planks in the wall behind her, hoping to see a thriving community that might help them. Her shoulders slumped. Just more barren countryside stretching away under gray clouds.

"Hold on, Mama. It can't be much farther."

Inge stared out at the desolate world. There was nothing here, so why had they stopped? Were they in a siding, waiting for another train to pass? Or was this just another time they'd be stationary for no discernible reason?

Inge bit her lip. "Come on. Move. Move!"

She twisted to see more through the hole.

Mama couldn't take wasting hours here only for the train to shuffle its way through the countryside for heaven only knew how many more days. They had to get going. Had to. Tears blurred Inge's vision.

Her voice cracking, she said, "Move. Please, move."

But as she stared out, the only things that moved were the clouds. Dread crept up Inge's spine as the world descended into gloom. But then...

Inge's eyes widened, a realization hitting her. She smiled. It was all going to be okay. Maybe someone truly was listening to her prayers after all.

8

The sun peeping above distant hills, long shadows crept across the camp. Rudi threw a red rubber ball and Bruno tore after it along the rough track running parallel to the perimeter fence.

Bruno returned and dropped the ball at Rudi's feet as a bald man with round glasses exited the SS accommodation block.

"Come on, boy." Rudi jogged to catch him, Bruno alongside. He shouted, "Baumann."

The man waited, standing to attention. "Herr Oberscharführer."

"I saw the sickness figures. Congratulations on getting things under control."

Baumann snorted. "I wouldn't exactly say 'under control.' We've had a good couple of weeks, is all."

"It's not something you're doing differently?"

"Have you seen the infirmary's supplies recently?"

Rudi said, "Everything's earmarked for the Front, so anything we requisition takes forever."

Baumann nodded. "I've traded a few things with the local doctor, but he's struggling to replenish stocks, too."

"I'll keep chasing things up. Maybe we'll get lucky."

They ambled around toward the front of the camp.

Baumann said, "Do you know Peeter Erm, the ice harvester?"

Rudi frowned.

Baumann held his hand above his head. "Big guy, red hair?"

"Not ringing any bells."

"Anyway, because the weather is his livelihood, he's like the local expert, and he's predicting a cold winter this year."

"Another?"

"No, I don't just mean cold, I mean *cold*. If he's right and what we had to deal with last winter is anything to go by, without supplies, we'll be lucky if we don't have to convert one of the other barracks into a second infirmary."

Rudi blew out his cheeks. "Okay. I hear you."

They parted, Rudi heading for the administration block, Baumann for the gates into the camp.

Rudi glanced back. "Hey."

Baumann turned and walked backward.

"That woman you were sent last night who'd been beaten...?"

Baumann shook his head.

Rudi heaved a breath. Another senseless death. Where was it going to end?

Away in the distance, thunder rumbled.

Baumann nodded toward the darkening horizon. "A storm's coming."

Rudi nodded. "I know."

9

In the cattle car, people leaped to their feet, shrieking with joy and reaching to the sky, but not in reverence to any God.

Thunder clapped like an artillery barrage and rain beat down on the car's roof. Droplets poured through the cracks into cupped hands and gaping mouths.

Inge thrust her hand through the gap in the wall, and water ran down the outside of the car into her palm. She withdrew it carefully and offered the pool of liquid to her mother.

Mama slurped the water up, her eyes already sparkling with more life than they had for days.

Inge smiled, but the expression faded. This was what the Germans had reduced them to – Inge giving her mother a drink like she would an animal? What could the Germans hope to gain from degrading them so?

Inge collected water for Robert, who swore he was doing okay but now couldn't stand, and then for Agata. Finally, she collected some for herself.

She slurped the first few drops. "Ohhh, wow." So sweet, so fresh, so cool.

She collected more and wiped it over her face. "Heaven."

In cities, the well-to-do spent a fortune on treatments in beauty salons that couldn't feel half as good as this. Bliss. Utter bliss.

She smeared water over her mother to cool her.

As if the moment couldn't become any more magical, an old couple, who'd spent most of the past twenty-four hours praying, waltzed in the middle of the car as the leaky roof showered them with life-giving water. Inge grinned at the most surreal thing she'd ever seen.

The door to a nearby car rumbled open. Inge flinched, and the dancing stopped. Everything stopped. Everyone stared at their door.

Outside, a dog barked, and German voices shouted, "Out! Everyone out!"

They'd arrived.

Their next-but-one neighbors clambered out.

It was hard for Inge to make out what was happening outside for the thunderstorm and the joyous commotion of her fellow travelers, but that hardly mattered. Like everybody else, she stared at their door, eager to discover the new life awaiting them in this distant land.

Everyone pressed forward, clutching their possessions, desperate to escape this hellish car. Inge heaved Robert up and slung her arm around his lower back to support him. He draped his arm over her shoulders.

And everyone stared at the door.

But the door didn't open. The sounds of the other passengers leaving drifted farther and farther away.

Agata frowned. "Have they forgotten us?"

Mama squeezed her hand. "Don't worry, they'll come back for us and you'll be sleeping in a proper bed tonight."

Agata beamed.

Minutes later, their neighbor's door opened and they were ordered out. Ten minutes later, finally, the metal latch on Inge's door clanged over, and the door juddered open.

A German soldier bawled, "Out! Out!"

Beside him, two others held barking dogs that strained at their leashes, and behind them, a muddy field stretched away to trees.

The people nearest the door jumped down.

Inge said, "I don't like this."

Mama took her arm. "It'll be fine, Inge. Why would they bring us all this way if there wasn't somewhere for us to go?"

With other passengers clambering out, Inge waited near the doorway while Mama and Agata helped each other down.

A line of people trudged across the mud toward the tree line, where trucks and blue buses were parked. Far ahead on her extreme left, the locomotive stood at a two-story station, its platform so small only the first three cattle cars had drawn level. How odd to have a station in the middle of nowhere. But what did that matter? They'd arrived. The hell was over!

Inge jumped out, then assisted Robert. Hobbling as if competing in a children's three-legged race, they set out across the field, both

40

holding their suitcase with their free hands. In seconds, mud caked Inge's pink sandals and squished between her toes.

She stared at the vehicles and the ocean of filth to reach them. Why hadn't the Germans parked next to the train to save the passengers this filthy hike and themselves all this wasted time? It was like the Germans wanted to watch them struggle across this quagmire, testing them to the very last moment. She rolled her eyes. Or was this an example of that German superiority they were always harping on about?

The cattle cars ahead of hers were already empty while those behind were still locked. If it hadn't been for the storm, she'd probably have heard the cars being emptied sooner. And that explained the wait — with limited road vehicles, the Germans were transporting only a few cars of passengers at a time.

She and Robert battled on through the mud, but because of his injury, people overtook them. Soon, a gap formed and they straggled farther and farther behind everyone else.

On the road, a bus rumbled off to the left and a truck to the right.

"Come on, Robert. We don't want them to go without us."

Inge quickened her pace, but her foot stuck in the mud. She yanked, but the mud held her tight. She heaved harder, but instead of breaking free, she lost her balance and fell forward. Her left hand disappeared into mud up to her wrist. She cursed.

Robert pulled her upright. She jerked her leg, and her foot came loose with a squelch.

Pelted by rain, they plodded on, mud splattering up their legs as they splashed through puddles. Inge prayed their new accommodation had a nice bathroom.

Under her breath, she said, "Warm bath. Warm bath. Warm bath."

"What?"

"Nothing." Ahead, people had already arrived at the vehicles and were being divided into groups. "Just hurry. We can't risk getting separated."

They hobbled quicker, Robert wincing.

From the road, a German with a huge nose shouted, "Move it!"

"Don't go," shouted Inge. "We're coming."

Robert clutched Inge tighter than ever before and lumbered for the road, sucking through his teeth with every step.

Trudging out of the mud onto the paved road, Inge smiled at Mama and Agata in a group of people piling onto a bus.

The big-nosed German held a whip in front of her, and she pulled up.

"You." He cracked Robert, making him flinch, then pointed to Mama's group. "There." He jabbed Inge and gestured to a truck with people crammed into the back. "You, there."

"But I'm with them." Inge pointed to her family.

"They're getting that transport. You're in this one."

Inge stepped toward her mother. "I'll go with them."

The German whacked Inge's thigh with his whip.

She squealed and jumped back.

Robert took her hand. "Go, Inge. We'll meet you there."

"But..." Tears welled in her eyes as a gaping hole ate away at her more than hunger ever could. She was stuck in a strange country and about to be dumped in a strange town. Alone. What if her family was taken to the wrong place and she couldn't find them?

Robert stroked her cheek. "It'll be okay, Inge. Trust me. After all we've been through to get here, what's the worst that can happen?"

"Okay, we'll meet in the town square."

The German whipped Robert. "Move!"

She ached to punch the horrible man, to splatter that big nose across his face. But she was a teenage girl carrying nothing but a suitcase; he was a soldier carrying a machine gun.

She forced a smile. As much for her own sake as Robert's.

Limping away, he said, "See you soon."

"The town square. Don't forget." Teary-eyed, she waved to Agata and Mama clutching each other. "Bye, Aga. Bye, Mama!"

They waved back.

Gritting her teeth, she backed toward the truck, sniffling away her tears — that vile German would not have the satisfaction of seeing how upset she was.

A beady-eyed German at the truck shouted, "In! In!"

Inge grabbed the side to climb in.

Beady Eyes pointed to a pile of luggage at the roadside. "No bags. It will be sent to you later."

"But it doesn't have my name on it. How will you know it's mine to know where to send it?"

"Will you recognize it?"

"Yes."

"Then you'll find it. Now in the truck. Hurry."

Inge placed her suitcase on the pile. Walking away from the very last thing she had from home, the last reminder of the life she'd loved, she screwed up her face as she battled to hold in her tears.

She climbed into the back of the truck where thirty or so women huddled.

Beady Eyes closed the tailgate and gestured to someone out of sight. The truck revved to life and moved off but only made it a few yards before juddering to a stop.

Beady Eyes dashed back and leveled his gun at them. "No one leaves the truck."

The truck engine spluttered and coughed like a man who'd worked down the mines all his life and whose lungs were ruined by dust.

Someone shouted from the front of the vehicle, and Beady Eyes disappeared.

A blue bus cruised past. In a window near the back, Mama stared out, wiping tears off her cheeks with Robert and Agata squashed beside her.

Inge shouted, "Mama!"

Mama pressed her palm against the window.

And the bus drove on. Hauling away her family, her life, her everything.

Inge gawked. The bus was going in the opposite direction to her truck.

"No way." Inge set her jaw. The Germans had stolen everything from her. Everything. They would not take her family.

She vaulted over the tailgate and ran after the bus.

Tears streaming her cheeks, she shouted, "Mama! Mama!"

She waved frantically. The bus driver had to hear her, had to see her, had to stop.

"Mama!" Her feet pounded into the road as she chased the bus. "Mama!"

A soldier stepped out in front of her and slammed his rifle butt into the side of her head. She fell to the road like a dropped vase.

Sprawled in the dirt, Inge reached a trembling hand toward the bus, the world a darkening smear of muddy colors.

Her voice a croaked whisper, she said, "Mama."

Inge's arm dropped. And blackness took her.

10

As Rudi and Kloser dawdled toward the compound gates, Rudi said, "Monthly income is down again but should pick up when we replenish our labor pool with a new intake. However, on a positive note, the suspected outbreak of typhus was a false alarm."

Kloser nodded. "Anything else?"

"The woman from the other day, the sister, she died of her injuries."

Kloser frowned. "Woman?"

Rudi chose his words carefully. "The woman who was beaten in her barracks."

"Oh, that one."

"She died of her injuries."

Kloser snorted. "Laziness."

"Excuse me, Herr Kommandant?"

"Laziness. She died of laziness. If she hadn't been lazy, she wouldn't have been in bed, so she wouldn't have been beaten. It's simple logic."

"I stand corrected."

The sentries on the gate saluted as Rudi and Kloser strolled in.

"You have to be firm with prisoners, Rudi. If you aren't, you're only making a rod for your own back." Kloser patted Rudi's shoulder like a father bestowing wisdom upon his son. "If you're too soft, I promise you, it'll come back and bite you."

Rudi nodded.

"Think about it. You can't train a dog or horse with kindness, can you? No, because they only respect the hand or the whip. It's the same here." Kloser gestured to the women at roll call. "They aren't like us. They can't comprehend logic and reason. Fear. Now, that works. And when it doesn't, pain."

Rudi had never struck Bruno. Never. Bruno was family, love, joy — everything that was right in a world that couldn't be more wrong.

To most folk, Bruno was just an animal, yet to Rudi, he was as much a person as anyone in the camp. More so than some.

Jews were subhuman, yes. No one could deny that, because the Fatherland's greatest minds universally agreed. But just because Jews weren't human didn't mean they weren't smart. Underestimating their capacity for reasoned thought was doing a disservice to them and to oneself. After all, underestimating the enemy was the quickest route to defeat. Which military man had never heard of Custer and the Battle of Little Big Horn?

"Herr Kommandant." Gruber clicked his heels, then looked at Rudi. "Oberscharführer."

"Carry on," said Kloser.

Gruber started roll call. "Barracks One."

Magda undertook her count, and when the numbers tallied, Gruber moved on. "Barracks Two."

"Barracks Two ready, Herr Unterscharführer," said Lena.

While the woman counted, Gruber ambled along the front row, monitoring proceedings.

At the end, Lena grimaced. "The count is 184, Herr Unterscharführer. One-eight-four."

Gruber shot Kloser an anxious glance, then gestured for her to start over. She scurried back to the beginning.

Kloser said, "Gruber, this is the barracks that caused the problem last time."

"Yes, Herr Kommandant."

Kloser shook his head at Rudi. "See what I mean? Spare the rod and..."

He snatched Gruber's records. After scanning the numbers, Kloser addressed the women. "Look around you and tell me who's missing or you'll be standing here till breakfast."

The women peered about.

"Five seconds," said Kloser. "Five... four... three..."

"My sister," said a feeble voice.

Blowing out a heavy breath, Kloser rubbed his brow. "Another sister? Dear Lord, they really do breed like vermin, don't they?" He squinted at the women. "Raise a hand, whoever said that."

Toward the back, far right, a hand tentatively rose.

Kloser waved away the ranks of women so they parted. A lone woman cowered, hand up, facedown.

"My apologies, Herr Kommandant. My younger sister died last week after being beaten, and now my older one has gone on strike and won't get out of bed."

"You see?" Kloser arched an eyebrow at Rudi. "This is the thanks I get for being so lenient." He sneered at the women. "That stops now."

He beckoned Gruber. "With me." He stormed for the barracks door, Gruber and Lena following. Rudi darted after them.

Inside the gloomy, stinking barracks, Kloser zigzagged between the bunks like before. Ahead, a woman lay under a flea-bitten blanket on a top bunk.

Kloser grabbed Lena's wooden bat and glared at the body in the bunk. "You've only got yourself to blame for this, you lazy, good-for-nothing Jew."

Kloser raised the bat to crash it down onto the unsuspecting woman.

But the woman leaped off the bunk and plunged a shiv into Kloser's chest. He toppled backward onto the dirt floor, throwing his arms up to shield himself. The woman fell with him, screaming and stabbing, stabbing, stabbing.

Rudi and Gruber dashed forward and hauled the woman off.

Blood dripping from her knife, she spat at Kloser. "You killed my sister, you Nazi pig."

Rudi twisted her arm until she squealed and dropped her weapon. "Get her out of here, Gruber. And get Baumann."

As Gruber hauled the woman away, Rudi crouched next to the commandant covered in blood on the floor.

Kloser cradled his left arm, which had multiple gashes across it. Rudi pressed his palm over the chest wound.

"You're lucky." Rudi smiled as reassuringly as he could. "It's more your shoulder than your chest, so you should be okay."

Kloser grabbed Rudi's wrist. "Then get me up."

"Let Baumann examine you first. We might need a stretcher to be safe."

"Like hell. Those vermin aren't going to have the satisfaction of seeing me carried out of here. Get me up."

"We should wait for Bau—"

"Get me up, Oberscharführer. That's an order."

"Yes, Herr Kommandant."

Rudi hoisted Kloser up, then, with his arm around Kloser's back to support him, they shuffled through the barracks.

"Wait." Kloser glanced at his blood-drenched chest in the light beaming through the doorway. He nodded to the nearest bed. "Use the blankets to hide the wounds."

"They're filthy. You could get an infection."

Kloser gripped Rudi's shoulder. "They can't see me weak, Rudi."

Propping the man against a bunk, Rudi grabbed two blankets and wrapped them around Kloser's shoulders to hide his injuries as best he could.

"Okay?" he asked.

Kloser nodded.

"Just a second." Rudi stepped outside and, in a loud voice, said, "Everyone facedown on the ground."

Anxious glances shot among the prisoners at the strange request.

"Now!" Rudi signaled the guards. They leveled their rifles, and the women dropped to the ground.

Rudi darted back inside, then he and the commandant lurched across the roll call area.

From the ground, the sister who'd spoken to Kloser earlier shouted, "I hope you die, you Nazi pig! Die!"

One of the guards ran over and grabbed her.

Kloser's legs buckled, but Rudi caught him and hoisted him up. "Hang on, Franz, we're almost there."

Baumann sprinted from the infirmary. He helped support Kloser, and they all lurched into the administration block. Through the first door on the right, they entered the staff infirmary. They lowered Kloser onto the nearest of the four vacant beds covered in crisp white linen, and Rudi lifted his feet to lay him down.

Delicately, Baumann removed the blankets stuck to Kloser with his own blood. "These weren't the best idea. God only knows what bacteria are hiding in all this filth."

Apart from the wound in the Kloser's chest, blood oozed from a gash in his right forearm, three in his left arm, and one in his left hand. Baumann inspected each wound, then rooted through his medicine cabinet across the room.

Rudi joined him. "How bad is it?"

"The chest isn't the problem, but the hand...?" He winced. "That's down to the bone."

"But you can treat it, right?"

"It isn't only the prisoner infirmary that's short on supplies." Baumann cast him a sideways glance, then filled a syringe and meandered back. "Herr Kommandant, I'm going to give you a shot of morphine for the pain so I can clean the wounds."

"Wait." Kloser grabbed Baumann's wrist. "Rudi?"

"Herr Kommandant?" Rudi stepped nearer.

"There's to be no punishment until I'm back on my feet. Understand? I'll be dealing with this scum personally."

"Yes, Herr Kommandant."

Kloser nodded to Baumann, who gave him the shot.

Rudi left.

Outside, he drew a weary breath. The attempted murder of an SS officer demanded an execution, but no way would Kloser be satisfied with a simple hanging. What was he planning?

Rudi cringed. "Oh God, no."

There could only be one thing – the Box.

11

Inge shivered, standing in the middle of one hundred or so women in a courtyard, facing a high brick wall topped with barbed wire. During her processing, they'd daubed something onto the back of her dress, and from seeing other prisoners now, she guessed it was a large white X. But that wasn't the strangest thing — they'd made her remove her yellow star. The law demanded that Jews wear those, so what was going on?

She glanced at the strip of white cloth she'd been forced to sew onto her dress in place of the star on her chest and the number stenciled on the fabric. So, this was her life now, was it? She was no longer eighteen-year-old Inge Zaleska, learner of languages, lover of strawberry ice cream, collector of postcards from places she dreamed of visiting... Now she was simply prisoner 3324.

Facing them, a woman with pockmarked cheeks and a white armband marked KAPO stood beside a hatchet-nosed SS officer. He'd been laying down rules forever: no talking, no moving, no eating...

"Finally," he said, "if any of you are thinking of escaping our cozy little establishment, think again. For every one escapee, ten prisoners will be shot. We'll also find your family and shoot every single one of them."

Beside Inge, a chubby girl said, "When can we see our families?"

Hatchet Nose smiled. "You'd like to see your family?"

"Yes, please."

He nodded to the pock-faced Kapo. She marched over and smashed a rubber truncheon into the girl's face. Blood poured from her nose.

Women all around flinched.

Inge stayed rooted to the spot, silent. She was skinny, not voluptuous, so she didn't turn heads from a distance. But close up?

She had stunning brown eyes and striking cheekbones. The last thing she wanted was a crooked nose to detract from the only features she had worth talking about. Mama always said...

Inge's chin trembled. She gritted her teeth and stared at the wall. Where were they? She prayed they were in a better place than this.

Hatchet Nose said, "Any other questions?"

Everyone stared at the ground.

"Good." He disappeared into a three-story stone building leaving them standing.

The sun slid down behind the wall and gloom descended. Finally, Pock Face ushered everyone into the building through a wooden door reinforced with metal strips and studs like something out of the Dark Ages.

They climbed a stone staircase, Inge heaving herself along using the wooden rail mounted on a wrought-iron balustrade. Still woozy after being hit on the road, she felt completely drained. Through another doorway, they entered an eerie world more akin to a cave than a building — a concrete chamber with a curved ceiling and reinforced doors to cells, while wide archways led to subsequent chambers.

They passed through another archway with a metal gate and Pock Face stopped next to a heavy door. She slid massive bolts over, top and bottom, then opened the door, its hinges squealing. She ordered the first ten women inside, Inge included.

They tramped into a dingy room lit by a single overhead light. The door squealed shut and its bolts slammed into place.

Inge's jaw dropped. They were supposed to sleep here?

The room was around nine feet wide and thirty long, with a ceiling that curved down to the left, as if it'd been a large, arched area that had been split into two. At the far end, evening gloom seeped through a barred window above a tiny sink and a hole in the floor that stank like a toilet. But it was wooden bunks that dominated the room, all pushed together to form two continuous beds.

There would have been ample space for Inge and her cellmates had it not been for the twenty-odd women already crammed in there.

The bloodied-nose woman said, "How are we supposed to sleep here?"

From a folding bed near the door, a voice said, "Shut up and find a place. It's lights out soon."

Some of the women exchanged glances, but Inge heaved up into a spot on the upper bunk. Thanks to her comrades' indecision, she had the first pick, which was about as good as it was going to get.

Inge ran a hand over the bed — solid wood with a mattress of sacking stuffed with straw. She lay between two women and pulled part of a threadbare blanket over her, but its owner yanked the material away, leaving her uncovered.

The other new arrivals squeezed in, met with the curses of those they disturbed.

Inge stared at the ceiling. Stuck in a cattle car and now sleeping on straw? Why were the Germans treating them like animals?

Still, at least tonight, she could sleep lying down. Maybe things were looking up.

Agata, Robert, and Mama flickered into her mind. Tears welled.

After Papa had disappeared, Inge had sworn to protect and provide for her family. And what? At the first true test, she'd failed.

Inge sobbed.

An elbow slammed into her ribs. "Shut the hell up."

She bit her lip and screwed her eyes closed. Things looking up? Things were only getting worse and worse. What new hell would she find awaiting her tomorrow?

12

A hand-cranked bell rang and woke Inge. Darkness still hung at the barred window.

Women clambered out of bed and dashed to crowd the sink and toilet hole. Inge yawned and shuffled off the bunk.

"New girls!" Standing next to the cot, a gaunt woman with a green armband clapped. "I'm Zofia, your room leader. Do what I say and we won't have a problem, but make me look bad and you'll wish you'd been shot the moment you got off the train." She glared at Inge and the others.

Zofia stalked to the lower bunk where the bloodied-nose woman was snoring. She punched the woman's shin. The woman shrieked and clutched her leg.

Returning to the doorway, Zofia said, "When this door opens, you have thirty minutes for the bathroom and breakfast. Do not waste it. Then it's roll call, where you will line up in columns of ten." She hammered her fist against the bunk. "Do not be late for roll call." Another hammer. "Do not move during roll call." Hammer. "Do not speak unless spoken to during roll call. Any questions?"

A straggly-haired woman said, "Why so little time in the bathroom? Will we get longer to wash properly later?"

"Good question." Zofia smiled and panned her gaze across everyone. "Everybody listening?"

Inge nodded. A chance to bathe? To scrub off the stench of that vile cattle car? Oh yes, things were definitely improving.

Zofia punched the straggly-haired woman in the gut. The woman doubled up, wheezing.

Raising an index finger, Zofia said, "Lesson one — you have *no questions*. You do what you are told, when you are told, and never — never — question anything."

Inge slumped. What hell had she been brought to?

Zofia said, "Okay, so get cleaning this place until the door opens."

Inge copied the old hands as they smoothed the sacking and folded the blankets, then picked stray bits of straw off the floor.

Out in the hall, hefty bolts scraped open. The old hands who weren't crowding the facilities at the back of the room shoved past the new inmates and lined up at the door. Inge did likewise.

Their door opened, and the women strode out, rushing in as orderly a fashion as was possible. They turned right, went through an archway, and into a "bathroom."

Inge froze.

A concrete block ran across the back wall, seven holes spaced out along its length. Women were already perched over four of the holes, so three of Inge's group darted over to sit on the remaining ones.

Inge gawked. *She* was supposed to use *that*?

The stench was bad enough, but the noises... what were they feeding these women?

To her right, women crowded a seven-foot-long stone trough standing on a spindly metal frame and filled with water. One was naked from the waist up, washing; another had a foot up on the trough, splashing her crotch. Inge could see everything — everything. Did these women have no shame?

The woman washing her privates rubbed herself dry with her skirt and waltzed past Inge for the door.

She sneered. "Get used to it, princess."

Inge thanked her stars she hadn't eaten for days and had barely drunk. No way was she squatting like an animal. A space appeared at the trough, so she dashed in.

Inge said, "Where's the soap?"

A redhead laughed.

The woman washing her breasts said, "Ask for a bar when you get your nails done. The lilac-scented one is lovely."

The redhead laughed again.

Inge washed her hands and face, then dried herself on her sleeve. She toddled out.

After the bathroom experience, things didn't bode well for a lavish breakfast feast, but boy, they couldn't get much worse.

Inge followed the women pouring down the stairs into a large hall on the ground floor. There, lines of women waited to be served breakfast from massive steaming metal vats. Inge waited, pulling out the battered bowl she'd received during processing from her pocket.

Finally her turn, Inge held out her bowl. The cook ladled in insipid brown liquid.

Inge peered at it. "What's this?"

"Coffee."

Inge sniggered. "Seriously?"

The cook grabbed Inge's bowl, tipped its contents back into the vat, and turned to the next prisoner.

"But..." Inge gawked.

The cook glared, so Inge slouched away, staring at her empty bowl. A few drops clung to the bottom, so she dribbled them into her mouth. Coffee? More like warmed puddle water.

At the other side of the hall, men filtered in.

Inge stared. "Robert?" She scanned the faces, desperate for that one special one.

Nothing.

What had happened to her family?

A bell sounded, and the old hands filed out. That must be roll call — whatever that was. Inge merged into the crowd. In the courtyard, women formed columns of ten, so Inge lined up behind others from her room.

Okay, she'd adhered to Zofia's first rule — she was on time. Now she just had to keep still and keep quiet. Easy. The Germans were backing the wrong horse if they thought this would break her. Some people picked up a rifle to become a freedom fighter, but her resistance struggle was going to be different — she was going to survive to tell the world of the atrocities she'd witnessed. They were never going to break her. Never.

And then she felt it.

Oh God, no. Not now. Please!

13

The dawn air bitingly fresh, Bruno snuffled through the undergrowth in a forest clearing. Rudi sat on the ground and leaned against the trunk of a great oak, basking in the only real companionship he had. The only one he needed. Bruno didn't care about expanding the Fatherland, didn't despise people because of their race, didn't believe himself superior to anyone or anything. And why would he? He was just an animal – a "subhuman."

Bruno ambled back and Rudi ruffled the dog's neck fur. Maybe there was something to be said for being subhuman.

Wagging his tail, Bruno lavished Rudi with so much tongue-licking, Rudi fell sideways, laughing.

No, Rudi didn't need anyone else. He hugged Bruno.

Rudi stared at the towering trees. "Shall we build a cabin out here and never leave the woods, boy?"

He sighed. As if that could ever happen. The world was a mental asylum, and he was a patient strapped into a straitjacket with no chance of escape.

He checked his watch and patted Bruno. "Sorry, Bruno, work time."

They wandered back.

In the administration block, Rudi looked in on the commandant.

Sitting up in bed, Kloser stuffed a forkful of ham and egg into his mouth with his right hand, his left arm and hand heavily strapped.

Baumann stood preparing some treatment at a table but turned and saluted. Rudi gestured for him to continue.

Rudi said, "How are you feeling, Herr Kommandant?"

"In pain, but you can't keep a good man down, Rudi. That scum is going to learn that the hard way."

"Could I ask what you have in mind?"

Kloser snorted. "Put it this way, Baumann can pump whatever concoction into me he likes, but nothing is going to feel as good as seeing justice done this morning. You did cancel the work details."

Rudi nodded. An attack on an SS officer couldn't go unpunished. But the problem was twofold: what barbaric punishment was Kloser planning, and how many people were going to be dragged into it?

Rudi said, "Would you like me to make any preparations?"

Staring into space, Kloser chewed. "Prepare four nooses."

"Four?"

"Yes."

"For the two sisters and...?"

"Nah-huh." Kloser guzzled more food.

Rudi waited. Who the devil was he hanging if it wasn't the people responsible?

Kloser swallowed. "The bunks are three-tier. That means, apart from the two sisters, four people could've stopped this."

Rudi grimaced. "Those sisters would've kept their attack secret for fear someone would sell them out for a food ration. Their bunkmates are probably innocent."

"Innocent? They're Jews, Rudi. *Jews!* Save your compassion for the German people after what the Jews have done to them over the decades."

Historians said Jews were responsible for Germany losing the Great War. But that was another generation. Should children suffer for the sins of their parents?

"With respect, Herr Kommandant, with the Allies advancing from the west and the Soviets from the east, isn't it a disservice to the Reich to indiscriminately slaughter workers? Shouldn't we keep as many alive as possible to maximize productivity and guarantee the victory we deserve?"

Kloser squinted at him. Was he weighing the needs of the Reich against his need for vengeance?

Baumann removed Kloser's chest dressing. "I'm sorry, Herr Kommandant, but this is going to sting."

As he disinfected the wound, Kloser grimaced and grabbed Rudi's arm with his uninjured hand. He sucked through his teeth. "If those pigs didn't know what was being planned, they should've made it their business to find out. They'll police themselves or they'll swing. Simple."

"If you're sure, Herr Kommandant."

"Do you remember '23, Rudi, or were you too young?"

Rudi hung his head. In 1923, the German economy had collapsed and hyperinflation had run riot.

"I remember my father burning bundles of cash on the fire because it was cheaper than burning coal."

"Exactly. And that was the Jews. They caused that because we gave them all the freedoms we give to people. Germany almost ended there and then. All because of the Jews."

Rudi nodded. "We were taught about it in school."

"So enough with all this talk of compassion. They're animals, Rudi. Animals. They can't help themselves. All they understand is the whip, so we have no choice but to punish them, or we won't be carrying reichsmarks in our wallets but in wheelbarrows again."

Rudi sighed. "So be it."

He didn't hold with the brutality that came so easily to many of his colleagues, justifying his reticence with that argument about productivity being of benefit to the Reich. Which was a sound argument. Except, there was more to it. That *subhuman* element. Whenever he punished a Jew, he felt almost as guilty as if he was punishing Bruno. Why? It made no sense. Jews were destroying the Fatherland, so why did it feel so wrong to punish them the way they deserved?

Not that *his* thoughts mattered. His commanding officer had given him a direct order, so what choice did he have?

14

Still standing in her column in the courtyard, Inge squeezed her thighs together. Of all the times for it to happen, it had to be here, now?

She watched the kapos marching about and scrutinizing the women while a couple of SS guards chatted in the corner. One of the golden rules was not to move, but if Inge timed things right, she could get away with it.

Once Pock Face strutted past, Inge slowly tilted forward and craned her neck.

The woman beside her whispered, "Don't move."

Inge ignored her. She had to know.

She tipped forward farther and farther. Finally, her legs came into view. As did a trickle of blood wending its way down the side of her left shin.

Inge gasped. Leaning upright, she screwed her eyes shut. "Oh God, no."

Using the toilet in front of strangers had seemed as bad as things could get, but menstrual blood running down her leg in public? She cringed. The shame. She ached to run to the bathroom and scrub and scrub until she was red raw. How had she missed the signs?

How? Simple. She'd figured the stomach cramps were from hunger, so she'd ignored them. Headache, back pain, fatigue — who wouldn't suffer all those after what she'd been through?

Inge screwed her eyes shut and bit her lip. This couldn't be happening. It just couldn't. She glared at the SS.

Why the devil were they being made to stand here for so long anyway? What point could it possibly serve? And the longer they were here, the more time someone had to spot her problem. She cringed again. She'd die if someone noticed.

But maybe there was a chance she could get away with it. She had to try.

With Pock Face squawking at another prisoner behind her somewhere, Inge flicked her gaze from far right to far left, making sure no one was looking her way to catch her.

Safe. Maybe.

Inge crossed her right leg over her left. She couldn't wipe the blood away without bending or using a cloth, but maybe she could at least hide it. Once more, she slowly tilted forward.

Another muffled whisper. "Stop moving."

Inge ignored the woman and craned her neck. Her right shin hid her left, completely concealing the blood. From the front at least. Under her breath, she said, "Thank God."

"You!"

Inge froze, shooting her gaze to the far left.

She gasped. A male SS officer stabbed his whip at her.

"Yes, you." He marched between the rows. "You weren't instructed to move." He whipped her left arm.

A stinging pain shot through her bicep. "I'm sorry, it's my p—"

He whipped her again.

Inge clutched her arm but resisted looking at him for fear she'd anger him more.

"Did I ask you to speak?" He struck a third time.

Pain searing her left side, she floundered. Was that a genuine question or was it rhetorical? Her heart pounded in her ears. What was she supposed to do? What?

His whip lashed her shoulder. "I asked you a question."

"I'm sorry. No, you didn't ask me to speak."

The whip bit again. He pointed to the silver stripes on the black patch on his left collar. "No, Herr Rottenführer."

She repeated, "No, Herr Rottenführer."

"Didn't your room leader explain the rules?"

"She did, Herr Rottenführer."

"Then stand to attention."

Inge straightened up.

He stood directly in front of her, so close his stale nicotine breath enveloped her, but still she didn't look at him.

He said, "So what makes you so special that the rules don't apply?"

"Nothing, Herr Rottenführer."

Sneering, he eyed her up and down. His jaw dropped. He pointed at her left shin, now revealed with her standing properly. "What the hell is that?"

"I'm sorry, Herr Rottenführer. I lost track of the days and didn't realize it was that time of the month."

"Do you think we want to see that? You dirty Jew whore!" He whipped her arm. "Dirty, dirty Jew whore." He lashed once more.

Inge squealed, flinching with each stroke but having no way to avoid them. He struck harder, and she cried out.

Finally, he pointed at the blood. "If I ever see that again, you'll see the end of a rope. Understand, Jew?"

Her voice faltering, she said, "Y-yes, Herr R-Rottenführer."

He strode away, head high as if basking in his triumph.

A quivering mess, Inge didn't follow much of what happened next, focusing all her strength on staying upright and still, despite the pain burning inside her.

Eventually, the women were dismissed, but instead of being allowed back to their cells, they were divided into groups.

As Inge cradled her left arm, a woman with curly brown hair sidled over and grabbed her dress. Inge flinched, ready for a new assault. But the woman didn't hit her. Instead, she ripped one of the pockets off and handed the scrap of fabric to Inge.

The woman said, "Either pad it or plug it. Your choice."

"Thank you."

"Don't worry, it'll only be a problem for a few months." The woman sauntered away, which seemed an odd way to end a conversation, not least because women usually menstruated into their forties. However, Inge was just thankful for the help.

She folded the piece of cloth, turned her back on everyone, and shoved the makeshift pad inside her panties.

Dawn had barely broken and yet, already, the day was a nightmare. Surely things could only get better. Surely.

***

Twenty minutes later, Inge and eighty-nine other women trudged along a country road three abreast, a guard at the front, one at the back, kapos alongside.

Ahead, the curly-haired woman did a double take at something in the roadside grass, then looked over her shoulder to see where the nearest escort was.

The person behind her looked into the grass too.

And the next.

A woman from her cattle car, two people ahead of Inge, reached into the grass and picked up a bread bun. A kapo scooted up from behind and clobbered her with a rubber truncheon. The bread fell onto the road and the kapo ground it into the dirt.

Bread lying in the middle of nowhere? How odd.

The group struggled on.

Directly in front of Inge, a woman limped along in a blue jacket, white padding bursting out of the shoulders. Hobbling, she dragged her left leg. Inge hadn't noticed at first, but the woman had only a right shoe, her left foot walking on a small rectangle of wood held in place by a thin leather strap over her instep.

Inge gazed at the feet ahead of her. Some women had proper footwear, but many had the wood-and-strap clog things.

The limping woman lurched onward but became slower and slower, then stumbled and fell onto her palms. She pushed up and struggled on.

A kapo battered the woman across the back. "Move, you worthless Jew."

Already weak, the woman crumpled onto the road.

Inge stopped, but the kapo shoved her. "Keep moving."

As Inge passed, the kapo kicked the fallen woman.

Biting her tongue at the injustice, Inge scurried on. Getting involved would end only one way — pain and misery for the woman *and* for her.

At a large elm, they turned onto a dirt track and marched up an incline to the brow. A quarry lay below, men working at the stone face.

Pock Face pointed into the bottom of the quarry. "Report to the shack." She then pointed to a flat area beside her. "Pile the stones here."

Inge gazed at the uneven stone steps that climbed up and up and up to finally reach the storage spot the kapo had specified.

Under her breath, she said, "Seriously?"

"Any questions?" asked Pock Face.

Unsurprisingly, no one had any.

The women descended, kapos stationing themselves every twenty or so steps. Inge tramped down what felt like a thousand but in reality was about a hundred. She muttered, "So the Nazis can invade half the civilized world, but they've never heard of a conveyor belt?"

In front of her, the curly-haired woman sniggered.

At the shed, a man in civilian clothes issued various tools. Inge received a wooden yoke with a metal bucket on either end.

Copying women with similar equipment, Inge tramped to a pile of stones and loaded her buckets. She filled one, making sure a huge stone stuck out for the guards to see she was working hard in the hope they wouldn't beat her, then started filling her second bucket.

Filling her own buckets, Curly Hair whispered, "Putting a lot in won't impress the guards. But if they're less than half full, they'll fill them for you, and believe me, you do not want that."

Inge moved the huge stone to the other bucket. "So fill to just below the rim?"

The woman nodded, picked up her yoke, and plodded away.

Her buckets suitably filled, Inge scuttled after her, the yoke across her shoulders, a hand steadying each bucket. This woman seemed to know the ins and outs of this place, and of all the people Inge had encountered, she was the only one who'd been remotely friendly.

Inge started up the uneven steps. The first two dozen were fine, but after that, the crushing weight of her load dragged her down. She slogged on, breathing hard. By halfway, she was panting like a seventy-year-old with a lung condition, so she paused for a breather.

A kapo cracked Inge across the back with a whip. "Move!"

Inge flinched, then trudged on.

Her leg muscles burned and her shoulders hurt from the punishing yoke. As she lifted her foot to conquer a particularly big step, her load tipped her backward. She pictured herself tumbling down the steps to land in a mangled heap but lurched forward and caught herself. She heaved on.

The summit in sight, Inge gasped with every step, sweat plastering her dress to her. Finally, she made it onto level ground.

"Dear Lord." She shuffled over to the growing pile of stone, her legs quivering, and let the yoke drop near to Curly Hair.

She rolled her shoulders, the release from the torturous weight feeling tremendous.

Unloading, Curly Hair said, "Don't let them see you wasting time."

Inge crouched to empty her buckets.

A truck rumbled up the track and reversed toward the pile of stones.

Inge said, "If they were bringing a truck anyway, couldn't they have given us a lift?"

Curly Hair chuckled. "Man, you're a riot."

"What? It's a reasonable question."

"Yes, because there's nothing the Nazis like more than a reasonable Jew."

Inge massaged her shoulders where the yoke had dug in. "Does that mean we won't be getting a back rub later to help with this chafing?"

The woman laughed again.

Inge tapped her bucket. "Thanks for the advice. And for helping earlier."

"Forget it." She fiddled with the clasp holding one of the buckets to her yoke, even though it appeared secure. "Wash that rag this evening, then sleep on it for your body heat to dry. Don't leave it somewhere to dry because someone will take it – like everything else here, rags are currency. Have you got something to use overnight?"

A cotton handkerchief embroidered with pink roses nestled in her pocket with her bowl. "Yes."

"So you're all set."

"Thank you."

The woman nodded. Grabbing her yoke, she stood.

"I'm Inge."

Curly Hair glanced around, as if anxious about someone catching them being civil. She headed for the steps. "Greta."

Inge smiled. She might be in hell, but at least she was no longer imprisoned there alone.

With renewed energy, Inge marched down into the quarry and loaded her buckets again. And again. And again.

136 steps.

Inge counted them. Twice. Which was a mistake because then she couldn't stop counting them. She guessed 136 was the equivalent of climbing a ten-story building. That was high!

Trudging up, it took forever to reach 136. She hated every single step, every drop of sweat, every gasped breath. It was torture.

Then she discovered a secret.

If she counted backward from 136, as if by magic, the climb became less daunting because instead of struggling up with the

63

number growing bigger and bigger, the number consistently shrank smaller and smaller. It was especially good for those last few steps. Counting down from ten to zero felt infinitely easier than trudging up from 126 to 136. She experimented and discovered counting in different languages also lightened the burden. These were nothing but psychological tricks, but they worked.

Later, she'd share her secret with her new friend. Sharing something useful, apart from encouraging a friendship, might motivate Greta to share more of her secrets to surviving this place.

And maybe not just this place. Maybe about the arrival, that field, the buses.

No!

Inge's chin trembled. Right now, her family was still alive because she had no proof to the contrary, but if she learned they weren't, that would break her. And she couldn't break. She was going to survive this — survive to tell the world of the horrors she'd witnessed. To do that, her family had to stay alive, even if they lived only in her mind.

As Inge tramped over to ascend, the woman with only one shoe started up, but her clog caught on the first step, and she tripped. She crunched into the staircase and lay gasping.

Pock Face rushed over. She pounded the woman with her truncheon. "Get up, you lazy Jew. Up!"

The woman threw her arms up to shield herself, but the kapo was relentless.

"Get up!" Another strike.

Eventually, the woman forsook protecting herself in favor of pushing to her feet.

Pock Face stopped hitting her and jabbed at the spilled stones. "Get them to the top. Unless you want another beating."

In tears, the woman refilled her buckets.

Inge scooted past and jerked her way upward as quickly as she could. Once she'd put twenty steps between her and Pock Face, she slowed, panting.

So the hill itself wasn't the only battle to be faced. What other dangers lurked yet to be discovered?

15

Following orders, Rudi marched eight machine-gun-wielding personnel into the compound, where the women were lined up.

Gruber glared, Baumann wiped the sweat off his brow, and Krebs fidgeted with his weapon. Everyone was on edge. Unsurprisingly. Whenever there was a mass execution, there was always the possibility of a prisoner revolt. Even unarmed, if the prisoners swarmed the guards, it would be touch and go who got out alive.

His men strategically placed, Rudi gave the order he always hated giving to a guard waiting with a stepladder. The guard mounted the wooden platform and hung a noose from the gallows permanently erected in the roll call area as a deterrent.

The women stared indifferently as that and a second one went up, probably appreciating that the two sisters had to die. But when the guard hung a third noose, shuffling feet and whispered voices filled the air.

Gruber shouted, "Silence!"

Kapos marched along the rows, battering random women as warnings.

Finally, the fourth noose dangled from the scaffolding.

Some women from Barracks 02 cried, undoubtedly knowing that some of them were to die, but not knowing who. The problem was, four nooses made no sense — a couple were obviously for the sisters, but who could the extra two be for?

As the four nooses swayed in the breeze, Rudi and Baumann trudged back to the administration block. They said nothing. Behind them, hundreds of women stared at the gallows, each probably imagining it could be they dangling from one of the nooses. Terrifying though it was, there was no denying Kloser's flair for the dramatic.

At his desk, Rudi shoved aside a report on the income generated by local companies hiring prisoners at four reichsmarks per day and gazed out of the window at the women. This forced labor was necessary to power the Fatherland to the victory it deserved, so why did he feel pangs of...? He didn't know what. Guilt? Shame? Injustice? All of those?

But how was that possible?

He didn't feel guilt at imprisoning a cow and forcing it to provide milk, or shame at a horse pulling a plow. And where was the injustice in forcing their guard dogs to patrol the camp perimeter?

Okay, their dogs were better fed than the prisoners, cows didn't exactly work to produce milk but after calving, just wandered around eating, and horses... well, horses got the worst of the three, but they still got food, shelter, maybe even to gallop around a field for the joy of it. What elevated Jews so far above other beasts that he should suffer such an odd combination of feelings?

"Herr Oberscharführer?"

Rudi turned from the window.

Baumann stood in the doorway. "The commandant would like a word."

"Of course."

Moving closer, Baumann said quieter, "But first, what do you make of this?" He offered him the shiv the sister had used in the attack.

Rudi examined the bloodstained weapon — a bit of wood bound by cord to a strip of metal that looked to have been sharpened on a stone. Nothing special. "And?"

"Smell it," said Baumann.

Rudi frowned. An odd request, but Rudi did so. He wrinkled his nose at the unmistakable scent of excrement.

"Exactly," said Baumann. "I think they dipped it in the latrines, hoping if they didn't kill him outright, an infected wound might do the job for them."

"Have you told him?"

"There's no point worrying him at this stage. I'm treating him with sulfonamides, which should get rid of any infection. If my supplies hold out."

"See they do." Rudi accompanied him into the infirmary and clicked his heels. "Herr Kommandant."

Kloser struggled to pull a boot on one-handed. "Is everything prepared?"

"The prisoners are at attention and four nooses are hung, yes."

Fumbling the boot, Kloser cursed and hurled it across the room. It hit a shelf and knocked off rolls of bandages and boxes of medical supplies.

"Allow me." Rudi picked up the footwear, then crouched to help Kloser put it on.

"When you've brought the sisters out," said Kloser, "bring the Box around."

Rudi cringed, sliding Kloser's foot into the boot. He'd hoped he'd been wrong about the Box, but...

Kloser must have sensed Rudi's unease.

"Rudi?"

Holding Kloser's left calf, Rudi looked up. "Yes?"

"I know you don't always approve of my methods, but don't be deceived by these Jews. They're experts at making you see one thing while they're secretly doing another. Look at how sneaky their attack on me was."

Rudi nodded. It was very cunning and deceitful.

Kloser said, "Don't be fooled into thinking they're like us. They might look like us, talk like us, even behave like us, but believe me, they aren't us. They're vermin, Rudi. We have to protect the Fatherland from them."

Kloser was right — Rudi couldn't allow himself to be fooled into thinking they were like him. And why would he? He'd seen a chameleon in Berlin Zoo change color; as a kid, he'd kept a caterpillar in a jar and witnessed it transform into a butterfly; he'd even heard a parrot in Oskar's Café speak — just like a person. Animals were capable of astounding trickery. Sometimes they did it innocently, but many a time it was to deceive, to lure prey into a trap. Just like the two sisters had. The establishment was right — Jews were dangerous. So dangerous. Both to individual Germans and to the Fatherland as a whole.

He slammed his palm into the heel of Kloser's boot to ensure it was on firmly and stood. "Ready, Herr Kommandant."

But his gaze was drawn to the window and the herd of women standing to attention in the baking sun. If they were any other animal, he'd have tubs of water sent out to them. When he appreciated what Kloser was doing was right, why did it feel so wrong? And more importantly, what could he do about it?

16

Rudi waited at the far side of the prisoners' infirmary block, the last third of which was split between a kapo accommodation section and a small detention area. Two kapos opened Standing Cell 01.

The older, knife-wielding sister tumbled out of a "room" barely bigger than an upright coffin, so she'd been unable to lie down or even sit for days. Two kapos hauled the sister outside, where she squinted in the daylight, while two others opened Cell 04 and dragged out the equally disheveled middle sister, her legs jelly from the torture of standing for so long.

Following Kloser's orders, Rudi and his entourage lugged the sisters to the roll call area and forced them onto their knees in front of the gallows.

With everyone assembled, Kloser swaggered out of the administration block. He stood on the veranda, hands on his hips, the left heavily bandaged, and surveyed his empire like a conquering hero.

Whispers and anxious glances shot through the crowd.

No doubt pumped full of every drug Baumann could find, Kloser hobbled unaided down the track and into the compound. He stood beside the gallows, chest puffed, chin up. He gave a single nod.

Block Leader Lena identified the first of the sisters' four bunkmates: a woman whose ears stuck out. Kapos marched the bemused woman up the steps to the scaffold, where they stood her on a trapdoor. She never made a sound as the guard lowered the noose over her head, just stared wild-eyed as if she didn't believe what was happening.

The second woman cried as Lena pointed her out. Her legs gave, so the guards heaved her to her spot on the gallows.

Relief swept across the remaining women; they obviously assumed that now there were four women awaiting punishment, all four places on the gallows were accounted for.

Kloser smirked.

Lena identified the third bunkmate and the kapos grabbed her. She kicked and bucked to break free. "No! No!"

One of the men slammed his rifle butt into her gut, and she crumpled, face twisted in pain.

By now, the fourth bunkmate had obviously guessed what was to come and resigned herself to it, because when the kapos collected her, she didn't struggle. Instead, she recited what sounded like a prayer in a language Rudi didn't understand.

It always amazed Rudi how willingly some people went to their deaths. All four of these women knew they were going to die, and yet only one of them had wanted to live enough to fight. What was wrong with them? Did someone who refused to fight for life actually deserve to have it?

With four heads in four nooses, Kloser swaggered to center stage.

He pointed at the sisters. "These would-be murderesses tried to kill me." Turning, he gestured to the scaffold. "While these women were either collaborators by remaining silent or too stupid to fathom what was going on. Either way, these four failed in their duty to police this camp for the benefit of us all."

Kloser raised his right arm and snapped his fingers. A guard pulled a lever. The trapdoor under the first woman opened and she dropped, her neck snapping with a crack, eyes staring in disbelief.

The rope creaked as it rubbed on the wood scaffold. Kloser smirked.

Three more times, the commandant snapped his fingers, until four bodies swung like a macabre line of laundry in a breeze.

He stared at the two sisters, and his smirk widened. "Bring the Box."

Closing her eyes, the older sister bowed her head.

The other groveled on her hands and knees. "Please, not the Box. Hang us. Please! In the name of God, hang us."

Kloser said, "You've brought this on yourself."

"Please, not the Box. Please." She sobbed at Kloser's feet.

He shuffled back from her. With a supercilious tone, he said, "It's no use begging me — I'm just an innocent bystander, so what happens next is out of my hands. Your sister, however..." He chuckled.

The older sister spat at him.

Two guards carried a battered wooden trunk over, its edges and corners reinforced with metal. They placed it next to the older sister, resting the thing on one end so the lid opened vertically.

The younger woman wailed. The other reached out to comfort her, but a kapo whipped her hand.

The older sister said, "I love you, Barta."

Barta's face twisted into more pain than a person should ever know. "I can't, Dara. No."

Unbelievably calm, Dara said, "Do it, Barta. You must. Or it will be worse for you."

Saliva stringing from her gaping mouth, Barta couldn't speak for crying. She shook her head, staring at her sister.

"Barta, do it. For me."

Barta screamed. She jumped up and ran.

A guard leveled his rifle at her, but Kloser thrust his hand out. "Hold your fire." He sneered. "I like this part."

Barta raced to the fence and leaped onto the electrified barbed wire. Her body jerked as the deadly voltage ripped through her, then, fingers locked around the wire, she dangled like a broken marionette in a nightmare.

Dara glowered at Kloser. "I curse you. I curse you, your wife, your children, and your children's children. I curse each of you to die in agony, alone and unloved."

Kloser gestured to the trunk. "Get her in."

Resigned to her fate, Dara allowed two guards to shut her into the Box.

Her voice muffled, Dara said, "I curse you, Franz Kloser! I curse you!"

"You." Kloser pointed at Lena.

Her jaw dropped.

"You should have known what was happening in your own barracks, so you'll do the honors."

A guard handed her a hammer and a bundle of six-inch nails.

She said, "I'm sorry, Herr Kommandant. They planned in secret. There was nothing I could do."

"So make amends now."

"Of course, Herr Kommandant." She tottered over to the trunk, placed a nail on the top and hammered it in.

Shuffling came from inside. "Missed me, you pig!"

Kloser glared at Lena. "You'll do a proper job, or you'll be in there next!"

"Yes, Herr Kommandant."

Lena hammered a nail into the side, then another a few inches lower. She then moved to the far side and hammered one in the middle.

A scream came from the Box. Kloser smiled.

Lena pounded another nail in, and another, and another, choosing different sides and different levels. Some elicited a scream, others didn't.

Once around sixteen nails stuck into the box in an assortment of places, Kloser said, "Enough. You know what to do now. And remember, a proper job, or you're in there next."

Her head hung, Lena whispered something Rudi didn't catch. Maybe a prayer or a plea for forgiveness. Her shoulder against the top edge of the Box, she pushed. It slammed over into the dirt. Dara screamed as she fell onto the nails sticking in from the side that was now on the ground.

Lena heaved on one of the leather handles and tumbled the trunk over again. The sister wailed as more nails pierced more of her body. A third time, Lena rolled the trunk like some evil game of dice, and a third time, Dara screeched. Blood streaked the Box's sides from holes where nails had previously been hammered and later removed.

And the game went on.

Rudi swallowed hard as a sickness rose inside him. He ached to look away, to run to his quarters and down a bottle of schnapps to purge this day from his mind. But he couldn't. He couldn't show such weakness in front of the prisoners, in front of his commanding officer. So he stood. Silent. Watching the gruesome spectacle. And hating himself for doing so.

Sweat glistened on Lena's face as she tossed the trunk over again. Dara wailed, but her cries were weaker now. Again, Lena heaved the Box over, the woman inside whimpering.

"Again," said Kloser.

Pushing her shoulder against the top of the trunk, Lena lunged, and the Box crashed onto another side. The wailing stopped abruptly.

Gasping for air, Lena stared at the Box. The silent Box. With no scuffling or moaning coming from the occupant, Lena stood to attention, as if awaiting praise for a job well done.

Kloser unholstered his pistol and shot her.

He smiled at Rudi. "That's a good day's work, and it isn't even lunchtime, don't you think, Oberscharführer?"

"Congratulations on restoring order, Herr Kommandant." Rudi hoped he might yet prevent even more suffering – there was no telling who the commandant might target if he felt he was on a roll. Rudi leaned closer. "With respect, maybe it would be wise for you to rest after exerting yourself. I can take things from here."

Kloser nodded. "Maybe you're right." He lurched away.

Rudi addressed the women. "Let this be a lesson to you all. Kommandant Kloser will accept nothing but unquestioning obedience. Anything else will be met with the harshest of justice."

He glanced around; Kloser hobbled toward the administration block.

Rudi gestured to the hanged women. "This treacherous scum will be left as a reminder of what happens to those who disobey the rules. When you look at them, think how lucky you are that he saw fit to punish so few of you."

He looked around again. Kloser disappeared inside and the door shut.

Rudi drew a breath. "Dismissed."

The women dashed away, probably fearful he'd change his mind and make an example of a random target.

Rudi stared at the ground. He couldn't let things carry on like this. But he was only second-in-command, so what could he do? And more crucially, how could he get away with doing it?

17

Midday, a whistle sounded. Everyone downed tools and tramped toward the shack. Inge swung her yoke off and bent double, hands on her knees, gasping. In the past, she'd believed she'd been tired after working hard, but boy, had she been wrong.

The shack door swung open, and a cook stood behind a huge pot. Her legs wobbling, Inge staggered over.

The old hands stood to one side, allowing the new arrivals to line up first. Maybe they remembered how tough the first few days were, so they wanted to help the newcomers ease into things. How nice of them.

Slowly, the line shuffled forward until Inge reached the front. She held out her bowl, and the cook ladled in scummy gunk that looked as appealing as what went down the plughole after she'd bathed.

Inge doddered away, swirling her cloudy, watery dinner. Tiny specks floated in it, masquerading as meat, or vegetables, or for all she knew, grass. She sniffed it. Either the gunk had no fragrance or the recent assault on her senses had been so severe, she was now dulled to all but the most extreme of smells.

She sipped it. Yes, it complemented the breakfast "coffee" perfectly: tasteless, nutritionless, *almost* worthless. Almost — bad food was still food.

Inge moseyed past the old hands waiting close by, Greta among them. "I see they managed to poach a chef from the London Ritz."

Greta laughed. "No, that's the breakfast chef. This one's from Maxim's, Paris."

Inge snickered. "You're not hungry?"

"Starving."

"So why aren't you queuing?"

Greta leaned closer and whispered, "Never be first to be served — it's all water."

"You're telling me."

"But don't wait too long either or it might all be gone."

"So be in the middle?" asked Inge.

"And make a friend of the cook, then they'll dig the ladle down to the good stuff that's sunk to the bottom."

Inge sighed. Thank heaven she'd made such a great first impression on the breakfast cook.

The old hands formed a line, Greta joining them.

Inge sat on a nearby rock.

When Greta returned, she sat beside Inge. She had the same gunk, but what looked like chunks of turnip lurked in it.

Inge nodded. A valuable lesson learned. "You seem to know a lot about this place."

Greta sniggered. "Unfortunately." She slurped her soup. "Is it still August?"

Inge shook her head. "September." She'd thought she was doing badly to lose track of the days for her period to sneak up on her, but how bad must things be to lose track of the month?

Greta said, "I try not to think about how long I've been here. You can't dwell on the past, this work, or the horrendous things you see... not if you want to survive."

"Yes, I discovered it's easier to get up the steps if I occupy my mind."

Greta nodded. "What do you do? Picture climbing a hill with your boyfriend?"

"Nah-huh. Count backward from 136 in different languages."

"Hmmm... I might try that, because I tell you"– she nodded to the steps –"my Markus is getting sick to death of me dragging him up that darn thing."

They both laughed.

Inge said, "So apart from the line for the soup, is there anything else I should know about?"

Greta snorted. "Where to start." She ate more soup. "Okay, one of the main things is to never leave your shoes unattended. Shoes are like gold, you put them down for a second, and they'll be gone."

"Shoes?" How could shoes be so important?

"If you can't walk, you can't work, and if you can't work, you're no use to the Germans, so..." She swept her hand across her throat.

"Really?"

74

"Do you think there's a nice little retirement village for worn-out prisoners?"

"So if I refuse to pick up my yoke after dinner..."

"They'll shoot you in the back of the head." Greta said it so matter-of-factly, Inge shuddered.

She gulped. She'd been blasé about this place because the appalling living conditions had distracted her, but in reality, it was utterly terrifying, with life hanging in the balance over the tiniest of things.

"Anything else?" she asked.

Chewing turnip, Greta said, "Get a top bunk. The last thing you want is to be below someone with dysentery. I tell you, being woken up by—"

"Urgh, I get it, I get it." Inge grimaced.

"Oh, and never — I mean never — let them see you're sick."

"Never?"

"Well, unless you're almost dying, then it doesn't matter anyway."

"Isn't there a doctor?"

Greta lapped every last drop of soup from her bowl like an animal. "There's an infirmary. But they don't waste resources on us when they can just ship in more prisoners. It's not like they're going to run out anytime soon, is it?"

"So if you can't work, it's all over?"

Greta nodded.

Remembering their first exchange, Inge frowned. "What did you mean this morning when you said my period would only be a problem for a few months?"

Greta winced. "They stop."

"What do you mean?"

"They just stop. As in no more periods."

"Ever?"

Greta shrugged. "I haven't had one this year."

"*This year?*"

"Maybe it's the lack of food, maybe something they put in the coffee." She shrugged again. "But what's it matter? They stop, and there's not a darn thing you can do about it."

Inge stared agape. She'd always dreamed of one day having a family. While the Nazis had robbed her of her freedom, someday that would end. But to rob her of motherhood...

Greta touched Inge's arm. "Hey, I'm not a doctor. Who knows, maybe they'll start again if we ever get out of here."

No children? Sickness rose from her stomach. They'd taken her family, her home, her past... now they were stealing her future, too.

Inge gritted her teeth.

No. Whatever it took, she'd beat this. The Nazis could have the time during which she was imprisoned, but once liberation came, that was her time. And she would live it to the fullest, children and all.

A whistle sounded to end the break, even though they couldn't have been resting for more than thirty minutes. The torture resumed. And it went on and on and on. Inge had never known a day last so long, and when the whistle was finally blown to end it, she collapsed onto all fours, panting. But then she remembered what Greta had said about appearing unfit for work.

Groaning with the effort, Inge clambered up and, wavering from exhaustion, hauled herself to the steps. For the last time that day, she trudged up, huffing and puffing.

The walk to the prison was a hard slog, Inge pushing her body on through strength of will, not muscle. When the building finally came into view, she smiled. She'd never have believed she could be so happy to see such a horrible place. However, instead of being allowed to fall into bed, they were herded into the courtyard and lined up.

Inge stood swaying. Her eyelids drooping, breath long, slow heaves, she prayed for it to end. But what was "it" anyway? The guards chatted while the kapos and room leaders wandered around hitting people at random, but no one was actually doing anything. It was as if this was simply another form of torture.

Her left leg buckled, but she managed to catch herself. She straightened, still swaying.

Finally, someone counted them and they were dismissed. Her feet all but glued to the ground, Inge trudged toward the entrance but crumpled. On her knees, she gasped. Two minutes. She'd go inside in two minutes.

Ten minutes later, Inge heaved herself up and wobbled into the mess hall, only to find herself exactly where Greta had said not to be – the back of the line.

Trembling with the effort of standing, Inge scanned the faces of the women on this side of the room, then beyond the line of kapos separating them, the faces of the men on the other side.

She slumped. No Mama. No Agata. No Robert.

The line moving, Inge watched people collect bread and soup, then guzzle it down. Her mouth watered and her stomach rumbled. She didn't care how vile the food looked, she was going to smile at the cook and say thank you. Food was food. And she needed it.

But what if there was none left? Greta had said they sometimes ran out.

Someone nearby slurped loudly from their bowl. Inge's mouth watered all the more while her stomach hurt like someone was kicking her from the inside.

If there was no food left when she got there, she couldn't go on. She might as well assault a guard and let them shoot her.

The fourth woman in front of Inge held out her bowl, and the cook ladled in food. The third woman offered her bowl, but the cook tipped the massive metal pot at an angle, scooped something out of the corner, and dropped that in. The woman directly before Inge held out her bowl, and again, the cook scraped into the very corner of the pot.

That was it. All gone. Inge had never been lucky, as ending up here had proven, but now, to rub it in, fate had played yet another cruel joke. Tears welled. She'd always thought of herself as a strong person, but even the strongest had their limits.

She shuffled along, vainly held out her bowl to the cook, and waited for the woman to smirk and turn away. But she didn't. She scraped the bottom of the pot and splattered a massive dollop of thick vegetable gunk into Inge's bowl. Inge stared at the mound. Even at home, it would be a decent-sized meal. She smiled.

The cook offered a piece of bread as well.

Inge's smile broadened. "Thank you. Have a nice evening."

The cook frowned but said, "You're welcome."

Still beaming, Inge shuffled over to Greta, who was licking her bowl.

Her friend froze when she saw the pile in Inge's bowl. "Is it your birthday? Because if it is, I didn't get you a present."

Inge chuckled. "I was the last one. I didn't think there was going to be anything left, then I got all this."

"Man, talk about lucky."

Inge offered her bowl. "Have some."

Greta squinted. "Really?"

"I'll never eat it all. Think of it as a thank-you for all the advice." Inge nibbled her bread in her left hand.

Greta scraped a couple mouthfuls into her bowl. "Thanks. But you might want to get into the habit of not eating with that hand."

Inge frowned. "Why?"

"Put it this way, there's no toilet paper, no soap, and little water, but you've got to wipe with something."

Her hand? Queasiness roiled in her stomach. Just when she figured she'd gotten a handle on this place and that things couldn't get any worse, the Germans had another surprise.

Inge put the bread in her pocket. "Maybe I'll save it for breakfast."

"A lot do that." Greta pointed to Inge's bowl. "Or as you've got so much soup, give half your bread to the big Pole with the scar." She nodded to a woman across the room. "If you ever need a favor, she'll remember and treat you well."

A powerful friend was a good idea. Inge ambled over to where four prisoners chatted, one tall with a jagged scar along her left jawline.

"Hi." Inge smiled.

The Pole stared impassively.

"I thought you might like some extra bread." Inge offered half.

The Pole said, "And what do you want?"

"For you to one day remember that I gave it to you." She placed the bread in the Pole's bowl and offered her hand to shake. "I'm Inge."

The Pole didn't shake. "I'll remember." She resumed her conversation.

Inge returned to Greta. Her spirits lifted, something that had puzzled her earlier sprang to her mind. "What was with that bread in the grass this morning?"

Chomping a chunk of turnip, Greta said, "Some of the locals know how tough the prison is, so they leave little gifts for us. Problem is, you can only grab them if no one's watching."

Extra food? Sympathetic locals? A fixer who owed her? Maybe surviving this place wasn't just a matter of dogged determination but learning all its little secrets. What secret would she uncover next?

18

The bell woke Inge. She pushed to get up to be one of the first to the bathroom, but she groaned. Every muscle hurt. Arms, legs, back, stomach, chest... everything. Nothing wanted to move.

Wincing, she shuffled to the edge of the bunk and, with a squeal, dropped to the floor. She stood, clinging to one of the bed uprights for support.

How was she going to manage the quarry? The steps would kill her. And if they didn't, the guards would because she'd be so slow.

Sucking through her teeth with every movement, she straightened her bedding, then when the door opened, she hobbled out, fists balled, jaw clenched. The bathroom was so busy, she had to wait for a toilet. She cursed for having eaten so much.

A woman left one of the holes, so Inge shuffled toward it, but someone scooted past and grabbed it. In no state to argue, Inge slumped beside the stinking row of women, cringing at the sounds of bodily functions.

Another spot free, she tried to lower herself over the hole, but her screaming muscles gave and she collapsed onto it.

Now what?

She looked at the crowd waiting their turn. How was she supposed to go with so many people watching?

Someone beside her let rip.

Grimacing, she closed her eyes and turned away. And that was when an idea struck her. Keeping her eyes closed, she covered her ears and pictured herself locked in her bathroom at home.

And the illusion worked. Until the next dilemma came. Greta was right – there was no toilet paper.

Inge dropped her face into her hands. Did she really have to do what Greta had suggested? It was either that or rip away another piece of her dress to use, but then what? Even if she washed the rag — without soap — there were only so many times she could reuse it. After a month, how much dress would be left?

The woman beside her reached back with her left hand. Inge cringed.

"Hey!" A scrawny woman waiting in line glared at Inge. "Get a move on."

Inge stared at her left hand. Was she really going to do this?

She reached behind her and...

She gagged but swallowed hard to keep from vomiting.

Job done, she pushed to stand, but her legs didn't have the strength. Gritting her teeth, she heaved with all her might, only to collapse in a gasping mess.

"For the love of..." The scrawny woman rolled her eyes. She grabbed Inge's right arm and yanked her up.

Inge squealed but then said, "Thank you." She shuffled toward the water trough, holding her left hand away from her.

"Oh, no, you don't," said a washing woman. She jabbed to a bucket on a table.

Inge staggered over. Twisting her face away to avoid seeing what others had left behind from their cleansing, she washed her hand as well as she could, then returned to the trough and washed her face using her right hand.

Finally, she tottered to breakfast. She nibbled her saved bread and drank her "coffee" while holding her left hand behind her back.

Greta appeared, smirking. "Let me guess — you conquered the toilet."

"I think *it* conquered me." She wiggled her left shoulder. "I can't imagine ever using this hand again."

"Trust me, you'll get used to it. Or there are women who'll do it for you for a scrap of bread."

"Seriously?" Inge swigged more coffee.

"Hey, if you're hungry enough, you'll do anything. Mind you, with that job, you have to ask if they're doing it for food or for kicks."

Inge laughed. "You know you said to never show you're sick — what do you do if you can't move?"

"Feeling it after yesterday, huh?"

"I can barely stand, so how the devil am I going to carry stones up that hill?"

Greta winced. "If you don't, you're going to feel the whip. Or worse."

80

"Just now, someone had to literally lift me off the toilet. Literally."

"Sorry, but you're going to have to find a way."

Breakfast over, Inge was the sixth to last to roll call, only beating a few other newcomers straining to move too.

After they were counted, Inge stood waiting for the work details to be organized for construction, the trench, the factory...

Under her breath, she said, "Anything but the quarry, anything but the quarry, anything but—"

Pock Face pointed at Inge's column of women. "Quarry."

Oh Lord, this was it. The end. If the quarry didn't kill her, the guards would.

But what could she do? She wasn't sick, so no doctor would declare her unfit for work. And even if one did, Greta had warned that being sick could be as good as a death sentence. Inge had no choice. Somehow, she had to work the quarry.

Inge staggered toward the quarry work detail.

Zofia grabbed Inge's shoulder. "Oh no, you don't. I haven't forgotten how you embarrassed me yesterday with your antics during roll call." She nodded to Pock Face. "This one's for bathroom detail."

Bathroom detail? Inge could have kissed the woman. Splash disinfectant around, a little mopping, light scrubbing with a sponge... talk about cushy. Yesterday, her menstrual cycle had gotten her a beating, but today, it had probably saved her life. And she'd thought she was unlucky.

Her good fortune boosting her energy, Inge fought her way up to the bathroom.

Zofia pointed at the toilets. "Those need cleaning."

"No problem. Where's the mop and scrubbing brush, please?"

Zofia laughed. "I forgot you're new."

She ambled into the far left corner and patted a rusty pipe eight inches in diameter that came through the ceiling and disappeared into the floor. "This is the waste pipe. An outlet connects the toilets to it inside here." She kicked the far left end of the concrete block with the toilet holes in the top. "All the waste needs sluicing through."

Uh-oh. This cushy bathroom duty had suddenly taken an unexpected and extremely unpleasant turn. "So I have to stick a rod down or something?"

Zofia laughed again. "Or something, yes."

Inge cupped her face, then remembered where her left hand had been and whipped it away. "A brush? Please say there's a brush."

She smirked. "Do I really have to spell it out for you?"

Inge cringed.

Again, Zofia pointed at the concrete block. "The incline inside isn't steep enough, so every so often, the waste needs to be pushed from that end"— she pointed to the far right toilet, then swept her hand to the far left one —"to that end."

Inge swallowed, sickness gurgling in her gut. "But there's no rod and no brush."

"No."

"And obviously no gloves."

"Oh yes, there are gloves."

Inge smiled, clutching her chest. "Oh, thank God."

"Ooops. No, sorry, my mistake."

Inge stared at the toilet block, picturing all the women who'd sat on it, including her. And she'd thought wiping herself with her hand was the most disgusting thing she was ever going to have to do.

She glared at the toilets, but then her gaze softened. She'd be able to sit to do this, so while the job might be the most disgusting thing imaginable, at least she could actually do it, so she wouldn't be beaten, or at worst, shot. Who would've thought scooping sewage would have a silver lining?

Zofia said, "Fetch me when you've finished here, and I'll let you into the top-floor bathroom."

Inge's jaw dropped. "I've got to do two floors?"

"No."

"Oh, thank heaven."

"Three. There's the ground floor as well. Two bathrooms on each."

Inge stared wide-eyed. Six bathrooms. All bursting with... she gagged and clutched her mouth.

Zofia left, chuckling.

Inge hobbled to the toilet block. Her face screwed up, she leaned forward to peep into one of the holes but jerked back before she saw anything. She shuffled closer, staring down her nose into the dark interior, wanting to see but also not wanting to. But she saw. She lurched forward and vomited into the toilet.

Wiping her mouth on the back of her hand, she cursed. Great, now she was going to have to stick her hands in that as well.

She stepped back and studied the line of holes. There was no way she could get out of doing this. None. She had to put her hand in and shove whatever she found to the waste pipe. Period. That accepted, the question wasn't how she could avoid the job but how she could distract herself enough to get through it. She needed another psychological trick. But what on earth could distract her from something so vile?

Inge knelt on the floor beside the far right hole. Turning her face away and squinting from the corner of her eye, she raised her left hand and hovered it over the hole.

She repeated, "I'm kneading bread. I'm kneading bread…"

Screwing her eyes closed, she lowered her arm. Her fingertips disappeared below the rim but stopped.

Grimacing, she said, "I'm kneading bread…"

She strained to lower her hand farther, but it didn't budge. She knew she had to do this, but it was as if her arm had a will of its own and would not go deeper. Gasping, she slumped forward.

How was she going to do this job? And if she didn't, would she be facing a whip or a pistol?

"No!" She shook her head. They would not break her.

Inge screamed. And plunged her hand deep into the gungy contents.

Retching, she clutched her mouth with her clean hand and tensed her muscles, fighting the impulse to drag her left arm out.

She wiped her brow and forced herself to draw a couple of steadying breaths.

Finally, she scooped with her left hand. But it was *not* like kneading bread.

She retched again.

But then a distant memory clawed its way from the back of her mind: maybe five years old, sitting in the garden after it had rained, giggling as she made mud pies for her one-eyed doll and teddy.

She scooped backward again. "Just making mud pies. Just making mud pies…"

Her hand now unable to become any dirtier, the job became just another job. Hole by hole, she shoved the waste along and down the outlet.

Eventually, she sat staring into space, her left arm dangling into the last toilet.

She'd done it. She sniggered. The filthiest job ever imagined, and she'd done it. This wasn't a punishment but a blessing. Not only had she been reprieved from the torture of the quarry, but the gentle exercise had eased her aching muscles. And she'd discovered the most important thing anyone could ever learn about themselves – there was nothing she couldn't do to survive. Break her? Let them try.

After Inge had cleaned all six bathrooms, Zofia took her to a small white-tiled bathroom reserved for kapos and functionaries like herself.

Zofia wagged a finger. "Don't be thinking this is me looking out for you – this is me looking out for me. Hell knows what illnesses you'd bring into our room if you didn't scrub yourself." She sauntered out.

Inge stood to the side of a shower jetting lukewarm water and scoured her soiled hand and arm, then she stripped and washed her dress to remove any splatters. Finally, she stepped under the water and lathered her hands with a piece of soap smaller than her thumb. Washing for the first time in over a week, she closed her eyes, luxuriating in freshness.

Heaven.

She smiled. Cleaning the toilets was a punishment that kept on giving.

Something slammed her in the middle of the back. She smacked into the wall and her head crunched into the tiles.

An arm pinned her to the wall by her neck. From the corner of her eye, she saw an SS guard.

He leaned into her ear. "You're going to enjoy this, Jew. This is what a real man feels like."

Dear Lord, no. Not like this. She'd dreamed of her first time, but never this nightmare. She whimpered.

He thrust a hand between her legs and poked at her.

She squealed. "Please, no. Please."

He laughed, but then he released her and staggered back. "What the...?"

He shoved his hand in her face, menstrual blood smeared on his fingers. "What's this?"

Still pressing herself against the wall, not daring to move, Inge said, "I'm sorry, it's—"

He yanked her head back by the hair and slammed it into the wall. "You dirty Jew whore!"

The bathroom blurred. Inge slid down the tiles and slumped in a heap on the floor. A kick slammed into her side, but the world was already turning dark, darker, black...

19

Inge's eyes flickered open to a blurry world.

Crouched before her, Zofia said, "Can you hear me?"

Why was everything sideways? And why was she lying on a bathroom floor?

Zofia grabbed Inge's chin and turned her face. "Can you hear me?"

"I..." Inge shook her head to clear it. "What? Yes, I can hear you. Wh-what happened?"

"You don't remember? Good."

Inge frowned. She'd cleaned the toilets, then gone for a shower — her eyes widened — and someone had grabbed her.

She gasped and jerked to get up and escape.

Zofia eased her down. With an unusual tone of concern, she said, "It's okay. We're alone."

Cowering, Inge scanned the bathroom. Was he still here?

Zofia shook her. "Listen, I can guess what happened, but you have to forget about it, okay? If you report him, nothing good will come of it. Nothing."

"But—"

"No buts! Listen to me — if you report this, the soldier will be punished not for raping you but for touching a Jew, I'll be punished for leaving a prisoner unsupervised, and you'll be punished for daring to bring a complaint. Do you understand?"

Inge nodded.

"Good. Can you stand?"

"I don't know."

Zofia offered her hand.

Inge heaved herself up but tottered back, hitting the wall. "Give me a moment."

Her face feeling swollen, she touched her left eye. Pain shot through her face and she winced. Likewise, touching her lip hurt. Had the monster hit her?

"When you're ready." Zofia handed her a threadbare gray towel and her clothes.

Inge toweled herself and dressed in her soggy clothes, then hobbled for the door but stumbled. Zofia caught her. Together, they shuffled out.

Inge glanced at Zofia. Why was the woman helping her? Did she genuinely care or was it that she hated rapists? Or was it simply concern that any report would cause her problems?

They lurched back to their cell, where Inge slumped against the bunks.

Heading for the door, Zofia said, "You've got the rest of the day off, okay?"

Inge said nothing. She now realized the full horror of this place. That traits she'd held dear — honesty, decency, kindness — wouldn't furnish what she needed to survive.

Zofia turned. "Okay?"

Inge gulped. "Two days off."

"Excuse me?" Zofia glared.

"I want two days off. And the rest of today." Two days would give her time to recover for whatever horrendous task she was assigned next.

"I thought we'd agreed this never happened?"

Inge held her gaze. "Because you'd be punished?"

"And so would you."

Inge smirked. "What are they going to do to me that they haven't already done? But you? You'd have to kiss goodbye to that cozy little private cot of yours and all your other privileges."

Zofia rubbed her mouth, studying Inge. "The rest of today and tomorrow. Now don't push it. Okay?"

"And..."

"And?" Zofia adjusted her grip on her rubber truncheon.

Unblinking, Inge locked her gaze. "No more quarry. For me or Greta."

Zofia snorted and shook her head. "Fine." She left.

Inge snuggled down in her bed. Yes, this bathroom punishment just went on giving and giving. What would it give her next?

20

Rudi swished a stick through the forest grass as he ambled after Bruno, wisps of morning mist creeping between the trees like something out of a fairy tale.

What was he going to do about the other day's events?

He snorted. What could he do?

The prisoners had broken the rules and been punished. SS Command would find no issue there. Except, there was a big difference between a noose and the Box. Plus, some of those hanged may have been innocent. This was the twentieth century, yet it felt more like the Dark Ages, where barbarism and superstition reigned.

If only he could get out of this hellish place.

Bruno had stopped to sniff an elm tree but gazed up at Rudi, tail wagging.

Rudi crouched, ruffling the thick fur around his friend's neck. "What would I do without you, huh?"

Bruno licked Rudi's cheek, again and again. Rudi laughed.

In this godforsaken place, doing these godforsaken things, Bruno was Rudi's one tiny piece of normality — the only splinter of joy in his war-shattered life.

Rudi hugged his dog, basking in the warmth of their shared love.

Breaking away, Rudi glanced at his watch and sighed. "Time to face the world, boy."

He scratched Bruno's head, his gaze drifting through the trees toward the camp. He squinted. What was that?

Training his binoculars on the rear of Barracks 02, he panned to two figures hunched together and occasionally glancing anxiously about. So early after dawn, all the prisoners should be busy with breakfast, so what was going on? But more puzzling, why was one a female prisoner and the other a German soldier?

"What the devil are they doing?"

Illegal dealings were impossible to quash. And while trading for food could be tolerated, trading for weapons or a camera that could be used to forge identity papers was a constant worry.

Rudi crept through the undergrowth, hoping to identify those involved. However, for security reasons, the vegetation had been hacked away to leave a fifty-yard clearing between the fence and the forest, and the figures rejoined the general populace before he could get close enough.

The encounter was likely a simple trade for food, but from their behavior, it didn't seem like a one-off event. To be safe, he'd surveil the area over the next few days to try to catch the culprits again.

Rudi and Bruno made their way back through the forest and emerged at Watchtower 03.

A guard raced toward them.

Under his breath, Rudi said, "We didn't even make it back to camp before it started."

The soldier saluted Rudi. "Herr Oberscharführer, you're needed in the administration block."

Needed? That didn't sound good.

Rudi said, "Do you know why?"

"Sorry, no, Herr Oberscharführer."

"Who is it that needs me?"

"I was only ordered to find you and nothing else, Herr Oberscharführer."

"Okay. Dismissed."

The soldier clicked his heels and ran back toward the camp buildings.

Rudi winced. What if the commandant hadn't had his fill of revenge? Rudi had only so much influence, and if he pushed too hard, it could be seen as insubordination. But he couldn't allow a repeat of the other day. Not more senseless killing. He'd rather face the slaughter of the Eastern Front than more slaughter here. At least then he could look at himself in the mirror.

He trudged up the incline alongside the fence. At the other side, the prisoners lined up for morning roll call. Rudi prayed he wouldn't see Kloser barking orders for even more nightmarish punishments. Luckily, he didn't.

So who needed him?

Ahead, nothing stirred in the commandant's house, the SS accommodation looked quiet, and the administration block appeared eerily still.

Maybe today was his lucky day and he was "needed" because a particularly attractive local woman had called hoping to sell her wares of chocolate-covered cookies. He sniggered. Yes, because that happened so regularly it had become something of a chore.

His smile dropped as the door of the administration block opened and a figure trudged out.

21

Baumann scurried over. "Herr Oberscharführer, it's bad news, I'm afraid"— he shrugged —"or maybe good news. It's one of those weird situations where it could be either, depending on how you view things."

"Then stop babbling and tell me what it is. And please don't say it's the commandant insisting on even more retribution."

Baumann grinned. "That's your choice now."

"What?" Rudi narrowed his eyes. He was in no mood for games.

Baumann checked his watch. "As of seventeen minutes ago, you're acting commandant. Congratulations, Kommandant Kruse."

"Kommandant Kloser isn't..."

"No, but if he isn't sent for proper surgical care soon, he might as well be."

"I thought he was on the mend."

"Have you heard of hospital gangrene?"

Rudi shook his head. "Ordinary gangrene, sure, but *hospital* gangrene?"

"Think gangrene, but instead of it being caused by the blood supply being cut off, it's caused by infection."

"Hell." Rudi blew out his cheeks. Gangrene literally killed parts of a person's body while they were still alive. It was horrific. "And this infection is because the knife was dipped in the latrines?"

"Or bacterial contamination from a prisoner. Or that filthy blanket he wrapped his arm in. Take your pick. To be honest, I'd have been surprised if the wound hadn't become infected. Whatever the cause, I've used all the sulfonamides we had, but they've barely touched it, so I've sent Krebs to requisition whatever the town doctor has."

Rudi pointed to the administration block. "Can I see him?"

Baumann gestured for him to proceed.

90

Rudi patted Bruno. "Go play, boy." There was no point in Bruno being cooped up inside. Bruno wandered away, nose to the ground.

Polishing his glasses, Baumann said, "I'm not one hundred percent about my prognosis, but fever, black blisters, puss... it's not looking good, and I don't want to take any risks."

They ambled toward the door.

Rudi said, "But why does he have to leave? Can't you treat him?"

"Sure — if you want him six feet under within the week."

Rudi's jaw dropped. "It's that bad?"

"It's heading that way. I've been saying for months I don't have the supplies I need, but has anyone listened?"

Rudi regularly requested items that never materialized because the camp was low-priority, so it wasn't surprising Baumann had so little.

Baumann said, "But even if we were fully stocked, I don't have the skills for something like this. He needs a qualified surgeon to cut out all the dead tissue. If it's not done properly — and soon — he could lose his whole arm. Or worse."

"How about the town doctor?"

Baumann shook his head. "He's just a country quack."

Rudi grabbed Baumann's forearm. "Look, you've got to do something. Anything. Don't make me responsible for this hellhole."

"Sorry, Herr Kommandant, but as you're Kloser's deputy, it's already done. Command confirmed it."

Rudi hung his head. He couldn't brutalize the prisoners the way Kloser did, whether the Reich mandated it or not.

Baumann patted him on the arm. "Rudi, don't look at it as a problem, look at it as a gift."

He snorted. "A gift? Oh yeah, it's what I've always dreamed of."

"But isn't it? It's no secret you've struggled to make changes here — worthwhile changes. Well, now's your chance."

Rudi squinted at him.

Baumann smiled. "Seriously. You can make a real difference now. A tiny camp at the back of beyond means nothing to Berlin, but to them"— he gestured to the rows of prisoners —"it's their entire world."

Rudi gazed at the pitiful wretches lined up — filthy, exhausted, half-starved. Was this his chance to bring a glimmer of hope to this godforsaken place? Or would anything positive be quickly overturned, with the prisoners punished for their indulgence and him sent to the Front for his audacity?

22

Inge tramped across grassland, staring at a small copse ahead. True to her word, Zofia had ensured Inge and Greta weren't assigned to the quarry, but what lay beyond those trees that demanded the attention of a fifty-strong work detail?

Inge groaned, jumping over a boggy patch of ground, her muscles still sore. Her top lip was split, her face swollen, and her side bruised, but after resting for a day and a half, she felt more herself. And with their new work placement, things could only improve.

As if God was playing a cruel joke, they passed a bush heavy with ripe blackberries.

Inge's mouth watered. So tauntingly close, yet so far beyond her reach. She dreamed of biting into one and its sweet juice bursting onto her tongue. A kapo stood in front of the bush, smiling and slapping her truncheon into her hand.

Inge looked away.

At the other side of the trees, more grassland was interrupted by a trench around twenty feet wide, nine feet deep, and three hundred feet long. An assortment of equipment lay amid the mud and puddles inside.

One of the kapos shouted, "Get digging!"

With the other prisoners, Inge slid down the slippery bank at the far end. Her feet sank so deep into the mud at the bottom, they disappeared. Some prisoners hacked at the bank with picks, others filled buckets using spades. It looking the easier job, Inge grabbed a spade.

"Do you know what we're doing?" asked Inge.

Greta chose a spade too. "I think it's an antitank trench."

Possibly. The trench was so deep and its sides so steep, if a tank drove in, it would tip forward and never get out.

Inge's eyes widened. "Does this mean the Soviets are almost here?" If they were, liberation couldn't be far off.

"Maybe. Why else dig it?"

A woman heaving a pick said, "Could be Finland."

Inge frowned. "Finland? I thought they were with the Nazis?"

Pounding the bank, the woman said, "If the Soviets take Finland, it's only forty or fifty miles across the Gulf. Maybe the Germans think the Soviets are planning to sneak in through the back door."

Above them, a kapo shouted, "Shut up and dig."

Inge dumped mud in a bucket and whispered to Greta, nodding to the pick woman, "She doesn't know what she's talking about. We're nowhere near that close to Finland."

Greta sniggered. "You don't know where we are, do you?"

"Of course I do. Someone saw a sign from our train. Latvia."

Greta patted Inge on the shoulder. "Welcome to Estonia."

Estonia? That was about as far north as it was possible to get without being in Scandinavia or Russia. Thank heaven it was September, because their winters had to be brutal. Not that she'd be witnessing one — if the Soviets were so close, the war was almost over. At least for her.

23

The sun dipping below the horizon to leave the heavens aglow with warm oranges and lush reds, Rudi stood before the women at the end of roll call. He said loudly, "Kommandant Kloser has been called away indefinitely, leaving me to assume command." Kloser and his wife had gone to Reval, the nearest place with a major medical facility.

Many women shot each other sideways glances, probably wondering if this was good news or bad.

Rudi answered that question. "After our recent typhus scare, with immediate effect, disinfection and showers using soap will be changed from monthly to weekly."

Gasps flitted about, and faces lit up at the prospect of regular bathing.

Rudi signaled four kapos, who carried buckets of soap and disinfectant toward the shower block.

"Dismissed."

The women scurried toward the showers, whoops of delight filling the air.

Rudi marched away, a warmth filling his chest as if he'd thrown a scrap of meat to a starving dog. It felt odd over something so trivial. Odd, yet not unwelcome.

Implementing showers was easy. Considering how close he and his men had to get to the prisoners and that typhus showed no respect for ethnicity or rank, it was impossible for anyone to object. Not every positive change would be so unobjectionable, however. That meant he couldn't roll out a wealth of changes simultaneously because if it was reported to Command and he was unable to justify his actions, everything would be overruled and someone worse than Kloser might take over. No, change demanded careful planning, and even more careful execution.

That night, as acting commandant, Rudi moved into the guest bedroom of Kloser's house. This wouldn't just give him extra comfort but time to research and to plan — in complete secrecy. Unless his housekeeper turned out to be a snoop. But that was highly unlikely because Kloser had used her for years and would've had her in the Box if he'd suspected anything untoward.

However, before getting ahead of himself, Rudi needed to investigate the shenanigans he'd witnessed from the forest.

As dawn broke, Rudi hid behind a bush on the edge of the cleared perimeter, peering through his binoculars at Barracks 02.

Bruno whimpered and nudged the stick he'd dropped at Rudi's feet. He was exceptionally well behaved in the camp or in town, but he knew this was *his* playtime, so obviously he couldn't fathom why they weren't playing.

Without moving from his eyepieces, Rudi patted him. "Sorry, Bruno. Just a few more minutes, then we'll play. I promise."

Waiting for something to happen was eating into his precious time with Bruno, but this job had to be done. Rudi sighed. Because of his added responsibilities, many things would be eating into their special time going forward. He wished he could explain so Bruno wouldn't feel dejected. However, once the camp was running the way Rudi wanted it to, he'd make it up to Bruno. A few weeks. A couple of months tops. There would probably be snow by then. Rudi smiled — how Bruno loved grabbing snowballs out of the air so they exploded in his mouth.

Rudi rubbed his eyes. Maybe he'd been wrong and whatever had gone down had been an isolated incident.

Pawing Rudi's leg, Bruno whined.

Rudi shook his head. This was a waste of time. "Okay, we—"

A soldier waltzed around the back of Barracks 02, and a moment later, a prisoner appeared. Some sort of trade occurred, then they parted. Rudi having a better vantage point, identified the German — Stolze, a cook with a pencil mustache.

That was one mystery solved, but what were they trading? Unfortunately, uncovering that would have to wait. First, Rudi needed to know the frequency with which this trading happened.

Using Bruno's early-morning walk as subterfuge, Rudi spied on the barracks the next day and again witnessed Stolze involved in some illegal trade, but with a different prisoner. Nothing happened the third day; however, the following one, the same thing happened with yet another prisoner, then a two-day break before another trade. That was five days out of eight, making it impossible for Stolze to claim he was not regularly lining his pockets at the prisoners' expense. But what was he trading?

Stolze was a cook, so the obvious answer was food. However, the prisoners were on starvation rations, so was Stolze buying extra food in town and selling it on at a huge markup? Rudi hoped so. The alternative was too disgusting to comprehend — Stolze could be stealing the prisoners' food and selling it back to them. There was only one way to find out.

The following breakfast, Rudi spied on the camp from his new bedroom. The administration block would've provided a better view, but here provided privacy.

Two prisoners from each barracks tramped out of the camp kitchen. Carrying poles on their shoulders, each pair lugged an enormous steaming vat of coffee suspended between them. Rudi hated that stuff — it was as much like coffee as mud was like chocolate.

Escorted by two of Rudi's most trusted men, and overseen by Stolze, the six vat-carriers trudged through the gate and to their respective barracks for their block leader to dish out the rations.

Rudi's guards made for the gate to leave, giving Stolze the all clear to head for the back of Barracks 02. But the guards doubled back, circling around either side of the building.

Slinging his binoculars onto the bed, Rudi dashed through the house and out of the door. He raced around the perimeter and shot into the compound.

He trusted his men; he didn't trust Stolze. However, he needed to be there in person so he didn't have to rely on someone else's "interpretation" of events. He sprinted between Barracks 02 and 03, voices coming as he neared the rear.

"Guys, come on," said Stolze. "It's just a little trade. We all do it, I—"

Rudi rounded the corner. Stolze and the guards immediately stood to attention while a redheaded prisoner hunched over as if hoping to dissolve into the ground.

"What did you find?" asked Rudi.

Schumacher, the taller of his two men, held out his hands — three hunks of bread in one, a gold tooth in the other.

Stolze said, "Herr Haupt—sorry, Herr Kommandant, it's a little harmless trade, is all."

"Harmless?" Rudi held up the tooth, which was streaked with dried blood.

Rudi jabbed at the prisoner. "Show me your teeth." He prayed she'd have a missing tooth and that she hadn't pinned down an innocent victim to rip out gold to sell.

The woman trembled. Schumacher lifted his rifle to batter her for not complying. Though the woman cowered, she didn't try to dodge, no doubt knowing if she did, the punishment would be twice as bad.

"No!" Rudi thrust his arm out and the soldier relaxed. Rudi checked the number sewn to the front of the woman's blue dress. "Show me your teeth, please, 958."

The guards flashed glances to one another at his politeness.

Avoiding eye contact, the woman bared her teeth, revealing a bloody gap top left.

Stolze gulped.

Rudi shook a piece of bread in Stolze's face. "You made her mutilate herself for this?"

"She begged me. I've never done anything like this before, believe me, but she just wouldn't stop begging."

Rudi clenched his fists, adrenaline coursing through his body. He ached to flatten this liar, but a bloody nose would be quickly forgotten.

He stepped closer to Stolze. Too close. So close he felt uncomfortable, so Stolze had to feel ten times worse. His voice unnervingly calm, he said, "Do you think I'm soft compared to Kommandant Kloser, soldier?"

Struggling to lean away from Rudi without stepping back, Stolze said, "Of course not, Herr Kommandant."

"Then why do you feel so comfortable lying to me?"

"Herr Kommandant, I—"

"Tell me, Stolze, have you ever wondered what it must be like to be locked in the Box?"

Stolze's mouth dropped open.

"One more lie and you're going to find out. Understand?"

Stolze's voice tremored. "Y-yes, Herr K-Kommandant."

But Rudi wasn't waiting for his bluff to be called. Without removing his glare from Stolze, he said, "Schumacher, have the Box brought to the roll call square."

No one moved.

"Is there a problem, Schumacher?"

"With respect, Herr Kommandant," said Schumacher, "we've never put one of our own in the Box."

Rudi didn't shift his gaze. "And have we ever had 'one of our own' blatantly lie to his commanding officer like this before?"

"No, Herr Kommandant."

"Then fetch the Box."

"Yes, Herr Kommandant." Schumacher dashed away.

"Where did this come from?" Rudi held the bread so close to Stolze's face, the man had to pull back.

"The kitchen, H-herr Kommandant."

"You stole food from the mouths of our men?"

"No, Herr Kommandant. From the prisoners' supplies."

"Bearing in mind we're going to rip apart the accommodation block, so we'll find whatever you have stashed, what—"

"Please, Herr Kommandant, you don't have to. I'll show you. Please."

The entire camp had witnessed how gruesome the Box was, so it was no surprise Stolze would do anything to avoid such torture.

Rudi stepped back. "Show me."

Stolze slumped with such relief that Rudi thought he was going to collapse.

Fifteen minutes later, Rudi sat in the commandant's office, staring at the heap in the middle of the desk: rubies, diamonds, emeralds, gold teeth, necklaces, rings, earrings, zlotys, reichsmarks, francs... there was also a large amount of State Credit Fund currency – the money they'd issued for use in Estonia when they'd ousted the Soviets. This proved Stolze wasn't just selling to the prisoners but to the locals.

Baumann scratched his head. "It beats me how they manage to smuggle in so much."

The majority of their prisoners came through other camps, most of which conducted cavity searches to find valuables, but even such invasive tactics weren't foolproof. At the hint of a body search, some prisoners stashed items somewhere, while the more cunning swallowed them to "retrieve" later.

Rudi nodded. "It's quite a haul."

"So what are you going to do with it all?"

"I've got an idea."

Baumann said, "Regulations say it should be sent to Berlin as property of the Reich."

"I know."

"So is that what you're going to do?"

Rudi arched an eyebrow at him.

"If they find out..." Baumann grimaced.

"Who's going to tell them? Stolze? You?" Only he, Baumann, and Stolze knew about this treasure.

"Talking about Stolze, what are you going to do with him?"

"He's expecting a reposting. He begged for the Western Front."

"I'm not surprised. Who in their right mind would want to go east?"

Not all war was created equal. Waging it was bad enough, but waging it during a Soviet winter? Whoever said war was hell had never fought in subzero temperatures. The Ukrainians who'd attacked Darja could probably vouch for that personally by now.

Baumann said, "What was he intending to do with it all?"

Rudi snorted. "He was worried the Soviets were getting too close, so he was going to escape to Sweden." Stolze wasn't just a thief and a liar but a coward.

Baumann shrugged. "As plans go, that's not the worst."

Rudi smirked. "Thinking of deserting, Scharführer?"

"Like you never have." Baumann pawed the pile of jewelry, gold, gems, and banknotes. "There's a small fortune here. You could do some real good with this."

"I know."

"So it's not going to Berlin?"

Silent, Rudi held Baumann's gaze.

"But you do have a plan for it?"

Rudi couldn't stifle a sly smile.

24

Early the next morning, Rudi walked to the town, Bruno running ahead and then coming back, as if to make sure everything was okay, before running on again. Approaching the bridge, Rudi called, "Bruno, side."

As always, one call was enough and Bruno charged back. Rudi attached his leash — the road to the camp had little traffic, but it became busier after the junction across the river, and while he trusted Bruno to be careful, the local drivers were another matter.

They strolled across the bridge. Water swirled under the stone arches and headed toward the coast on the Gulf of Finland two miles away.

Outside the white stucco church in the town square, Rudi waited for a horse-drawn carriage to pass, then a truck and a blue car. The town was so small it had no tram system, and there seemed as many horse-drawn vehicles as motorized ones. Strangely, instead of this making the place feel sad and dated, it made it feel quaint. The type of place Rudi could imagine bringing a young woman for a romantic getaway.

He crossed the cobbled area in the center, cutting through an assortment of stalls selling farm produce to a sidewalk café where people chatted at tables beneath green-and-white parasols.

It was all so tranquil. So civilized.

Was war really raging across most of the continent?

Farther along, Rudi eased open the door to the town's one jewelry store, the door's top clipping a small brass bell, which jingled. Rudi peered in from outside.

Wooden cases displayed watches, bracelets, rings, necklaces... all spaced out more than necessary, probably to try to hide the fact that the store had little stock.

A balding, chubby-faced man emerged through a navy curtain behind the main counter.

"Come, come." The jeweler smiled, beckoning. His gaze dropped to the three pips and two silver stripes on Rudi's left collar patch. "The military is always most welcome, Herr Oberscharführer."

To recognize Rudi's rank, the man had done his homework. Whether because of fear, greed, or politeness was immaterial. What mattered was the man spoke German well, which would make this infinitely easier.

Rudi asked, "May I bring my dog in?"

"A dog?"

Rudi eased the door wider to reveal Bruno.

The man's smile dropped. "Does it bite?"

"Oh, yes."

The man's eyes widened and he clutched his chest.

Rudi smiled. "But only when I tell him to."

The jeweler twitched a smile. "Ah, I see the Oberscharführer has a sense of humor. How wonderful. Yes, bring your"— he gulped —"very big and very scary dog inside."

"Thank you." They entered.

"Now how may I help you, Herr Oberscharführer?" He gestured to his wares. "A necklace for a mother? A ring for a lover? A timepiece for a father?"

"Actually, I'm hoping to sell you something."

The jeweler's gaze flicked to Rudi's wristwatch, then his hands, presumably checking for rings. "I rarely buy military memorabilia, but of course, I'll take a look."

Rudi swung a canvas satchel off his shoulder. While he placed various packages wrapped in cloth on the counter, the jeweler leaned over to pet Bruno.

The jeweler said, "He doesn't really bite, does he?"

"He does, yes."

The jeweler jerked his hand back.

"And he never lets go until I give the command."

The jeweler shuffled sideways, away from Bruno.

Rudi smiled. "Don't worry, he's eaten two jewelers today, so I don't think he can manage a third."

The jeweler laughed nervously, then reached for one of the packages. "Okay, let's see what you have." He unwrapped a collection of silver jewelry. His eyebrows rose, and he gestured to the other packages. "Is it all silverware?"

"See for yourself."

Opening the second package revealed gold jewelry. "Oh!" The next one was filled with gold teeth. The jeweler frowned. "Oh..." Finally, the chubby man unwrapped the last one. Eight diamonds sparkled, plus a sapphire, five rubies, three emeralds, and some stones Rudi couldn't identify. "Ohhh."

Rudi said, "For a fair price, you get the lot."

The man grimaced. "If only it were that simple. This is a small town, and the war takes all our young and all our money. Unfortunately, what would be a fair price for me wouldn't be a fair price for you."

"So how about this — you buy what you want, then broker the rest to jewelers in other towns at twenty percent commission." Rudi would get rid of everything with the least effort, and the jeweler would push for the best prices to maximize his cut. A win-win.

The jeweler said, "It might take weeks to sell so much, and I could only offer a small upfront payment."

"No problem." Rudi winked while patting Bruno. "My debt collection service knows where you live."

The jeweler chuckled. "Quite a sales tactic. But I bet the dog's never bitten anyone in his life, has he?"

Rudi smiled. "Bruno, menace."

Bruno bared his fangs, snarling as if he'd rip the limbs off anything within reach.

Eyes big as saucers, the jeweler said, "Give me five minutes to pop to the bank."

25

Rudi spoke on the phone, sitting at the polished maple table in the commandant's dining room. "Yes, that was me you spoke to."

The man with the nasal whine said, "Boots and winter coats, right?"

"Six hundred of each, yes." He twiddled a pen.

"Nothing's changed. It's still awaiting authorization."

"You don't need to check?"

"If it had been authorized, it would have come through me."

Rudi doodled on a sheet of paper resting on a book he'd taken from the bookcase to avoid leaving an impression in the wood. "So, are you directly involved in ordering from the actual companies?"

"Yes."

"And it could still be months before it's even authorized, let alone delivered?"

"I'm afraid so."

"Just out of interest, where would you source an order like this?"

"Why?" He sniggered. "Do you have a rich uncle?"

"No, but I'm fascinated by the requisition process. I mean, the men on the front lines get all the medals, but without you guys, they wouldn't even have guns to shoot, would they?"

"Are you messing with me?"

"What? No! My father was a procurement specialist for IG Farben, so I've always been fascinated by the supply chain process. Crazy deadlines, shipping disasters, suppliers going bust... man, you have to be a genius to fit all the pieces together so everything falls into place." He winced. Had he gone overboard?

"You've got that right. The stories I could tell you."

"I bet." Not that he wanted to hear a single one. "So, boots and coats, who'd be your go-to guy?" Rudi poised his pen. "I'll tell you what, let me take a stab."

The guy snorted. "Okay, give it your best shot."

Excellent. Nothing made a person more willing to provide information than the desire to prove how superior they were.

Rudi said, "Hugo Boss."

The man laughed. "Good effort. But no. Hugo Boss is our go-to for uniforms, but for what you're talking about, I'd say..."

"Yes?"

"For the coats, the first one that comes to mind is VGF, but for your order, one of the smaller companies might be a better fit, so Bemberg Fabriken in Cologne or Schweizer GmbH in Hamburg. As for boots... the obvious one is T and A Bata, but trust me, you want Munich's finest — BKB Produktion if they can fit your time frame, and if not, Bahlsen and Voss of Stuttgart."

Rudi scrawled everything down. "Wow, you really know your stuff."

"That's why everything comes through my desk. One time I had just thirty—"

"Excuse me a moment." Rudi held the receiver away and raised his voice as if talking to someone. "Now? I'm taking an important call, so get Krebs to deal with it." He paused as if listening to a reply. "Okay, give me a second." He returned to the call. "I'm sorry, but one of my staff is missing and something's come up. Listen, it's been fascinating chatting with you, so I look forward to our next call."

"You're welcome, Herr Oberscharführer."

Rudi hung up. His contact had been allowed to shine and been left believing only an emergency had dragged Rudi away. If ever Rudi needed help again, the man would hopefully be eager to display his expertise.

He circled the conservative valuation on the scrap of paper the jeweler had given him. It seemed a lot, but would it be enough?

On returning from town, he'd completed the day's most urgent administrative duties and then given himself the rest of the day off — being boss came with hellish responsibilities, but it wasn't without its perks.

Rudi obtained the phone numbers for the clothing companies and set to work finding a supplier, expecting to be able to pick and choose to get the best deal. Unfortunately, because of his available funds and the companies' outstanding commitments, he had to grab the only two options he could, which meant that neither the coats nor the boots were likely to arrive before the first snows. Worse, the jeweler's valuation fell short of what he needed by thirteen percent.

Luckily, however, as commandant, Rudi now had access to the camp's discretionary fund. A small subsidy was nothing considering the amount of stock he was getting.

The deals done, he snatched his hat and tunic from the hallway coatrack and marched outside. He whistled. "Bruno!"

Bruno replied with a single bark as he'd been taught. A moment later, he emerged from behind the administration block and tore down the track, tail wagging.

"It's your lucky day, boy — we've another trip into town." Rudi patted him. Since these orders went through none of the official channels, both companies wanted a deposit.

Rudi and Bruno moseyed back into town and to the bank he'd visited after the jeweler's to inquire about exchanging the foreign currency Stolze had amassed. The manager arranged both advance payments and then, at Rudi's request, phoned each of the company's banks to confirm such. That wasn't strictly necessary, but Rudi's deal was so unorthodox, he needed to take every precaution to ensure it didn't go south.

Dawdling over the bridge back to the camp, Rudi gazed into the river's swirling waters. Hours ago, he'd been just a guy with a dream; now, he was an entrepreneur doing international trade deals with money he'd stolen from his government. And all to ease the lives of the Fatherland's enemies. Did that make him a criminal or a good Samaritan? Only Berlin could decide. If they ever found out.

Across the bridge, he let Bruno off his leash, and Bruno ambled away, sniffing the ground.

Rudi frowned. Had he really stolen from the Reich? Or had he merely bought the items the Reich was supposed to buy, thus doing its job for it? That was one way to look at things. Though he doubted a court-martial hearing would see his actions in such clear terms.

Sitting at the dining table again, Rudi dragged his fingers through his hair and exhaled loudly. Weary from all his dealings, he doodled on the paper resting on the book again. As long as the jeweler delivered the rest of his financing, everything was set. But if the valuation had been overly conservative and there was a surplus, what was he going to do with it?

A woman with a mole on her left cheek appeared in the doorway, head bowed, arms so spindly they looked like those of a child. "Herr Kommandant, I'm sorry to disturb you, but Kommandant Kloser always enjoyed afternoon tea and cake at this time. Will you be partaking as well?"

"Sorry, what was your name again?" His head was so full of grand plans, everything else was a blur.

She said, "1036. But Kommandant Kloser said that was too much of a mouthful, so he just called me Six."

"No, your name."

Even though she stared at the floor, he saw her frown. In a tone of voice more akin to asking a question than making a statement, she said, "Elena, Herr Kommandant."

Rudi's best friend was called Bruno, not Dog #3 because he'd had two as a child. Why? Because Bruno was a one-of-a-kind animal with a unique personality. Jews might be subhuman, but that didn't mean they didn't each have a personality all their own. And anything with a personality deserved a name.

"Then, yes, tea and cake would be nice. Thank you, Elena."

She frowned again at being thanked but toddled away. Minutes later, she returned carrying a gold tray. She placed a cup and saucer decorated with small red roses on a coaster on the table, the cup filled with steaming black tea.

He said, "Two sugars?"

"Yes, Herr Kommandant."

"You remembered how I take my tea?" Kloser had raved about her cooking, and from what Rudi had sampled at their officers' dinners, it was remarkably good, but he'd never taken notice of the person behind the food.

"Of course, Herr Kommandant." She cut into a cake that had chocolate sculpted over the top and cream oozing from the side, then hovered the knife two inches farther around. "How big a piece, Herr Kommandant?"

"There's fine."

She cut a slice, put it on a matching plate, and put that on a placemat before him.

"Thank you," he said.

As she toddled away with the cake on her tray, he bit into his slice. The cream dissolved into a buttery delight on his tongue and mixed with the melting chocolate to form a velvety gooeyness. Delicious.

"Elena?"

She turned but avoided eye contact. "Herr Kommandant?"

"That was a brand-new cake you hadn't cut into."

"I baked it especially this morning, Herr Kommandant."

"Did you taste it while baking it?"

She shook her head. "That's forbidden."

"So if you haven't sampled it, how do you know it tastes nice?"

She gasped and scurried back. "I'm so sorry, Herr Kommandant. Is it the cream? Has it turned? I—"

"I didn't mean that."

"Let me fetch you something else." She reached for the plate.

He held his plate. "That's not what I mean."

"Or I can make something. Just tell me what you'd like."

He held up his palm. "Elena, stop."

She stood. Trembling.

He held his slice up to her. "Bite."

She flinched, nibbled the tiniest bit, and screwed her eyes shut. Waiting.

"Elena, don't panic. You aren't in trouble."

She peeked. "I'm not?"

He smiled. "No."

Her chin quivered and a tear rolled down her cheek.

"All I meant was, if you don't sample the food while you're cooking, how do you know what it tastes like?"

Her voice broke as she spoke. "I've cooked for as long as I can remember, so I know all these recipes and what they taste like when they're made."

"Could you cut another slice, please?"

"You like it?"

"It's lovely."

A smile flickered. She placed the tray down and again hovered the knife.

He said, "A little bigger, please."

She cut a hefty slice and lifted it toward his plate.

Rudi cupped the plate with his hand so she couldn't put the second slice down. "Now take that to the kitchen and eat it."

"Excuse me?"

"That's an order, Elena. Take that slice to the kitchen and eat it. Now. Or are we going to have a problem?"

"No, Herr Kommandant. Thank you, Herr Kommandant." She scampered away.

Rudi felt guilty sending her away to eat, but in private, she could savor the cake, whereas sitting with him, she'd have been so anxious the experience would have been more of a trial than a treat.

Eating the cake, he scrawled more figures on his paper, thankful he'd rested on a book as the use of coasters and placemats suggested Kloser's wife was house-proud.

Elena returned. "More tea, Herr Kommandant?"

"No, thank you."

Instead of leaving, Elena removed a book with a black cover from the bookcase and ambled over. "Herr Kommandant, this book would be better to rest on."

He didn't look up. "This is fine, thanks."

"But this one is bigger, Herr Kommandant."

"No, thanks."

"It's got a better feel to it."

Oh, no. He'd shown the woman a little kindness and now, she was taking liberties. Why couldn't she just accept the cake and leave him in peace? After showing her kindness, was he now going to have to show her cruelty?

He waved her away. "Elena, leave."

"But you don't understand, Herr Kommandant. You don't understand."

He slung his pen down and glared. "What don't I understand?" He waved his book at her. "It's a book. Just a darn book. Like that one"— he pointed at hers, then at the bookcase —"and all those."

"But it isn't." Tears welled in her eyes.

"What isn't?"

She smoothed her hand over the black cover of her book. "This is leather. That..." Tears ran down her cheeks.

He twisted his book around. It was pinky-brown leather, as opposed to black, and the texture was more tactile than ordinary leather. Unusual. But nice.

He said, "This what?"

"It's skin."

"I know. Leather is skin, yes."

She shook her head. "Human skin."

He dropped the book. The cup smashed and tea splashed across the table.

26

Inge tramped along the road to the trench in a column of women. Her stomach screamed for food, Inge having eaten only coffee and half a bread ration saved from the previous evening.

A bitter wind swept over her and the hairs on her arms rose. She'd lost track of the date, so was that just a cool breeze, or was the weather changing already? The roadside trees were still green, but winter came early this far north.

Under her breath, she said, "God help us." The work was torturous in good weather, so in snow...

Surely the Germans wouldn't make them work in subzero temperatures. Even they couldn't be so inhumane.

Ahead, a woman with broken glasses glanced either way, then grabbed something from the grass shoulder. Then another woman dipped her hand into the grass and nonchalantly marched on.

Was there food? Inge checked behind her. The nearest kapo was looking the other way. She scoured the grass.

Nothing.

But there must have been food — what else would those women have been picking up? Had she missed her chance? Her stomach rumbled again, so she couldn't help but scrutinize the roadside.

Behind her, a voice shouted, "Keep up! Quicker!"

Inge glanced back. The guard was moving closer. If they got too close, even if Inge saw something, she wouldn't have time to grab it.

"I said, quicker!" The guard's whip bit the back of Inge's thigh.

Inge winced.

"Move it!" Passing Inge, the guard whipped another woman, then stalked farther.

Inge rubbed her stinging leg.

There! Something oval and light brown in the grass. A bread roll.

Extra bread would be worth a lash. Her mouth watered.

Cautiously, Inge swerved right. Her heart hammered as her gaze swished back and forth between the food and the guard.

"Move!" The guard struck someone else.

The food loomed closer and closer. Inge swerved a fraction more, eager to be close enough to grab the treasure, but not so far out of line to alert a guard.

Nearing the bread, she tensed, ready for action. The move had to be lightning fast — bend, grab, straighten. One fluid movement. If she bungled it, there was no second chance.

Eyeing the bread, she licked her lips, stomach growling in hungry anticipation.

A couple more steps. Her mouth watered so much she swallowed.

Almost there, Inge dropped her right shoulder, bringing her a fraction closer to her prize.

Inge tensed, ready to dive into the grass. But the woman in front bent, shot her arm down, then coolly moseyed on. A moment later, she surreptitiously munched on something.

Cursing, Inge trudged on.

The procession tramped across the boggy grassland, through the copse, and to the trench.

Half sliding, Inge scrambled into the muddy bottom. And the day's torture began.

The quarry had been a nightmare — all those stones and all the steps — but at least it had been dry. Here, the trench bottom always seemed waterlogged, making moving doubly arduous. If that wasn't bad enough, with no hot water and no soap, Inge ended every day caked in filth she couldn't scrub off. She couldn't remember the last time she'd felt clean — felt like a woman.

Inge dumped mounds of earth into a bucket while Greta filled another. With both buckets full, Inge grabbed a hunk of grass sprouting from the side of the trench and hauled herself off the bottom.

"It's my turn." Greta beckoned Inge back.

Inge jumped down, her feet sinking deep into the mud. Over the days, they'd cooperated to find shortcuts to ease their workload, the most obvious being that instead of both of them struggling up the slippery bank with a bucket each, one would go and haul up both loads. Inexplicably, the guards occasionally stopped them doing this, almost as if efficiency was secondary to the prisoners being worked to death. Crazy.

At the top, Greta slung down a rope, which Inge tied to the first bucket. Greta hauled it up and emptied it, then lowered it again. Inge moved to attach the second bucket, but her feet were sucked so deep in the mud, she fell.

She pushed up and heaved with her right leg. Her right foot squelched free, so she placed it on firmer ground, then pulled with her left leg. The muddy suction held her fast.

Jerking and jerking, she cursed but couldn't get out.

Greta slid back down and grabbed Inge's hands.

Bracing, Greta said, "On three — one, two, three."

Greta heaved as Inge hauled. With an enormous slurping sound, the mud released Inge. But off-balance, she and Greta splattered into the filth.

Inge pushed up from lying facedown.

On her back in the muck, Greta laughed. "You look like you've been dipped in chocolate."

Inge glanced down at herself — mud plastered her. She sniggered and reached toward Greta's face. "Want a lick?"

Greta wailed and pulled back, but too late. Inge smeared a muddy handprint down her cheek.

They chuckled.

A kapo shouted from above, "Back to work. Now!"

Inge struggled up. "I'll go. Tie your bucket on."

She grabbed a clump of grass and kicked off with her left leg to start climbing, but something slapped underneath her foot.

Puzzled, Inge lifted and twisted her leg to look. The sole of her pink sandal hung off.

"No!"

"What's wrong?" asked Greta.

Inge twisted her foot for Greta to see.

"Oh, no."

"What am I going to do?" Only the healthiest prisoners survived. Without a shoe, she'd damage her foot, and if she couldn't walk, she couldn't work. And everyone knew what happened to those unfit for work. She pictured the woman with only one shoe being beaten at the quarry when her footwear had tripped her. Inge hadn't seen the woman since.

"Don't panic," said Greta. "We'll think of something."

The kapo shouted, "If I have to come down there, you'll be sorry."

Inge gulped. She stared at her shoe. Her useless shoe. What was she going to do? Being forced to wear wooden clogs would be a death sentence.

27

Inge struggled on in the trench, hobbling around so her left shoe took as little impact as possible.

The buckets full, she moved to climb the bank, but Greta caught her arm. "I'll do it. You can't risk damaging that shoe more."

"Wait." Inge bent. "I'll take the darn thing off."

"No!" Greta thrust out her hand. "If you cut your foot and get an infection, that will be even worse."

"It's just soft mud."

"And buried sticks, spiky roots, sharp-edged stones..."

Inge held her forehead. "I don't know what I'm going to do."

"Don't panic. We'll fix it."

"How? I never got my suitcase back, so I've nothing to trade."

"Just get through today and worry about that later. Okay?"

Inge slumped. Was this the beginning of the end for her? Who'd have thought her darn shoes would be what broke her rather than the Germans?

"I've got an idea." Greta unfastened the white belt around Inge's waist and pulled it loose. "Fasten this around your foot."

Inge bound her shoe with the belt, then stamped a few times. The belt was uncomfortable, yet it held. But for how long?

She soldiered on. However, no matter how she tried, she couldn't shake the image of that one-shoed woman being beaten.

Finally, a whistle ended the day's torture.

Lurching along the road, Inge gazed at the grassy shoulder. Things could have turned out so differently if she'd been the one to grab the bread that morning. That tiny change could have altered everything — her mood would've been different, the way she approached her work would've been different, how she moved would've been different. And with everything different, she wouldn't have been standing in that precise spot for the mud to rip her shoe apart. But she wasn't the one who'd grabbed the bread.

She frowned. The bread. That was the key. How had she been so stupid?

Inge's lumbering gait transformed into a confident stride. She could fix this.

As usual, they stood in the courtyard for an hour or more, even though roll call appeared to go without a hitch. Inge had always imagined that a prison sentence simply took a person's liberty from them and that other than spending most of every day in a cell, physically and mentally, that was where the punishment ended. The Germans seemed to have a very different view. They didn't just take a person's freedom, they took their individuality, their health, and even their sanity. This wasn't a prison but a house of physical and psychological destruction.

Inge smirked. She had a plan, so they could go to hell — they would not break her.

But as the time passed, a niggling doubt clawed at her. Her plan hinged on one specific prisoner, so what if something had happened to them? In this hellhole, any life could be snuffed out at any time. No matter how strong, how cunning, how connected a person was, one wrong move and that was it.

Inge ached to glance about to confirm the woman she needed was still there. But she couldn't. Doing anything other than facing forward in silence, eyes down, guaranteed a whipping.

Eventually dismissed, the prisoners entered the mess hall. Instead of jostling for a position in the food line somewhere between the middle and the end, Inge scurried to the front. She had to be one of the first to ensure she didn't miss the person.

As she'd imagined, her "soup" had as much nutritional value as the bog water in the bottom of the trench. However, along with this delightful course, she received a bread ration.

She took the food nearer to the doorway. Sipping her soup, she monitored the comings and goings, waiting for that one special prisoner.

Women crowded around eating, and Inge shifted position to maintain watch on the line. What would she do if the woman was gone?

Anxiety clawing, she lifted the bowl to her mouth and tipped in the last few drops while peering over the rim. Where the devil was she?

Inge spotted a couple of the woman's friends in the line, so she scanned backward and forward, making sure she hadn't missed anyone.

No sign.

Her bowl as empty as her stomach, Inge eyed her bread. That was her breakfast, so she popped it in her pocket to avoid being tempted.

But her mouth watered.

And no matter how she fought to ignore the bread, she knew it was there because her hunger made the tiny bulge in her pocket feel like a boulder.

Her stomach growled.

She took out the bread. Stared at it.

Just a nibble wouldn't hurt. Just a mouse-sized bite...

She lifted it to her lips.

"No!" Inge crammed the bread back in her pocket. She hoped she wouldn't need it, but in case she did, she couldn't jeopardize her plan simply because she couldn't control her baser instincts. What was she? An animal?

She paced, studying the line. "Where are you?"

Greta joined her, but Inge didn't take her eyes off the women.

"How's the shoe?" asked Greta. "Holding up?"

"Yes."

"Are you looking for someone?"

"Yes, but something's wrong. She's usually here by now." Inge slumped, the line dwindling and dwindling.

Her plan had been sound. In a normal world. Unfortunately, the Germans' propensity for random brutality meant even the best-laid plan could founder at any moment for the most ridiculous of reasons. What was she going to do now?

"Who?" asked Greta. "Maybe I've seen them."

"It's too late, I—" She gasped. There! Inge smiled as a big woman with a scar on her jaw strode in. Inge dashed over.

Greta shouted, "Good luck."

Inge scampered close enough not to lose the woman, but far enough away to allow her to get her meal before the vat ran dry.

The woman finally served, Inge swooped. "Hi."

With a blank expression, the Pole stared down at Inge.

"You do remember me? You said you would." If the woman didn't, Inge's plan fell apart, as did her life.

The Pole looked her up and down, then fixed on Inge's shoe held together with a belt.

Stony-faced, the Pole said, "No." She strode away.

No? How could she not remember? Inge had given her bread and asked for nothing in return. That must never happen here, so how could anyone forget?

And there was the answer — the woman hadn't forgotten but simply didn't want to honor her debt.

Like that was going to happen!

She scurried after the Pole.

"Hey!" She grabbed the Pole's arm.

The Pole glared at Inge's hand, then down into Inge's face. Inge swallowed but didn't let go.

Inge said, "You said you'd remember."

"I remember. But I see what you want, and the answer is no." She ripped her arm free and marched on.

Inge glanced at her feet. Yes, it was obvious, but so what?

"Wait!" She scuttled after the woman again. "I need shoes. You have to help. Please."

"Everybody needs shoes."

"But I gave you bread."

The woman stopped, her blank expression turning darker. "You think half a ration of bread buys a pair of shoes?"

Inge didn't want to do this, but she had no choice. "How about one and a half rations?" She thrust out her fresh bread.

The Pole looked at it, then at Inge's damaged shoe. Her expression softened. "That"— she nodded to the bread —"buys you a repair kit."

"What's a repair kit?"

"A needle and strong thread."

Inge rubbed her brow. Her sandals couldn't cope with hard labor in summer — snow and ice would destroy them completely.

"So, one repair kit?" The Pole reached for the bread.

Inge snatched it away. "How much for new shoes?"

The Pole nodded to the bread. "That, and one more piece, and your shoes."

Inge frowned at her wrecked shoes. "You want these?"

"To some people, those will be the best pair of shoes they've seen this year."

Inge hadn't thought of it that way, but yes, bad shoes were better than no shoes. Even wrecked, her footwear could buy someone a few more weeks, enough to hope that the Allies would arrive before the footwear — and their chances of survival — wore out.

"Deal." Inge offered her hand to shake.

The woman ignored Inge's hand. "Wait here tomorrow night." She grabbed Inge's bread and waltzed off.

Inge called after her, "Don't you want to know my shoe size?"

The Pole turned. For the first time, she smiled. "Does this look like a shoe store?"

She shook her head, bit into Inge's bread, and sauntered away.

Fair point. What had Inge been expecting — a range of styles and colors? As long as the shoes fit or could be padded to make them do so, the size was irrelevant.

Inge said, "Then I suppose something in a slim heel to show off my calves is out of the question?"

The Pole didn't turn, but her shoulders juddered as if she was laughing. Good. Humor was an excellent way for people to connect.

Now all Inge had to do was get through one more day. Just twenty-four hours. In the normal world, that wouldn't be too much to expect. Here...?

28

Sitting at the commandant's desk in the administration block, Rudi ran his finger down the ledger giving statistics on prisoner sickness and unavailability for work.

Bruno whimpered next to the door.

"Sorry, boy. Just a second." Rudi had been so busy, he hadn't noticed poor Bruno politely waiting at the door, indicating it was toilet time.

Rudi opened the door and Bruno snaked through. "Krebs, let Bruno out and watch for him coming back, please."

A voice called, "Yes, Herr Kommandant."

Opening another ledger, Rudi flipped through to the figures on the income the camp generated through companies hiring prisoners as cheap labor, with all the money feeding back to Berlin. He scanned the column where companies had paid six reichsmarks per day for each skilled laborer, then the column for unskilled laborers costing four reichsmarks per day. The total was disappointing. But companies couldn't hire prisoners who were laid up in the infirmary. Or buried in the pits on the edge of the forest.

Putting the ledgers side by side, Rudi checked the sickness statistics against the corresponding date's income, hoping to identify a pattern — other than the obvious one — and thereby find a suitable solution.

The SS mandate to work prisoners to death was ludicrous. Philosophers could argue the morality of it, but any fool could look at these ledgers and see that prisoners were vital for the labor they rendered, which powered Germany's war.

Gruber lurched into the doorway and stood glaring.

Rudi didn't look up. "A problem, Unterscharführer Gruber?"

"May I speak freely, Herr Kommandant?"

Rudi leaned back and waved for Gruber to continue, though he already knew what was eating at the man.

Gruber said, "The prisoners are to get an extra ration of bread at breakfast?"

"They are."

"But that's just tomorrow, right?"

"No."

Gruber pursed his lips. "With respect, Herr Kommandant, I get you like animals, but there is a limit." He pointed toward the compound. "Why in God's name would you give that vermin more food?"

Rudi shoved the ledgers across the desk. "You want to win the war, don't you, Unterscharführer?"

"Of course!"

"And how do you suggest we do that?"

"We're the superior race. One German is worth ten of any other nation on the planet."

"While I imagine the Allies might dispute your math, which is understandable considering how they're advancing, how do you propose we Germans dispatch those ten inferior soldiers?"

"With our bare hands, if we have to."

Rudi pointed at him. "And that's exactly how we're going to have to do it, if we fight stupid instead of fighting smart."

Gruber sneered. "What?"

"Our camp, just like all the others we've established, isn't just a detention center, it's a source of labor." He counted off on his fingers. "Our prisoners lay roads, extend the rail network, mine resources, dig tunnels, and of course work in factories, not least to produce many of the munitions our military relies on."

Gruber shrugged. "So?"

"So the Allies took Africa from us and are now pushing up through Italy, while the Soviets gave us a hammering at Kursk and are now advancing at a hellish pace. Isn't it worth a little extra bread if it boosts output and thereby boosts our chance of victory?"

Gruber snorted. "You think wasting money on bread will win the war?"

"Last month, we averaged seventy-three prisoners in the infirmary every day. Do you know how much all those lost work hours cost us in company payments?"

Gruber shook his head.

"Just shy of nine thousand reichsmarks. *Nine thousand.* And much of that is down to malnutrition. Don't you think a better plan would be to feed prisoners more so we can work them harder?"

"There are more than enough to replace those we lose without wasting money feeding them."

Rudi had spent days poring over the reports to be able to a riposte any argument. "It takes a new arrival up to three weeks to reach the productivity of the average prisoner. Why waste the experience we develop for the sake of a few crumbs?"

"Kommandant Kloser never saw the need to increase rations."

"If you check what is being issued per prisoner per day, you'll see it lies within the daily calorific range stipulated in SS regulations. Or should we let what happened in Crasneanca last year happen here?"

Gruber frowned. "Crasneanca?"

"Prisoners were so hungry they ate their dead."

Gruber's jaw dropped. He stared into space, obviously struggling to process something so shocking.

Morality aside, if losing the war and cannibalism weren't sufficient argument to get Gruber on side, nothing was.

"Anything else, Unterscharführer?"

"Uh..."

"Good." Rudi looked back down at the ledgers. "Shut the door as you leave."

Gruber closed the door behind him.

Rudi blew out a huge breath. Some of the men were always going to be a problem, Gruber especially. All it would take would be an official complaint and a zealous SS investigator to uphold it, and at best, Rudi would be stripped of his captaincy. At worst? He'd be labeled a Jewish sympathizer and sent to the Front while his family back home would face endless persecution from the Führer's most ardent local supporters.

It was one thing to risk his career, maybe his life, but he couldn't put those he loved in jeopardy.

29

The next day at the trench, Inge struggled to treat both her shoes with the utmost care. She'd be getting a new pair of shoes that night, but if her left shoe fell apart completely or her right sustained damage, the Pole would likely demand extra bread. And Inge couldn't give up even more food.

Treading carefully, Inge carted a full bucket to the nearby mountain of earth taken from the trench and emptied the contents. She panted and dragged her forearm across her brow. Whether it was from having had only "coffee" for breakfast or from having to take extra care with her shoes, she was utterly drained.

A kapo shouted, "Move it!"

As Inge lumbered back, the kapo swished her whip, so Inge gritted her teeth and lurched quicker. She clambered down the bank but slipped and splattered into the bottom.

Greta offered her hand. "Are you okay?"

Inge heaved up. "I will be when I get those shoes tonight."

She picked up her bucket but slumped. Getting those shoes meant giving up more bread. How could she survive without food? All she'd eaten for two days was that filth they called coffee and that muck they called soup. If she didn't get something substantial soon, she'd collapse or have an accident, either of which would see a kapo beat the daylights out of her.

The finish whistle finally blew and they set off back. Inge stumbled along the road, eyelids drooped so low she was more asleep than awake. Something whipped her legs, jolting her lucid. A kapo stalked by.

Inge hauled herself along, functioning more on an instinctual level than a rational one. Her feet dragging on the road, she tripped and stumbled forward. A hand grabbed her arm and stopped her from falling into the woman in front.

She glanced around. Greta smiled, only for a kapo to lash each of them across the back.

During roll call, Inge swayed left, so she shuffled her feet to keep from falling, only to sway the other way. She'd always sworn that the Germans would never break her, but if she only got watery soup again tonight, how would she make it through tomorrow?

Roll call was mercifully short, but Inge was too dazed to bother about her position in the food line. Having been served, she leaned against a stone column and stared at her bread. Dear Lord, how she wanted to eat it. Instead, she swirled murky liquid around in her bowl.

Something bobbed.

Inge's eyes widened. She swished again. A lump. Fishing it out, she gasped at a chunk of potato the size of her thumb.

Was her luck changing? About time.

Chomping off a quarter of the potato, Inge closed her eyes and chewed while counting to sixty, feeling the texture, reveling in the taste, fooling herself into believing she was eating more than she was. She savored each quarter the same way. Delicious.

But then the chunk was gone.

Inge swished and swished for another piece but found only liquid. She gazed at her bread. Maybe she could eat part of it and give the Pole half today and half tomorrow. And what? Get only one shoe tonight? Or get no shoes because someone else was eager to make the deal she'd welshed on?

She cursed, stuffed the bread in her pocket, and downed her soup.

Walking away from the food line, the Pole nodded to her. Inge trudged over. They and three others ambled into a corner.

With her friends obscuring proceedings, the Pole said, "You've got the bread?"

Inge nodded. "You've got shoes?"

The woman produced a pair of black shoes from inside her jacket. "You're lucky, these are some of the best I've had for ages."

Inge examined them. Black, sturdy, functional. Ugly as sin, but easily capable of handling a winter. Fantastic. Finally, something was going right. Work would be so much easier with such strong shoes.

Her spirits soaring, Inge crouched and tried the left shoe. She winced, struggling to push in her heel. Forcing it in, she stood and stamped to test the footwear. Her hunger and weariness flooded back

— the shoe crushed her toes. If she wore them for even a few minutes, they'd rub her feet raw.

Inge said, "Have you got anything else?"

The Pole shook her head.

"How long until you can get something?"

"How long until someone else dies?"

"Excuse me?"

"Where do you think these came from? The shoe fairy?" The Pole snatched them and hid them again. "Be here tomorrow. With bread." She marched away.

As deflated as an old tire with a nail in it, Inge slouched against the wall. What was she going to do? Work was torturous with decent shoes, but the state of hers made everything twice as bad.

She'd tried her best. Tried so hard. Fought and fought, but this was too much. She couldn't do it anymore. Her face scrunched up and tears streamed. She couldn't go on. Couldn't.

Inge slid down the wall and, in a heap on the floor, blubbered. She was done.

Sobbing so hard her chest hurt like a kapo had prized her ribs apart and was stomping on her heart, Inge sat, the room a blur through her tears. The Germans had won.

Her breath shuddering, she pulled the hem of her dress up to wipe her eyes. And that was when she felt it.

She laughed — laughed like a crazy person — as she fumbled with her bunched-up dress and rived at her pocket. Bread! She had bread!

She wiped her face on her dress, then smiled at her magnificent lump of floury goodness. She bit a chunk and closed her eyes to savor her prize. It was dry, chewy, and probably contained as much sawdust as flour, but, boy, did it taste spectacular.

Munching another mouthful, she grinned. That saying about clouds and silver linings couldn't be more right. She'd learned a valuable lesson here — from now on, no matter what they threw at her, she'd find a way to twist it to her advantage.

Beaten? She wasn't beaten. They were never going to beat her. Let them try their worst.

30

The following evening, Inge waited with her bread, but the Pole had no shoes. Prisoners had died, but resolving Inge's predicament didn't depend solely on a prisoner with the right shoe size dying but on them dying *and* the Pole being first to scavenge.

The next night was the same story. And the next. But when the Pole did strike lucky, boy, did she hit the jackpot — two pairs.

The Pole offered Inge brown fur-lined boots with a good tread.

"Wow." Inge beamed. They'd be warm and give enough grip to handle snow. Perfect.

Inge tried one, but it was so tight she couldn't get her foot past the ankle. She snorted and handed it back.

The Pole next gave her a pair so creased and scuffed, they'd obviously been well worn, but they were still sturdy.

Again, they were too small.

The Pole scowled. "How can someone so skinny have such fat feet?"

Inge pursed her lips. "I do *not* have fat feet."

"So why doesn't anything fit?"

"I don't know. Are you taking them off dwarves?"

Further evening meals came and went, and Inge became more and more desperate as the days grew colder and colder. Once the snows came, no amount of belt-wrapping would hold her shoe together, let alone stop her foot from freezing. She needed shoes. Fast.

Another night, and the Pole handed her a black leather shoe. Crouching, Inge pulled it on but immediately slumped.

"Oh, come on." The Pole threw her arms up. "Are you even trying?"

"What do you want me to do? Cut my toes off?"

"Those fitted Basia and look at the size of her."

Blocking the kapos' view of proceedings, Basia nodded over her shoulder. The woman was Inge's height but twice the width.

"So Basia must have particularly dainty feet." Inge gave the shoe back. "I'm sorry, but if they don't fit, they'll never get me through the winter, will they?"

The Pole couldn't argue with logic, so she snatched them and left.

Inge trudged to Greta.

"No luck?"

Inge grimaced.

Greta glanced around, then slipped something into Inge's pocket. "This should help. I found it walking back but didn't have a chance to give it to you."

Dipping her hand in her pocket, Inge felt a coil of something hard. "Fantastic! Thank you."

She hugged Greta.

"You're welcome."

Things looking up, curiosity once more clawed at Inge. "You know, there's something I've wondered for ages now." She patted her left breast. "Why no stars when you could be whipped for not wearing them at home?"

Greta said, "Estonia is officially free of Jews. I guess the Nazis don't want to upset the locals by admitting they're importing new ones."

Was there no end to how devious and deceitful the Nazis were?

That night, Inge sat in bed and wound Greta's strip of wire around and around her left shoe. To be safe, she snapped a piece off, then wound that around the right, too. The result wasn't perfect, but it was a strong repair. For now.

She sighed. Her shoes were protected, but what about her feet? Her toes and soles were puckered and blotchy from being constantly wet, and today, her left foot tingled. That couldn't be good.

More days passed, and though her shoes held, her feet suffered. Inge became so concerned, she traded bread for thick woolen socks. Every night, she'd wash her feet, then keep them as elevated and as warm as possible.

One morning in the bathroom, Inge gawked at her breath billowing before her. "Oh God."

If that was inside, how cold was it outside?

After trudging out for roll call, she shivered in sleet.

Surely the Germans wouldn't send them to work in this. There was no point in killing their workforce, especially when all the labor was free. But the work details left as usual.

In the trench, Inge's footsteps shattered the ice covering the puddles. She threw herself into digging, praying the exertion would keep her warm. And it did, until cold seeped through her sandals and worked its way up her body. Then, as if God wanted to play a cruel joke, snow began to fall.

Shivering so much it looked like she had a medical condition, Inge continued working.

Nearby, a woman collapsed facedown in the filth. Everyone carried on. Inge looked at the nearest kapo, expecting an order to help. But none came.

Inge crouched. "Are you okay?"

No response.

She eased the woman's head around. Vacant eyes stared at nothing and no breath billowed.

Someone shouted, "You!"

Inge looked up.

A kapo jabbed her whip. "Back to work."

Trembling, Inge staggered to her bucket. As she scooped in soil, she couldn't stop staring at the dead woman. That would be her. If she didn't get shoes, the cold would kill her just as surely as it had that poor soul.

She shook her head and imagined the bread she'd eat later, the socks that would warm her feet, and the sleep that would give her dreams of better times. But then she glanced at the dead woman again. That would be her. Not today, but in a week. Maybe a month, if she was really, really lucky. Her.

31

Ambling into camp, Rudi threw a stick for Bruno, who raced after it. With the jeweler having sold the rest of the cook's stash, Rudi had completed payment for the winter wear at the bank using a small subsidy from the camp's finances.

As Rudi headed to the administration block, Baumann waved, exiting the compound. "Herr Kommandant, do you have a minute?"

Rudi joined him. "Is there a problem?"

Baumann smirked. "You'll see."

They strolled to the infirmary on the far left of the compound.

Inside, two rows of ten bunk beds strewn with dirty linen accommodated sweaty bodies, and coughing, moaning, and wheezing filled the air. The same as always.

Rudi scanned the sick and the dying. There had to be something out of the ordinary, but what? He scratched his head.

Baumann grinned. "Incredible, huh?"

Rudi frowned. "Sorry, what am I looking at?"

"You can't see it?"

Rudi squinted. In the nearest lower bunk, a woman coughed up yellowy gunge onto her chest; in the bunk above, a pale woman lay so still Rudi wondered if she was dead; from the bunk opposite, a patient's breathing gurgled like a pot of boiling stew.

What the devil was he looking for?

Baumann chuckled. "Seriously? You don't see it?"

"See what?"

Shaking his head, Baumann trailed along the aisle and thrust both arms out to one particular bed. "Ta-da!"

"Ahhh." Rudi grinned. "An empty bed."

"No, no, no. Not just an empty bed. The first bed to ever stay empty for a full twenty-four hours."

"Congratulations, Baumann." Rudi held out his hand to shake.

Baumann held his hands away. "Don't look at me. Showers for improved hygiene, extra bread for improved nutrition – this is you, Rudi. All you."

"Really? So quickly?" Could such simple changes make such a difference in little over a week?

"That's all it takes." Baumann pointed up the room. "And look – not a single bed with more than one patient."

The last time Rudi had visited, most beds had had patients crammed in top to tail. This was amazing. And so far, the only negative comment was Gruber's. Rudi had seen no dirty looks, heard no whisperings, sensed no form of dissent... but that didn't mean there'd been none.

He lowered his voice. "Have you heard any talk about the changes? Any discontent?"

Baumann shook his head. "You?"

"Gruber. About increasing the bread ration."

Baumann snorted. "What did you expect?"

Rudi smiled. He was going to be able to do this. By making small changes that he could justify on the grounds of improved productivity or personnel well-being, he was going to be able to save the entire camp.

Since childhood, he'd been conditioned to believe that Jews were animals. But were they? The longer he spent with them, the more his observations cast doubt on that. If they were animals, a subhuman species closer to vermin than decent Aryan stock, why were they virtually identical to people? Any fool could tell the difference between people and any other animal on the planet. No one ever mistook Bruno for a person. From half a mile away, a cow was a cow, no mistake. A bird? Who in their right mind would ever imagine a bird was a person?

But a Jew? Rudi had been inches away from them. Inches. He'd looked into their eyes, smelled their breath, heard them speak just the way he did, as if they were having similar thoughts. And what? It was impossible to discern the difference. Impossible!

If he stood naked in a darkened room with a Jew of similar build, he'd wager a thousand reichsmarks that no one could tell them apart, no matter how much they poked or prodded. Not even the Führer himself.

The most logical conclusion was both terrifying and enlightening because it changed *everything* — a Jew might be just as much a person as he was.

That was the only answer that made sense. But could it be true?

"Give me a list of supplies you need," said Rudi. "But keep in mind that treating someone who can return to work is one thing, whereas treating someone who can't..." Medication to increase productivity was viewed vastly differently from medication to ease suffering, and though he was now commandant, he still had limited power. If they wanted more supplies, they had to play the odds.

"Got you."

Rudi patted Baumann on the back. "This is fantastic."

The doors burst open and a guard ran in. "Herr Kommandant, there's been an accident."

Rudi sighed at the empty bed. "Well, you had it for a day."

But his nonchalance vanished when two prisoners carried in Elena, her face twisted in pain, a broken bone jutting through a gash in her right shin.

Baumann guided them to the empty bed.

When she saw Rudi, she struggled to get up. "I'm so sorry, Herr Kommandant."

Rudi pointed to the bed. "Elena, lie down."

"Please, lie still." Baumann pressed her shoulder until she lay flat again.

She said, "I tripped on that blasted stair carpet. But I'll be back to work after a little rest, don't worry."

Rudi said, "Elena, you'll stay right there until Scharführer Baumann says otherwise. Understand?"

"But who'll make your meals?"

"Don't worry about that."

Baumann examined her and turned to Rudi. "Her tibia needs to be reset, so she'll be off her feet for at least two months, if not three."

Elena said, "I'm so sorry to let you down, Herr Kommandant. Let me recommend someone to look after you."

"Elena, I'll be fine." Rudi hadn't known her long and had never seen the need to consult her records. Was she imprisoned for being a Jew? A Slav? A political undesirable? A criminal? She might be none of those or all of them, but one thing he did know — she was a caring soul. Animal or human was incidental; she'd get the care she needed

128

as if it was his mother or Bruno needing help. And if anyone objected, let them try to challenge him on it.

He turned to Baumann. "She gets whatever she needs. Understand?"

"She'll get what I can manage, just like every patient."

Rudi left. As he exited the compound, Bruno bounded over.

"Hey, boy." Rudi scratched the dog's head. "Had a good sniff about?"

Back at his desk, Bruno lying at his feet, Rudi pored over another ledger. He had to justify extra medical supplies, which would be tough on top of his other plans. He studied statistics on various aspects of the camp and its prisoners.

Believing the prisoners were animals or merely numbers in a ledger made turning a blind eye to their suffering easy, but Rudi defied anyone to look at one of them — truly look — and not reassess that belief.

If only there was a way he could make more of his countrymen question the world the way he did.

32

Her teeth chattering, Inge staggered into the mess hall from evening roll call, arms clutched tightly about her chest, snow in her hair. She'd figured her shoes were her biggest problem, but she was wrong — her dress was. She'd loved flaunting the pink-and-white striped outfit around town and seeing the admiring looks, but here, in the cold, her dress was going to be the death of her.

If she had her suitcase, she'd have a fighting chance. But a thin cotton dress when the temperature was likely to plunge to minus ten or lower...

Shivering, she tottered along in line, stuffed her bread in her pocket, then, cupping her bowl with both hands, leaned against a column. However, instead of eating, she hunched over her bowl to soak up what little heat it emitted.

Her teeth chattering too, Greta appeared. "E-eat."

"I'm t-trying to get w-warm."

Greta shook her head. "E-eat while it's h-hot. That's b-better."

Inge slurped her soup. It radiated heat as it went down to warm her from the inside. How could she survive the winter? If a pair of shoes cost three days' bread, an overcoat might cost three times that. And if she had to go without bread for a week or more, she'd never have the strength to work. What was she going to do?

A few minutes later, the Pole ambled by and patted her jacket. She nodded to the corner of the room. "It's your lucky day."

Trembling, Inge followed.

The Pole reached into her jacket. "This is a great pair of—"

"No! I d-don't want sh-shoes."

Frowning, the woman snorted at Inge's wrecked sandals. "You think those will get your through an Estonian winter?"

"A c-coat. How much for a coat?"

The Pole shook her head. "You need shoes."

"No, I n-need a coat."

The Pole leaned closer and whispered, "Trust me, take the shoes."

Inge shook her head. "A coat. Get me a coat."

The Pole checked who was nearby, then leaned even closer. "I'm not supposed to know this, but you aren't staying here. And if you don't have good shoes, you won't make it to where you're going."

33

"Bruno!" Rudi whistled from the administration block's doorway. He waited and waited, straining to hear a barked reply.

Silence.

"Bruno!" He whistled for longer, then again, listened.

Silence.

Rudi looked up at the snow falling from the black sky. Bruno loved snow, but it was unusual for him to go to relieve himself and stay away so long. As for not responding to Rudi's calls, that was unheard of.

"Bruno!" He listened.

Nothing.

Rudi marched back through the general office toward his own.

"Herr Kommandant?" Krebs held up a telephone receiver. "Sturmbannführer Söllner."

"Deal with it." Rudi grabbed his winter coat from his office, then paced back through.

Krebs covered the mouthpiece. "Herr Kommandant, I said it's the Sturmbannführer."

Rudi didn't even look at him. "And I said I'm not here."

He stormed out.

Bruno had never gone missing before. Something was wrong. Very wrong.

34

Rudi tramped through the forest, snow crunching underfoot, his flashlight beam slicing through the darkness. "Bruno! ... Bruno!"

He stalked deeper into the shadows, hunting for footprints to lead him to his best friend. The snow might be a godsend in that if Bruno had been attacked by a bear or gored by a bison, Rudi would be able to track him and save him. On the other hand, if Bruno *was* injured, the snow could bury him and suffocate him. Rudi had to find him. Fast.

He cursed. If he hadn't been so intent on helping the prisoners, he'd have paid more attention to Bruno and realized something was wrong earlier. So this was his reward for fighting to do the decent thing, was it? He cursed again.

Sweeping his flashlight back and forth, Rudi scoured their usual paths as the wind howled through the treetops.

There was no trace of Bruno.

What if Rudi was looking in the wrong place?

Emerging from the forest, he dashed to the nearest watchtower. Inside, a guard peered over a mounted machine gun and saluted.

Rudi shouted, "Have you seen Bruno?"

"Sorry, no, Herr Kommandant."

The sentries on the main gate hadn't seen him either, nor the other watchtower guards.

Baumann jogged over. "Anything?"

Rudi shook his head.

"Go get some rest. We'll organize a proper search in the morning."

"I'm not leaving him out there alone." Rudi marched for the road into town. "Hold things down here."

Baumann called, "Rudi... Rudi..."

35

On the toilet the next morning, Inge stared at her new shoes. Sturdy, comfortable, well made. Everything she'd hoped for. But had she made a diabolical mistake in trusting the Pole?

Inge addressed a lanky woman beside her. "Have you heard anything about anyone leaving here?"

"Leaving? What do you mean 'leaving?'"

A curly-haired woman sniggered. "Yes, I'm thinking of partying in Paris at the weekend. You?"

Lanky laughed.

No one knew anything. That darn Pole. The woman had just wanted rid of Inge because she'd been an awkward customer.

Inge cursed. Why had she been so stupid to listen? The only way anyone left here was in a box.

Over breakfast, she fumed. That Pole was not getting away with this. Cheating her into getting shoes when what she needed was a coat. It didn't matter how big the woman was or what connections she had, Inge was not going to be conned.

The Pole waltzed into the hall. She caught Inge's gaze and smiled.

Inge clenched her fists. The woman had cheated her and now had the audacity to laugh at her?

Inge marched toward her. Breath snorting. Anger making her tingle with pent-up energy.

Someone caught her arm.

Inge jumped. Turned.

Zofia said, "Get your blanket before you go to roll call."

Inge frowned. "Why?"

"Just do it. Okay?"

"Okay."

Zofia strode away.

"Hey." A voice came from behind Inge. She spun. The Pole held out her hand. "Good luck, Inge."

"What's happening?"

"Haven't they told you? You're being transferred."

"Where to?"

She shrugged. "Whatever happens, keep walking, okay? Never stop. Not for anything."

That was an odd thing to say. "Okay."

The Pole left.

Inge stared into space. So she was leaving. But going where? Did it matter? Wherever it was, it had to be better than this hellhole. She groaned. No, it would be worse. Every day she'd tried to put a positive twist on things, yet every day, things only got worse. Why would this be any different? The Germans wouldn't transfer her to be kind.

Roll call was mercifully quick. Probably because of what the Germans had planned. After that, Inge, Greta, and seventy other women were led three abreast along a road she didn't know.

A light covering of snow crunching underfoot, Inge pulled her blanket around her shoulders and glanced at her new shoes. She smirked. Supportive, with a good grip. The Pole had been right — when she had her blanket, good shoes were far more important than a coat. She strode on.

Apart from a number of kapos, two German guards headed the group with another two at the rear. Each carried a backpack with a bedroll. Wherever they were going, it needed at least a full day's march and an overnight stop. Thank heaven for her shoes!

But...

She glared at the guards' backpacks again. They'd have provisions in there. Where were the supplies for the prisoners?

36

The new day bitingly fresh, Rudi slammed the door to the commandant's house behind him and dragged on his coat. He glanced down at the bowl on the veranda, a faint glimmer of hope glowing inside him. But the food he'd left out was untouched. He cursed. Glaring at the world, he stormed toward the road into town.

Bruno had never done anything like this. Never. If anything had happened to him, Rudi didn't know what he'd do.

To his right, someone exited the administration block. He ignored them.

Someone shouted, "Herr Kommandant!"

Rudi held his palm to them and marched on. Turning toward the town, he stalked down the grassy left shoulder, scrutinizing the undergrowth. He prayed to hear a whimper, see the flick of a tail, or spot paw prints in the snow — something he'd missed the previous night because of the dark and the howling wind. But inside, a black pit was sucking the life out of him to leave nothing but an empty husk.

Footsteps pounded into the road behind him. He didn't turn. He didn't care. He strode on, peering into the shadows.

"Rudi!"

Baumann. Still Rudi didn't turn. The camp could manage a day without him. Heaven knows it had managed often enough without Kloser.

"Rudi!" Baumann caught up, breathing hard.

"I don't care what it is. Deal with it, Scharführer."

"I'm not here for the camp, I'm here for you."

"You left Gruber in charge?"

"Even he can't destroy the place in just a morning. How can I help?"

136

Rudi pointed to the other side of the road. "Check the undergrowth. If a car hit him, he might have crawled away to find shelter."

"You got it." Baumann turned to cross the road, but Rudi caught his arm.

"Thank you, Klaus."

Baumann nodded, then crossed and began searching.

On either side of the road, they walked all the way into the town. There, Rudi asked passersby if they'd seen Bruno, but no one had.

On the return journey, they switched sides to make sure nothing had been missed. Not wanting to, but knowing he had to, Rudi also checked the road surface for blood.

A hollowness clawed at Rudi. A confused dread of wanting to find something but also not wanting to. Last night, Rudi had pictured finding Bruno injured, taking him home, and nursing him back to health. When he'd set out that morning, that was harder to imagine, but not impossible. However, now?

Tears welled in Rudi's eyes. Now, he couldn't picture carrying his injured friend home; now, he pictured carrying a body.

As they neared the camp, instead of turning onto the track down to it, they continued on for another hour. But they found nothing.

Trudging back, Rudi stared into the distance. Unthinking. Unfeeling.

Baumann said, "There's still a chance. Who knows, he might even be there waiting when we get back. Or he might have wandered so far, he got lost and will turn up in a few days."

"A dog can't just disappear into thin air." Something had happened. And Rudi wouldn't rest until he found out what.

37

Inge stumbled along the road, gloom devouring nearby fields as the sun sank below distant hills. Her feet throbbed, her back hurt, her legs ached...

A kapo whipped her arm. "Move it!"

Panting, she glared as the woman strolled by. Unlike their escorts, the prisoners hadn't eaten or drunk since breakfast. As for the walking, Inge had never walked so far in one day.

The procession rounded a clump of trees. Ahead, the road split into two, with the left branch curving down into a hamlet nestled in a valley while the right snaked over a hill.

In the valley, shadowy buildings surrounded a small green. That had to be where they were heading. Which dark shape was big enough for eighty people? Inge squinted. There. A church. A night in a pew or even on a floor would be fantastic after the day she'd had. Thank heaven. Maybe they'd even get something to eat.

Nearing the junction, she wasn't the only one who felt rejuvenated at the prospect of their torturous day coming to an end – the column moved with a sense of urgency.

But at the junction, the guards didn't turn left.

Inge cringed. "Oh please, God, no."

The road climbed away before them. Sobbing came from behind her, but she didn't turn. The only thing that mattered was putting one foot in front of the other to get up this nightmare and down the other side.

Her column slowed, so the kapos marched back and forth, bawling and cracking prisoners with their whips.

Inge glared at a hook-nosed kapo as she raised her whip. Was she punishing them because she enjoyed it or because if she didn't, she knew someone else would be punishing her?

Ten or twelve places ahead, a woman fell and didn't get up.

A square-jawed guard raced over.

He stood over her. "Get up! Up, you lazy pig!"

Hook Nose beat the prisoners onward, passing the woman.

"Up!" Square Jaw kicked her in the side.

The woman clambered onto all fours but collapsed again.

Square Jaw slung his rifle off his shoulder. He aimed at her head. "You have five seconds. One..."

The woman whimpered, heaving with her arms but not moving.

"Two... three..."

She pushed onto all fours again. However, instead of heaving to stand, she sank to her knees and elbows, forehead on the road.

"Four..."

She shook her head just as Inge staggered past.

"Five."

The gun blasted.

Inge jumped as blood splattered her shins. She stared, wide-eyed. Square Jaw had warned the woman, yes, but it had seemed like an idle threat to motivate her to stand. No way had Inge believed he'd pull the trigger.

Square Jaw slapped Inge's arm. She jumped again.

"You"— he hit another prisoner —"and you. Get rid of the body."

Get rid of the body? They were in the middle of nowhere, so what the devil were they supposed to do?

Eyes even wider, Inge looked at the other prisoner, who stared back, equally bewildered.

Square Jaw trained his gun on Inge. "Move it or carry it. I don't care which."

Inge cowered. She had to do something or her brains would be spattered all over the road too, but what?

She lifted the dead woman's arms. Her comrade took the hint and grabbed the legs.

Inge nodded to a ditch. They hauled the woman over and dumped her in a dark, boggy hole. Inge looked down, trying to think of something to say, something she'd like said over her if the roles were reversed.

Hook Nose whipped her. "Move! Or you'll be in there, too."

Inge trudged on.

The procession reached a hairpin bend. Inge rounded it only to find the incline rose sharply. Wheezing, she heaved herself on, thighs burning with the effort. But her foot skidded on compacted snow and she tumbled to the ground.

She lay on her back, gasping. She had to get up. Had to. But just lying there was absolute ecstasy.

Square Jaw reared over her. He kicked her in the ribs. "Up!"

Inge squealed but pushed onto her elbows and twisted onto all fours. However, her arms gave and she fell flat on her face.

"One..." He cocked his rifle.

She had to get up. Now.

"Two..."

She positioned her hands on either side of her chest and tensed her muscles to heave up.

"Three..."

She didn't move. Why should she get up? What was the point? To suffer months, possibly even years, of this hell? Why? That wasn't living.

"Four..."

Why? Because these evil Nazis couldn't be allowed to win. Grimacing, she strained with all her might and pushed to all fours.

"Fi—"

She stood. And dared to shoot Square Jaw a sideways glance. "Tell the Führer I saved him a bullet."

Square Jaw slammed his rifle butt into her back. She staggered but didn't fall. They weren't going to break her. No way in hell.

38

A new dawn bringing renewed heartbreak, Rudi stared at the bowl on the veranda. Still full. He swallowed hard. Bruno was the only thing that had kept him sane in this godforsaken place. Those stolen walks had given him a glimpse of a different life, of a world overflowing with love and sharing, not horror and greed. How stupid he'd been to think that could survive.

Much of the snow now slush, making tracking impossible, he marched into the compound, where the prisoners were lined up after morning roll call. He escorted the thirty healthiest-looking prisoners outside the gates to where a group of guards waited with Gruber.

He addressed the prisoners. "Form a line, two arm's lengths apart."

The prisoners shuffled into position, holding their arms out so their fingertips touched.

"Remaining this distance apart, you're to scour the forest for any signs of my dog, a fight, or anything unusual. Understand?" One way or another, he was going to find Bruno.

In unison, the prisoners said, "Yes, Herr Kommandant."

"Anyone who tries to escape will be shot. No warning. Understand?" His morality could take a holiday — anyone who took advantage of this situation would pay.

"Yes, Herr Kommandant."

Rudi said, "Unterscharführer, sweep the forest as we discussed, a guard on either end of the line and one every six prisoners, twenty feet back."

Gruber said, "Yes, Herr Kommandant."

"Dismissed." Rudi tramped into the administration block while Gruber marched the search party toward the forest.

Rudi stared into space at his desk. He pulled over some files, then tossed them aside. Nothing else mattered.

"Herr Kommandant?" Krebs stood in the doorway. "Sturmbannführer Söllner is expecting your call today."

Rudi nodded.

"And, er, I'm sorry about Bruno. I hope they find him."

"Thank you, Krebs."

Krebs left.

Rudi was in no mood to play politics with Söllner, but he couldn't leave a superior hanging for too long.

He sighed. Things couldn't carry on like this. Somehow, he had to dig himself out of this hole. He removed a file from one of his drawers and took his Brunsviga mechanical calculating machine from a shelf. Maybe he could lose himself in figures.

Reading the total of a column of numbers, he positioned the machine's six small metal levers to the correct setting on each of the numbered dials in the front. He cranked the handle. The gearing inside turned so the device displayed the total from the ledger. Rudi set the levers to the next column's total and cranked the handle again. The gears added the first total to the second and displayed the result.

He smirked. It was like magic — how could a lump of metal and cogs compute such complex mathematical problems with just the turn of a handle? Not only did the Brunsviga minimize the risk of errors and perform calculations at lightning speed, but at only three kilograms and a mere nine inches by seven, it was portable — if he were a businessman, one of these would live in his briefcase.

Rudi continued his calculations, doing many that were totally unnecessary, just to keep occupied.

Baumann appeared in his doorway. "No news?"

Rudi shook his head.

"I'm sorry, Rudi."

Rudi gestured for him to sit, so he did.

Baumann scratched his head. "You know, maybe there's another option that's worth a try."

Rudi shoved the calculator aside. "Go on."

"Well, a scent is a scent, right?"

Rudi's eyes widened. "The dogs." Why hadn't he thought of that?

Baumann nodded. "If they can track a prisoner, they might be able to track another dog."

"Klaus, you're a genius." He dashed away. "I'll get Bruno's blanket."

Ten minutes later, Rudi stood outside the administration block with Draxler, the camp's best dog handler, and a German shepherd on a leash beside him.

Rudi handed the dumpy man a red blanket. "When he's not sleeping on my bed, he curls up on this."

"That should work. Where was the last place you saw him?"

Rudi pointed to the commandant's house. "Outside the house."

They marched down.

Rudi said, "The snow isn't a problem? Or that he went missing two days ago?"

Draxler patted the dog. "Kaiser's the best tracker I've ever known, so while conditions aren't ideal, if there's a chance, he's the one who'll find Bruno."

Draxler pointed at the prisoners forming work details. "It would be best to postpone that until after we've searched the area. The last thing we want is them trampling the scent trail even more."

Rudi gave a guard instructions to confine the prisoners to barracks.

Gnawing anxiety still ate at Rudi's stomach, making him feel queasy, but at least now, a glimmer of hope calmed his dark thoughts.

Draxler shoved Bruno's blanket against his dog's snout. "Find, Kaiser. Find."

Kaiser trotted away, sniffing the ground, leading Draxler and Rudi.

The dog veered between the commandant's house and the personnel block and set out across the scrubland.

"He's definitely picked up something," said Draxler.

They looped around up to the road.

Rudi cringed. That had been his one fear – some careless driver hitting Bruno. But instead of following the road into town, Kaiser guided them back into the camp, between two of the camp trucks, and around to where a work detail was constructing another barracks outside the compound.

Massive wood columns rose out of the ground, beams and joists spanning the gaps between them like the skeleton of some great fallen beast. With prisoners confined to barracks, the site was empty.

Rudi expected Kaiser to head straight past for the forest, but he didn't. Nose to the ground, the dog headed into the structure, around some of the partially constructed walls, then out on the side nearest the compound.

Kaiser pulled toward the fence.

Rudi shook his head. "This can't be right."

Draxler yanked Kaiser away, but the dog kept on pulling.

"Give him another smell." Draxler gestured to the blanket.

Rudi did so. Again, the dog heaved toward the fence.

"No," said Rudi. "Bruno knows to stay away from the fence. Besides, he'd never get under it without electrocuting himself." There was no sign of digging anywhere along the fence, which confirmed Bruno hadn't entered the compound.

"There's only one way to find out, Herr Kommandant. Let Kaiser follow the scent trail."

They traipsed around to the gates. The sentries opened up, but Rudi stopped. This was a waste of time.

Draxler pointed inside. "Herr Kommandant, believe me, if Kaiser says Bruno's been in there, he's been in there. Maybe he went in there but got out in a different spot."

That didn't make sense. Bruno never entered the compound. Never.

Rudi dragged his fingers through his hair. Nothing about this situation made sense. But he had to find Bruno.

They entered.

Draxler guided Kaiser to the area of the fence the dog had been interested in on the other side.

From there, without deviating, Kaiser led them toward the rear of the compound behind the infirmary block.

Rudi frowned. "Draxler, there's only one thing back here."

"I know, but"— Draxler scratched his head —"Kaiser's never let me down yet, so..."

Rudi stopped. "Look, thanks, but this isn't working." He turned to leave.

"Herr Kommandant, you trust me and I trust Kaiser."

Rudi hung his head.

"We've come this far," said Draxler. "If there *is* a scent trail, there's only so long before it fades so much even Kaiser can't follow it."

Rudi waved for Draxler to proceed.

Kaiser led them to the back of the compound, a putrid smell getting stronger and stronger. At the end of the infirmary, he guided them around the corner and sat before the door to a small wooden shack. He stared up at Draxler.

Rudi threw his hands up. "I told you it was a waste of time."

"But he's signaling this is where the scent ends."

Rudi glared at the dog, then the shack. "We both know what scent he's followed."

Draxler reached for the blanket in Rudi's hand. "Could I have that, please?"

Rolling his eyes, Rudi handed it over.

Draxler gave his dog another sniff. "Find, Kaiser. Find."

Kaiser whined and pawed the door.

Rudi wanted to leave, to forget about this farce and wait for the search party to return. Covering his eyes, he heaved a breath.

No, he'd started this, so he had to see it through.

He trudged to the shack door. Could Bruno have gotten into the compound and been shut in here by accident? The odds were so high that even his magical calculator would struggle to compute them, but a slender chance was still a chance...

Cupping a handkerchief over his nose and mouth, he pulled the door. It creaked open. Flies swirled around him as he stepped inside. In the gloom, four naked bodies lay awaiting the once-weekly mass burial, their worldly possessions already having found new homes. There was no Bruno.

He scanned the interior, checking for claw marks in case Bruno had been shut in and had tried to get out. Yet if that had been the case, the scent trail would've continued. Nothing made any sense. He cursed and turned for the door. What a complete waste—

He froze. What was that?

He gulped. Knowing he had to examine what had caught his eye, but dreading doing so, he closed his eyes and turned back. He didn't want to look, he didn't want to look, he didn't want to look...

But maybe he'd been wrong. He'd only caught a glimpse.

Rudi opened his eyes. His face twisted into so much pain that an onlooker could be forgiven for thinking he'd been stabbed.

His voice breaking, Rudi said, "Bruno?"

He shoved one of the bodies off what looked like a dog's tail.

Rudi lurched sideways and vomited.

Draxler peered inside. "Herr Kommandant, do you need help?"

"Get Baumann. Now!"

39

Rudi stared at his office wall. He couldn't think of anything except stuffing the person responsible inside the Box and smiling as he pounded in nails. He wanted to hear screams. Bloodcurdling screams.

He dropped his face into his hands and sobbed.

But more than anything, he wanted to hear just one last bark.

A voice said quietly, "Rudi?"

Rudi wiped his eyes.

Baumann stood in the doorway. "I can come back later."

Rudi beckoned. "No, I want to know now."

Baumann carried in a large brown suitcase, holding it horizontally, and placed it on Rudi's desk.

Rudi rested a hand on the case. Tears rolled down his cheeks.

Baumann said, "Are you sure you want to know? We could just bury him."

"Tell me."

Baumann said, "His cranium was crushed, the indentation suggesting a piece of cut wood. Other than that, he has what looks like an electrical burn on his right side, presumably from the fence. I'm guessing someone tied a rope around him, threw it under the fence, then dragged him into the compound from the other side during the night."

Rudi balled his fists and clenched his jaw. "And?"

Baumann took a breath. "He's been"— he swallowed —"he's been partially skinned and much of the flesh, particularly on his chest and hindquarters, has been cut away."

Rudi gulped. "So they..." He choked on the words he was about to say.

Baumann lowered his gaze. "Yes."

Gruber barged in, sweat on his brow. "Herr Kommandant, we got back as quickly as we could." His gaze fell to the suitcase. "Is that...?"

Baumann nodded.

Gruber said, "What did they do to him?"

Rudi hammered his fist onto his desk. "They ate him."

Baumann said, "I'm guessing they killed him when he was sniffing around the new barracks, then hid him near the fence."

"I'll line a dozen against the wall as an example." Gruber patted his pistol. "Then a dozen more every half hour until someone talks."

"No." Rudi placed his hand back on the case. "That makes us as bad as them. Even after this, I won't slaughter innocent people."

Gruber snorted. "They're Jews. None of them are innocent."

Rudi stroked the smooth leather of the case. It was cold, unfeeling, hard.

Was Gruber right?

Rudi had come to question if, deep down, Jews were real people. Not subhuman, but thinking, feeling beings just like him. Now? He couldn't imagine ever being able to look at a single one of them and not want to rip out their throat.

Rudi shouted, "Krebs!"

Krebs darted in.

Rudi said, "Check how many prisoners were on the construction detail for the new barracks the day Bruno disappeared."

"Eighty-three, Herr Kommandant."

"You don't need to check?"

Baumann said, "I already had Krebs verify that. It's a sixth of the camp. Way too many to question."

"Line all the prisoners up." Rudi stood. "And bring the Box."

Gruber smiled. "Now we're talking." He dashed away.

Baumann winced. "Rudi, you just said you didn't want to kill the innocent."

"I've said a lot of things and look where it's gotten me." There was being a good person, then there was being a good Nazi. He'd tried one...

Rudi rested a standard-issue folding shovel on the suitcase and eased it up in both arms.

Baumann reached for the shovel. "I can help."

Rudi swung the case away. "No."

He cradled it and walked outside.

In the compound, Gruber barked orders while guards beat prisoners as they exited their barracks. Turning away, Rudi marched toward the forest — toward their private world where all the troubles of the war had never existed.

The sun glinted on the snow while shadows from trunks lay across the ground like fallen trees. A robin fluttered by.

"It's a nice day, Bruno." Tears streaked Rudi's face. "Winter is definitely here, but you like winter, don't you, boy?"

Rudi smiled, seeing Bruno leap up and bite a snowball out of the air. He trudged on.

This didn't feel real. As if he'd wake any moment to find a wet nose and a long tongue slobbering over him. It couldn't be real. How could someone do that to Bruno?

But no matter how far he walked, how long he cradled his friend, he never woke.

They entered a small clearing. "Shall we have a rest by our tree?"

Crouching carefully, Rudi laid Bruno on the ground next to the oak he'd often leaned against while Bruno sniffed about.

Rudi sat against the trunk, his hand on Bruno beside him. Time disappeared as he pictured Bruno nuzzling undergrowth, peeing against a boulder, snapping at an insect buzzing past...

Rudi patted Bruno. "Time to go, boy."

After clearing the snow, Rudi dug. The ground was hard, and more than once, he had to hack through a root, but on he dug. Finally satisfied Bruno wouldn't be disturbed, Rudi laid his casket in the deep, dark hole.

Rudi placed his hand on the case. "Thank you."

He filled in the hole and patted the dirt flat.

Scooping up snow, he made a snowball. He hurled it and immediately closed his eyes. When he opened them, the snowball was gone — Bruno having bitten it out of the air. Rudi smiled.

Rudi trudged away, seeing Bruno running on ahead as usual, only this time he kept on running and running and running, disappearing into the trees.

"See you again one day, boy."

40

Rudi walked alongside the perimeter fence, the prisoners lined up at the other side. Approaching the gate, he looked down, about to say, "Go play, Bruno," but caught himself.

He clenched his fists as pain exploded inside him.

Entering the compound, he reminded himself that most of the prisoners were innocent. He snorted. Like that mattered anymore.

At the front of the roll call area, he trailed a hand over the Box — not that a single prisoner would need it pointed out to them — before joining Gruber and six of his men. He glowered at the shivering wretches staring at the ground in fear.

In such cramped conditions, no one could catch, kill, and eat an animal in complete secrecy, so other prisoners had to know who was responsible. If they wouldn't give up the guilty, to hell with the lot of them.

Rudi said, "Look at me."

No one moved.

Rudi shouted, "Look at me!"

He signaled his men, who raised machine guns.

The women cowered, hunching into ever smaller balls, but none of them dared to run.

"Unterscharführer Gruber."

"Herr Kommandant?"

"If even just a single pair of eyes isn't looking at me in three seconds, open fire."

"Yes, Herr Kommandant."

"One..."

Some of the faces looked up.

"Two..."

More faces joined them. Prisoners nudged their neighbors to look.

"Three..."

He scanned the rows. Even though some still had their heads bowed, they were looking at him. Good. He needed them to see his pain, to see his earnestness.

"One of you killed my dog." He paused. Not for dramatic effect, but to swallow the agony trying to claw him into a blubbering heap on the ground. He gritted his teeth and scanned the faces. But froze, shocked.

Staring, he narrowed his eyes at the rows of powerless wretches. Something he'd never imagined in his vengeance-fueled rage filled their gazes — horror, sympathy, understanding.

No!

That was more deceit. Like how the sisters had lulled Kloser into a carefully staged trap. Kloser had been right: "*They're animals, Rudi. Animals. They can't help themselves. All they understand is the whip.*"

Rudi glared. "You all know me. You all know I'm not like Kommandant Kloser. You might think that makes me soft. That I'll let you get away with murder." He pointed, dragging his finger along the women. "And don't be fooled, *this is murder.*"

Some of the prisoners were even crying now. How deceitful could they get?

He said, "I want those responsible. Until I get them, you're all going to stand here, whether it takes a day, a week, or a month."

Striding away, he said to Gruber, "If anyone falls, they stay where they drop."

"Yes, Herr Kommandant."

As Rudi marched out, Baumann scurried over from the infirmary. "Rudi, with respect, the only reason the sickness levels are under control is your hard work. But if you go through with this, by morning, you'll have undone all the good you've done."

"They have to learn, Baumann. They'll police themselves or they'll suffer."

"You sound like Kloser."

Rudi stopped. Glared at him. "Then maybe he had it right all along."

Baumann touched Rudi's arm. "Rudi, you don't mean that."

"It's Herr Kommandant." He shrugged Baumann off and strode away. Kloser was right — Rudi had been soft. Too soft. That ended now. If the prisoners wanted to test his resolve, they had only themselves to blame for the consequences.

41

Inge trudged along the country lane in the middle of the column, dusk creeping across a hillside.

Behind her, Square Jaw said, "One... two..."

Cringing, Inge glanced back. A woman from the trench lay facedown on the road, unmoving, maybe dead from exhaustion.

"Three... four... five..."

The rifle blasted and Inge flinched. That was the fourth execution, yet even if it was the four hundredth, the gruesome shock of it would still jolt her.

A woman in front of her began praying. Inge snorted. She'd never been a practicing Jew, which would have made winding up in her current predicament hilarious if it wasn't so tragic. She'd always believed in something, though, even if she couldn't put her finger on exactly what. However, religion taught that God was everywhere. That meant He was walking with them now, watching them being beaten, starved, shot... And He did nothing. God? There was no God. At least not an all-powerful being that loved everyone.

Around a bend, the road curved downward. Thank the stars — walking would be easier with gravity's aid.

Letting the incline pull her, Inge tramped down the hill.

A guard at the front pointed to two dark structures across a field. Wherever they were going, they weren't getting there today.

Soon, the guards guided them along a track to a barn while Square Jaw spoke to a farmer outside a house.

Standing beside a well, Hook Nose said, "Ten minutes for water."

The women raced over and crowded around it. Someone lifted the wooden cover and Greta turned the metal handle, lowering a bucket on a chain into the hole. It splashed. Greta reeled it back up and desperate hands dipped in.

Fresh water.

Smiling, Inge drank. Champagne at a royal banquet wouldn't taste as good. She rolled her eyes. How far her life had fallen for something so trivial to be such a cause for jubilation.

Still, the well was a step up from the horse trough they'd had to use the previous night.

After drinking, they were crammed into the barn and forced to sit on the compacted earth. A horse whinnied. The beast was so skinny it looked like it would struggle to drag itself out to the barn let alone haul a plow across a field.

The guards spread hay across the floor at the other side, then cooked goulash on a gas-fueled field stove. They laughed as they wafted the meaty fragrance across the barn.

Inge's stomach growled so loudly it was like she had an animal stuffed inside her dress. She pulled her blanket tighter around her and tried to think of anything but food.

Greta said, "Can you believe these cruel—"

"Quiet!" Square Jaw raised his rifle. "Anyone who speaks will be sleeping outside chained to the well."

Silence.

Sleep took Inge.

But the night seemed to disappear in an instant.

"Up! Up!"

Groggy, Inge peered about. Sunlight shafted through the cracks in the barn wall.

How could it be morning already? She'd only just closed her eyes.

"Up!" shouted a guard.

The prisoners clambered up.

"Fifteen minutes for water and bathroom."

Under her breath, Inge said, "Bathroom? Why didn't someone say we had an en suite."

"Quiet!"

Greta stifled a chuckle.

Most of the women rushed to the well, so Inge walked around the side of the barn and, under the scrutiny of a guard, crouched beside the wall to use the "bathroom" with other women.

After, she dawdled over to the well, where someone hauled up another bucket of water, chunks of ice floating in the top. Inge drank her breakfast.

Greta scurried past with others to use the impromptu facilities. "Don't go anywhere without me."

Inge didn't know how far they still had to go, or how long it would be before they drank again, so she cupped more water.

"Line up!"

Women scuttled to form a column to avoid the whip. Greta hared around the corner of the barn but hit a frozen puddle. Her feet flew from under her and she crashed to the ground.

Inge dashed over. "Are you okay?"

Rubbing her head, Greta grimaced. "I think so."

Offering her hand, Inge pulled Greta up only for her friend to wail like she'd been jabbed with a spike. Greta clutched her left knee.

"You!" a kapo shouted and pointed a whip. "Line up!"

"You've got to get up, Greta." Inge held Greta's arm. "Come on."

Straining, they hauled her up to stand on her right leg.

"How's it feel?" asked Inge.

Greta winced. "Give me a moment."

A guard marched over. "In line. Now!"

Inge pulled her friend's elbow. "Come on."

Greta took a step but squealed. Her knee gave and she crashed to the ground again.

The guard slung his rifle off his shoulder. "In line."

Tears running down her face, Greta peered at Inge. "I can't walk."

Crouching, Inge took her arm. "Greta, please. Get up."

"I can't."

The guard leveled his rifle at them. "Five seconds."

Inge thrust her palms toward him. "Wait. Please. We can do it."

Crying, Greta said, "I can't, Inge. I can't."

Inge shook Greta. "Yes, you can."

"One..."

Inge wound her blanket around Greta's knee.

"Two..."

Pulled it as tight as possible.

"Three..."

Folded the material in on itself to secure it.

"Four..."

Bound the leg as best she could.

"Five..."

She shouted, "Wait! We're ready. We're ready!"

Inge leaped up and grabbed Greta's hand. "I'm not leaving you." She prayed the makeshift bandage provided enough support for Greta to hobble. She heaved.

Greta's face twisted as she hauled up to stand. Tentatively, she placed weight on her injured leg. It held.

The guard jabbed toward the line. "Move. And if you fall behind, that's it."

Inge put her arm around Greta. "I've got you."

Together, they lurched to the column. The procession headed out.

Inge sighed. Dragging herself across the Estonian countryside had been torture enough, but dragging the two of them? Their destination better be close. Darn close.

42

Rudi slung a half-eaten piece of bread and marmalade onto his plate at the commandant's dining table. He had to eat. He knew that. But he couldn't.

He stared at the wall in the silent, silent house. He could almost hear the *tap-tap-tap* of claws on the wooden floor. Almost. Shoving the plate away, he rose.

As he trudged toward the administration block, he scanned the compound. Under guard, the women were still lined up. Or most of them were. Dotted here and there, a body lay on the ground.

He looked away. This wasn't his fault. He'd ordered that if anyone provided verifiable information, he should be notified and the prisoners returned to their barracks. They had only themselves to blame for their suffering.

Baumann was waiting near the building. Rudi rolled his eyes and tramped past the man.

Baumann saluted. "Herr Kommandant, I'd like to give my report."

"If you must." Rudi plodded inside, Baumann trailing behind him.

"As per your orders, the prisoners have been standing to attention throughout the night, so I conducted an inspection fifteen minutes ago."

Rudi slunk to his office, slung his coat in the corner, and collapsed into his chair. "Are you getting to a point, Scharführer?"

"Herr Kommandant, I have to report that there are five dead and at least twenty-seven in need of medical attention."

Rudi looked down at a ledger. "Duly noted, Scharführer."

"So what should I do about those needing assistance?"

Rudi didn't look up. "My orders stand."

"Blast it, Rudi, this isn't you. I feel for you, believe me, I do. But hundreds of the people out there had nothing to do with what happened to Bruno. They're suffering needlessly, but you could stop it. Right now."

Unblinking, he stared at Baumann. "Have they delivered Bruno's killer?"

"Most of them don't know who that is." Baumann threw his hands up. "Heck, the killer could even be one of the dead, so you could keep them all standing there till next year, but no one is ever going to come forward. You're punishing people for things they have no control over."

"I'm punishing the guilty!" Rudi hammered the desk. "And anyone who isn't guilty of the crime but knows who is, is guilty of collaboration." He stabbed a finger at the window and the compound beyond. "Any one of them could stop this right now. Because they know. Believe me, *they know.* So *I'm* not hurting anyone. *They're* hurting themselves."

"But—"

Adrenaline subsiding, Rudi held his palm to Baumann. "Thank you for your report, Scharführer. Now, I have work." He returned to his ledger.

"Rudi, please, end this."

Rudi hurled the ledger across the room. "I said, thank you, Scharführer."

Baumann pursed his lips but saluted and left.

Krebs appeared in the doorway. "Herr Kommandant?"

Rudi shouted, "What?"

Krebs shrank back. "I'm sorry to disturb you, Herr Kommandant, but Kraus Construction's site manager asked if the meeting at the excavation today could be pushed from 1400 hours to 1500."

"Cancel it."

"We canceled yesterday."

"And we're canceling today."

"Yes, Herr Kommandant. Shall I say tomorrow at 1000?"

"If you must." Rudi dragged a hand through his hair, but Krebs didn't leave. "Is that all?"

"A delivery truck has arrived."

"So deal with it."

"Herr Kommandant, this shipment hasn't come through normal channels, so I don't know how you'd like it processed."

"What?" Frowning, Rudi marched outside. A black truck stood in front of the building, and a small man with a mustache leaned

156

against one of eight wooden crates. Two guards unloaded another from the rear.

"I'm Kommandant Kruse. What's all this?"

The deliveryman handed him a paper. "Sign at the bottom, Herr Kommandant, and it's all yours."

"What is?"

The deliveryman shrugged. "I'm only a driver."

Rudi gestured to a guard standing nearby with a crowbar. The man levered open one of the crates and lifted out a gray winter coat.

Rudi's jaw dropped. It was the special shipment he'd paid for with the cook's stash. What the devil was he going to do with six hundred coats now?

The deliveryman pointed to the paper. "If I can get a signature, please."

Rudi signed and the man left.

Gruber marched over. "Is there a problem, Herr Kommandant?"

"It's winter coats for the prisoners."

Gruber laughed. "Well, let's get straight on handing those out." He laughed again.

Rudi stared at the trembling women in the compound.

Krebs said, "Herr Kommandant, where should we store these? We don't have so much space available in the supply room."

Rudi marched back toward the door. "Give them to the prisoners."

Gruber snorted. "Herr Kommandant, you can't be serious."

"Those are my orders, Unterscharführer." He disappeared inside. What he intended to do was the cruelest thing he'd ever done, possibly the cruelest thing anyone had ever done. But he had to do it. They'd given him no choice.

43

At the back of the column, Inge and Greta lurched away from a small town back into the countryside, their arms around each other.

"Hold on, Greta. We'll be there soon."

Greta limped on, face in a permanent grimace. "You said we were there."

"I thought we were." The town was the biggest place they'd encountered, so it had made sense for it to have been their destination.

One of the two rear guards whipped Greta across the back. "Faster."

Greta collapsed, pulling Inge down too.

The guard raised his whip. "Get up!"

Inge clambered up and hauled on Greta's arm. "We're getting up. Please, give us a second."

On her back, Greta shook her head. "Leave me."

"Get up, Greta. Please." Inge heaved, but Greta didn't budge.

Crying, Greta said, "I can't."

"Move!" The guard whipped Inge.

Inge recoiled as pain sliced across her shoulders. "Greta, please."

"I can't."

The guard slung his rifle off his shoulder.

"Please." Inge hauled on Greta's arm with all her might. But she couldn't get Greta up without help.

"Leave me, Inge."

"No." What could she do? She couldn't lose her only friend.

Inge did the only thing she could — as snow started falling, she sat on the ground.

Greta said, "What are you doing?"

"If you're giving up, so am I."

The guard leveled his gun at them.

"Inge, you can't."

Inge folded her arms.

The guard aimed at Inge. "One..."

"Inge!"

"I'm not moving."

"Two..."

"Inge, please."

Inge shook her head.

Greta rolled onto all fours.

"Three..."

Greta screamed as she stood.

"Four..."

Greta grabbed Inge's hand and pulled. Inge scrambled to her feet. The guard lowered his weapon.

Arms around each other, Inge and Greta lumbered across a stone bridge as dark water swirled through its arches.

44

Rudi paced behind his desk. Back and forth, back and forth. Just like his thoughts.

Was Baumann right? Was he turning into Kloser? He dragged his fingers through his hair. What was he supposed to do? They'd killed Bruno.

Bruno!

Justice had to be done.

But was justice at any cost *really* justice?

He held his head. He was a soldier, not a philosopher. How was he supposed to judge what was right?

Kloser would have no qualms about doing what Rudi intended to do. Neither would most of his comrades. But in ten years, when Rudi looked back on today, what would he see — a wounded soldier seeking justice or a vengeful monster inflicting torture?

He slumped into the studded leather armchair Kloser had bought on a trip to Reval with his wife. Bruno deserved justice. Doing anything else was a betrayal of their friendship. He had to see this through. Had to.

But if what he had planned was right, why did it feel so wrong? He did a double take as his gaze drifted past the window. His mouth fell agape at the sight in the compound. Faces that only moments ago had been filled with horror, pain, and despair had transformed into something he'd only ever seen once — on his father's face the day he came home from work to find Rudi's mother had given birth to their daughter early.

Pure joy.

Hundreds of prisoners wearing new coats danced and twirled and posed and hugged. Who would've thought such a sight could grace a place like this?

He buried his head into his hands. That made what he intended to do even harder. But how else could he find the justice Bruno deserved?

"For Bruno." Rudi slammed his fist onto the chair arm.

Under falling snow, he marched into the compound while the prisoners celebrated, every face aglow like a child's on Christmas morning. Voices quietened as he resumed his position front and center beside one of the empty crates.

Barely a few hours earlier, these women had only dared to look at him under threat of execution. Now, he scanned the faces staring at him like he was some sort of savior.

He said, "Back in line."

Some shuffled into loose rows, but most didn't move.

Rudi glanced at Gruber.

The unterscharführer barked commands and the rows reformed.

So many faces glowed with happiness. He'd known they'd appreciate coats but had never expected such joy over something that, before the war, would have been so ordinary as to be mundane for most of them.

Rudi gritted his teeth. *For Bruno.*

"You." He pointed his swagger stick at a woman with a crooked smile on the front row, then gestured to a spot six feet in front of him.

Her smile faded. She glanced around as if hoping for support but received none.

Gruber shouted, "Move!"

She scuttled before Rudi, her joy snuffed out, her gaze once more nailed to the ground.

The next five seconds would define the next fifty years of Rudi's life. He swallowed hard. *For Bruno.*

With a calm, level tone, he said, "Who killed my dog?"

"I'm sorry, Herr Kommandant, I don't know." She cowered, probably expecting to be struck.

"That's okay." Could he really do this? He gulped again. They'd given him no choice. "Take off your coat."

Her brow furrowed with bewilderment. "Herr Kommandant?"

Rudi drew his pistol. "Take ... off ... your ... coat."

Whimpering, she removed her coat and offered it to him.

"In the crate."

She dropped it in.

"Set it alight." He held out a box of matches and a tiny can of naphtha that he used to refill his cigarette lighter.

Her expression collapsed, but she poured fluid onto her coat and dropped in a lit match. Flames illuminated the inside of the crate and smoke rose.

Rudi gestured for her to return to her row. She scooted back. He beckoned the woman beside her. Crying, the woman shuffled over, arms wrapped around her chest, clinging to her coat.

"Who killed my dog?" asked Rudi.

Shaking her head, her breaking voice squeaked, "I don't know."

Rudi pointed at the burning crate.

Sobbing, the woman removed her coat and threw it into the flames. He waved her away and pointed at the next woman. She slouched over.

Rudi turned to Gruber. "Take over, Unterscharführer. If you don't get a name we can verify, burn the lot."

"Yes, Herr Kommandant."

Rudi marched away. Feeling as hollow as if a grenade had blown out his insides. His heart ached. Ached for Bruno. Ached for what he'd done. Seeing justice served was supposed to feel satisfying, yet all he felt was emptiness. Emptiness mixed with shame.

Maybe this was why Kloser had done as little as he had – he wasn't lazy but plagued by the agonizing responsibility of having to make hard decisions. From now on, Rudi would follow that same path. He liked working with figures, so that was what the prisoners would be – not people, but numbers.

Kloser had warned him they were animals. Animals that couldn't help acting on their impulses, no matter how immoral or depraved. So that was how he'd have to treat them.

Striding back to his office, he hung his head. Could he live such a cold life? Turn off that part of himself that made him care, that part that had made him leap into a raging river to save a drowning stray dog?

He snorted. Bruno, the war, Crasneanca... there was no beauty in the world, only varying degrees of ugliness. He was better as distanced from everything as he could get. And that started now.

45

Greta stumbled on the country road, but Inge caught her. "Keep going, Greta. You can do it."

Panting, Greta hobbled on, head hung, seemingly too tired to speak.

Beyond some conifers ahead, smoke rose. Inge had been disappointed so many times, she didn't even pray they'd reached their destination.

She plodded on.

Past the trees, the road stretched endlessly into the distance.

Inge's legs gave and she dropped to her knees, dragging Greta with her. Under her breath, she said, "God help us."

They were never going to get there. Never. She and Greta were going to die on this road. What was the point of carrying on for another day, another hour, another minute? This journey was going to kill them, so why endure the nightmare one second longer than they had to? Greta had been right about wanting to stop, to end it all. How selfish Inge had been to force her to carry on.

"Greta, shall we stop?"

Greta nodded.

"You know what that means?"

Greta nodded again.

"Okay."

Wheezing, Greta said, "Thank you."

The rear guards waltzed up behind them.

"Move," said a tall guard.

Inge glared at him. "No."

"Move!" He shoved her with his foot.

"Count to five and end it, you Nazi scum." Inge looked him square in the eye, unafraid. He was going to remember her and how she didn't plead. She clenched her fists and waited to look down his rifle barrel.

Instead of shooting her, he burst out laughing. He pointed ahead. "You dumb Jew, we're there."

Inge looked. The front of the column had turned off the road and was disappearing down a small incline, toward that smoke.

His comrade rolled his eyes and fished a chocolate bar from his pocket. He handed it to the tall guard. "Okay, you called it."

Inge glowered. "You bet on whether we'd make it?" What kind of sick human being wagered on whether they'd have to shoot another person or not?

Tall Guard waved his chocolate. "This gets you a pass on the 'Nazi scum' comment, but don't push it. Now move."

Helping Greta, Inge heaved up. They trudged on and down a track. Hidden from the road, a double barbed wire fence enclosed four one-story wooden buildings inside a compound where columns of smoke curled. Outside the fence, three wooden buildings lay in an L-shape.

Relief overwhelming Inge, tears streamed down her cheeks. "We made it, Greta. And they've got heating." She laughed. "Heating! Look at the smoke."

She couldn't remember the last time she hadn't shivered through an entire day.

Hope giving them strength, they doddered faster. But as they neared, Inge frowned. What crazy heating was this? Inside the compound, nine bonfires blazed with prisoners lined up so far from them, they'd feel no benefit. Whoever was in charge had to be a complete imbecile. Or just plain cruel.

She clutched her mouth. Some prisoners lay on the ground unconscious, maybe even dead, and everyone was ignoring them. A number had obviously been there for some time because the falling snow had settled on them. There was her answer — the commandant wasn't an imbecile; he was a monster.

As part of her group's processing, they were paraded in front of a bald man with round glasses and a doctor's coat. He selected a number of prisoners to examine, including Inge and Greta. She waited outside the one-story infirmary until it was her turn, then entered.

Inge stood in a curtained-off area. A locked medicine cabinet and a three-section operating table suggested this was as close as the prisoners got to a surgical unit.

"I'm Scharführer Baumann. Take off your dress, please."

164

Please? She immediately checked beneath the white coat — he wore a German uniform. How odd.

She removed her dress. Bruises old and new hugged her body.

Baumann sighed at the brown, yellow, blue, and purple blotches, then checked her pulse. "Any fever, headaches, coughing?"

"No."

Listening to her lungs, he said, "Rash, nausea, vomiting?"

"No."

He looked down her throat. "Aching muscles, swollen glands, chills?"

She made an *ahhh*.

Pulling back, he said, "Was that a yes?"

"Aching muscles." She'd like to meet someone who'd suffered what she had and didn't ache all day, every day.

"But no rash, fever...?"

"No."

"So it's likely work-related."

"You think?"

"Sorry."

Please and sorry? Did this guy know he was in the German military? Such politeness suggested she had some leeway, so she chanced her luck. What was the worst that could happen — she'd get a couple more bruises?

Inge said, "May I ask what all this is about, please?"

"After the last transfer from the prison, we had a typhus outbreak."

Typhus was deadly. If the prison spread that, maybe she'd struck lucky getting out of there.

"Okay, get dressed. You're done." He handed her a scrap of paper, then scribbled in his notes. "Give that to your block leader."

She pulled on her dress and moved to leave but hesitated. He was the most decent German she'd ever met. But how truly decent was he? "Will we be getting any food, please? We've had nothing for three days."

He grimaced. "As you might've guessed from the scene outside, the camp is"— he sucked through his teeth —"going through something right now. So I'm sorry, I honestly can't say."

"Thank you." She left.

Outside, she scratched her head, staring at the women shivering in the cold while fires raged just beyond reach.

"Going through something?" Her shoulders slumped. "Talk about out of the frying pan..."

Greta hobbled past for her examination, and she squeezed Inge's arm. "Thank you. For everything."

Inge replied with a smile.

Some women were admitted to the infirmary, including Greta, while everyone else was processed, which included being assigned a new number and a barracks. Inge became prisoner 1582 of Barracks 03.

As Inge was led away, Baumann left the infirmary. She smirked. Just her luck — the only decent German she'd ever met and he was too low in rank to help.

Trudging behind the rows of shivering women, Inge looked at the paper Baumann had given her. Next to her number at the top was the date. She froze.

Inge sank to her knees, tears in her eyes.

46

Sitting in his office's armchair, Rudi glared when Baumann appeared in the doorway.

"Herr Kommandant, the transfer from the prison has arrived."

"I see that."

"The documentation states seventy-two. Sixty-four are fit for work, one has a sprained knee, three have frostbite, four died in transit."

"Thank you. Dismissed."

But Baumann didn't leave. Rudi rolled his eyes.

"Herr Kommandant, they've been denied food for three days. Obviously, they had nothing to do with what happened to Bruno. Permission to authorize rations?"

Rudi held Baumann's gaze. Kloser would say a Jew was a Jew and deny them food. But of all the people in the camp, that group was guaranteed to be innocent. At least of the only crime he cared about.

"Bread and soup." He turned to the window.

"Herr Kommandant?"

His eyes shut, Rudi rubbed his brow. "What now, Scharführer?"

"What about the other prisoners?"

"What about them?"

"It's still snowing. If they all freeze to death, how are you going to explain that to Sturmbannführer Söllner?"

Rudi sighed. Was Baumann doing him a favor by giving him a way to save face while letting the prisoners off the hook, or was he genuinely more concerned about the prisoners than their friendship and Bruno?

Rudi glared at Baumann.

"Please, Rudi."

In ten years, how would Rudi judge his actions today?

Covering his eyes, he nodded.

"Thank you, Rudi." He left. In the main office, he said, "Krebs, inform the kitchen to prepare soup."

Rudi turned back to the window as both men appeared outside and marched away — Baumann for the compound, Krebs for the kitchen.

Except for twenty-two of them, the prisoners were dismissed and all darted for shelter. Of those remaining, twelve rushed to carry the food, and ten helped Baumann with the sick and the dead.

Rudi watched everybody disappear.

He stared out. Lost in the falling snow. So lost.

Sometime later, six prisoners trudged back with soup vats suspended on poles while six others carried bread rations.

Once again, everyone disappeared inside.

So it was over. Bruno had been killed, and Rudi would never know who was responsible. How was that honoring his best friend?

Trailing his coat across the floor, he trudged to the door. He felt like he was disappearing, too. Fading away. Diluted. Like too little coffee in too much water.

Slinging the coat around his shoulders, he tramped down the track. He was drowning in this place. As surely as if he'd been thrown into a river with his arms and legs bound. His only hope was to get away. It didn't matter where, just away. Even the Front. At least there it was straightforward war — kill or be killed. Simple. Here? Ugliness. Nothing but twisted ugliness.

And then he saw it.

He stopped. Stared. What the...?

The compound wasn't deserted. A woman with flowing black hair and a blanket pulled around her shoulders sat on a rock, hunched over a soup bowl.

Why on earth would she choose to be outside instead of in her barracks out of the snow?

Intrigued, he watched her.

A robin fluttered through the compound and landed twenty feet from the woman. As she ate, the red-breasted bird hopped closer and closer, testing if it was safe to approach. Because of the angle, Rudi couldn't see the woman's face properly, but he could tell from her head movement that she was watching the bird, too.

The bird stopped six feet from her. She tore off a piece of her bread and threw it to the creature.

168

Rudi's jaw dropped.

The bird ate the scrap, so she threw a second. Again, the bird devoured it. The woman threw a third piece. Clutching its treasure in its beak, the bird flew away.

Rudi stared. Frozen with disbelief.

Only moments ago, he'd committed to leaving this place to take his chances on the Front, the ugliness that drenched this world being overwhelming.

But this?

He drilled his gaze into the woman. Who was she? Why was she behaving so... oddly?

He marched back up the track. The sentries opened the gate for him and he strode in.

"Herr Kommandant?"

He glanced back.

A sentry said, "With respect, after what happened to Kommandant Kloser, Unterscharführer Gruber has ordered that no personnel enter the compound alone."

Rudi beckoned him and continued on. The sentry dashed to catch him up. They marched around to the side of Barracks 03 that faced the commandant's house.

The woman saw him, jumped up, and scurried for the sanctuary of her barracks.

"Stop!" Rudi pointed his swagger stick at her, even though she was the only person in sight.

She froze thirty feet from the barracks, hunched in the cower that prisoners always adopted in the presence of a German.

Rudi stared at her. Snowflakes had caught in her raven hair, which, when twinned with her pale complexion, gave her an almost ethereal look. With her head bowed to avoid eye contact, he couldn't see much of her face, though from what was visible, she looked plain.

But now he stood before her, what the devil was he going to say? Well, why not start with the obvious?

"Why are you outside?" he asked.

"I needed some air, Herr..."

"Kommandant."

She gulped. "I needed some air, Herr Kommandant."

"Air? It's below zero? Are your barracks too hot?"

"I..." She stared at the ground.

The sentry raised his gun, "Kommandant Kruse asked you a question."

She flinched, pulling back without daring to step away.

Rudi gestured for his man to stand down. "Why are you outside?"

"I..."

Though her head was bowed, he saw her chin tremble. She had to be hiding something to be so frightened. However, to get to the truth, he needed to see her properly — see how her face twitched when she spoke, how her eyes shifted when she lied.

He pushed the tip of his swagger stick under her chin and lifted. Her gaze flicked up for a fraction of a second, then shot back down. When she wasn't struck, she raised her face and looked at him.

Above cheekbones that would make any of Michelangelo's creations envious, her eyes blazed the darkest amber. Plain? That had been a foolish assumption.

Eye contact making her seem almost human, he softened his voice. "Why are you outside?"

"There was too much noise — grieving, shouting, joking, praying, complaining... I couldn't stand it."

"You don't like people, or you don't like noise?"

"I just discovered it's my sister's twelfth birthday today. I can't be with her, so I needed to be alone."

"So why feed the bird?"

She squinted at him, as if mystified.

"You fed a bird. Why?"

"I'm sorry, I've only just arrived. I didn't know that was against the rules."

"But why feed it? Are we giving you too much food?"

She gestured to the surroundings. "Everything's frozen. Where's it going to find something to eat?"

"Aren't *you* hungry?"

She sniggered. "Starving." She bowed her head. "Sorry. I shouldn't have said that."

He frowned. She was right — that would have been viewed as a complaint by most guards and punished accordingly. "If you're so hungry, why give away your food?"

She shrugged. "A few crumbs isn't life and death to me, but it is to a tiny creature like that."

She looked up again, her gaze as captivating as a sunset over a desert.

170

He rubbed his chin. Instead of cowering, she stood tall. Defiant, even though she thought she was to be punished for a crime. And of what was she guilty? Compassion. What hell the world would suffer if only it were brimming with such "criminals."

"Wait there."

47

Inge cringed as the commandant swaggered away, his backup trailing behind him like a lost dog. What was she thinking to complain about being starved? And to the commandant of all people? That brute had made prisoners stand in the snow to watch fires they couldn't feel burn.

And she'd insulted him to his face.

Talk about stupid!

She stared at the gallows and dragged her fingers through her hair. She'd crawled through hell to get here, hauling her only friend most of the way. And now she was going to die over something so trivial? Why the devil had she opened her big mouth?

The commandant marched through the gates and turned left. She watched. Watched that swagger. That chin-up, chest-puffed-out, overentitled gait that all SS adopted. Did they practice in mirrors? And where was he swaggering to? Probably to fetch more men because only two of them wasn't enough to deal with one tiny woman.

He turned left again and entered the building nearest the tree line.

She glanced at her barracks. Maybe she should run and hide. Jews were animals to men like him. Oh, he'd bluster about, but he'd never recognize one filthy Jew lost among two hundred others. Just like she'd never recognize one particular sheep in a flock.

Inge scurried toward her sanctuary, downing the last of her turnip soup, but stopped. He might not recognize her, but he'd choose someone to punish. His kind always did. She couldn't let someone innocent suffer for something she'd done.

She waited.

A few minutes later, he strutted back around. This time, he entered the compound alone and marched toward her.

Shivering, she stood tall, hoping he didn't mistake her reaction to the cold as fear. She'd had enough. She couldn't live her life on a knife edge, not knowing if an innocent look or comment would become her death sentence.

She glowered at him. Under her breath, she said, "Do your worst. Because I promise you, it's nothing compared to what's been done to me already."

Instead of drawing his pistol or raising his whip, he stared with an almost serene expression. "Have you ever seen a parrot?"

She frowned. "What?"

"A parrot. A real parrot."

What the...? This had to be how crazy people experienced the world — as disjointed, unassociated fragments. Had the brutal imprisonment she'd suffered sent her over the edge?

"Have you ever seen one?" he asked again.

Wait, this was really happening.

He gazed at her expectantly. He had a small crescent-shaped scar under his left eye. Had he seen action on the Front?

She said, "Uh... no, I haven't."

"When I was a kid, my father used to take me to Oskar's Café as a birthday treat — the most popular place in town. People traveled from miles around to eat there, not because of the food, but because there was a green parrot that talked. I mean, it didn't talk like people talk, but it repeated things it had heard." Wistful, he gazed past her.

Talk about surreal. This guy was clearly a raving loon and needed psychiatric help. The last thing he needed was to be responsible for the lives of hundreds of prisoners.

But that didn't help her right now. What was she supposed to do? Say something? That wasn't allowed if she hadn't been given permission or asked a question.

However, he hadn't finished. "The first time I gave this parrot a nut, it said, '*I'm Mendie. Pleased to meet you.*' It must have said that to thousands of people over the years, but in that moment, the way it tilted its head and the glint in its eye, I swear, it was like the bird really was saying those words for the very first time, just for me."

Inge floundered. She had no clue how to handle the mentally unbalanced.

She stared at him. Stared at eyes as sad as any she'd ever seen, even having witnessed what she had. Such darkness. Both terrifying

173

and alluring. Like a magnificent tiger in a zoo that had once prowled the jungles as master of all but was now resigned to existence in a cage. Such unimaginable loss. The poor—

Wait.

Was that pity? *For a Nazi?* What the hell? He was SS. The Devil incarnate. He was not a tortured soul who'd had a tough break; *he* was the torturer who did the breaking. And now the psycho had noticed her.

She stared down. Trembling.

He said, "My father always used to say, *'Compassion is contagious. Always spread it around.'*"

He held out a brown paper bag.

Lost for what else to do, she took it.

He shuffled backward with an almost embarrassed toothless smile, then strutted away, never looking around.

Inge watched, rooted to the spot, until he disappeared inside that same building. She stared at the bag. Talk about weird. What evil stunt was he pulling? Delicately parting the top of the bag, she winced as she peeped in.

Her jaw dropped and her eyes popped wider — two thick slices of bread with butter and marmalade oozing from between them.

She clutched the bag to her chest and glanced around, expecting someone to be bearing down on her to snatch it away as some sick joke.

There was no one.

She peeked at her sandwich again. Her mouth watered. Was it really for her? Once more, she checked no one was hurtling toward her to spring a cruel prank.

She was alone. Just her. And *her* sandwich.

She gazed at the building into which the commandant had disappeared. To feel such pain, yet do this, was there a heart beating under all that hate? A real person? But she could ponder that later.

Instead of taking the sandwich out, she reached into the bag and tore a hunk away, then pretending to rub her chin, she sneaked it into her mouth.

She chewed, then stopped and closed her eyes, letting the food lie on her tongue. "Ohhh..."

She'd forgotten food could taste like this. Buttery, orangey, bitter, juicy, tart... a rainbow of taste exploded.

Eyes shut, she chewed torturously slowly to savor what was, without a doubt, the tastiest thing in the history of the world.

She swallowed, then stole another look into the bag and sniggered. Such a huge sandwich. And all hers! Or should she take it inside and share it?

She popped another chunk in her mouth and again melted as its fruity, gooey lusciousness danced on her tongue.

As she ate the fifth piece, she realized that after her soup, bread, and now this, she was actually pretty full. That gave her two options — save the rest for later or, as she had with the Pole, make an ally in her new home.

Or... maybe she could have just one more piece. Maybe two.

***

From the bedroom window of the commandant's house, Rudi gazed through his binoculars as the woman munched another piece of sandwich, her eyes shut, seeming to bask in the heavenly taste of homemade marmalade. He smiled.

Drowning in ugliness?

If a Jew could see beauty in a camp so filled with horror, maybe there was hope for him too.

48

Sitting on the rock near her barracks, Inge said, "Wherever you are, happy birthday, Aga."

A single tear trickled down her cheek. Considering what she'd endured, the chance her family was still alive was diabolically slim, but until she had undeniable evidence, she had to cling to that slender hope. It was one of the few things from which she drew strength to keep going.

With no idea about who had influence in her new accommodation, Inge's only option for benefiting from sharing her sandwich was to use a scattergun approach. She tore what remained into six bite-size pieces and ambled into her barracks.

A gang of jabbering women mobbed her: "What did he say?", "Did you know him before the war?", "What did he give you?", "Why you?"

Like a movie star ambushed by paparazzi, Inge froze.

A broad-faced woman with a booming voice said, "Give her space and she might tell us."

Quietening, the women backed off.

Inge gazed at the faces bursting with eager anticipation. The last thing she wanted was to be the center of attention, but someone had obviously seen her encounter from a window and announced it for everybody to watch. Now, she had no choice.

"I, uh, I was just sitting, and he came over. He'd seen me feed a bird—"

One listener nodded to another. "He does like birds."

"— and asked why I'd done it. So I told him — because the bird was hungry. He asked if I wasn't hungry, and I said of course I was, I was starving."

Another said, "You said that to his face?"

"Uh-huh. As soon as I said it, I figured I was going to be whipped or even shot. But no, he disappeared, and when he came back, he gave me this."

She tore open the bag and presented the contents across both hands. Gasps filled the air and wide eyes grew even wider.

Inge said, "Please, take one."

Letting the prisoners help themselves was risky, but she hoped the natural pecking order would see the main players get the lion's share.

Hands dove in. The food disappeared in a second.

A curly-haired woman said, "Did you know him before the war?"

"No."

A gaunt woman said, "So why give you that?"

Inge shrugged.

A Polish woman with a pig nose said, "He's expecting to bed her."

Inge snorted. "He can expect all he wants, it doesn't mean he'll get it."

"Like you'll have a choice."

Curly Hair said, "You must have done something to get free food."

"No."

Pig Nose smirked. "So we're supposed to believe he gave you this out of the goodness of his heart?"

"No," said Inge. "Because I fed a bird."

Laughter erupted.

While Inge fielded more questions — and requests for favors, should the commandant approach her again — she couldn't help but dwell on one particular comment: *He's expecting to bed her.*

Was he? Was that behind his kindness? Queasiness turned her stomach. How insulting for him to think he could buy her for as little as a marmalade sandwich.

The commotion died down, so Inge found a bunk to rest. The prisoners seemed to have joined one of two camps: those who looked at her with a kind of awe and those who whispered about her like churchgoers commenting on a scantily clad woman on a street corner.

She pulled her blanket around her. So the commandant intended to rape her, and half the prisoners condemned her as a whore. Yet again, she'd made one heck of a first impression.

Despite being exhausted, even after lights out, she couldn't sleep. What would she do if the commandant sent for her? "Oh, God." What if it wasn't just him? What if she was to be handed around to all the officers?

Intimate relations between a German and a Jew were illegal. But the soldier who'd beaten her in the shower hadn't cared about that, so who was going to give one red cent out here in the back of

177

beyond? The work in the prison had been torturous, but it had been honest labor. Here? Was the majority of her work going to be done on her back, with her first time being a gang rape? Her face screwed up and tears streamed.

When she finally slept, nightmares tortured her. Nightmares of being chased but being unable to run.

Inge woke, queasy at what might happen if she encountered the commandant again.

Roll call and breakfast came and went, then Inge was assigned to a work detail.

Without her blanket wrapped around her shoulders, the wind sliced through her as she and her group tramped along the road toward town. After a few minutes, they cut up a track across country.

In front of her, a woman in clogs tripped over a root and sprawled in the mud ruts left by a farm cart. She clambered up and continued on. Again, Inge thanked her stars she had shoes.

But falling wasn't what worried her — queasiness still gripped her stomach.

As they clambered over a stile, she realized the gaunt woman behind her was one who'd taken a piece of her sandwich, and presumably she had eaten a soup and bread ration, exactly like Inge.

"Is your stomach okay?" asked Inge.

"As good as it ever is with the filth they give us. Why?"

"I don't feel so good."

She sniggered. "Are you thinking that sandwich was poisoned?"

Inge gawked. "I am now."

"Quiet!" shouted a kapo from the other side of the wall.

Inge frowned. She'd eaten ten times more of that sandwich than anyone else, so if it was poisoned, it would obviously affect her far more. But surely if the commandant wanted a prisoner dead, he'd just shoot them. Why would he waste his time poisoning them?

Because he was a twisted monster. Look how he'd tortured the prisoners by having them stand in the snow out of reach of blazing fires.

Oh dear Lord, why had she been stupid enough to eat that sandwich? Why hadn't she waited for him to be out of sight, then thrown it away?

They trudged on through the countryside. Eventually, they crossed a swaying rope bridge over a river to emerge onto another road, where they headed right.

178

At the foot of a hill, they marched into a construction site dotted with shacks and a number of vehicles with *Kraus Construction* emblazoned on them. There, Inge joined the wheelbarrow crew.

Armed with shovels, a group of prisoners mixed sand, cement, water, and gravel to make concrete. One of them filled Inge's barrow, then she trundled away, following others pushing barrows, all heading directly toward the hill. Her barrow's wheel wonky, the thing pulled left, so she struggled to keep it on the planks laid on the ground.

Rounding the last shack, Inge stopped and gazed at the hillside. A gigantic hole had been gouged in it, into which the wheelbarrow crew headed.

Someone whipped her across the back. "Move!"

She didn't even bother looking who'd done it. Like that mattered.

Entering the hole, she craned her neck to take everything in. It had to be twenty or thirty feet high and double that across. What was it? A railway tunnel? A shortcut for road vehicles? Maybe even some sort of secret underground facility?

Whatever it was, surviving it was more important than making sense of it.

Her barrow drifting left again, she heaved right, fighting to make it go straight. Someone directed her, and she tipped her load next to women reinforcing the walls. Farther in, men worked, undertaking the more specialized tasks to enlarge the excavated area.

Inge returned for another load and stood panting while someone filled her barrow. She dragged her hand across her brow. Considering she'd had a decent meal yesterday and spent a good few hours resting, why was she already exhausted?

Her barrow full, she heaved it up, trundled inside, and emptied it. Then back again.

The next load, her arms trembled as she picked up the barrow. Halfway to the excavation, the wonky wheel drove her off the planks and into a mud rut. She struggled to prevent the barrow from falling over, but her feet slipped, and the barrow tipped sideways. Inge shoved a knee under one of the handles and saved it.

Gasping, she hauled the barrow back onto the planks.

However, her intestines suddenly twisted like someone was crushing them in their fists. She dropped the barrow's handles and darted behind the nearest shack, clutching her stomach. She crouched beside a bush and ripped her panties down before she had an accident.

Grimacing, she defecated. It gushed like hand-pumped beer. Something was seriously wrong. That monster had poisoned her. It was the only answer.

"You!"

Oh dear Lord, not now.

A guard marched over.

Still squatting, Inge said, "I'm sick. Please, give me a minute."

"You can't do that there, you filthy Jew!"

He whipped her. She flung her arms up defensively but fell sideways and sprawled on the ground. He whipped and whipped and whipped.

Standing over her, sweat beading on his face, he pointed at the mess on the ground. "Clean that, then get back to work." He marched away

Inge pulled herself back together. Having nothing to "clean" with, she tossed dead leaves and twigs onto the soiled area, then scooped the lot up with her hands and threw it under a bush.

While next waiting for her barrow refilling, she thrust her hands into a bucket of water to wash while no one was looking.

Each subsequent load felt heavier, and by the afternoon, being whipped for slowness had become part of each trip.

Stumbling back with her barrow, Inge swayed with lightheadedness, her pink-and-white striped dress sodden with sweat even though it was cold enough for snow. She slumped over her barrow and took a deep breath. Once she felt stable again, she started back, only for a horrifying thought to dawn. Nausea, aching muscles, fever — those were the symptoms the doctor had asked about. Oh dear Lord, what if she'd contracted typhus? He'd said the prison had it.

With another load, she plodded toward the man-made cavern, her mind awhirl. But the wonky wheel took her off the planks again. She heaved to stop the barrow from tipping sideways, but dizziness swept over her. Concrete spilled across the ground and Inge collapsed into it.

Someone whipped her. They bawled, "Get up! Up!"

The world blurred.

"Up!" Whipped.

"You again. You lazy whore!" A shiny black boot kicked her in the side.

Her voice frail, she said, "Five."

Another kick. "Get up, lazy whore. Up!"

Gasping, she said, "Count to five."

180

49

Semiconscious in a bunk, Inge caught a blurred glimpse of a large room in which sounds drawled as if someone were stretching them.

Her arm. A shape was touching her arm — a man. Wrapping it. Nearby, a male voice. "That's what you're using?"

The man wrapping replied, "Paper bandages and aspirin are all we've got. Everything else is reserved for emergencies. Not that there's much, so fingers crossed."

"I'll see what I can do." Footsteps clomped away.

The world darkened again.

The next time she woke, moaning, wheezing, and whimpering surrounded her. Where was she?

She wanted to push onto her elbows and look around, but she didn't have the strength.

A woman's voice said, "Hey."

Inge peered from the corner of her eyes.

Greta hobbled over from the next bed, her knee in a brace. "How are you feeling?"

"Like I've been scraped off the bottom of someone's shoe."

"That good, huh?"

Greta sat on the edge of her bed. But Inge's eyes widened as memories flooded back. Fear energizing her muscles, she shoved Greta. "Stay away."

Inge pulled back, but something blocked the bed behind her. She turned — a pair of feet rested on the pillow beside her head. She was sharing the bed?

"Inge, calm down. You're safe."

Inge scrambled to get away from her bunkmate while shoving Greta away. She tumbled out of bed and sprawled across the floor.

Greta shouted, "Scharführer Baumann!"

Baumann rushed over. "Oh, dear Lord."

Inge thrust her hands out. "Stay back. You need to put me in isolation."

He frowned. "Isolation? Why?"

"I've got typhus."

He laughed. "You haven't got typhus. Food poisoning, that's all."

"Food poisoning?"

He grasped her hand and eased her up to sit on the edge of her bed.

Taking her pulse, he said, "Food poisoning, severe dehydration, and exhaustion, which, combined, caused you to collapse. You should consider yourself very lucky, young lady"— releasing her wrist, he put his stethoscope on her chest —"not many people get special treatment from the commandant himself."

"The commandant? He's the one who poisoned me."

"Kommandant Kruse poisoned you?"

"With marmalade."

Baumann laughed again. "It was the commandant who stopped the guards from beating you. Why would he poison you?"

She frowned. She remembered being beaten, but then everything had gone black. "He stopped the guards?"

"You're lucky he'd rescheduled his inspection with Sturmbannführer Söllner, or you'd have suffered far more than just bruises."

"But he gave me marmalade and then I got sick."

Baumann scratched his head. "The commandant gave you marmalade?"

She held her hands apart. "A huge sandwich. After he saw me feeding a bird."

"Ahhh. A bird. You stumbled upon the commandant's soft spot. But what did you have before the marmalade?"

"Soup and bread from the kitchen."

"And before that?"

"Nothing on the march here."

"Did you drink?"

"From a well on the second night and a horse trough the first."

He smiled. "A horse trough? But it's the commandant's marmalade that made you sick?"

"Ohhh, I suppose that makes more sense."

"Good." He handed her two charcoal tablets. "Chew these before swallowing and drink plenty of water."

"Can I get up?"

"To stretch your legs, of course. By rights, you could return to work, but I'm penciling you in for barracks rest tomorrow and work the day after. Okay?"

"Thank you."

He dawdled to another patient. Inge snuggled down in bed. The mattress the softest thing she'd slept on for months, she squeezed it.

"Wood shavings," said Greta.

"I wish we had these in the barracks."

"Too right. It's almost worth being sick." She nodded at Baumann. "Especially when he's so nice. Why can't all Germans be like him?"

"I suppose that's why he became a doctor."

"I don't think he is a doctor. I think he's a medical orderly or something. But he knows his stuff, which is what counts."

Baumann disappeared into the area in which he'd examined Inge that first day.

"I don't get it," said Inge. "Why is he so great while the rest of the German military are such monsters?"

"There's the commandant too, don't forget."

Inge wrinkled her nose. "Maybe."

"Maybe? He saved you from a beating, didn't he?" Greta smirked. "And gave you that poisoned marmalade?"

Inge rolled her eyes. "Yes, but when we arrived, he was torturing the whole camp by forcing them to stand in the snow."

Greta shrugged. "I was so out of it, that didn't really register. What was all that about?"

"I don't know." Inge stood. "But I know who will."

The commandant was a conundrum, appearing kind from one angle but a monster from another. Inge needed to know more. Not least because he'd done her two favors now — and Nazis did not do favors — so what was he going to demand of her in return?

She shuffled to the curtained area, hoping Baumann was as approachable as he appeared.

"Dr. Baumann?"

He looked up from making notes. "Scharführer Baumann."

"Sorry, Scharführer. Could I ask a question, please?"

"Of course."

"The commandant... uh... how can I put this?" Even if Baumann was friendly, she still had to be respectful about his commanding officer. "Uh... when we arrived, all the prisoners were freezing in the snow, and some had even collapsed, yet—"

Baumann held up his hand. He sighed and closed his file, his cheery demeanor darkening. "Some of the prisoners killed his dog."

She gasped.

"Last year, the commandant saw a dog drowning in the river during a storm surge, so he dove in. No hesitation. Just straight in. It's the darnedest thing I've ever seen. I thought they were both going to drown, but Rudi— sorry, the commandant —got this close"— he held his thumb and forefinger a fraction of an inch apart —"to making the swimming team for the Berlin Olympics, so he managed to get them both ashore. They'd been inseparable ever since. Bruno was like family to him."

She clutched her heart. "That's awful."

"What you saw was his attempt to make the prisoners talk, to identify those responsible, but..." He shrugged.

"So he didn't catch the killer?"

Baumann shook his head.

That poor man. To risk his own life to save a dog only to have someone kill it. If it were her and she had men with machine guns at her command, she doubted she'd have been as restrained as he'd been.

**

The following day, Inge attended the evening roll call, and the day after, she resumed work at the excavation site. Word had spread about the commandant stepping in to save her, so, again, women bombarded her with questions she couldn't answer.

After that evening's roll call, she returned to her barracks and joined the food line.

The pig-nosed Pole said, "So, has he stuck his hand up your dress yet?"

Two other women snickered.

"No. I'd ask you the same, but..." Inge snickered.

Glowering, Pig Nose shoved Inge. "What's that supposed to mean?"

The gaunt woman jumped between them. "Cool it, Berta. Take your attitude to the back of the line."

Gaunt Woman was one of the women who'd snagged a piece of the marmalade sandwich. Inge had hoped the barracks' natural pecking order would come into play, and thankfully, it had.

184

Muttering, Berta stalked away.

"Thank you," said Inge.

"You didn't have to share your sandwich, so the fact you did means something." Gaunt Woman glared at Berta. "At least to some of us."

Inge collected her evening meal — bread and "coffee." She ate sitting with Gaunt Woman, who introduced herself as Marta.

Inge said, "In the prison, we got bread *and* soup in the evening."

"Get away."

"Uh-huh. And not just turnip. Sometimes potato."

"No way." Marta nibbled her bread.

A woman with glasses joined them.

"Kristina, get this," said Marta, "Inge got soup twice a day in the prison."

"No!"

Marta smirked. "Sometimes potato."

"Oh, I'd kill for potato," said Kristina. "Or cabbage. Anything but turnip again."

Inge wrinkled her nose. "But we only got bread once a day, not twice like here."

"That's a recent change, thanks to the commandant." Marta slurped her coffee and arched an eyebrow at Inge. "Talking about him, the word is you 'bumped' into each other again. What's the story this time?"

Inge shrugged. "I never even saw him. It was Baumann who told me he stopped a guard beating me."

Marta nodded. "He's okay, Baumann is. Of course, we used to say that about Kruse, but..."

"Kruse?"

"The commandant — Heinz Rudolf Kruse," said Marta. "He used to be decent, then he went and pulled that stunt with the coats."

"What coats?" Inge frowned. What did coats have to do with anything?

"You saw the fires?"

"Uh-huh."

"They were our winter coats. He burned every single one."

Kristina sighed. "And seven prisoners died of the cold while another thirty-one ended up in the infirmary."

Inge scratched her head. "I thought it was about finding who killed his dog."

"It was," said Marta.

"So couldn't someone have told him who the killer was to stop it?" asked Inge. "Or didn't anyone know?"

Kristina said, "Monika Volz from Barracks One. Everyone knew she was the ringleader."

Marta nodded again.

Inge frowned. "So if everyone knew, why didn't anyone say anything to end it all?"

"Because it was *Monika Volz!*" Marta winced. "She was an evil witch from Munich who'd cut your throat while you slept for crossing her."

"She killed one prisoner for her shoes." Kristina nibbled her bread as if such violence was an everyday occurrence.

Inge tensed. She had good shoes. What if this Volz saw them?

Marta said, "The irony is, Volz was one of the first to drop dead from the cold."

Inge relaxed. "So why didn't you tell the commandant then?"

"Oh yeah, that would've been convincing." Marta laughed. She pointed away. "That's the one, Herr Kommandant. That dead one who can't deny it. Can we have our coats back now?"

Kristina said, "And Volz didn't do it alone, so if you ratted her out, the others would cut you for fear you'd rat them out as well."

"Too right." Marta screwed up her nose. "That Lilly Hasse is as crazy as Volz ever was, and she was in on it, but who else...?" She shrugged.

Inge said, "It must have been a horrible situation."

"You can say that again." Kristina clicked her tongue. "I can't believe Kruse did it to us — it was just a dog."

"And you're just a Jew." Inge sipped coffee.

"What?" Kristina gawked.

Inge said, "You look at his dog as a worthless animal, so what's it matter that it died? How do you think they look at us — as worthless animals, so it doesn't matter if we die. It's all about perspective."

"But we're not animals."

Inge snorted. "We are to them. That's how they can treat us the way they do without feeling it's wrong."

Kristina jabbed a finger at Inge. "So you're defending him now? He gives you a sandwich and suddenly he's a victim, not a murderer?"

Inge shrugged. "Like I said, it's all about perspective. To him, some of us are murderers and the rest are collaborators for not giving up the killers."

Kristina nudged Marta. "Do you believe this bull?"

Marta pursed her lips. "Actually, she kind of makes sense."

They finished eating in silence.

After, Inge lay on her bunk, the straw mattress unbelievably lumpy compared to the luxury of the infirmary. She sighed. She'd believed the commandant was a monster, but was he?

Yes, he'd forced the prisoners to stand in the snow for hours, which had killed seven, but at any time, the prisoners could have told him what he wanted to know to end their suffering. The prisoners were just as much to blame for the dead as the commandant. Maybe more so.

What an odd place. Things weren't as clear-cut here as at the prison. She'd have to be careful – in a place like this, someone with a smart-mouth could quickly run into all kinds of trouble. Or all kinds of opportunities. The prospect was both tantalizing and terrifying. But could she find the nerve to do what she was thinking?

50

Rudi's breath billowed in his bathroom as he shaved, wearing his greatcoat over his underwear like a bathrobe. Elena used to light the fires every morning, and initially, after she'd taken up residence in the infirmary, he'd taken over that duty. But with only him wandering the big empty house...

Dressed and downstairs, he chomped into a slice of bread spread with marmalade. He rolled the tasteless mass around his mouth, chewing with as much enthusiasm as a child learning algebra. The kettle whistled on the stove.

Rudi took one more bite, then tossed the bread onto a plate on a counter piled with dirty dishes. He poured boiling water into his mug and his coffee steamed to life, its bitter aroma as tempting as the bread.

It was usually now Bruno would whimper.

Rudi gritted his teeth. Bruno had known coffee was the last element of Rudi's morning routine before their first walk, so the smell always set him off. The two bowls on the floor caught Rudi's attention. Those would have to be cleared away. One day. He'd bent to remove them umpteen times, but each time he'd pulled back, unable to do it.

He sipped his coffee. How was he going to carry on in this soulless place?

He banged his mug down, coffee sloshing out. Bruno wouldn't want him to be like this. In the same way a terminally ill wife would demand her soon-to-be widower find someone else to share his life, Bruno would wish Rudi a decent future too.

Bruno was joy and wonder, curiosity and playfulness. Everything that life was supposed to be. He'd changed Rudi's world. Made this hellish place into a home — somewhere not just bearable, but somewhere Rudi had smiled, laughed, lived...

Shutting the world out was doing his best friend a disservice. Maybe the best way to honor Bruno's memory was to somehow change the world for the better, just as Bruno had.

But how? The reason he was in this mess was because he'd tried to change things. Without Bruno, why would he think anything could possibly get any better?

He tramped into the living room and collapsed onto the studded red leather sofa beside a plate of half-eaten ham and eggs. An assortment of cups and glasses sat on a coffee table as if there'd been a party.

Elena wouldn't be returning as housekeeper for weeks and weeks. Maybe he should accept her offer of recommending a replacement. But even though he could ignore whichever prisoner gained the position, it would still mean having someone else in the house, someone invading his solitude. Could he stomach that?

He had to do something. Anything. Maybe the Front. Experience good, honest war, where there was a real enemy who shot back, not frightened women who withered under his gaze.

That was something to consider.

Above the mantel, a lake with piercing blue water beneath the snowcapped mountains of the Bavarian Alps invited the viewer into an idyllic world where the war didn't rage. Rudi stared at it. Did such a place still exist?

He drew his hands down his face. Whether such a place did or didn't, his life — if it could be called a life — was here. And right now, he had an inspection to undertake.

Fastening his greatcoat, he marched outside. Snow crunched under his fur-lined boots. Being Sunday, a rest day, the prisoners were in their barracks as Rudi strode toward the perimeter fence, scanning for signs of tampering with the cabling, digging under the wire, tunneling causing impressions...

He stopped dead.

All the prisoners were inside. Understandable on such a bitter day. All except one who was sitting on a rock with her back to him. He frowned. Her. Again?

"You're not angling for another sandwich, are you?"

The girl who'd fed the robin twisted around. Her mouth gaped. She jumped up, back straight, gaze down. "No, Herr Kommandant, I wouldn't be so presumptuous."

Presumptuous? Her German was excellent.

He gestured to the barracks. "Prisoners usually can't wait to get inside, yet here you are sitting in the snow. Again."

He waited for her to say something, but she didn't.

"It's quite puzzling."

Still nothing.

He beckoned her to come closer. She shot a wary glance to the watchtower, where the sentry stood with his machine gun leveled toward her.

Rudi waved and the man lowered his weapon.

He said, "You seem to enjoy being outside in the cold."

She stared at the ground.

"You proved you speak fluent German a moment ago. Is there a reason you won't speak it now?"

"Yes, Herr Kommandant."

"So...?"

She flinched, her body tensing. "I meant no offense, Herr Kommandant, but you didn't ask a question."

She hadn't "answered" because he'd asked no "question" to answer. Though he'd never felt the need to do it himself, he'd witnessed prisoners flogged for speaking without permission or a question having been posed. How stupid of him to approach this as an ordinary interaction. "I stand corrected. So let me try again, why are you outside when you could be warm inside?"

She sniggered.

He said, "And now I've made a joke, have I?"

"Sorry, Herr Kommandant. Again, I meant no offense."

"Then why laugh at me?"

"I wasn't laughing at you, Herr Kommandant, but at what you said."

"And it was funny because...?"

"Have you been in our barracks?"

He frowned. "I don't follow."

"To feel how *warm* it is?"

He folded his arms and studied her. She was an odd one. And yet... "So why don't you show me?"

Panic flashed over her face, and for a split second, her gaze flicked up to him. "I..."

She stared back at the ground.

He said, "Wait there."

190

Rudi marched around and into the compound, accompanied by two guards with machine guns. Robin Girl was waiting as instructed, but seeing his escort, she shrank back.

"My predecessor was lured into a trap in a barracks just like this one, so excuse me if I appear overly cautious. Now, show me."

She shuffled into her barracks.

The block leader, Hilde, gaped when Rudi waltzed in behind Robin Girl, then she shouted, "Stand by your bunks. Now!"

The two guards strolled in. One leveled his gun at the women. "Move toward the back of the barracks."

With a mixture of fear and bewilderment, the prisoners scrambled away.

After the initial confusion, whispers flittered around as Rudi followed Robin Girl deeper inside. While all heads were bowed, Rudi saw furtive glances and shocked expressions. He ignored them, focusing instead on his breath billowing before him. She was right.

"Is it always so cold in here?" he asked.

Robin Girl said, "Yes, Herr Kommandant."

Hilde stepped forward. "If I may, Herr Kommandant, she's only just arrived, so—"

"No, you may not." Rudi didn't want what some sycophant thought he wanted to hear. He pointed at a small woman cowering behind another one. "You. Step forward."

Lines of fear twisted the woman's face, but she shuffled closer.

"Don't worry, you aren't going to be punished. How long have you been here?"

"I'm not sure, Herr Kommandant. I think about eleven months."

"So is it always this cold? Speak freely. This isn't a trick." He cringed as he said it because he knew colleagues who'd say that as a trick in itself.

She glanced at the other women. Some nodded, some shook their heads.

"Well...?" The hesitation already suggested the answer, but he wanted to hear them say the words.

"Yes, it's always cold, Herr Kommandant." She grimaced as if expecting to be hit.

He pointed at the brick stove. "How long does your average fuel ration last?"

Many prisoners exchanged blank looks.

Rudi said, "Your fuel — coal, wood, whatever — how long does it last?"

Robin Girl said, "I'm sorry, Herr Kommandant, but I haven't seen any coal or wood." She looked to the small woman. "Have you?"

The woman shook her head.

Rudi rubbed his brow. Why wasn't the camp's stock of fuel being distributed? Was he really so stupid that he'd never wondered why smoke didn't curl from the barracks' chimneys? Or deep down, was he far more of a Nazi than he'd ever imagined?

"Let me look into this." He and his men left. As he marched away, the barracks door creaked behind him. He turned.

Robin Girl stood there.

He said, "Was there something else?"

"I wanted to say..." She fidgeted, hands clasped in front of her.

"Yes?"

"I wanted to say thank you. For saving me." A smile flickered across her face. "And for looking into the fuel for us."

He waved her away. "I'm protecting the Reich's investment. You're here to work, aren't you, not to freeze to death?"

"Sometimes, it feels like you'd rather we freeze." She clutched her mouth.

He squinted, then marched back to her.

She cowered. Head bowed. Face twisted as if waiting to be struck. It twisted even more when he raised his whip.

He poked the end under her chin and lifted her face.

Even though he'd raised her head, she averted her eyes so as not to offend him. And trembled.

Guilt clawed at him.

Such fear. If he approached a dog that knew him and it was this terrified, he'd be ashamed.

He spoke softly. As a man, not a commandant. "I'm not going to hurt you. Look at me."

She looked.

Dazzling eyes met his. Wells of deep, dark amber.

He gazed into them. The insanity of a world at war melted away, and for a moment, it was as though he was facing another person. A living, breathing, vibrant person. A person just like him.

He said, "If you and I meet again, feel free to speak, even if a question hasn't been asked. Okay?"

192

"Yes, Herr Kommandant."

He gazed into those eyes a moment longer — eyes that could swallow a lifetime — then dragged himself back.

"I *will* look into this matter, you have my word, but if there's nothing else, I have work." He pointed to the administration block but frowned. Why had he felt he needed to explain himself to a prisoner?

She nodded. "Thank you."

He strode away.

"Feel free to call back anytime," said Robin Girl. "I'm usually in."

Rudi froze. Then squinted at her.

The girl smirked as if she'd made a joke to a friend.

He strode back and scrutinized her. Her mischievous smile dropped.

Rudi said, "I know I've given you a sandwich and stopped you from being beaten, but don't mistake decency for friendship."

Gaze screwed to the ground, she said, "I'm sorry, Herr Kommandant. I forgot my place after you told me to speak freely. It won't happen again."

"See it doesn't. Prisoners can be shot for such impertinence." Though he had been the one who'd told her to speak freely, so...

"Yes, Herr Kommandant. Sorry, Herr Kommandant."

"Now, if you'll excuse me, duty calls." He caught himself and rolled his eyes. What the devil was it about this prisoner that had him justifying himself?

As he marched away, he muttered to himself, "Call back anytime. I'm usually in."

He chuckled.

A person. Just like him. Was that truly possible?

51

Gazing at the supplies ledger, Rudi ambled to his office door. He scanned a column detailing the shipments of coal they'd received, but stopped at the sound of laughter in the main office. Voices whispered and led to more laughter.

Rudi leaned against the doorjamb, straining to hear what was being said and who was saying it.

Someone whispered, "At least this one's more beddable than the last."

Another hushed voice said, "Oh God, no. If I had to, I'd bed a dog over a Jew any day."

The first voice. "Seriously? And get bitten to hell?"

Rudi scowled. So he and his bird-feeding acquaintance were the latest gossip, were they?

He meandered back to his desk chair and shouted, "Krebs."

Krebs appeared. "Herr Kommandant?"

"What happens to the coal shipments for the prisoner barracks?"

"We sell it to a couple of stores in the town."

"And the trees we fell for firewood?"

"Those too."

"On whose orders?"

"Kommandant Kloser's."

Rudi slung the file onto his desk. "New orders. With immediate effect, two sacks of coal or two barrows of logs are to be released to each barracks, and the infirmary, every Sunday until further notice."

"Does that mean today, too, Herr Kommandant?"

"Did I say with immediate effect?"

"Yes, Herr Kommandant."

"And make sure they understand this is a ration that must last a week."

"I'll organize a work detail, Herr Kommandant." He turned to go.

Rudi looked at his ledger. "Krebs?"

He poked his head around the door. "Herr Kommandant?"

Rudi didn't look up, not reading anything, but just to make the man wait. "You and the Administration Team deliver the rations personally."

Krebs's brow knitted. "Us, Herr Kommandant?"

Rudi shot the man a glare. "Is that a problem, Oberschütze Krebs?"

"Of course not, Herr Kommandant. We'll get right on it."

Rudi returned to his ledger. "I trust you will. Because if I don't see smoke curling from those chimneys within fifteen minutes, the personnel's cigarette ration will be halved for the next month."

Krebs darted away.

Eleven minutes later, Rudi smirked as smoke drifted from the chimneys of all three barracks and the infirmary.

Bruno was joy and wonder. Rudi hoped he'd brought a little of each into the world today to honor his friend.

***

Rudi woke in bed at the whistles sounding to rouse the prisoners. He got up and pulled on his greatcoat. Still gloomy outside, he did not switch on the bedroom light because he didn't want to attract attention from those outside.

He made coffee, carried the steaming mug upstairs, and sat in the gloom beside the window, his binoculars in his lap.

Once the prisoners had eaten their breakfast and used the bathroom, they filed out for roll call, the security lighting illuminating them.

Through his binoculars, Rudi studied them as he would a rare bird in the forest. A tall prisoner had a permanently shaking left hand, probably due to illness or injury. One had lopsided hair, likely hacked off with a knife. Another wiped her nose on her sleeve whenever the kapos weren't watching to see her moving. In a gray jacket, another swayed to one side, then jerked back, as if she were dozing off.

Clothing and hygiene issues aside, he'd wager he would see good people with similar traits in any town in Germany.

He scanned along the rows of women.

A short one jigged up and down, thighs pressed together. Exactly the behavior of a person wanting to use the toilet. Exactly.

He scanned farther. "There you are."

Robin Girl stood toward the rear, raven hair wafting in the breeze.

She was a conundrum, that one. So innocent, and yet so savvy. He stroked his chin. What had possessed her to feed that bird?

If something looked like chalk, wrote like chalk, and tasted like chalk, he'd confidently wager it was chalk. So why was telling these supposed "subhumans" from decent Aryan stock so unbelievably difficult? It made no sense.

There was only one logical possibility. He'd pondered the idea for some time now, but idle speculation was hugely different from accepting such an outlandish concept. Could everything he'd been told for as long as he could remember be wrong? Investigating that possibility might cost him his career, but he was going to uncover the truth.

He snorted. His career? If he wasn't careful, it would cost him his life.

52

The sun setting, Inge trembled in the middle of the prisoners at evening roll call. But she wasn't shaking from the cold. What she planned on doing was likely to backfire so badly, she'd likely be shot within the next ten minutes. But if the gamble paid off, it could change everything.

Turning her head as much as she could without a kapo whipping her, she peered from the corner of her eyes toward the gate. SS waltzed in to oversee the proceedings – the one called Gruber, who she'd been warned to stay clear of, a couple of guards, and...

Under her breath, she said, "Oh God, he's here."

She gulped as the commandant strolled in. He hadn't attended roll call for three days, and she hadn't spotted him outside the compound after she'd returned from work. Yet, now that the chance she'd prayed for had arrived, her heart pounded so hard she thought it would rupture.

She tensed, fighting to control the trembling, but she couldn't.

Gruber signaled the Barracks 01 block leader to begin.

Inge sharing her sandwich had gained her a handful of friends in her barracks, but obtaining fuel that benefited everyone? That had elevated her to the kind of status usually reserved for movie stars.

Everyone wanted to be her friend now. Some for the protection they thought that offered, some for the favors they imagined it might see granted, but most for the scraps they figured would come their way when the commandant next bestowed a gift upon his favorite prisoner.

Inge welcomed them all. Even sharing portions of her bread ration to endear herself to the most promising contacts. That had meant starving herself for the best part of a week, but it had finally paid off. She'd struck the motherlode – the answer to surviving this hell. She hoped.

Barracks 01 count complete, Gruber moved on to Barracks 02.

The count for Barracks 03 — the last barracks — getting closer and closer, Inge's breath came hard and heavy. She was running out of time.

So she could wait. Do it tomorrow. Or the next day.

But in this place, there was no guarantee tomorrow would ever come. This was her chance. The blood drained from her face, and she shook so much that some women frowned at her, probably imagining she was sick.

At the front, the commandant gazed past everybody into the night sky. What he was thinking, only he knew, but it seemed little to do with prisoners. She'd tested the water with him by allowing her big mouth to do its thing. Unsurprisingly, he'd threatened her with being shot.

Maybe this was a bad idea. Way too dangerous. Maybe keeping her head down and her mouth shut was the best approach to surviving.

But was it? She'd figured the only danger came from the SS and the kapos, but it didn't: the prisoners could be just as dangerous. Some had murdered over footwear; others had incurred the commandant's wrath to cause the deaths of six innocent people. If Inge was to stand a chance of surviving, maybe keeping her mouth shut was the worst thing she could do.

And it wasn't like this was only for her. A safer camp would benefit everyone.

Plus, of course, it was the right thing for him.

Her heart pounded. She had to do this. On so many levels, it was the right thing to do. She gulped. So why did it feel so wrong?

Inge stared at the gallows. At the uprights, the crossbeam, the wood worn smooth by the rubbing of rope...

It felt wrong because some here would be lucky to see another dawn. And she'd be responsible for that.

Under her breath, she said. "God, forgive me."

In the nearest watchtower, a guard aimed a massive mounted machine gun into the compound. Inge winced and shut her eyes. Dear Lord, the moment she put her plan into action, she'd be sliced in two. They'd slam so many bullets into her that the prisoners would have to clean up her remains with a mop.

The count for Barracks 02 was accepted.

Why was roll call going so smoothly tonight? Why weren't there the usual miscounts and inexplicable waiting that so often made it last for hours?

Hilde, her block leader, started the Barracks 03 count.

Oh God, this was it. Inge wiped her palms on her dress and tried to swallow, but her mouth was too dry.

In a blink, the count was over and documented. Roll call done.

The officers started walking away.

It was now or never. *Now or never.*

She opened her mouth, but no sound came out.

Oh God, oh God, oh God. Another few seconds and he'd be too far away. She had to do it. But she couldn't. But she had to!

She shouted, "Herr Kommandant!"

Everyone around her gasped and shrank back, even though they weren't supposed to move. A circle of space formed around her. Hilde dashed over while Gruber peered around the woman, trying to judge who'd shouted.

But the commandant kept on walking.

Inge tried again. "Kommandant Kruse!"

Gruber marched over, drawing his pistol.

Hilde hammered Inge with a length of hard rubber pipe. Inge staggered, pain slicing through her as Hilde raised her weapon again.

"What the hell do you think you're doing?" She cracked Inge over the head.

Inge crumpled to the ground, the world awhirl.

Gruber aimed his pistol at Inge.

And still, the commandant strolled away.

The rubber pipe slammed Inge in the back. She cried out.

She was going to die. Die because she'd made a horrible mistake. But the name the doctor had used flashed into her mind.

With the last of her strength, Inge shouted, "Rudi!"

This time, the commandant turned.

Hilde pounded Inge again.

"Wait!" Rudi strode back.

Cowering, Inge stared up at the pipe about to smash into her skull and the gun about to blast her from this earth. There was no way to back out now. The next five seconds would either transform her life, or end it.

She shouted, "Monika Volz, Helena Goldberg, Lilly Hasse, Maria Meyer. They killed Bruno."

Rudi stopped dead. He raised a trembling hand to his face.

Gruber cocked his pistol, aiming at Inge's head. "Herr Kommandant, let me deal with this for you."

Inge screwed her eyes shut. This was the end. She prayed she'd be reunited with her family, but having witnessed the world God allowed to flourish, she wasn't sure she believed in Him and His glory anymore.

"Unterscharführer, stand down." Rudi waved the women aside, and they parted.

Blood running down her face, Inge gazed up.

Rudi reared over her. "What did you say?"

"Monika Volz, Helena Goldberg, Lilly Hasse, Maria Meyer. They killed Bruno."

Gesturing to Gruber, he said, "Write that down."

He stared intently at Inge, as if deciding whether he should believe her or have her immediately hanged as a warning to the entire camp.

Finally, he said, "How do you know they did it?"

"I investigated, Herr Kommandant. Many prisoners believe I'm the camp's golden girl because I got fuel for everyone. They think if they're my friend, I'll take care of them, so to impress me, they shared their secrets."

"And Bruno's killers matter to you because...?"

"I'm not sure what happened to my family, but I think they were all murdered." Inge gulped, fighting back the tears as loss clawed inside her chest. "So I know the pain you're feeling at losing your best friend, and the injustice you've suffered. I hoped knowing the truth might help."

Rudi drilled his gaze. Jaw set. "And why do you care about a German's suffering?"

"For the same reason you cared about a Jew's — because compassion is contagious, so we should spread it everywhere." She hoped reminding him of his father's favorite platitude would hit home.

Motionless, Rudi stared away into the night for an eternity.

Gruber said, "Allow me handle this, Herr Kommandant." He gestured to a guard. "Prepare the scaffold. One noose."

Gruber spat on Inge. To Hilde, he said, "Get the lying whore on her feet."

Hilde hauled Inge up.

Inge didn't cry, didn't scream, didn't do anything. There was no point. She'd tried her best to survive, but it hadn't been good enough. It was over.

Hilde dragged Inge toward the gallows.

"Wait!"

200

The world held its breath.

Rudi pointed at Inge. "Take her to the infirmary."

"Yes, Herr Kommandant," said Hilde.

"You." Rudi pointed to a kapo. "Help her."

"Yes, Herr Kommandant." Taking an arm each, the kapo and Hilde helped Inge stumble away.

"Unterscharführer, go with them. Tell Scharführer Baumann that this is the emergency he's been waiting for, so she gets only the best."

Scowling, Gruber said, "Yes, Herr Kommandant."

In a loud voice, Rudi said, "You should all have now learned that I am not soft." He pointed at Inge. "If anything happens to that woman because she had the decency to tell the truth — anything at all — I'll lock those gates and burn this camp to the ground with every single one of you in it. Do not test me on this." He paused, no doubt to let the gravity of his words sink in. "Dismissed."

Hobbling, Inge touched her head and winced. Blood covered her hand.

But bruises and a minor head wound were nothing.

She'd done it. Volz and her crew were monsters. Now that Inge had given them up, relief swept over her. She'd imagined remorse would eat her alive, but it didn't. Should a witness for the prosecution at a murder trial regret making the world a safer place? Feel shame over what punishment the guilty would receive?

The commandant could now have his closure, and she and her fellow prisoners would be safer without a gang of violent psychopaths roaming free among them.

Inge had done the right thing. Except after a trial, a witness got to go home and resume their life. What happened to her now?

53

The next morning, Rudi strolled into the infirmary. A place over which he had total command. So why was his heart fluttering, as if he were attending a job interview?

He wiped his palms on his greatcoat. Maybe he'd eaten something that was off.

Who did he think he was fooling?

It was her. *Her!*

She was unlike any woman he'd ever met, yet she was a Jew. He'd rationalized his interest in her by equating it to a scientist studying a disease, a detective investigating a murder, a coroner conducting an autopsy... Professional men all desperate to solve a grisly puzzle.

He rubbed his hand over his mouth. After the previous evening's events... there was no puzzle. He wasn't only drawn to her intellectually, he was drawn to her as a man was drawn to a woman.

But that was impossible. She was a Jew. A Jew!

What was wrong with him?

He stared at the rows of beds, two patients squashed into most, unlike on his previous visit. This was the aftermath of his failed attempt to catch Bruno's killers. He hung his head.

Halfway down the room, prisoner 1582, otherwise known as Inge Zaleska, according to camp records, was sitting up in bed, her head bandaged.

He blew out a weary breath. Despite all his power and all his armed men, this delicate woman who had nothing — literally nothing — had done what he couldn't. How could he not be drawn to her?

Baumann momentarily stood from dealing with a patient and saluted, then returned to his work. Rudi trudged down the aisle and stopped three beds away from Inge.

He handed Elena a tin. "It's a little dry now, but it still tastes good."

Elena grinned. "Herr Kommandant, thank you. I hope you're managing. I feel so guilty letting you down like this."

"Just get well, Elena. Now, if you'll excuse me."

"Of course." She opened the tin. "Oh, my cake. Lovely."

Rudi shuffled to the foot of Inge's bed. Folding his arms, he sighed.

Inge said, "I'm sorry, Herr Kommandant, but I didn't know how else to speak with you."

"So it's Herr Kommandant now, is it? Not Rudi?"

"Sorry." She glanced down. "Did you—did you get the killers?"

She sounded uncertain. Was she struggling with her decision to give them up, knowing it could mean their death?

He nodded. "Volz is dead. Hasse and Meyer denied it, but Goldberg corroborated what you said in the hope I'd be lenient on her."

"Were you?"

He'd dreamed of hearing the creak of rope on wood as bodies swung from nooses, but... "They're being transferred to a subcamp better equipped to handle violent criminals."

A subcamp where Kommandant Kloser would appear kindhearted.

She nodded, her expression brightening. Was that because they were leaving the camp, so she'd be safe from reprisals, or because they were still alive?

Who cared?

She'd given him Bruno's killers. That was all that mattered.

Hands on his hips, he said, "So what was your little stunt about? Are you looking to be made block leader to get more food and your own bed?"

Grimacing, she clutched her chest. "And have to beat people?"

He threw his hands up. "So what are you after?"

She shrugged. "We all have to live here together, so can't we do that — live together? Like people, and not crazed beasts? Wouldn't that make it more pleasant for your men as well as for us?"

That was logical. Except... "You appreciate this is a concentration camp, and you are all prisoners?"

"So work us. But don't starve and beat us."

"And that's all you want?"

She nodded.

"No special treatment for you?"

She shook her head.

He pursed his lips. How the devil was he supposed to make sense of her? Was she genuinely a good soul, or did she have some hidden agenda he couldn't yet fathom?

He said, "Can you cook?"

She squinted. "What?"

"Cook? You know, what women do in a kitchen with food."

"Well, I am a girl, aren't I?"

Was that an innocent reply or a dig that he was saying a woman's place was in the kitchen?

The idea he was toying with was dumb. So dumb. It could only end one way. He turned to leave but heaved a breath. He'd come here for answers and was going to get them, no matter what it took.

Rudi said, "Scharführer Baumann says you aren't concussed and nothing is broken, so you're being discharged. First thing tomorrow, one of my men will escort you to the commandant's house. Understand?"

"Uh…"

"Good." He marched away.

So instead of distancing himself from someone he knew he should avoid at all costs because he was drawn to her, he'd invited her into his home. Smart.

But he was indebted to her. She'd given him such a gift – at great risk – and he needed to know why. Plus, she was only going to cook for him, so what was the worst that could happen?

The worst? If he allowed emotion to cloud reason?

The best was he'd be court-martialed. The worst – he'd be shot. He smirked. Just another day at war.

54

Dawn struggling to break, Inge shivered at roll call as dawn struggled to break. Sleet driven by a cruel wind meant that, for once, the other women were eager to get to work to move and warm themselves. Inge?

She stared at the commandant's house. Why was she to report there to "cook?" As a "superior" Aryan, surely he could butter bread or boil a kettle all by himself.

A guard marched over to Gruber at the front, who singled her out, and she was escorted to the house. The guard knocked on the door.

Inge's heart hammered. Was she really here to cook? The Germans treated prisoners like objects to do with as they wished, so maybe the gossip was right – he would be demanding more than a warm meal.

What would she do if he assaulted her?

She wiped her palms on her dress, but it was wet from the sleet.

What would she do? What *could* she do? He was a big, powerful man – with a gun. Would it be better to lie there and let him have his way or to fight in the hope he appreciated her courage and relented? Yes, because showing restraint over taking what didn't belong to it was what the German military was renowned for.

Inge struggled to swallow. "Oh God."

The guard shot her a sideways glance, but before he could say anything, the commandant answered. Dismissing the guard, he showed her into his hallway and slammed the door, trapping her inside.

"Now, before we go any further." He raised his hand.

She flinched and shut her eyes. She couldn't fight him because that would only make the situation worse. It was better to just lie there and pray the ordeal was over quickly. She waited. And waited. But nothing happened. She peeked.

His arms folded, he said, "What are you doing?"

"Sorry, Herr Kommandant, I thought you were going to— never mind."

"You appreciate I'm taking a gamble on you?"

"Yes, Herr Kommandant."

He held up both palms. "Unless we're in company, you can stop saying 'Herr Kommandant' every time you open your mouth."

"Sorry, Herr— sorry."

He clapped. "Okay, down to business. You can cook, can't you?"

She remembered the comment he'd made suggesting women belonged in the kitchen. Had he never heard of suffrage? Or how some men had even mastered the intricacies of stirring a pot to become chefs?

She wanted to say something cutting, but this was likely the cushiest job in camp. "Uh..."

"You know — you take food, heat it, serve it."

"Yes, I've done that. On occasion." Maybe not with a great deal of success, but like she was going to tell him that and be shoved back out to push barrows in the sleet.

"Good. The previous commandant often hosted informal dinners for the higher ranks to bolster morale. That responsibility has now passed to me, so we're dining tonight. I'll leave the menu to you."

She gulped. "Tonight?"

"Tonight." He pointed up the stairs. "If you want to get ready, the bathroom is the first door on the left."

"You want me to cook in your bathroom?"

He frowned. "What? No, you'll be cooking in the kitchen."

"So where's the kitchen?"

He swung an arm down the hall behind him. "But you'll want the bathroom first."

"Thanks, but I don't need the bathroom."

"Believe me, you do. Or do you really expect me to keep my food down with you stinking like that?"

Inge's jaw dropped. With such charm, it was a miracle the people of Germany ever managed to procreate. She ached to say something clever, but his next comment floored her before she could think of a suitable riposte.

"There's a drawn bath and fresh clothes on the ottoman." He ambled away.

"Excuse me?"

Smirking, he glanced back. "Hot water? Soap? Clean clothes? I assume you have those where you come from." He resumed strolling away. "Come downstairs when you're done and I'll explain your duties."

A drawn bath? Fresh clothes? She raced upstairs, feet pounding into the steps.

Inge opened the bathroom door and clutched her mouth. In a white-tiled room with gold fittings, steam rose from the bubbly water in the bathtub, and the air hung heavy with the scent of lavender. She closed her eyes, drew a slow breath in through her nose, then exhaled with a loud *ahhh*. The smell was... all day every day, she was engulfed by the stench of excrement, urine, vomit, sweat, illness, and death. This was heaven.

Fluffy white towels hung on a gold rail. Inge reached to caress one but pulled back, the grime on her hands so noticeable against the virgin cloth.

She dipped a finger in the bathwater. It was the ideal temperature.

Was this real? She snickered. Was she honestly about to take her first bath in what felt like years?

She locked the door but bit her lip. This was too good to be true.

A white chair with a gold-padded seat sat in the corner of the room. She angled the backrest against the door handle to prevent anyone from getting in.

With a smile, she ripped off her clothes. She didn't know how much time she had, so she wasn't wasting a single second.

Stepping one foot into the tub, she closed her eyes and moaned with pleasure. "Ohhh."

She chuckled. But as she climbed in, she glimpsed herself in a mirror and froze.

Wide-eyed, she caressed her shrunken breasts, then tried to pinch her stomach, but there was nothing to pinch. She'd only been a prisoner for a few months, yet she was wasting away. What would she be like if she were here a year?

She twisted to see her butt and shook her head. She'd never had an hourglass figure, but she'd never looked so much like a boy.

But she couldn't let that ruin this special moment, because she might never have another. She sank into the water, closed her eyes, and moaned with delight. She'd forgotten the joy of warm water. How strange it was to treasure what she'd taken for granted for so long.

She didn't want to move but to luxuriate for hours. Unfortunately, the Germans had conquered most of Europe in just a few months, so it wouldn't take them long to get through that flimsy door if they wanted to. She couldn't risk running out of time and missing this one chance to bathe properly.

With a sigh, she took the soap from a gold clam-shaped holder and smiled as she worked up a lather. Something else she'd taken for granted — proper soap, not that stuff in the shower block.

After washing, she reached for the shampoo but hesitated. Baumann had said not to get the bandage on her head wet. She snorted. Miss out on washing her hair and finally feeling like a woman again? Like that was ever going to happen.

She whipped the bandage off and shampooed her hair.

No one had yet pounded on the door, but she knew if she took liberties, she would be punished and lose any possibility of using this room again. With a heaved breath, she clambered out of the tub.

She gawked at the bathwater — so dirty, it looked like it had come from a bog.

Drying with a fluffy towel felt like being caressed with a kitten. On a padded chest lay white underwear, a thick brown woolen dress, and a heavy brown jacket, plus a large paper bag. She dressed. Functional, but far from stylish.

Finally, she rinsed the grime out of the bathtub, put her filthy clothes in the bag, washed her hands, and went downstairs.

If this was how the commandant's staff lived, she was going to do everything she could to ensure she kept this position.

From the hall, she heard Rudi talking on the phone in the living room. She waited in the doorway, so he could see she was available to start work.

He covered the receiver and nodded behind her. "Wait in the dining room, please."

As he returned to his call, Inge dawdled into the dining room, where a highly polished dark wood table dominated. She ran a finger over the surface, then turned to the shelving unit behind her. Old-fashioned ceramics dotted the shelves, but two rows of books caught her eye. Removing one, she caressed its pinky-brown cover. It was some of the softest leather she'd ever felt.

Rudi strolled in.

She stroked the book. "This feels lovely."

"Don't!" He snatched it.

"Sorry, I didn't know they were valuable." Charming. The Germans had taken everything she owned, but let her touch one little book...

He slid the book back into place. "They're not valuable, they're vile."

She shrugged. "Each to his own. But they feel nice. Pigskin, yes?"

"No." He rubbed his face. "It's... uh... it's human. Cut from the bodies of the dead. My predecessor's wife collects them."

"Human?" She snorted. "Come on. Why would anyone collect something so revolting? It's pigskin. Must be."

He grimaced and shook his head.

"What makes you so sure?"

He removed one of the books. The cover displayed a rose tattoo. "Have you ever seen a tattooed pig?"

Inge's stomach churned.

"She's got lampshades upstairs, too. I had to hide the one in the guest bedroom because it gives me the creeps."

The old commandant and his wife sounded like complete monsters. Thank heaven they'd left.

Rudi gestured to the doorway at the other end of the room. "Let me show you what's involved."

"I thought I was just cooking?"

"And general housekeeping duties. Unless you'd like to go back to pouring concrete."

A cushy indoor job or backbreaking work exposed to the elements? "Where would you like me to start?"

In the kitchen, the sink, counter, and table were covered with dirty dishes. He'd obviously been without a housekeeper for some time. Though she figured the mess was less to do with the length of time and more to do with losing his dog.

While he listed her responsibilities, she studied him. Tall, athletic, square-jawed, blue-eyed, fair-haired – he could have been a poster boy for the Aryan race. But he did have his imperfections: the crescent-shaped scar below his left eye.

But that was on the outside. Inside? A darkness clung to him, which probably wasn't just about his dog. Maybe because, in a way, he was as imprisoned here as she was. Oh, his cell was luxurious, no one beat him for the most inexplicable of reasons, and he could roam free whenever off-duty, but he was chained to this camp just like the rest of them.

Rudi described where to obtain what she needed to undertake her duties, during which he leaned across her to demonstrate how she'd sometimes have to knock the cold water tap for it to work.

His breath enveloped her in the aroma of coffee — real coffee, not puddle water. Inge closed her eyes and savored a nutty, smoky smell with a hint of chocolate. She yearned to taste it. Mouth watering, she licked her lips.

"Are you okay?"

She opened her eyes to find him frowning. "Yes. Just locking everything in here." She tapped her head.

"Right." He narrowed his eyes but pointed to the dining room. "Regarding tonight, nothing fancy — three courses will be fine. There'll be four of us, with the meal to commence at eight o'clock. Okay?"

"Okay."

He left.

Inge slumped over the counter. He'd asked if she could cook, not prepare a three-course meal for dinner guests. What was she going to do?

55

At 7:30 p.m., Inge stirred a saucepan of brown gloop on the stove.

Rudi poked his head into the kitchen. "Everything good for eight?"

She glanced at the carriage clock she'd taken into the kitchen from the living room mantel. "Yes."

He ducked out.

She tasted the gloop again, and again grimaced. No matter what she added, it tasted bitter. How was that possible?

She dashed back into the pantry. There was probably plenty of food with which someone knowledgeable could prepare a good meal, but with no recipe, Inge was lost. Scouring the shelves, she muttered, "Sweet, sweet, sweet..."

Nothing.

Inge scampered back to the stove and tipped in more of the canned drink she'd found earlier. Normally, Fanta tasted sweet, but it wasn't helping her meal at all. Why? Didn't sweet cancel bitter?

She tasted again. For a meat dish, it left a strange fruity aftertaste. "Oh, Lord, what am I going to do?"

Okay, so the food wasn't delicious, but it wasn't as revolting as some of her previous attempts at cooking. And if nothing else, the meal would certainly be memorable. Yes, memorable. That was good. Every host wanted their party to be memorable, so maybe tonight could be a success after all.

Back to stirring.

At 7:59 p.m. and 50 seconds, Inge carried two white bowls of soup into the dining room. As she entered, Rudi glanced at his watch — so far, so good.

She placed one bowl before Rudi and the other in front of Baumann. The next two, she placed in front of Gruber and a man

211

with a mustache they'd called Hofmann, then she stood at a respectful distance in case anyone needed anything.

She mouthed to herself, "Please like it, please like it."

Spoons scraped on porcelain as they started.

Gruber tapped his wineglass without saying a word.

Inge dashed over. She filled the glass from the bottle beside him, then returned to her spot.

Rudi gestured to the kitchen. "If you need to prepare the next course, Inge..."

"Thank you, Herr Kommandant." She scurried back to the kitchen.

Inside the doorway, she craned her neck to listen.

"This is..." Baumann smacked his lips. "Beef, is it?"

"And... turnip?" said Gruber. "Does that look like turnip to you?"

"I think so," said Rudi.

Gruber snorted. "So this is what's all the rage in Czechoslovakia, is it? Beef and turnip soup?"

Rudi said, "It's her first day, Gruber. Let's give her a little slack, huh?"

Inge left to prepare the next dish.

After the first course, Inge collected the bowls, none of which were empty, then served the main course in the same order.

Gruber poked the brown gloop studded with boiled potatoes and turnip with his fork. "Isn't this the soup we've just had?"

Rudi said, "I'm not sure."

"It's similar, Herr Kommandant," said Inge. She'd thought using the same main ingredients to create a theme was a good idea, but this muddy mass looked too much like the last course. And that hadn't gone down well.

"Similar?" asked Rudi.

"Don't tell me." Gruber laughed and swigged wine. "The first course was beef and turnip soup while this is beef and turnip stew."

She forced a smile. Unfortunately, he was right. What was she thinking?

Rudi said, "Is it a traditional Czech dish?"

"No, Herr Kommandant."

Baumann said, "A family recipe?"

Inge said, "No, Scharführer. On such short notice, and with such limited ingredients, it's the best I could do. I apologize."

212

"Never mind," said Baumann, "I'm sure it tastes even better than it looks. Not that it looks bad, of course." He had a forkful and nodded, smacking his lips again. "Hmmm, it certainly tastes different from the soup. Tangy. Kind of fruity."

Gruber chuckled. "And we all know that the sign of a good meat dish is how fruity it is."

Hofmann laughed. Rudi and Baumann didn't.

Rudi ambled to the liquor cabinet and took out a bottle of clear liquid with a handwritten label. "You know your drinks, Gruber, tell me what you think of this."

He poured a small measure into a shot glass and gave it to Gruber, then tipped the bottle to Baumann, who declined with a wave.

Gruber sniffed the drink, then sipped. Blowing out noisily, he wrinkled his brow. "Hell's teeth, that's got a kick. What is it?"

Rudi handed him the bottle. "A gift from a friend in town."

Baumann said, "I didn't know you were friendly with any of the locals?"

Rudi had done what any decent person would do in saving a girl from two monsters, so there'd been no reason to brag about it, even to Baumann.

Gruber studied the label. "Tilga '37. Is that the year or the mileage-per-gallon this would get in a truck?" He laughed, then had another sip.

Inge watched Rudi till he nodded to the kitchen, then she scuttled away.

This was a disaster. Why hadn't she listened when Mama had nagged her to help in the kitchen so she could learn how to run a household. Why? Because Inge had believed she was going to travel the world with a high-flying job, so she had thrown herself into learning languages. And how was that working out for her?

The second course ended, and Inge collected the dishes as Rudi topped up Gruber's glass. Was he plying his guests with alcohol to divert their attention from the food?

Rudi said, "That was... interesting, Inge. Some unusual textures and different flavors."

"Yes," said Baumann, "you made some, uh, shall we say, brave choices."

Gruber snorted again and shoved his plate away. "Brave choices are best left for the battlefield, not the kitchen. How about another glass of Tilga? I need to cleanse my palate."

Inge bowed her head. "I'm sorry, Herr Kommandant. I did say I'd only cooked on occasion."

Hofmann said, "How long before your regular cook comes back?"

"A month or two," said Rudi.

Two months? The dishes clattered in Inge's hands. "Sorry, Herr Kommandant."

Gruber picked something from between his teeth and studied it. "I don't think your Jew is too enamored at the thought of your company for so long, Herr Kommandant." He flicked whatever he'd picked onto the floor.

"I'm sure that's not the case," said Baumann.

Gruber gestured to her. "Would you like to cook here for another two months, Jew?"

"If that's what the commandant wishes, of course, Herr Unterscharführer."

Hofmann said, "That might just be long enough for her to learn how to cook."

He and Gruber sniggered.

"Let's give her the benefit of the doubt, gentlemen," said Rudi. "She was thrown in at the deep end at the last second and has obviously never cooked a big meal before."

Gruber reached for his wine. "Or any kind of meal, if this is anything to go by."

"Ignore them, Inge," said Rudi. "You did well for your first time."

The guests shot each other curious glances.

Inge winced a smile. "Thank you, Herr Kommandant."

"Yes," said Gruber, "I can't wait to see what's for dessert. I bet beef and turnip strudel is an absolute delight." He laughed.

She scuttled into the kitchen, cradling dishes.

Gruber said, "I see you've got a new pet, Herr Kommandant."

Inge strained to hear the reply, but he said nothing.

"Better be careful," said Gruber. "These animals are far more trouble than your last one."

In the kitchen, Inge served a chocolate torte she'd found in a red tin onto side plates. She made sure no one had wandered in, then spat on one plate before placing a slice of cake onto it. Under her breath, she said, "An animal, huh? Think yourself lucky this animal doesn't need to pee."

She strolled back in and served dessert.

214

56

Baumann stood in the front doorway, Gruber and Hofmann already having left. "Thank you for an interesting evening, Rudi." He offered his hand.

Rudi shook it. "You're welcome, Klaus."

But Baumann didn't release his grip. He leaned closer, even though they were alone. "I don't know what your plan is, but as your friend, I have to say that Gruber has a point – be careful."

"There's no plan, Klaus. Inge's a temporary housekeeper. End of story."

"Are you sure? I get how devastating losing Bruno was. Maybe your grief is making you look for a surrogate, something else you can take care of."

"I tried throwing a stick for Inge, but..." Rudi shrugged.

Baumann arched an eyebrow. "I've seen how you look at her."

Rudi yanked his hand free. "Okay, I find her interesting. So what? It's not like we have a lot of entertainment in this backwater hellhole, is it?"

"If it's entertainment you're after, there are women in town more than eager to oblige. And associating with them won't see you marched before a firing squad under the racial defilement laws."

Rudi shook his head. "Those women might be fine for Gruber, but..."

"Seriously, they'd convene a special court so they could make an example of you."

Rudi rubbed the back of his neck. He knew what he was doing.

"Rudi, if you won't do it for yourself, do it for her. They'll hang her. You know they will."

He patted Baumann on the shoulder. "Klaus, thanks, but it's not like that. She's smart and she's funny, so when I need a housekeeper, why not have one I enjoy being around?"

Baumann nodded. "As long as that's all it is."

"It is. Good night, Klaus."

Baumann left and Rudi ambled to the kitchen. Standing at the sink washing dishes, Inge didn't hear him enter, so he silently watched her.

What was he doing? He'd been kind of truthful with Baumann, but that was probably because he was only being *kind of* truthful with himself.

Could his men be right? Was this a coping mechanism and he was pushing his feelings for Bruno onto another "animal"? Or was there more to it? Bruno could give unbounded love and loyalty, but he couldn't talk, couldn't exchange ideas, couldn't truly share Rudi's world. Life with Bruno was ultimately life with a dog, not life with a partner, another soul.

Another soul?

He stared at Inge. It was one thing to believe a Jew could share his world because she talked and understood him, but could one of them really be all that he was?

The answer was obvious: it was his grief. Like an Aryan could ever develop true feelings for a Jew with all their lying, dirty, greedy ways. Talk about stupid. He snorted. Gruber was right – he'd found a new pet.

Inge turned and jumped. "Sorry, I didn't hear you come in." She dried her hands on a cream towel. "Everything's finished here. Is there something else I can do for you, Herr Kommandant?"

She smiled, and those dark amber eyes nailed him. Before he knew it, he'd smiled back.

"No. If you change, I'll escort you to the compound."

Inge changed into her old clothes and met him at the foot of the stairs. "Ready."

She smiled again. This time, he didn't.

Side by side, strolling up the track parallel to the fence, Inge said, "I'm sorry I messed up tonight."

"That's okay. I should have explained more when I asked if you could cook."

He looked her up and down from the corner of his eye. Why had she fed that bird? It made no sense. Jews didn't do philanthropy. At least not for anything outside their precious faith. Why would a hungry Jew feed an animal? Where was the profit, the deception,

216

the trap? There had to be something, because what she'd done was just so wrong.

And if there was no nefarious motivation...

He cringed. That wasn't worth contemplating. The implications were just too terrifying because they challenged everything he'd ever been taught. Literally everything. Yes, he'd wondered about the possibility for some time, but now that he was staring into that abyss, he dearly wanted to step back from the edge, back onto safe ground and into a world he knew, even if it was far from perfect.

They walked around the fence toward the gate in an awkward silence.

Hinges squealed as a sentry pushed a gate open.

Inge said, "So, I guess you're in the market for a housekeeper again."

Surprised, before Rudi could process the implications, he instinctively said, "You don't want the job?"

She laughed. "Of course I want the job, but I figured after tonight, you'd want someone more experienced."

She'd given him an out. Should he grasp it? "Everyone has to learn. I'll make arrangements for you to get some pointers from Elena, my previous cook. Okay?"

She beamed. "It will be my pleasure, Herr Kommandant."

"And it will be my pleasure to smile at all your brave experiments with food." He smirked.

Her smile dropped and she stared at the ground. "With respect, Herr Kommandant, if you dislike my cooking so much, maybe it would be best if you did find someone else."

"I'm sorry, Inge. That was supposed to be a joke. Forgive me."

"Okay."

"So you'll continue as my housekeeper?"

"Of course. And it will be my pleasure to smile at all your brave experiments with humor." She sauntered through the gate without looking back.

Rudi laughed. "Good night, Inge."

She strolled toward her barracks, her shadow swinging across the ground as she walked from the area covered by one security light to another.

Rudi turned to leave, but one of the sentries stared at him, agog.

Rudi scowled. "Something to say, soldier?"

The sentry clicked his heels to stand to attention. "No, Herr Kommandant."

Rudi glanced back as Inge disappeared around the side of a building. She was a Jew. An enemy of the state. According to the Nuremberg Laws.

It was easy to identify a Jew when they had big ears, a hook nose, or those telltale sidelocks. But he'd wager if he stuck Inge in a group of pure-blood Germans, no one would ever single her out as a Jew. Not even if they conducted a barrage of scientific tests. Not surprising. Germany's greatest minds all agreed that Jews were subhuman, yet even with the Reich's latest technology, it had thus far proven impossible to differentiate Jews biologically from real people. Why? That made no sense.

Shaking his head, Rudi tramped back along the track.

For a person to be deemed a Jew, at least three of their grandparents had to have been born into the Jewish religious community. *Born into* — not practicing within, *born into*.

If a person had not been raised a Jew, and their parents had not been raised as Jews, and their grandparents had not been raised as Jews, how could that person be Jewish because seventy, eighty, maybe even a hundred years earlier, their great-grandparents had been practicing Jews? Should a person be accountable for what their ancestors had done a century ago?

Crazy.

He sighed as he yanked the house door open.

A pet? No, this Jew was no pet. But exactly what was she? And more to the point, what was she to him?

57

The next morning, a guard escorted Inge to Rudi's house again. She washed and changed, then lit the fires and prepared the breakfast he'd requested — strong black coffee and four slices of bread, one with marmalade, one cheese, two ham. Extremely simple. Probably for her benefit after the previous evening's fiasco.

It was strange how they'd made such a connection. She'd have never thought a Jew and a Nazi could ever be civil, let alone be friends.

Friends? Was that what they were?

She'd been friends with men her own age, and even dated a few, but she'd never connected with any of them.

And this connection was real — she was not imagining it. When he laughed, it was genuine; when he looked at her, it was with kindness; when he listened, it was with interest. So yes, they were friends. What else could such a relationship be called?

She sniggered. The first man with whom she could imagine forming a proper relationship just happened to be a Nazi. And not just any Nazi, but the Nazi imprisoning her. "Good one, Inge. Real good."

Footsteps clomped down the staircase. Inge scurried into the dining room, where she'd laid everything out for him. After the previous night's disaster, she wanted today to be perfect.

Standing at a respectable distance from his chair, she waited, hands clasped in front of her stomach.

Rudi strode in, studying some papers.

Inge smiled, waiting to catch his eye. But he never looked.

He took his seat, munched his bread, and sipped his coffee, all the while reading.

She waited.

And waited.

Maybe he wasn't a morning person. Or maybe he hadn't slept well. Whatever the reason, she wasn't there to socialize but to do her job. And do it well.

"Can I get you anything else, Herr Kommandant?"

He turned a paper. "No."

She waited.

Leaving a piece of bread and half the cup of coffee, he rose and wandered back upstairs.

Inge collected the dishes. "Okay, so definitely not a morning person."

She poured the coffee down the sink, washed the dishes, and tidied the kitchen. Footsteps clomped downstairs again, so she scooted to the front door to await any final instructions before he left.

But Rudi didn't leave. He drifted back into the dining room. "Where's my coffee?"

Inge trailed behind him. "I'm sorry, Herr Kommandant, I thought you'd finished."

"Was it empty?"

"No."

"Then why would I have finished?"

Shaking his head, he grabbed his greatcoat from the stand in the hall and stormed out, slamming the front door.

Inge froze. What just happened? That wasn't the man she'd joked with only hours earlier. Maybe that was the problem — she'd been overfamiliar. But he'd laughed. He'd joked back.

She slumped against the table. Yes, but he was allowed to joke, just like he was allowed to do anything else he wanted because he was German.

"So much for being friends."

She trudged to the kitchen and rooted through the cleaning supplies in a cupboard. What was she to do now? Easy — whatever necessary to avoid returning to backbreaking outdoor labor.

Reading the instructions on a floor cleaner, she sighed. Why his sudden about-face? What had she done wrong? Everything had been fine when they'd parted. Well, as fine as a Jew-prisoner-Nazi-jailer friendship could be. Maybe that was the reason — he'd reconsidered and wanted a strict prisoner-jailer relationship. Fine. That she could do. In fact, that was better because she'd know exactly where she stood.

Inge brushed the hardwood floor with a broom.

But if this was so much better, why did it feel like she'd lost something? And not just the chance to improve her life with lighter work, but...

She snorted. But what? What did she think was happening here? That this Nazi, who wasn't really a Nazi, was going to save a Jew because she wasn't a real Jew? She shook her head. She wasn't usually prone to pathetic teenage fantasies, so why now? She was a Jew; he was an SS officer — any sort of "friendship" was probably a death sentence for both of them.

She continued sweeping, working her way around the whole ground floor, then got down on her hands and knees with a cloth and cleaning agent to start buffing. She crawled over every inch of the floor from the front door to the kitchen sink and from the far side of the living room to the far side of the dining room.

Finished, she wiped her brow on the back of her arm and arched her aching back to stretch.

As she scrubbed her hands in the kitchen, footsteps clomped down the hallway.

A guard appeared in the doorway. "You're to come with me."

He gestured to the front door, a trail of dirty footprints leading from it. So much for everything being perfect.

She bit her tongue. "Of course."

Outside, the wind buffeted her as she trailed after the guard. She clutched her arms around her chest. Rudi hadn't mentioned working anywhere other than the house. She cringed. Oh Lord, what was in store for her now?

58

Sitting on the edge of the infirmary bed, Inge jotted down notes on paper Baumann had provided.

Elena said, "But remember to baste it. If you forget, don't be surprised when the meat's dry."

"Uh-huh."

"And when you take it out, give it at least ten minutes before carving. That'll make it good and moist. Oh, and if you look on the top shelf in the pantry, there's a red tin. That torte won't last much longer, so it wants eating."

Inge nodded. "I found that, thanks. It was probably the only edible part of the meal."

Elena touched Inge's arm. "I'm sure it wasn't that bad."

"Believe me, it was. But this"— she tapped her notes —"is fantastic. If the commandant will let me, I'll cook you something as a thank-you."

"He's a good one, that one. Stay on his good side and he'll treat you right." Elena leaned closer and whispered, "He was going to change the camp, you know."

"Really?"

"I tried not to, but I overhead some of his phone calls, and I saw some of his notes while I was tidying. Believe me, we'd never have had it so good if those halfwits hadn't gone and killed Bruno and ruined everything." She patted Inge's hand. "But thanks to you, he got them, so who knows what might happen now?"

So Rudi wasn't just kind to her but kind in general. That couldn't be easy as an SS officer. Maybe that was why he'd been so cold that morning — he wasn't upset with her but was struggling with some issue. Thank heaven for that.

She smiled.

Yes, she'd bet things would be totally different when he came home tonight and could relax. Especially with her secret weapon — Elena's recipes.

Back in the kitchen, Inge set to work creating a meal Rudi would relish. She'd listed what she could recall being in the pantry, so Elena had recommended a piece of steak seasoned with her special selection of herbs and spices.

With the basics prepared, Inge baked a fruitcake, then cleaned up the guard's muddy footprints. After, she itemized everything in the pantry and cupboards so, should she be allowed to visit Elena again, they could discuss what meals could be made and what supplies should be ordered.

Finally, Inge cooked the meat and vegetables as much as she dared, then took them off the heat to finish once Rudi appeared. He showed at 7:30 p.m., the same as the previous night.

Inge dashed to the hallway. "Hi."

"Hello."

She helped him off with his coat and hung it on the stand, then gestured to the dining room. "Please."

Candles lighting the room, she guided him to his seat and poured him a glass of red wine from a bottle she'd let breathe. She ached to ask him about his day, but it wasn't her place. She repeated to herself — prisoner-jailer, keep it simple.

His expression dark, he silently scrutinized her.

She set the wine before him and smiled. "I just need a few minutes."

His eyes narrowing, as if suspicious of what she was doing, he nodded once.

Inge scooted to the kitchen. She finished cooking the meal and arranged the food on a plate. It smelled divine. She ached to dig in herself, but she carried everything out, with the side plate of bread, and presented it to Rudi.

Standing at a respectable distance, Inge waited while he ate.

Butterflies in her stomach, she ached for the tiniest hint of approval, the faintest murmur of enjoyment.

Nothing.

Finally, he pushed the plate away.

As she neared to remove the plate, she couldn't help herself — she just had to know. "I hope the food was an improvement on last night."

"It was... adequate."

Disappointment clawed inside her like he'd kicked her in the gut. But then she glanced at his plate. It was so clean, it looked like a starving man had licked every inch.

She drew a slow breath. Prisoner-jailer. Keep it simple.

She took Rudi a large slice of fruit cake, the inside still warm and moist, and topped up his glass. And waited.

Silence.

Like a flower wilting without water, Inge withered inside. She couldn't take this anymore.

Her head bowed, she stared at him from under her brow. "Herr Kommandant, have I done something wrong?"

Silent, he turned his glass, staring into its dark contents.

Her chin quivered as his rejection of all she'd done to please him overwhelmed her. She scurried for the kitchen but stopped.

No, she needed to know why he'd turned against her so viciously after being so warm earlier. If he was fearful of imprisonment or execution for fraternizing with a Jew, fine, but let him say that to her face.

"Herr Kommandant, may I speak?"

He didn't look up. "No."

Agape, she stared at him. She hadn't expected that.

He munched his cake as if everything was fine.

Her heart pounding, she balled her fists. She had to know. Had to. She opened her mouth, but no words came out.

And all the while, he kept stuffing his face with food she'd slaved to cook. Silent. Cold. Distant.

Why? He'd never acted like this before, so why now after how hard she'd worked?

Her breath quickened, and pain and confusion bubbled inside her as if she would explode if she didn't find a release.

She said, "The second time we met, you told me to feel free to speak, even if I hadn't been asked a question, so now I'm speaking. Why are you treating me like this? What have I done wrong?"

He ate another mouthful without even acknowledging she'd spoken.

She raised her voice. "Answer me."

Still nothing.

Stepping closer, she stabbed a finger at him. "This isn't right. You wouldn't treat a dog like this."

He threw his glass across the room. It shattered against the wall. "You're a Jew!"

Inge hammered her fist onto the table. "I'm a human being!"

They glowered at each other.

His eyes narrowed and his breath snorted, while a vein on his neck throbbed.

It was no good. She wasn't going to win this argument, no matter how right she was.

"I was a Jew when I fed that bird." As she snatched his empty plate, a tear trickled down her cheek. She clenched her jaw, fighting to contain her emotions. She would not cry. She would not.

Inge headed for the kitchen. "I'm sorry I disappointed you. Again." But she stopped. "You know, I really tried today. Really tried. Not because I had to, but because I wanted to. Because I hoped you'd be pleased."

The last two days had been a wonderful dream, but now she'd woken, so it was time to return to reality. "I'll leave my uniform in the kitchen. I hope you find someone more acceptable."

She skulked away.

Standing at the sink, she beat her fists into the soapy water. It splashed everywhere. She would not cry. She would not cry. SHE WOULD NOT CRY.

After washing and drying the last few dishes, she went to the bathroom. She stripped off her brown work dress, folded it neatly, and dragged on her pink-and-white one.

Trudging to the front door, she said loudly, "I'd like to go to my barracks, please." Even her freezing barracks would be warmer than this place.

His footsteps clomped toward her. She didn't look when he arrived but remained facing the door.

"Inge, I..."

He'd said her name.

She turned and peered up. Hoping. Expecting. Longing.

Gazing away, he dragged a hand through his hair.

"Yes?" She waited.

"I'll arrange an escort."

He strode away and gave orders over the phone. A few minutes later, a guard arrived.

Once tramping back to her barracks and out of his presence, she couldn't hold back the pain. She wept. But why? He was the

225

Nazi imprisoning her, so why was she so upset that he'd rejected her? Why?

She lay awake in her bunk, staring into the darkness. Whimpering.

Why? The answer was easy, but she didn't want to acknowledge it because of the terrifying reality it left her with — after being treated like an animal for so long, she'd finally met a man who treated her like a person. Like someone who was worth something. And now that was gone. Now she was worthless again. An animal. Vermin.

She sobbed.

59

Groaning, Inge heaved up the wheelbarrow and trundled along the planks as the wind howled across the excavation site, driving rain sideways. But on she trudged.

After her two days in the house, the cold felt colder, the work harder, the hours longer. But this was her life now. All it was ever going to be. Till she dropped dead from hunger, exhaustion, or a bullet for opening her mouth.

A kapo whipped her across the back. "Faster!"

Recoiling as pain slashed across her shoulders, she stumbled on. She emptied her barrow and lumbered back.

She'd spent two days living in a dream. A dream in which she was human. Then a real person had woken her, and the dream was over.

Life? This was hers.

60

Rudi rolled over in bed for the umpteenth time, the gloom smothering him. Those amber eyes still burned into him. Hurting. Questioning. Aching.

Dear Lord, he couldn't have abused her more if he'd kicked her. *But she was a Jew.*

That didn't mean she couldn't suffer. That look. Such sadness. Such anguish.

A Jew!

If an animal looked at him like that, he'd melt and do whatever the poor thing needed, so if Jews were animals, why was easing their suffering wrong?

Because consorting with the enemy was not only illegal, it was against everything he'd sworn to uphold as an SS officer. He was duty-bound to protect the Fatherland from its greatest threat for a generation.

Yes, because Inge was such a danger to Germany's standing as a world power.

He hammered his pillow. "She's a Jew!"

Rudi clambered out of bed, dragged on his greatcoat, and tramped downstairs.

Pouring a glass of water in the kitchen, he crumpled over the sink, forehead resting on his forearms.

How could he do that to her? Those eyes. Possibly the most forlorn thing he'd ever seen.

What he'd done was unforgivable. Instead of shutting her out like that, why hadn't he just told her the truth?

Because he didn't owe her anything. She was a prisoner. A Jew.

He slammed his fist on the sink.

No, *she* was right — *she* was a human being.

61

Inge shivered in the snow at roll call, the dawn an orangey smear over distant hills.

Gruber pointed to the first woman in the row for Barracks 02. Again. This would be the third recount, even though the numbers tallied. Why did the Germans love seeing them suffer so? Thank heaven it was Friday. Only two more days, then a rest day.

Her teeth chattered. If only she could have kept that brown dress to have two layers.

A kapo limped in her direction, flexing her grip on a length of heavy rubber tubing.

Uh-oh, someone was in for it. Inge lowered her face even more. At least she hadn't said or done anything that could be construed as having broken any rule. Not that that always mattered.

But her peripheral vision confirmed the feet were marching toward her.

Oh, dear Lord, no. Was it too much to ask to not be beaten for just one day in her godforsaken life?

The feet were almost upon her.

Inge tensed. *Please, not me. Just once, not me.* She hunched to make herself a smaller target so the blows would hit her arms, her back, her shoulders... places that would hurt but wouldn't cripple.

The feet stopped in front of her.

Face down, Inge screwed her eyes shut. Tight. So tight they might block out the entire world forever.

A voice snarled, more animal than person, "What the devil is that?"

Inge trembled. What was what? How could she answer if she didn't understand the question? But if she said nothing, the punishment would be even more brutal. What could she say that wouldn't make things worse?

"Answer me!"

Inge peeked, her voice faltering. "I'm sorry, I—"

The kapo backhanded Inge across the face. "Shut up."

"You." The kapo hit the person beside Inge. "Answer."

The woman said, "Paper."

"You lazy thief. How dare you steal paper." The kapo ripped open the woman's fastened blued jacket, popping buttons off, and wrenched out torn sheets of heavy-duty paper. She slung them on the ground — pieces of the bags in which cement arrived at the excavation site.

The kapo pounded the woman with her truncheon.

Some women stole paper to use as insulation inside their clothes, but Inge had been warned about the repercussions if caught, so she had chosen to freeze. Thank God she had.

Leaving the paper thief a whimpering wreck lying in the dirty snow, the kapo stalked away. She battered another woman. "Eyes down!"

On the front row, a woman collapsed and lay motionless. No one moved to help. Those who wanted to couldn't; those who could didn't want to.

A guard marched over to Gruber, who was leaning against the scaffold, smoking as if enjoying some outdoor spectacle. Gruber beckoned the limping kapo, and a moment later, the kapo lurched toward Inge again, adjusting her grip on her weapon.

Once more Inge shrank, praying the limping woman would march past and abuse someone else. It was a horrible thing to wish for, but Inge couldn't take any more. Her eyes shut, she prayed and prayed and prayed.

The footsteps stopped, so Inge peeked.

The feet directly in front of her, Inge gasped and braced for the onslaught.

A rubber truncheon prodded her in the chest. "Accompany the guard."

Inge gulped. Oh dear Lord, what was she going to be punished for this time?

"Now!" The kapo smashed her truncheon into Inge's arm.

Inge squealed but scuttled to the guard and was led through the compound and out.

Punishment was always administered in the compound, so what was happening? She gazed to the commandant's house. Light illuminated the downstairs windows.

They couldn't be going there. Surely not. Rudi had made her position abundantly clear.

The guard escorted her to the house and knocked on the door.

Inge's heart pounded and sweat ran down her spine despite the cold. Why was she here? Whatever the reason, it wasn't going to be good.

She looked back at the women freezing at roll call and wished she was still one of them.

The door opened.

The guard saluted Rudi and was dismissed. Without a word, Rudi stepped aside, inviting her in.

Stomach churning, she shuffled inside.

Avoiding eye contact, he stared at the wall.

She waited. What was happening? Had he brought her here to rub her face in the fact that she was a worthless Jew again?

However, instead of taunting her, he stared at the floor, like a prisoner worried a kapo might strike if they raised their head.

She frowned. Was he expecting her to say something? Apologize, maybe? Like that was ever going to happen.

"I think"— he rubbed his face —"I owe you an explanation."

She snorted. "You think?"

He flicked his gaze up. "I'm trying to apologize."

Stunned, she gestured for him to continue.

He drew a breath and again looked at the floor. "I'm sorry."

Part of her wanted to say something cutting to make him feel the pain he'd caused her, but another part appreciated the courage required for a man of his stature to apologize to someone of hers. She said nothing.

He said, "Believe it or not, I didn't want to hurt you."

"You've got a funny way of showing it."

"You don't understand." He pointed toward the outside. "If my superiors thought for just one second that you were anything more than a housekeeper, they'd hang you. No hearing, no jury, no judge. Just a noose."

"So I'm supposed to believe you were being cruel to be kind?"

"I was."

"But you never thought to ask how I felt about it?" She folded her arms. "Because I'm just a Jew?"

"I was trying to protect you." He reached to guide her into the living room, but she dodged.

"Protect me? So I can enjoy a lifetime of that?" She gestured to the compound. "I'd rather have a single year of happiness than fifty of misery."

"Inge, I'm serious. They'd hang you."

"So am I." Again, she motioned toward the compound. "Do you think that's living?"

He drew a heavy breath. "I can imagine."

She clutched her mouth. "Oh, you've got to be kidding me. You're seriously going to stand there and tell me you can imagine what it's like being a prisoner in this hellhole? You in your heated house, with your pantry, your bathtub, and your dinner parties? *You* are going to tell *me* you can imagine what it's like to live in filth, frozen, starving, and literally worked to death?"

His gaze was nailed to the floor as tightly as the floorboards.

"Well? Are you?"

"I..."

"No, I didn't think so."

She stared at him, shaking her head.

Finally, he met her gaze. "I'm sorry, Inge. I'm really struggling with everything that's happening."

"Oh, you poor thing. Yes, it must be awful for you having lost your home, your family, and any chance of a future. No, wait, that's me. Me!" She hit her chest, then flung her arm out toward the compound. "And every other poor wretch you've dragged here."

"So help me change that."

"What?"

62

Sitting at the dining room table, Rudi said, "No, no, no. How many times do I have to say it?"

"Why not?" Inge threw her hands up, sitting opposite. "That's not only the most obvious improvement but the one most desperately needed."

"The daily food ration is mandated by SS regulations. I'd never get away with going over that, so I'd probably be replaced, and heaven only knows who'd take over."

"But food's the most important thing."

"And the most unfeasible. To improve the camp, we have to make small changes we can justify that will benefit — not the prisoners — but the personnel, the war effort, or the Reich. Preferably, all three."

She snorted. "All three?"

He nodded.

Rolling her eyes, Inge doodled on a piece of paper. He studied her. With severe limitations on what he could get away with, it was vital he didn't waste a single resource but only implemented changes that would mean something. Inge's help was invaluable because she could provide insights into what prisoners actually needed, as opposed to what he guessed they did.

Inge said, "So clothes."

His elbow on the table, Rudi rested his head on his hand. "I tried that. It didn't end well."

"So try again."

He pursed his lips, then slid a paper to her. "It's funny you should say that."

She read, then gasped. Beaming, she looked up. "Boots? When do they arrive?"

"Ten days. Six hundred pairs, fur-lined, various sizes." Rudi smiled. Thank heaven they hadn't arrived at the same time as the coats.

Inge gaped. "Fur-lined? That's fantastic, Rudi."

He smirked. "So it's Rudi again, is it, not Herr Kommandant?"

She clutched her mouth as if she thought she'd done something wrong. "Sorry."

"Be careful." He arched an eyebrow. "In private, it's okay. But out there"— he pointed outside —"remember what I said about being hanged?"

"Okay."

He tapped his notes with his pen. "What else?"

"Shorter working hours."

He arched an eyebrow again.

"You're working us to death. Literally."

"And while I'm at it, why don't I give you the whole weekend off, not just Sundays, and grant you two weeks' annual vacation?"

She gazed like a kid seeing a giant chocolate bar. "You can do that?"

"Of course not. Berlin would never go for any of it. Where's the benefit to the personnel, the war effort, the Reich?"

Inge stared into space, then pointed her pen at him. "Couldn't you say—"

"No."

"But you haven't heard what I was going to suggest."

"I don't have to. Fewer working hours could never be of benefit to the Fatherland. Period."

"How about..." Inge rattled her pen between her teeth. "Increasing productivity by..."

Increasing productivity would have legs with Berlin. Where was she going with this? "Yes?"

"By...?" She pointed her pen at him. "Driving the prisoners to work in those trucks of yours."

"So your solution to increasing productivity is to chauffeur prisoners about?"

She wagged her pen. "No. My solution is to not exhaust prisoners by having them walk to and from work but to transport them, so they have more energy to be exploited for the actual labor."

"Hmmm." Rudi stroked his chin. Having the prisoners walk everywhere had been instituted by Kommandant Kloser as another means of passive punishment, but with regard to productivity, it did more harm than good. "You know, I might be able to swing that."

"Excellent. So after all that extra work, how about rewarding prisoners with extra food? If productivity is up—"

234

"Seriously, I can't do anything about that."

"But you're the commandant."

"Now, yes. But who'd be commandant if Gruber reported me for flouting regulations and treating prisoners too well?"

Inge scrunched up her face. "Okay. So... hot water for washing?"

He shook his head. "Sorry."

"But you could say it benefits your personnel because they don't have to smell us. And better hygiene would mean less sickness, so increased productivity."

"Won't work."

"But I've just said how you can justify it."

He shook his head again. "The tiny benefit wouldn't justify the considerable expense for the extra coal."

"We could cut down more trees for firewood ourselves."

"When?" The prisoners never had free time. Even their rest days were spent maintaining their barracks.

She threw her pen down. "Then I don't know. Nothing I say is any good because your precious Reich won't like it."

"No, I've said I'll look at transportation. That was your idea."

She shrugged, staring at her paper. Her enthusiasm was dying before his eyes because he was shooting down almost every suggestion. He wished he didn't have to, but he had no choice. What could he give her to show there was still hope?

He said, "Would you like shorter roll calls?"

She gasped. "You can do that?"

"I *am* the commandant."

"Yes. Please, please, yes." She jabbed his paper. "Write it down. Write it down."

"You seem a little undecided. Shall we circle back to that one?"

She scowled.

Rudi said, "I'll pencil it in as a maybe."

"Do you really want to annoy the person who can spit in every meal you're going to eat for the next few months?"

He held his hands defensively. "Okay, okay. I'll instruct my men." He noted it.

"Oh, thank you." She reached across the table to take his hand but must have realized how inappropriate it would be, so she pulled back. "Thank you. You won't believe what a difference that will make." She smiled. And those burning amber eyes nailed him.

"You're welcome."

Seeing her so happy and knowing he'd caused it filled him with a glow as if he were bathing in warmed honey. He smiled. Joy and wonder. Who'd have thought he'd find what his life was lacking in something as mundane as shortening roll call?

He tapped his paper. "You do realize these changes might have to be introduced over a few weeks, not all at once." Although his ledgers might hold the key to moving things along quicker.

Inge frowned. "Why?"

"I need to keep my men on side."

"But they're your men. Won't they just follow orders?"

"Yes. Unless they believe I'm not following mine."

"What would happen then?"

He'd be reported, leading to any number of possibilities: demotion, court-martial, a posting to the Front, imprisonment, even execution. And Inge, his coconspirator? The men would take great pleasure in resurrecting the Box.

He held her gaze. "Let's just say it wouldn't be good for either of us."

Yes, sitting here planning with Inge was one thing, but getting any of these changes implemented...

63

Someone knocked on Rudi's office door. Rudi rarely shut it, wanting to appear approachable, but for this meeting, he wanted a moment to prepare.

At his desk, Rudi wiped his palms on his pants. "Here we go." He raised his voice. "Come."

Gruber entered. "Herr Kommandant, you wanted to see me?"

Rudi gestured to the chair opposite. "I'd like to pick your brains, Unterscharführer."

Gruber sat. "Of course, Herr Kommandant. Fire away."

Being asked to sit and offer an opinion by a commanding officer was quite a compliment. While the gesture wouldn't placate Gruber once Rudi unveiled his plan, Rudi hoped it might at least put the man on the back foot.

Rudi said, "Our trucks. What do you estimate their maximum capacity for transporting personnel over a short distance?"

"Hmmm..." He puckered his lips. "What kit would they be carrying?"

"None."

"Roads or cross-country?"

"Roads."

"Twenty-three — seven on the benches either side and nine crouched down the middle in two staggered rows. More in the enclosed truck because it's high enough for passengers to stand."

"And if we remove the benches?"

"Maybe an extra two or three."

That was Rudi's estimate too. However, the prisoners being much smaller than the average man, twenty plus a guard and a kapo or two in each truck would be easy.

Gruber said, "Who are we transporting?"

Rudi's heart hammered at the conflict he was marching into. He held Gruber's gaze. "The prisoners."

Gruber frowned. "We've had a transfer order?"

"No. From tomorrow, we're transporting them to and from the excavation site."

Gruber snorted.

Rudi opened his palms. "Speak freely, Unterscharführer, I value your input."

"I'm sorry, Herr Kommandant, but we're driving them to work now? Why in God's name are we making things so easy for them?"

Easy? Rudi would like to hear Inge's take on that. "Easy, Unterscharführer?"

Gruber counted on his fingers. "We've given them a weekly shower, fuel, extra bread. Now we're chauffeuring them to work?" He held his arms wide. "Where's it going to end?"

Rudi nodded. "I hear what you're saying, Unterscharführer, but there are other considerations."

"Other considerations?" Gruber sniggered and pointed toward the compound. "The SS directive is not just to imprison this vermin, not just to work them, but — literally — to work them to death." He chopped the side of one hand into the other. "To death, Herr Kommandant."

Rudi smiled. "Exactly. I knew you'd see it."

Gruber scratched his head. "See what, Herr Kommandant?"

"That something's going wrong because so few are dying from being overworked."

Gruber narrowed his eyes. "So how is providing a taxi service going to help?"

"Unterscharführer, during Kommandant Kloser's last full month of command, how many prisoners do you think were — literally — worked to death?"

Gruber shrugged. "Twenty-five?"

Rudi shook his head.

"Thirty?" said Gruber.

Rudi shook his head again. He tapped his ledger. "Two."

"What? No, that's—"

Rudi held up his palm. "In that last month, three died in their sleep, one died walking to work, two died walking from work, one was electrocuted when she jumped on the fence, one was crushed when a truck backed up, four died in the infirmary, two were beaten to

238

death, three dropped dead during extended roll calls, and two died undertaking their work duties. Do you see?"

Gruber looked bewildered.

"Of the nineteen who died, only two were worked to death. Two." Rudi leaned forward. "Do you think that's good enough, Unterscharführer? Because I don't."

"With respect, Herr Kommandant, all those deaths could indirectly be considered work-related."

"Indirectly? So I'm supposed to report to Berlin that we are *indirectly* doing our duty, am I?"

"No, Herr—"

Rudi held up his hand again. "For God's sake, man, three died in their sleep. *In their sleep!* Why are we killing prisoners in their leisure time instead of following our directive to work them to death? It's not good enough, Gruber."

"No, Herr Kommandant."

Rudi slammed his hand down on his desk. "This farce ends now. Kommandant Kloser might have believed prisoners dying in their free time was acceptable, but I won't have it. From this moment forward, I want every second of work possible out of this vermin. Understand?"

"Yes, Herr Kommandant."

"Look at this." Rudi stabbed a column in his ledger. "Three died during roll call. *Three.* How did that loss of labor serve the Fatherland? Why are we forcing prisoners to endure torturous roll calls for hours and then complaining that productivity has dropped? And this." He stabbed another figure. "Another two were beaten to death. Why?"

"We have to punish the lazy ones to motivate them to work harder, Herr Kommandant."

Rudi sniggered. "Well, you won't find a lazier worker than a dead one, will you, Unterscharführer? This inefficiency has to stop. Allowing it to continue is doing a disservice to the Reich. We need to work prisoners harder, not have them waste their strength standing in the snow for hours or working slower because they've been beaten half-dead." Rudi raised his eyebrows. "Yes?"

"Yes, Herr Kommandant."

"Good." Rudi nodded. "From now on, every prisoner will be worked harder for longer to better serve the Fatherland. No exceptions. Have I made myself clear?"

"Yes, Herr Kommandant."

"Dismissed."

Gruber left. Rudi leaned back and blew out a mighty breath. Thank heaven that was over. The meeting had gone smoother than he'd imagined, but that was because he'd caught Gruber unprepared. Once the man processed everything, would he accept it, seeing some perverse logic in Rudi's argument, or had Rudi just set in motion his own end?

Krebs appeared. "Herr Commandant, we've received a radio message from the excavation site. You're needed immediately."

64

Kneeling on the bathroom floor, Inge scrubbed the tub. A faint brown stain encircled the inside, and no amount of rubbing was budging it. She tipped more white scouring powder onto her brush and laid into the mark again. Papa had always sworn there was a secret to completing any job — elbow grease.

Downstairs, a door slammed.

Inge checked the clock she carried around to monitor her progress through her duties. "Four fifteen?"

Rudi had requested his meal for 7:00 p.m., so it wouldn't be him. Who the devil was in the house?

She crept onto the landing and peered down the stairs, anxiety churning her gut. No one stood in the hallway. Maybe a guard had a message and was wandering around the house. She strained to hear footsteps. Nothing.

"Hello?" She crept downstairs. The dining room was empty, so she peered into the living room. "You?"

Slouched on the leather sofa, staring at the ceiling, Rudi said, "Hey."

"I'm sorry, but I haven't even started on dinner yet."

"No problem."

"If I start now, I can maybe have it ready for..." She glanced at the clock.

"Sit."

"What?"

He patted the sofa. "Sit."

"I have jobs to finish."

He patted again.

She dutifully sat, back upright as if at attention. This was odd. Even for their situation.

He said, "Tell me about your day."

"My day?" She laughed. "Unless you want to be bored rigid, you do *not* want to hear about my day. Believe me."

"Tell me. I just need to hear about something ordinary."

She shrugged. "Okay. So, I swept the floors, reorganized that big kitchen cupboard, washed the bedding in the guest bedroom, and now, I'm scrubbing the bathroom. As you can see, it's been a wonderful, fun-filled day. You?"

He drew his hands down his face. "I've been ordered to squeeze in an extra two hundred prisoners, even though we're already over capacity. I discovered our work detail building that new train embankment has gone off course, which will take weeks to correct. And I oversaw the digging of a mass grave after four prisoners stole a van and were shot trying to escape."

Inge gazed at her lap. Mundanity certainly had its benefits. "I prefer my day."

He nodded. "Me too."

"So why do you do it?"

"What?"

"Be a commandant."

He shrugged. "It's not like I planned it. It just kind of happened. One posting led to another, and before I knew it, here I was in sunny Estonia, punishing Jews because..." He stared into space.

"Because?"

"You know, I really wonder that myself."

She smiled. "It could be worse."

He turned to her. "You think?"

"You could live on my side of the fence."

He smirked. "True."

"So seriously, why do you do it?"

"When you were a girl at school, did you believe what your teachers told you?"

"Why wouldn't I?"

"Exactly. And after the Führer's rise, German teachers started teaching German kids that Jews weren't human, that they were desperate to cripple our country again like they did in the twenties. Not that it was just teachers. The radio, newspapers, politicians, friends, street placards, and even family all said the same thing: Jews aren't like us — they're animals who want to destroy everything we

242

love. If you hear that enough times from enough different sources, you can't help but believe it."

"You found a way."

He snorted. "Did I? I'm stuck here, aren't I?"

She'd put her hopes in liberation by the Soviets or the Allies, but she'd been praying for that for years and rescue was nowhere in sight. She'd never thought some Germans might be praying for the same thing. Rudi was a prisoner just like her. Oh, his cell was far more luxurious than hers, but it was no less a cell. There was no escape for either of them.

Inge frowned. Or was there?

Pulling a bent leg onto the sofa, Inge twisted to him. "Tell me about birds."

He shot her a sideways glance. "Birds?"

"Birds. You like birds. Tell me about them."

He let his head fall back. "You don't want to know about birds."

"But it was vital you knew about me scrubbing the bathroom, was it?" She dared to touch his arm. Just for a second. Just to give the situation the gravity it deserved. "Tell me."

He squinted at his arm, then her. She could imagine the cogs whirring as he struggled to understand her angle. "They have feathers."

She said with mock surprise, "Really?"

"Yes."

"Anything else?"

He puffed out his cheeks.

"Come on. Tell me."

"Okay. Some scientists believe birds descended from thecodonts, which are like ancient crocodiles."

Inge turned away. "If you're just going to mess with of me, forget it."

"I'm being serious. They believe birds were once a kind of reptile, like a crocodile."

"But birds look nothing like crocodiles."

"Exactly. Except they've found fossils that seem to connect them, showing birds with teeth and arms."

She smirked. "Stop messing with me."

"Honest."

"Birds with teeth?"

He smiled. "They're amazing creatures that can do so many incredible things. That's why they're so fascinating."

243

"What can they do?"

"Well, hummingbirds can fly backward."

"A bird that flies backward? How does it see where it's going?"

He laughed. "It doesn't fly backward all the time, only when it wants to."

"Really?"

"Really." He twisted to face her. "They burn so much energy, they have to eat their own weight in food every day, which sounds like a lot, but"— he fished a tiny coin out of his pocket and offered it to her —"the smallest species weighs less than one reichspfennig."

"Wow." She held out her hand. He dropped the coin into her palm and she weighed it.

"Their eggs are the size of a pea."

She chuckled. "You'd need a lot of those for an omelet."

He sniggered. "Maybe a hundred. Unlike an ostrich egg, which is about"— he held his hands as if encircling a baby's head —"this big. But then, ostriches can be nine feet tall and weigh three hundred pounds."

"Nine feet? That's like me sitting on your shoulders."

He nodded.

She smiled. "How do you know all this?"

"Do you think I was born an SS officer?"

Somehow, she kind of did. The Germans had caused so much suffering throughout the world, she struggled to imagine them as anything but one great war machine, with their women doing nothing but lying on their backs, pumping out soldier after soldier after soldier. In the same way they looked at her and saw "Jew," she looked at them and saw "Nazi."

Except not here.

On this sofa was only a man who saw a woman and a woman who saw a man. Two friends. Talking. Feeling. Connecting. Yes, they were both imprisoned in their own ways with absolutely no chance of escape, but maybe they didn't have to. Maybe all they had to do was lock that front door to keep the horrors outside at bay and lose themselves in each other.

Maybe, if she tried hard, *really hard*, that dream she'd lost would return — she'd be a person living in the world once more, not vermin trapped in a cage.

244

65

All week, Inge carried the clock around the commandant's house, no longer to gauge how she was getting through her duties but to see how soon Rudi would be home. The time always crawled by, no matter how she threw herself into her work. Once he arrived, he ate the meal she'd cooked, then they sat in the living room, talking and laughing in their own private world.

On Sunday, Inge had a cold shower with her fellow prisoners, washed her clothes, helped clean their barracks, repaired a door, and changed the straw in her mattress. By the time she'd finished enjoying her "day of rest," it was late afternoon.

Inge dashed across the snowy expanse to the washroom, where water pipes lined with spigots ran above troughs. She scrubbed her hands after handling the filthy straw.

"Inge!"

Beaming at the familiar voice, she turned. "Greta."

They hugged.

Greta said, "I was starting to think I'd lost you."

"Says she after her relaxing stay at Hotel Baumann."

"You're not wrong there. Two days on that railway embankment and I'm already thinking of breaking my other knee." She nudged Inge, smirking. "So how's housekeeping for his lordship? Or shouldn't I ask?"

"It's good. Tiring, but compared to the trench, it's a cakewalk."

"Tiring, huh? He's very demanding, our commandant, is he?"

"Actually, the opposite," said Inge. "He's really easygoing."

Greta rolled her eyes. "You're really making me drag this out of you, aren't you?"

"Drag what?"

"What do you think? What he's like, you know"— she whispered —"in bed."

Inge frowned. "It's not like that."

"Oh, right." Greta winked. "I stand corrected."

Inge grabbed Greta's hand. "Seriously. He hasn't laid a finger on me."

"Oh." Greta gawked. "That's not what everyone is saying."

"I don't care what everyone's saying. I'm telling you what's happening — nothing."

"Why not? Look at you, you're gorgeous." Greta stroked Inge's arm. "You could slice cheese with those cheekbones. And as for those eyes..."

Inge elbowed her. "Stop it."

"It's true."

Inge's cheeks burned. "We talk. That's all. He's like Baumann — a decent guy."

"So he's the one who's made this place so weird?"

"Weird?"

"At the embankment, the work is absolute torture, but I haven't been hit once. Not once. Then there's roll call. What's all that about? It's like we barely have time to line up before it's over."

Inge grinned. She and Rudi were making a real difference. And more was to come. Lots more. One of the biggest in just two days.

66

Roll call finishing, Rudi strode into the compound, scanning the ranks of women. Even with their heads bowed, he could see some were crying, and others were trembling. But why? The improvements were working, Inge having confirmed how the women appreciated them.

He glanced across the compound for a possible cause. And then he saw it. He cringed. Had Gruber done this intentionally, or was it a genuine mistake?

Near the scaffold, seven crates stood almost exactly where the coats had been burned. The women had to be horrified that something had happened for which they were to be similarly punished.

Rudi addressed them. "You have my word that no one is to be punished tonight. Quite the opposite. You must have noticed that roll calls are quicker and that there are fewer beatings. If you'd like that to continue, you must show your appreciation by working harder."

Rudi paused for his words to sink in. The women still looked terrified, as if this was a trick. He sighed. Not surprising, considering how he'd lulled them into a false sense of security with the coats and then done what he had.

"As a gesture of good faith, I have a gift for each of you. And this time, I promise you get to keep it." With a crowbar, he levered open a crate and held up a pair of black fur-lined boots. "Winter boots for everyone."

Deathly silence.

Rudi scanned the women, picturing the jubilation when they'd received their coats. He'd suspected they'd be wary this time, but after the positive changes he'd implemented, he hadn't expected such fear. But could he blame them?

Rudi walked along and pried open each crate. "Block leaders, distribute the boots to your barracks."

The block leaders dashed to the crates. Nearest to Rudi, Hilde beckoned the first woman in line, who scurried over, grabbed the boots offered, then scurried back.

Rudi shouted, "Wait!"

The woman dropped her new boots and whimpered, obviously expecting to be whipped at best or, at worst, dragged to the scaffold and hanged.

Rudi picked up the boots. She flinched. Maybe thinking he was going to beat her with them.

He said, "Are these your size?"

"I-I'm sorry, Herr Kommandant, I don't-don't know."

This wasn't working.

On the advice of the company representative, two-thirds of the boots were in the three most common sizes, with bigger and smaller sizes making up the remainder. If distribution wasn't handled properly, some women would be stuck with either useless footwear or blistered feet, which could easily become infected.

Rudi ordered Inge fetched from the house. Three minutes later, she arrived, confused.

Rudi pointed at Inge and addressed his prisoners. "You know this woman. You know she's the reason you have warm barracks, so you know you can trust her. She will oversee the distribution of footwear and ensure, wherever possible, that each of you gets boots that fit." He turned to Inge and said quietly, "Got that?"

"Yes, Herr Kommandant."

Herr Kommandant? He stifled a smile, trying to remember the last time she had called him that and not Rudi, then dismissed the men, leaving Inge to supervise.

Rudi clicked his tongue, marching toward the commandant's house. That had been the ideal opportunity to give Inge the credit she deserved for the camp's improvements, but it was best his men remained ignorant of her influence. Not least for her sake. While everyone knew she was untouchable, "accidents" happened, and proving foul play could be impossible.

As he opened his front door, he glanced into the compound. Some prisoners were dancing in their new boots, some kicked up snow like children kicking leaves, and others simply gazed down at them in disbelief. And in the middle of it all stood Inge, handing out gifts like Santa Claus to poverty-stricken kids.

Joy and wonder.

And all because a Jew had fed a bird. If not for that, he dreaded to think of the state this place would be in. The state *he'd* be in.

Yes, joy and wonder. He smiled. She was special, this one. So special.

67

The following night Rudi tramped home around 7:30 p.m. and sighed as he hung up his greatcoat and cap. Though he was still wearing his uniform, removing his coat and hat was like removing his duties — he felt lighter.

Inge peeped out of the kitchen. "Better day today?"

"It didn't stink." He shrugged, but under his breath, he added, "Too much."

It was a sad life when days could only be differentiated by the degree to which they stank.

Inge said, "Go sit down. It's ready."

In the dining room, he sat at the head of the table, sipped a glass of red wine already poured, and stared at the flickering candles in the middle of the table. Okay, so maybe not every moment of every day stank. His sanctuary *had been* the forest with Bruno, but now... he gazed around at his tiny oasis in the bowels of hell. This was about as sane as he could hope for.

Inge shuffled in carrying a plate in both hands as if holding nitroglycerine. "I hope you're hungry. I kind of misjudged things, so there's loads left."

"You aren't following Elena's instructions?" The taste of many meals suggested she wasn't, but he was never going to say that with all the effort she was putting in.

"I am. But things never seem to go quite right."

She placed a plate before him. Some sort of meat and vegetables swam in so much gravy, it almost overflowed the plate.

He said, "Thank you."

She smiled and toddled away.

"Inge."

She raised her eyebrows.

250

He pushed out the chair to his left with his foot.

She frowned. "Me?"

"You said there's plenty."

"Yes, but..." She clutched her chest. "I can't, can I? What if someone finds out?"

A Jew could be punished for having food above the rationed amount. He grimaced. "You're probably right. I hear the commandant is a real monster."

He shoved the chair farther out.

Inge grinned and skipped into the kitchen. She returned with a small portion and a glass of water. She sat beside him.

He nodded. "Enjoy."

"Thank you." She picked up her cutlery. "In Czech, we say *dobrou chut'*."

"*Dobro...*"

She said it slowly. "*Dobrou chut'*."

"*Dobrou chut'*."

"*Děkuju.*"

They tucked in.

Rudi chewed a piece of meat.

And chewed.

And chewed.

The taste was... almost pleasant, mainly from some sort of seasoning, but the texture was like chewing a tire.

Inge said, "Sorry, the meat's a bit tough."

"Tough is a tad harsh."

She gestured to the kitchen. "If you want more, there's plenty."

"Good God, no." He rubbed his mouth. "Sorry. Yes, it's a little tough."

"But why? I did it exactly how Elena said."

"Exactly?"

"Well, maybe not exactly. I mean, what does cook 'slowly' mean? How slow is slow?"

Rudi shrugged, speared another hunk with his fork, and held it up. "But look on the bright side, at least we have something to repair the new boots with when their soles wear out."

She arched an eyebrow. "Someone's getting no pudding."

"That's good, because I'm already stuffed."

"Pity. I found the last of Elena's cakes."

"Well, maybe I can manage a small piece." He winked.

"We'll see." She wagged her knife at him. "But only if you're good and eat all your vegetables."

"Yes, Miss Inge."

She rolled her eyes.

Rudi said, "So what did you do back home in an evening?"

"Read. See friends. Listen to the radio. Go to dances." She shrugged. "Normal stuff. You?"

"I loved the cinema."

She nodded. "Me too."

"Romance? Mystery? Adventure?"

She grinned. "*Flip i Flap.*"

"What?"

"*Flip i Flap!* Come on, everybody knows *Flip i Flap.* I used to watch them with my Grandpa when I visited him in Poland. It was our special thing. But they're huge. You must know them."

Rudi stared blankly.

"They're two men — a fat one and a skinny one — and they wear round black hats and are always having hilarious adventures."

Mouth downturned, Rudi shook his head.

"The skinny one blows on his thumb and his hat lifts." She put her left thumb in her mouth and her other hand on her head. When she puffed out her cheeks blowing, she moved her right hand as if it were a hat tilting.

"Ohhh, *Dick und Doof.*"

"What and what?"

"In Germany, we call them *Dick und Doof.*" Rudi pretended to ruffle a tie while adopting an aggrieved tone and said in English, "*Another nice mess you've gotten me into.*"

"That's them!" Inge laughed and pointed at him. "I love them."

Rudi grinned. "Yes, they were very popular. They even did some movies in German. Their accents were awful, but they spoke real German."

"How wonderful. I like the one—" Inge laughed. "The one with the piano and they're—" Laughing, she pretended to push with both hands. "They're pushing—" She held her chest, giggling.

Rudi chuckled. "Up all the steps."

Still laughing, Inge nodded. She wiped her eyes and returned to her meal.

252

Rudi studied her. He'd imagined it was only their predicament that had thrown them together, but it wasn't. In a different world, he'd still be drawn to her.

She did a double take, realizing he was staring. She touched her mouth. "Is something stuck?"

"I don't have a cinema, but I have a radio."

She arched her eyebrows. "Music?"

He nodded.

She clasped her hands as if in prayer. "Oh, it feels like a lifetime since I heard music."

Picking up his wine, he nodded toward the living room. "Bring your glass."

"But the dishes."

"Forget the dishes." Moving into the other room, Rudi said, "Do you like swing?"

"I love swing."

"Please." He gestured to the sofa and ambled over to the brown Bakelite radio at the back of the room. "Have you heard of Charlie and his Orchestra?"

"No." She sat on the far left of the sofa.

He twiddled the radio's knob to find a station. "It's state-approved swing, which sounds horrendous but is surprisingly good."

Static and intermittent bursts of sound came from the big round speaker in the front. Finally, a swing band bathed the room with syncopated magic.

He sat at the opposite end of the sofa but pulled his knee up to twist toward her.

Inge told him how her parents didn't approve of her listening to jazz with her friends, but Rudi focused more on her than on her tale. How her eyes sparkled when she talked of a party they'd held, how her hands danced in time with her words, how her lips twitched smiles as memories enveloped her in love...

He glanced at the three feet of cold leather separating them. Why was he so wary of getting too close — both physically and emotionally? He liked this woman. No way in hell could he deny it any longer.

But liking a Jew was wrong. Which was why it was illegal. So what was wrong with him that he couldn't quell his yearning to be with her? Was he psychologically damaged — like a man who craved children?

It was wrong. Simple.

But was it?

Here, in their sanctuary from the horrors of the world, they weren't a superior Aryan and a verminous Jew — they were two people. *People.* Nothing more, nothing less.

He'd always thought being so close to a Jew would not just *be* wrong but *feel* wrong. The way incest or bestiality would. Except he felt nothing. Nothing except gratitude that she'd come into his life.

Maybe he'd lost it. Maybe the horrors he'd witnessed had sent him over the edge. Whatever the reason, something had changed. In him. The world was just the same cruel place it had always been, but now, it was as if he were looking at it from a different place, a distant place, a place where the rules were only rules if they meant something. And her being a Jew meant nothing.

But where did he go from here?

68

The weeks grew darker and the snow deeper. Any joy Rudi found from the reduced daylight hours shortening the working days was offset by the unforgiving cold.

Krebs peered into Rudi's office. "Herr Kommandant, are you expecting another of your 'special' shipments?"

"No. Why?"

"The shipping clerk from the railway station phoned. They have ten crates to be collected."

How odd. All the coats and boots he'd bought had arrived, so someone must have shipped items to the wrong facility.

"Do we know what the shipment is?" If it was something they needed, a crate or two might go astray before the shipping company was notified.

Krebs said, "Six hundred winter coats."

Oh, dear Lord. Because of the whole Bruno affair, he'd forgotten to cancel the order he'd placed back in May and left open in case his jewelry deal had fallen through.

And thank heaven for that.

Rudi said, "Send a truck."

"Yes, Herr Kommandant."

Rudi made a mental note to cancel the boot order.

That evening, snowflakes as big as postage stamps fell. At his front door, Rudi stamped his feet to knock off the excess snow, then entered.

He called out, "Sorry, Inge. Last-minute emergency at the excavation site."

Inge replied from the kitchen, "Everything's a little well done now, but it can't be helped."

"It'll be fine." Rudi hung his coat up. "You won't believe what Kraus Construction is trying to pull." He removed his boots, put them next to the coatrack, then strode for the kitchen. "They're only trying to—"

Inge stood in the doorway, arms folded. "What *they're* trying to pull? Aren't we forgetting something, Kommandant Kruse?" She arched an eyebrow.

He scampered back, dropped an old newspaper from the hall table on the floor, and stood his wet boots on it. "Sorry."

"Every night this week." Smirking, she shook her head. "I swear, it's like having an oversized child."

She wandered back into the kitchen. He followed and found Inge dishing food onto plates.

Rudi said, "Kraus is blaming the prisoners for being behind schedule, saying we should provide better-quality workers. And of course, because our workers are of such low quality, Kraus wants a price reduction."

"So what are you going to do?" Inge held up a ladle, asking if he wanted gravy.

He nodded. "Tell them to go hang."

Carrying a plate each, they ambled into the dining room and sat.

"There is one bit of good news, though," said Rudi.

"Yes?"

"Six hundred winter coats arrived. They'll be distributed tomorrow after roll call."

"Fantastic."

Rudi nodded. "It should make coping with this lovely Estonian weather more bearable."

Inge sipped water. "If they're warm."

"They should be. Russian winters aren't exactly balmy."

"They're Russian?"

"From Soviet POWs."

Inge paused, a forkful of food at her lips. "So what happened to the Russians who were wearing them?"

"It's probably better not to ask." Rudi grimaced. Rumors abounded of thousands of Soviet prisoners being denied food because the Reich either couldn't afford rations or didn't want to.

They enjoyed their meal, then retired to the living room and chatted.

The weeks grew darker still, and coldness bit like a rabid dog at the hand trying to catch it. And all the while, the war raged like the beast it was. But evenings in the house remained a tiny slice of sanity in a world gone crazy.

At the table, Inge stared at the wall opposite, chewing slowly. Rudi recognized the look — she had something to say. "What?"

She waved him away.

"I know there's something, so just tell me."

She dropped her cutlery and pursed her lips.

Rudi said, "Tell me."

"It's me. Okay. Me."

"What about you?"

She gestured to herself with both hands. "Look at me. Clean. Warm. Nice dress. Good food."

"I think *good food* is stretching things a bit, but..."

She glared at him.

"Sorry. What are you getting at?"

"How easy I have it compared to those poor devils." She gestured to the compound.

Rudi threw up his hands. "So what more can I do? The place is unrecognizable compared to six months ago."

"It's not enough."

"We've been through this – I can't give them more food."

"What if they earned it?"

"What?"

She handed him a folded piece of paper from her pocket.

He read. "*One chit equals one piece of bread. Two chits equals a bowl of soup.* What's a chit?"

"I want you to institute a reward system where, every day, the best ten workers get a chit they can exchange for things. I know you're going to say no, which is why I haven't–"

He waved the paper. "I've heard of camps running schemes like this. Dora definitely did because I contacted them for advice on our excavation."

She beamed as if Germany had just surrendered. "So we can do it?"

He grimaced. "Resources. My men are overstretched, and I wouldn't trust the kapos with anything to do with rewards."

"Then trust me."

"*You?*"

"Oh, thanks for the vote of confidence."

"Sorry, I didn't mean it like that. But you've always said you didn't want to be a functionary."

She tapped the paper. "This isn't beating people, this is rewarding them."

"But that would take you away from here."

She snorted. "Do you know how often I look for work so if one of your men comes, they'll find me up to my elbows? Let me trial this scheme two days a week for a month so I feel I'm doing something worthwhile."

"Two days?"

She nodded. "And if productivity goes up, it can become permanent, and I'll train a group of women I trust so we can roll it out across all the work details."

He'd become a soldier to protect his Fatherland, to serve his people. Could he deny Inge the chance to serve hers?

"Okay, one month."

Beaming, she grabbed his hand. "Thank you."

A tingle shot up his arm.

Inge gasped, whipping her hands under the table. "Sorry."

"It's okay."

"But thank you. This means a lot, so..." She couldn't stop grinning.

He wanted to smile, too. Oddly, making her happy somehow made him happy. He nudged the paper. "We might need to adjust some of your rewards."

"Which?"

"Five chits and they get a day off?"

"The rewards have to be worth it, or there's no incentive. Besides, it could take weeks for someone to be awarded five, so most will cash in long before that."

She was right. Plus, this would be an easy sell to the likes of Gruber because the prisoners would appear to be willingly working themselves to death.

Inge said, "I want to award ten chits per day, one per person, so people feel there's a decent chance of winning one. And I want to supervise the prisoners exchanging the chits to make sure it's done fairly."

"Okay. Give me a couple of days to organize everything, and we'll have a trial run. Maybe using the excavation detail because you know what's involved."

Inge grinned. "In that case, I've got a special treat for dessert."

Rudi cringed. The last cake she'd cooked had been as enjoyable as eating socks. "Lovely."

"I'll cut you an extra big piece."

"Just a sliver. I don't want to put on weight."

She arched an eyebrow. "And if I said it wasn't me who baked it? That I wanted to cheer Elena up after that infection nearly finished her off, so I took all the ingredients over for her to mix so I only cooked it?"

"Maybe a good slice wouldn't hurt."

Inge snickered, shaking her head.

Over cake, Inge further explained her idea. She'd obviously put in a lot of work, because she nailed every question he posed. But it wasn't just her clear thinking that impressed him, it was her passion — she had an easy life now, and where many people would keep their head down to avoid jeopardizing that, she longed to improve things for everyone.

In the living room later, music playing in the background, Rudi reclined at his end of the sofa. "Okay, so now I have something to tell you."

"Anything," said Inge at her end.

"I'm hosting another dinner to boost morale. If Elena is up to it, would you mind if she helps so it goes more smoothly than last time?"

She sniggered. "I'll drag her here by her hair, if I have to. And I promise not to spit in Gruber's food this time."

"What?"

She looked down. "Nothing."

"Please tell me you didn't."

Gesticulating wildly, she said, "He was being a complete monster. Making jokes about me, my country, my cooking. He's a vile little man. Vile."

Rudi faced her, his expression grave. "Inge, he doesn't know you like I do. If he'd suspected you'd done something like that, he could've taken out his pistol and shot you there and then."

Inge snorted.

"I'm not joking."

"Okay, I'm sorry. I'll be on my best behavior."

"Thank you."

Rudi could see her point. But was Gruber to blame? If Gruber had never met an articulate, compassionate Jew, why wouldn't he believe the poisonous propaganda Goebbels and his cronies spread? However, if the man got to know Inge the way Rudi had, got to see her as a real human being, could he remain filled with such hatred?

69

Inge buffed the final section of the dining table and admired the sheen. She'd already polished the cutlery and glassware, but the table was the most noticeable because they'd all be sitting around it, so she wanted the surface like a mirror. This meal was important to Rudi, so getting everything right was important to her.

She strode into the kitchen. Elena had made a sauce, mixed another cake, and given Inge detailed cooking instructions for everything. Even if one or two minor things went wrong, as long as the meat was cooked, the sauce would save the main course, and the cake would finish things off in style. Tonight was virtually guaranteed to be a success.

The guests arrived and Rudi entertained them in the living room. Laughter drifted through the house. A good sign.

At 7:55 p.m., Inge stood respectfully silent in the living room until someone noticed her. While Baumann and Rudi relaxed on the sofa, Gruber scanned the frequencies on the radio, and Hofmann sat in a chair.

Gruber's eyes narrowed when he saw her. "I think your Jew wants something, Herr Kommandant."

Rudi looked around. "Yes, Inge?"

"Sorry to disturb you, Herr Kommandant, but the food is ready when you are."

"Shall we, gentlemen?" Rudi gestured to the other room.

Gruber clapped. "Excellent. What beef and turnip delight have we in store tonight?" He laughed.

Rudi glanced at Inge, barely shaking his head. She shot him an even fainter acknowledgment. She would not be goaded. Tonight was going to be her night. Her triumph would be better than a gallon of saliva in Gruber's meal.

While the men relocated, Inge lifted carved lamb onto plates and drizzled the creamy sauce over it, a delicious scent wafting up. Inge's mouth watered like a stray dog's on sensing a discarded scrap, but she wouldn't nibble a piece. Not even lick the fork she'd used. She wouldn't give Gruber the satisfaction of catching her "stealing" extra rations.

The plates ready, she smiled. She'd made this? Okay, she'd had help, but... wow.

She served Rudi and Baumann first.

Rudi's eyebrows raised. "You cooked this?"

No, the kitchen pixies did. She resisted the urge. "Yes, Herr Kommandant."

Baumann sniffed his. "This smells lovely, Inge."

"Thank you, Scharführer." She desperately wanted to punch the air, but she refused to even smile.

"Hold the beef and turnip, Jew," said Gruber. "I'll have what they're having."

Again, Rudi barely shook his head.

Inge reassured Rudi with a glance. "Of course, Herr Unterscharführer. Maybe you'd like an extra slice of lamb. I cooked plenty."

He nodded. "Why not?"

Inge served the last two guests, then stood to one side to be called on when needed, head down.

Rudi said, "Inge?"

"Yes, Herr Kommandant?"

"Join us."

Her jaw dropped. She flicked her gaze to him, and he gestured to the chair beside Baumann. Feeling the blood drain from her face, she stared at the other faces fixed on her, all with the same horror and confusion she imagined she was expressing. She gulped.

Gruber cracked first. He laughed. "Good one, Herr Kommandant."

Rudi ignored him. "Inge, sit."

"I..." Inge pointed to the kitchen but was too thrown to think of what to say.

"Baumann, would you move along one?" said Rudi.

Head down toward Rudi, Baumann whispered, "Are you sure about this?"

Rudi nodded.

"As you wish, Herr Kommandant." Baumann shifted one seat over.

Rudi patted Baumann's vacated chair. "Sit."

He lifted a slice of lamb and a potato onto his side plate, then put that in the vacant spot.

Inge trembled, sweat beading on her brow. What the devil had possessed him?

That didn't matter. All that mattered was that the commandant had given her a direct order, and in this camp, his word was law.

She swallowed hard again.

Cringing, Inge tottered over. The chair screamed as she slid it out over the wooden floor. She sat, gaze buried in the tabletop.

Gruber frowned. "You can't be serious, Herr Kommandant."

Rudi said, "We're only enjoying a meal together, Unterscharführer, not reading from the Torah."

"With a Jew?" said Gruber. "You honestly expect us to eat *with a Jew?*"

Rudi glared at Gruber.

Inge pushed up. "Excuse me, I've—"

Still glaring at his comrade, Rudi clamped her hand to the table. "Sit."

She yanked her hand free. Bowing her head to avoid anyone's eye, she said, "I need to prepare the next course. Please excuse me, gentlemen."

She scurried away.

Gruber belly-laughed and applauded. "Wonderful. You had me there for a moment! Honestly, I really thought you were serious."

Rudi sighed and reached for his wine.

Gruber mimicked Rudi, *"We're enjoying a meal, not reading from the Torah."* He laughed again. "Classic! I'll have to remember that one."

"I'm pleased you're having a good time, Unterscharführer."

"Oh, I am indeed. But may I be candid, Herr Kommandant?"

Rudi gestured for him to continue.

Gruber leaned closer. "Be careful with that one. I see what she's doing, even if you don't."

Rudi frowned. "Meaning?"

"Some of these Jewesses — they're witches."

Baumann said, "Gruber, we haven't had witches for two hundred years. If ever."

Gruber sneered. "Only a fool thinks witches exist solely in fairy tales. They're all too real. You hear the stories — good Aryan men being corrupted by a smile, a sly word, a flash of skin, each injecting the Jew venom deeper and deeper until the poor wretch can't help but obey his evil Jew mistress."

"Thank you for your concern, Unterscharführer," said Rudi, "but I assure you, everything's under control."

"That's what the men always think. Then before they know it, it's too late."

Rudi raised his glass toward Gruber. "But none of them have such a stalwart unterscharführer watching out for them, do they?"

They clinked glasses and returned to their meal.

Tears welled in Inge's eyes. What had gotten into Rudi to do that to her? And now he was letting Gruber spout such poison. How could he?

As the main course neared its end, her heart pounded. She wiped her palms on her dress and shuffled in, praying no one would say anything. Especially not Rudi.

Luckily, everyone ignored her when she removed the plates and brought dessert. After that, she tidied the kitchen while the men retired to the living room for a nightcap. Finally, they left.

Her mouth dry, pulse racing, she stood with her hands in a sink full of suds, listening to Rudi clomping toward the kitchen.

He stopped in the doorway. "Inge, I'm sorry things went a little awry."

"Awry?" She slung a plate into the sink. Water splashed everywhere. "What were you thinking?"

"I... I don't know. You'd spent so long preparing the meal, it seemed only decent to have you join us."

"A Jew? Dining with four SS?"

"It was informal. Baumann's decent and Hofmann's spineless, so I hoped that if we all set our differences aside, they might see you the way I see you. Even Gruber."

"Differences?" She folded her arms. "You think there are 'differences' between us?" She snorted. "You throw hundreds of thousands of us into ghettos, send hundreds of thousands more to camps, and all because of 'differences'?"

"Change — real change — will only come if Germans see Jews as people. How are they going to do that if they never meet any socially?"

She threw her hands up. "Well, I'm sorry that our vacationing in all the lovely camps you've so kindly provided is spoiling Germany's cultural evolution."

"My mistake." He slumped against the doorjamb. "Do you ever have one of those days?"

She arched an eyebrow. "Seriously?"

"Sorry, I keep forgetting."

"Forgetting? That I'm a Jewish prisoner living in squalor while you're a Nazi commandant living in a luxurious house?"

"I've been thinking about that. Many people have live-in housekeepers, so..."

"Again — seriously? Or has Hitler converted to Judaism, so now everything's nice and *kosher*?"

He pointed toward the front door. "They're not stupid. They know something's going on, they just don't know what."

"I know how they feel."

"What's that supposed to mean?"

"What do you think it means?"

"If I knew, I wouldn't ask."

She cupped her brow. Were all men so downright dumb? He was intelligent in so many ways, so why couldn't he see how wrong all this was?

Inge gripped her hair in her fists. "I don't know what you want from me."

"To be honest"— he rubbed his chin —"I've wondered that myself."

"And?"

He shrugged.

She said, "So what am I doing here?"

"You're my housekeeper, my cook."

"You've tasted my cooking. No one's believing that." She gazed into space. What did she have to do to reach him? To make him look at their situation and decide what on earth was happening?

Head bowed, she said, "A lot of the women think I'm your whore."

He sniggered. "My men too."

She met his gaze. "So why aren't I?"

He squinted. "What?"

"Why aren't I your whore? At least then I'd know what this is." She pointed back and forth between them.

"Do I make you feel like a whore? Even though I've never touched you?"

"No."

"So what does it matter what everyone else thinks?"

"It matters what *I* think. I want to know why I'm here. What I mean to you."

"Don't you like being here? Having easier work, away from the filth and cold?"

"But it's still work. It's not like I've any choice about being here."

"If you don't want to be here, I can have you reassigned."

She pounded her chest. "Just tell me why? Why me?"

"Because…" He ran his fingers through his hair to clasp his hands behind his head.

"Because?"

He blew out a breath. "Do I *really* have to say it?"

She folded her arms, gaze burning into him.

"I like you," said Rudi. "Okay? I like you. I hoped you liked me."

"I'm your prisoner."

"I know."

"I'm a Jew."

"*I know!*"

"So what do you think is going to happen? That we'll step out for a few months, then you'll ask my father for my hand, and we'll get a nice little house in the suburbs?"

He slumped onto the edge of the table. He shrugged.

Inge said, "This is crazy. It's only going to end in suffering. For me, if not you as well."

"The whole world is crazy and suffering. That's war." He shook his head, then stared into her eyes. "But these moments with you, they're… they're the only thing that keeps me sane."

He took her hand. This time, she didn't yank it away.

She said, "This is going to end badly."

"I know."

She cupped his face.

He smiled.

They gazed at each other in silence as the night cocooned them in warmth, hiding the horrors of the war in its dark embrace. Two people lost in a world more lost than it had ever been.

70

The next day, Inge stood at the rear of one of the three trucks, gazing out over the makeshift tailgate-cum-safety-barrier at the snow-drenched landscape speeding by. Unlike the other trucks, which had a tarpaulin over the cargo area, hers was enclosed by solid panels tall enough for the women to stand, but the rear doors had been removed so they wouldn't suffocate.

The tall guard in the back eyed her suspiciously.

She ignored him.

The truck rumbled over the stone bridge, the river a snake of ice. She smiled. She loved to skate on the frozen pond back home with Robert. But she immediately pushed the picture out of her mind. Thinking about those she loved hurt like she'd been stabbed in the chest. She couldn't cope with that loss and everything here at the same time.

The vehicle turned right, swinging the twenty-odd occupants into each other. Inge clutched Greta to keep from falling. Traveling on the straight again, she shivered and pulled her Soviet coat tighter around her. She'd forgotten how bitter and precarious life in the outside world was.

At the excavation site, Inge dismounted from the vehicle as the other trucks pulled up behind them.

Helping others alight, Inge said loudly, "Remember, I'm not looking for anyone to kill themselves, just consistent, committed work throughout the day."

She'd explained the scheme at roll call. Some women had been apprehensive, but most seemed eager for the extra rations available. However, the last thing Inge wanted was for someone to go crazy and hurt themselves.

"Greta." Inge nodded her to one side.

Greta moved closer.

Inge whispered, "Don't knock yourself out, because I can't give my best friend a chit on the first day, or everyone will think it's a scam."

Greta nodded, but her expression dropped.

Inge touched her arm. "Maybe next week. But things are getting better, aren't they?"

Greta half-smiled. "He must really like you."

"What?"

She tugged her coat. "The coats, short roll calls, now rewards..."

"It's not all me. He's a decent—"

A kapo shoved Greta. "Get to work."

Greta stumbled away.

Inge opened her mouth to speak but stopped. She couldn't overstep her bounds in the very first minute of the very first day. Especially when the kapo had shoved Greta, not whipped her.

Work underway, Inge spent the morning monitoring the prisoners' performance to award a chit to the ten hardest workers. Each chit was numbered and featured her signature, so she could keep track of them and so they couldn't be forged. If the trial was a success, Rudi had said they'd have proper ones printed.

To start, she oversaw the concrete mixing team, then the wheelbarrow crew, and finally, the two groups inside — those laying the concrete and those carting away the debris from the face.

She sighed at her list of twenty-seven potential candidates. How could she possibly narrow that down to ten?

During lunch break, she sat with Greta beside a storage shack. "I don't know how I'm going to decide. I need thirty to give away, not ten."

"You know some of the women will work super hard when you're watching but slack off the moment you move on, don't you?"

"Yes, but how can I get around that?"

Greta shrugged. "Hide?"

"Hang on." Inge held up a finger. "Rudi's got binoculars. I could spy on them from a distance."

Greta nudged her and arched an eyebrow, smirking. "Rudi, is it? And what else has *Rudi* got?"

"I told you. It's not like that."

Greta snorted. "I bet."

"It's not." Inge glanced around to check no one could hear. "To be honest, I wish it was, but..." She shrugged.

"Seriously? You *still* haven't...?"

"No."

Greta whispered, "Do you think he has a war wound, so he can't get... you know?"

"Oh God, I hope not."

Greta laughed and slapped Inge's arm. "You hussy!"

Inge sniggered. "Well, you know, I..."

"Want him?"

Inge's cheeks burned. She didn't *want* him; she *ached* for him. She'd thought he felt the same, especially after he'd actually confessed to liking her, but he couldn't feel the same because he'd never even kissed her, let alone anything else. Maybe deep down, he still considered her a *filthy* Jew. If he'd had that sentiment drilled into him for years, maybe he just couldn't shake it.

Greta munched on a scrap of turnip. "You know, you could make the first move."

Inge's jaw dropped.

Greta said, "I don't mean be lying there legs akimbo when he walks in the door, but there are other ways."

"Like?"

"When you hold his gaze, lick your lips. Or when you look at him, don't just maintain eye contact, let him see you checking him out."

Inge nodded. "I could do that. Maybe."

"And if he doesn't get the message, brush against him so you accidentally touch his, you know..."

"Greta! He'll think I earned my money on a street corner."

"He won't."

"He will. I don't want him thinking I'm some cheap slut who's had dozens of men."

Greta touched Inge's arm. "Try it. You'll be amazed."

A whistle ended the break and everyone trudged back to work.

While Inge appeared to be monitoring the concrete workers, she surreptitiously scrutinized the wheelbarrow crew. Within thirty minutes, instead of adding more names, she'd crossed off four. However, she couldn't concentrate. Could she really initiate things with Rudi? They had a deep connection, which she was sure he felt too. Maybe a little nudge to let him know that she wouldn't reject him was all it would take.

Sunset came frighteningly early so far north, and with it, an even icier wind blew. Finally, the whistle sounded and the prisoners trudged to the trucks, some panting, some cradling an injury, some with barely the strength to walk. Once all were inside, the trucks departed.

Standing at the tailgate again, Inge stared at the women. Shadows danced on their faces cast by the headlights of the truck behind them, twisting exhaustion and pain into nightmarish demons. She'd forgotten how punishing the work details were. Her list had been narrowed to ten, but she longed to give everyone extra bread.

The truck sped parallel to the river, then stopped to join the road from town.

An ice-covered willow bent from the riverbank, its dangling branches strings of shimmering jewels, while moonlight bathed the winter scene in an ethereal glow to create something out of a fairy tale.

The truck turned left and accelerated across the bridge over the frozen river.

Halfway across, a horn blared. Brakes squealed.

The truck lurched right. Skidded. And the prisoners slammed into each other. Jolting, the vehicle smashed partway through the stone wall running down the side of the bridge with an almighty crack. Then stopped.

The prisoners clung to each other, terror scored across their faces by vehicle headlights.

Stillness descended. And fear eased into relief. Some women even dared to smile through their tears.

But the truck pivoted on the remains of the wall and tilted forward as if to drop. Wails erupted, like on some hellish slow-motion roller coaster, but then the vehicle rocked back.

Wanting to escape, some of the women struggled to untangle themselves, but as their weight shifted, the truck tilted again.

Inge thrust her hands up. "Stay still. We have to move carefully or we'll tip over."

Beside Inge, her face haggard with fear, a kapo gazed at the safety of the bridge.

"Please." Inge shook her head. "We'll all get out of this if we work together."

The tall guard raised his rifle. "Don't move."

Holding her hands up, the kapo said, "Okay. Okay."

But the moment the guard lowered his gun, the kapo leaped over the tailgate.

The vehicle rocked.

269

With the human ballast disrupted, Inge screwed her eyes shut and covered her head with her arms, waiting to drop to her death.

But nothing happened. The truck steadied.

Inge peeked. Had they gotten away with it?

A mustachioed guard from the second truck shouted in, "No one move. We're going to attach a cable and winch you back onto the bridge."

"Please, be quick," said Inge.

He glared. "Who the hell do you think you are to—"

Beside Inge, the tall guard shouted, "Get the darn cable, you fool!"

The mustachioed guard disappeared.

Inge turned to the other women. "It's going to be okay. Just stay still so we don't unbalance the truck."

The wall underneath the vehicle crunched and the truck jolted. Everybody gasped as it teetered on the precipice. It rocked back and forth. Back and forth. Back and forth...

Whimpering and terrified looks filled the cargo bay as no one dared to move, frozen in place as if encased in ice.

The truck tipped forward. Everyone gasped, faces bleeding horror. Inge prayed the vehicle would right itself again.

But instead of tipping back, the vehicle tipped farther and farther...

The women screamed as the truck plummeted off the side of the bridge. It nosedived through the air and hammered into the ice, hurling the women against the front wall of the cargo area in a gigantic tangle of arms and legs.

71

Inge gazed up from the knotted mass of limbs, but all she could see was a rectangle of stars over the tailgate. Beneath her, women struggled, some pleading, others praying, most wailing.

Lunging for the side of the truck, Inge grabbed one of the supports, which would normally be vertical but was now almost horizontal. Someone underneath her screamed.

"Sorry." Inge heaved to the side using her arms, striving not to kick anyone. As if climbing wall bars, she clawed her way up the side of the truck to the tailgate. She slung a leg over and hauled herself up. Gasping, she lay clinging to the tailgate as if she might somehow fall.

Finally daring to move, she glanced over the edge. The truck had nosedived into the ice and now stood like a leaning tower.

Someone shouted from above.

Inge peered up. Way up.

Twenty-odd feet above her, faces and flashlights peered over the side of the bridge.

Inge cupped her face. Help was too far. If they wanted to live, they had to save themselves.

Other than the wailing coming from inside, pounding and a desperate German voice shouted from the front of the truck — the driver was alive. Inge leaned out over the side, gripping the tailgate with one hand. Partly submerged, the cab was locked solid in the ice, the door wedged shut, the hood below the surface.

A hand clawed her foot.

She yanked herself back.

The guard reached up, his face bloody. "Help me. Please."

Inge grabbed the man's arm and heaved. A woman shrieked as he stamped on her to escape the grotesque monster of flailing limbs. Inge pulled him up to join her on the tailgate.

More hands reached.

Inge stretched down. "I'll get this one. Can you manage that one?"

She nodded to a woman closer to the guard. But he didn't lean down to help. He threw his legs over the other side of the tailgate.

"What are you doing?" Inge stared in disbelief.

He sneered at her, then leaped down and bolted for the riverbank. But a loud cracking came from the ice, the truck having damaged its integrity. He dashed over treacherous surface, but a sheet of ice tilted. Shrieking, he slid down and plunged into the black water.

Flashlights from the bridge scanned the river. Inge clutched her mouth as the guard clawed at the ice from underneath, screaming a scream no one would ever hear, before the current dragged him away. In seconds, he was gone.

Oh dear Lord, how were they going to escape?

Above, a man in a fur hat shouted, "Catch this." He slung a rope down.

Inge snagged it as more women dragged themselves from the monstrous mass of limbs.

"Greta!" Inge hauled her friend up and offered her the rope. "You go."

Greta clutched it and started to climb while Inge helped the next woman onto the tailgate.

"Inge!"

Inge looked up. Greta had stopped less than halfway to safety. "Go, Greta. Climb."

"I'm slipping."

"Keep going."

"I—" Greta screamed and slid backward, then fell. She hammered into one of the women who'd only just reached the tailgate, and they sprawled across it.

Inge grabbed them to save them from dropping to the ice.

Fur Hat shouted, "Someone else try."

"It won't work," said Inge. Healthy women would struggle to climb the rope, so half-starved women who'd been worked like slaves... "We need something else."

Beside Fur Hat, one of the guards spoke on a portable radio. He'd be contacting the camp, but how long would it take for help to arrive? Inge pictured the terror on the guard's face as the current dragged him under the ice. They needed saving now. Right now. Any

272

second, the ice could give and the black waters would swallow the truck to eat them all alive.

A moment later, Fur Hat and a man with a bushy beard grappled with a wooden ladder. They lowered it over the edge of the bridge and swung it toward Inge.

Inge and Greta dragged it over and propped the base on the tailgate.

Greta said, "You go first."

Inge shook her head. "I'm stronger than all of you. Get up there, Greta."

Greta climbed as Inge leaned down to help another woman up.

The second there was enough space behind Greta, another woman started climbing, then another.

With three women climbing, a fourth joined at the bottom. While helping up others, Inge checked over her shoulder. Finally, Greta reached the top, where hands pulled her to safety. This was going to work.

The next woman reached the top. And the next. More women hauled themselves to the sanctuary of the bridge.

Inge smiled. This really was going to work.

But the ice groaned. The truck jerked a few inches to one side.

Inge clutched the tailgate. The women on the ladder screamed, knuckles white as they clung on, the lowest one hugging it with both arms.

"Hurry!" shouted Fur Hat. "Before it gives."

The women climbed again.

More women hauled themselves to the tailgate, each bloodied, battered, and bruised, having been lower in the crush of bodies.

One tiny woman couldn't move her right arm, so Inge helped her onto the ladder. "Don't hold the side, curl your arm around the back so you can anchor yourself as you climb. Okay?"

Broken Arm nodded and started climbing, following a woman with big ears.

But the ice cracked again. And the truck jolted.

Big Ears screamed. She fell and smashed into Broken Arm. The pair crashed into the bottom of the truck again.

Fur Hat beckoned. "Hurry! Hurry!"

The last few women climbed onto the ladder, including Big Ears, who'd made it out a second time.

Inge gazed into the depths of the cargo area, at the women lying in a tangled, unmoving heap, Broken Arm among them. Inge didn't want to risk going down there — if the ice gave, she'd have no chance of getting out before the truck submerged — but the world had lost enough mothers, daughters, and sisters. She would not leave anyone behind who could be saved.

Her heart hammered as she clambered into the gloomy interior. She muttered, "Please hold. Please hold."

In the bottom, she strained to hear breathing, to see billowing breath, to discover life...

Something banged from below. She jumped. What the...?

She lugged motionless bodies aside. The driver pounded on the small window in the back of the cab. "Get me out!"

His face twisted with terror, he didn't look much older than she was.

She shouted up, "Flashlight!"

A beam of light corkscrewed through the blackness as a flashlight hurtled down and landed nearby. Inge grabbed it and shone light around the back of the cab. There had to be an access panel.

The truck jolted again. And dropped.

He banged on the glass. "Help me. Please! My foot's trapped."

"I'm trying."

There was no access and the window was way too narrow to climb through. She shone the flashlight into the cab. Water had already engulfed the dash. If he didn't drown, the cold would kill him before help arrived.

"Please." His eyes begged.

Again, she scoured the wall, praying for a hatch.

Nothing.

The water rose about him.

"I'm sorry." Tears welled in her eyes. "I'm so sorry."

Instead of screaming or cursing or praying, he gazed at her. Peaceful. And water swirled in around him. He pressed his hand against the glass, as if needing to connect — to feel another human being close by as his life ebbed away.

She placed her hand over his and stared into his face. "I won't leave you."

The ice creaked and the truck dropped again. Water engulfed him.

274

His hand dropped from the other side of glass. For a moment, Inge gazed into the flooded cab. No one should die alone, in such fear, so thank heaven she'd been there for him.

Someone calling her name dragged her back to the moment. How long they'd been shouting, she'd no idea.

"Inge! Inge, please!"

Greta.

Inge scrambled out of the pile of death and climbed to the tailgate. High above, Greta beckoned. "Quickly!"

Inge grabbed the ladder and climbed onto the first rung.

A huge crunching sound sliced through the air, and the truck jerked left. Dislodged, the ladder toppled sideways.

Inge fell.

She smashed into the ice and skidded across the frozen surface.

Lying on her side, Inge peered through fluttering eyelids.

Light beams cut through a blur of grays and blacks.

She shook her head but winced as pain enveloped her. She touched her forehead. Warm and wet. Her hand glistened red.

What was happening? Where was she?

Focus returning, she peered about. A ladder lay nearby, a jagged splintered crack in one side. Shouts drew her attention. People leaned over a bridge. Calling her.

The bridge. The crash. *The ice...*

Oh dear Lord, she had to get off the ice.

Grimacing, she rolled over to push up, but the ice tipped backward underneath her, and she slid toward the dark waters.

She gasped and splayed out, jamming her feet against edge of the adjoining ice sheet to stop her sliding.

The ice stabilized, but...

She was trapped.

If she moved, she'd slide into the abyss and never be seen again. How could she escape if she couldn't move? She was dead.

"Inge!"

She clutched her mouth. That voice. She twisted around. Smiled. Like the driver, at least she wouldn't die alone. "Rudi!"

Rudi shouted from the bridge, "Don't move. I'm coming."

"No!" She thrust her hands toward him. "It's too dangerous."

Gripping a rope with gloves, he jumped off the bridge. He slid through the air and landed on the surface.

"Stay back, Rudi. It's all broken."

Reaching out his foot, he tested the ice. When it held, he shuffled toward her.

"It's okay, Inge. I'm here." He tested another step. Safe. He moved again. "Can you move at all?"

"Maybe." If she was really careful.

He removed his gloves, slung the rope around his back, and tied it in front of his chest. He shouted up, "Be ready, Baumann."

"Ready when you are." Baumann crowded the top with other SS.

Rudi tested the ice once more. Stable. He shuffled nearer.

Inge smiled. He was going to save her.

But when he next pushed his foot down, the ice sank. He was twelve feet away. Way too far to reach her.

He poked the ice again, as if to test if he could run across it.

"Don't. Please." She shook her head. She was going to die here, but there was no reason he had to. Especially not for her.

He held up a palm. "Don't move."

"Do you really think you need to say that?"

He smiled. "Trust me. Baumann's got me, and I've got you."

She smiled back. "I trust you."

But instead of moving toward her, he backed away

Her face twisted at the horror of dying alone.

Rudi said, "I'm not leaving you, don't panic."

He retrieved the broken ladder and slid it over the fractured ice toward her. "Hold the ladder and I'll pull you over."

That could work.

Moving slowly to avoid shifting her weight too much, she reached for the bottom rung but couldn't hold on. "My hands are too cold. I can't grip."

"Okay, we'll try something else."

He slid more of the ladder over so it rested alongside her. "Can you roll onto it?"

"If I move, I'll slide in."

"Roll as fast as you can. Trust me, I've got you."

"I can't."

"You can. Listen to me — on three."

She was going to die. She was going to slide into the freezing water and never be seen again. Her face twisted in anguish.

"Inge, trust me. On three."

276

She nodded. It was her only hope.

"One ... two ... three."

She rolled onto the ladder. And it held. She gasped with relief. Rudi really was going to save her.

Rudi hauled the ladder toward him, straining to prevent it from tilting upward under her weight as the ice shifted beneath her.

Inch by inch, she drew closer and closer to safety.

But the wood crunched and the cracked side broke apart. Stability compromised, the ladder twisted. Inge tipped sideways. She grabbed at the rungs to hold on, but her fingers fell away.

The ice opened up.

Black water beckoned.

And Inge disappeared into the icy darkness.

The last thing she saw was the complete horror in Rudi's eyes.

She sank into the biting cold — so cold it was like her whole body was on fire. The shock made her gasp. She didn't want to but couldn't prevent it.

Choking, she flailed, beating at the ice imprisoning her as the current dragged her away from the light, away from her life.

A few miles downstream, the river joined the Gulf of Finland. No one would ever see her again. This was the end.

But something grabbed her wrist.

From behind, it encircled her chest and clamped about her.

Suddenly, she wasn't being dragged forward by the current but hauled backward by this guardian angel.

A moment later, she burst through the surface, coughing and spluttering. Her angel dragged her across the ice and up into the air, dangling her like a broken marionette.

"I told you I'd got you," said Rudi.

72

A blanket draped around him, Rudi closed Inge in the living room and showed Baumann out.

Baumann said, "Keep her warm to raise her core temperature, and if she exhibits any confusion, slurred speech—"

"Fetch you. I remember. Thanks, Klaus."

"You're sure it's wise to keep her here tonight and not the infirmary?"

"Where is she more likely to develop hypothermia?"

Baumann nodded. "The infirmary might be cold, but there's a lot of talk about what happened today."

Rudi shrugged. "So?"

"So some of the men are questioning why you risked your life to save a Jew but let one of our own drown in the cab."

"Blask was already dead."

"You didn't know that at the time."

Rudi pointed to the living room. "She could have been the first to climb to safety, but instead, she risked her life to save fourteen prisoners and then went back to save Blask."

Baumann held up his hands. "Hey, I'm with you, but some of the men?" He grimaced. "All they see is a live Jew and a dead German."

"They can see what the devil they like. I'm commandant here."

Baumann rubbed his brow. "About that..." He winced.

"If you've something to say it, say it."

Baumann shook his head. "It's Kloser. I think he's coming back."

Rudi's eyes widened. "What?"

"I received his medical file today. Why else would I need that if it wasn't to continue any ongoing treatment? I was going to discuss it with you after roll call, but then, all this happened."

"When's he arriving?"

278

"I don't know."

"I thought they'd taken his hand?"

"They did, but he's always been angling for a prestigious posting, hasn't he? My guess is he sees this not as an opportunity to be discharged but as a stepping stone to something bigger and better. It's not like he needs two hands to strut about barking orders, is it?"

Rudi stared into space. All his improvements would be overturned. But it wasn't productivity or prisoner well-being he was concerned about.

Inge.

She'd become just another prisoner, and he'd become just another SS officer. Separated. Isolated. Alone.

Baumann said, "So you haven't received any notification?"

Rudi shook his head. Inge. What was he going to do about Inge?

"It might not happen, but you need to prepare for it," said Baumann "Both of you."

Rudi stared at the wall. What was he going to do?

"Rudi?"

It was the end for them.

Baumann touched Rudi's arm. "Rudi?"

He looked.

"She doesn't know Kloser. You need to prepare her, or with her attitude, she'll be in the Box within a week."

"Yes." He patted Baumann's shoulder. "Thanks, Klaus."

Baumann left, and Rudi drew a couple of breaths to compose himself, then ambled into the living room.

Inge shivered, sitting on the floor in front of the coal fire. She shuffled closer to the heat, cupping a mug of steaming cocoa, a brown blanket around her shoulders.

"Any warmer?" he asked.

She nodded and held up her mug. "You know, it was almost worth dying for."

He smirked. "I've had cheap dates, but cocoa?"

She smiled as he stood over her. "So it's official now, is it? I'm your 'date?' We're a 'thing?' And that's why you rescued me?"

He sat beside her and stared at the dancing flames. Yes, they were definitely a "thing," and yes, it was definitely official. At the Totenkopf training camp in Dachau, he'd undertaken all manner of drills and acquired all kinds of skills, but diving into a frozen river to save a

Jewish prisoner from drowning? For some reason, Himmler hadn't put that top of the SS curriculum. If anyone had harbored doubts that he and Inge were in a relationship, they wouldn't any longer.

He shrugged. "You helped save fifteen prisoners. You deserved to be rescued."

"That's your story, is it?"

"As far as the men are concerned."

"And as far as Heinz Rudolf Kruse is concerned?"

Bathed in firelight, he gazed into her eyes. Her wondrous amber eyes. Eyes that he might soon never again see without a kapo beside her or barbed wire separating them. Clawing emptiness raked at his stomach as he felt her being dragged from his life. He couldn't let it end like this.

Rudi said, "May I kiss you?"

She laughed.

His expression fell. "Oh, great way to kill the moment. The thought of me kissing you is that funny, is it?

"*It* isn't, but the situation is, don't you think? I mean, in the history of the world, that must be the first time a captor has asked so politely to abuse his captive."

"Abuse?" He turned away, his gut hurting like he'd been battered with a rifle stock, the moment not just gone but butchered, burned, and buried in a pit.

She spun him by his shoulder and lunged.

Their lips met. Her tongue caressed his as he cocooned her in his arms. He sank backward to the floor, and they pressed together as if it was impossible to get close enough. Her breasts squashed against his chest, her fingers clawed his shoulders. She was warm. Inviting. Wrong. Oh, so wrong. And yet... so unbelievably right. Like the right key slotting into the right lock.

Their tongues danced. Velvety. Enveloping. Yielding. Like drowning in melted chocolate. Her fingers raked his hair, and he brushed her cheek and down her slender throat with his fingertips. Slowly. So tantalizingly slowly it could take a lifetime to explore her whole body.

Their embrace stretched for an eternity, yet when they separated, it was the same minute of the same hour of the same day. The laws of physics would have deemed it impossible that so much had happened in such a short time, and yet, there it was.

The back of his head on the floor, he smiled up at her.

Inge rested on her elbow beside him. She winked. "Next time, don't ask, just do it."

"Okay."

She trailed a finger over his chest, eyes fixed on her movements. "You know, Scharführer Baumann said it's vital I raise my core body temperature."

"It is. That's why I want you here tonight, where it's warm."

"Here where?"

"In my bed."

"But where will you sleep?" For a moment, she flicked her gaze to his.

He tipped his head backward. "On the sofa."

"Do you have to?" She flicked her gaze up again.

"Where else am I going to sleep?"

She didn't say anything, just burned those amber eyes into him. God, how he wanted to carry her upstairs and throw her onto his bed. But he pulled away. "No... Just no."

Confusion flashed across her face. They'd just kissed for the first time, yet now he was pushing her away. He could see how that would be perplexing, but how could he do anything else?

Her chin trembled. "Why not?"

"I just can't."

"Because I'm a Jew. A filthy, deceitful Jew. Just say it."

"No." He took her hand. "Inge, I could never think of you like that."

She snatched her hand away. "Then why don't you want me?"

"I do. But not like this. Not when I'm an SS officer and you're a prisoner. It wouldn't feel right. Like I'm exerting my control over you."

"You wouldn't be a guard raping a captive, you'd be a man making love to a woman."

"No." He shook his head over and over, as if saying the word wasn't enough. "I can't. Believe me, I want to – oh God, do I want to – but I can't. Not like this. Not until you can give yourself as a free woman instead of a glorified slave."

"The war could go on for years, so we might never be together."

"I've been thinking about that. Maybe we don't have to wait for the war to end."

She frowned. "What?"

Aside from his mother, Rudi couldn't imagine diving into a frozen river to save anyone other than Inge. That connection overwhelmed everything else, even his commitment to the Reich.

He said, "We have to escape."

"We? You can go anytime you like. It's me who's the prisoner."

"I'm an SS officer. If I 'go' anywhere, it's desertion. I'll be court-martialed and shot. Hell, they're even guillotining deserters in Berlin."

"So what are we going to do?"

"How do you feel about dying again?"

73

Rudi strode along a track toward a frozen lake glistening in the sunshine, a group of men working on the ice at the far side. Nearby, a man with a hooked pole guided a block of ice along a channel cut in the surface. At the shore, he shoved the block onto a wood-framed conveyor belt, which transported it up the bank and into a wooden building surrounded by trees. Huskies barked in an adjoining enclosure.

Rudi said, "Excuse me, I'm looking for Peeter Erm, please." Baumann had described the man as a redhead, but everyone was wearing hats.

The man pointed. "Fur hat on the sled."

"Thank you."

Rudi marched across the lake toward two men pulling a wooden sled over the ice. Inside a frame on the sled, what looked like a car engine powered a vertical circular saw that ate through the ice. Behind them, others pried apart cut blocks to make smaller, more manageable ones that bobbed in the water.

Desertion went against everything Rudi believed in: loyalty, honor, and justice. But there was no honor in working innocent people to death. Even before Inge, he'd questioned what was happening, but now? She'd changed everything. Unfortunately, he couldn't save the whole camp, but he could save her. Maybe...

The problem was that they couldn't just escape. A commandant deserting with a prisoner would be so abhorrent to the Reich — to the Führer himself — and set such a dangerous precedent that there would be nowhere to hide. He and Inge would be hunted down, dragged to Berlin, and guillotined before the largest audience imaginable. Maybe even on television.

No, escape wasn't enough. They had to disappear. Literally. There was only one way to achieve that — they both had to die.

The man with the fur hat using the sled noticed Rudi approaching and called for someone to take his place.

Rudi asked, "Peeter Erm?"

The man nodded. "Can I help you?"

"I need to hire you and your team."

Thirty minutes later, Rudi stood on the bridge with Peeter. Below, the truck sat wedged in the ice, leaning sharply.

Rudi said, "We tried to winch it out, but it's frozen solid."

Peeter nodded. "We can cut it free and ease it around to give you a better angle for your winch. When do you need it done?"

"The sooner the better."

Peeter clicked his tongue. "With all my best workers conscripted, business is—"

Rudi offered folded banknotes. "Today would be ideal."

Peeter plucked the bills. "My men will be on it by lunchtime."

"Great."

Rudi stared at the ice. It looked so solid. Impenetrable. Imprisoning. "How easy would it be to keep the hole from freezing over afterward?"

"If you're hoping to dredge for the man you lost, I'm sorry, but he's gone. It's possible the body caught on a sunken branch." Peeter pointed into the distance. "But it's more likely that it washed out into the Gulf, and that's frozen so solid you could walk all the way to Finland, so..." Peeter winced.

"No, it's not for dredging."

"If it's ice fishing you're wanting, I know a—"

Rudi held his hands up. "No, I just want a hole."

"Okay. That's doable."

"Also..." Rudi gestured for Peeter to follow. They strode across the bridge and Rudi pointed to the other side of the river. "I want a hole cut there, too."

"In line with the willow?"

Rudi nodded. "And with the other hole. Say, six feet across."

"Kept free of ice, too?"

Rudi nodded again. And offered another bundle of banknotes. "Everyone knows about the truck, but keeping the holes clear is just between us. Okay?"

Peeter glanced at the amount, then pocketed the money. "I'll clear them myself every evening once it's dark."

Rudi gazed at the frozen river. His idea was crazy. Totally insane. But in an insane world, sanity was only going to get them killed. This was their only chance. And though there was a slim possibility that it would work, the odds were it would end them both.

Back at camp, Rudi parked the car and ambled toward the administration block but stopped dead.

He stared into the compound, mouth agape.

Oh, dear Lord, it was true.

He stumbled into the virtually deserted compound, the prisoners undertaking their day's work. Gruber pointed at Barracks 03, and Kloser shook his head. Kloser's driver, Spengler, trailed along behind them like a military lap dog.

"Kommandant Kloser!" Rudi smiled. "I can't tell you what a joy it is to see you. And looking so healthy, too."

Kloser threw his arms up, his left hand replaced by a steel hook that glinted in the sun. "What have you done, Oberscharführer?"

Oberscharführer – Rudi's old rank. Instantly, he fell from being in complete control of the camp to being a tiny cog in a massive war machine.

"Productivity has increased by twenty-eight percent. As for—"

Kloser held up his palm. "Rudi, please, don't embarrass yourself. Unterscharführer Gruber has already apprised me of the 'improvements' you've made. What were you thinking? Winter coats is one thing, but heating fuel, transport to work, extra bread...? I trusted my camp to you, and look what you've done to it."

"With respect, Herr Kommandant, Unterscharführer Gruber doesn't have access to the figures on the increased income we're generating, all of which feeds back to Berlin to fund our war effort."

"Talk figures all you want, Rudi, but here's the only one I'm interested in — why are two of my men dead?"

"That was an unfortunate road accident that happened because—"

"Because you were transporting prisoners to work like a taxi service. Whatever possessed you?"

Rudi gestured to the administration block for his ledgers to save him. "If you'll come to my office, the ledgers will show—"

"*Your* office?"

A stupid slip. But if Kloser wouldn't listen to reason, wouldn't look at the ledgers, Rudi had no defense. He lost his train of thought. "I... uh..."

"What I want is an explanation for why sixteen women survived that frozen river with not a single one developing so much as the sniffles, yet we lost two brave warriors."

Rudi gulped. Saving Inge had been all that mattered. "I..."

Kloser said, "I've heard about your Jewess. The men think you're bewitched."

Gruber smirked. This had to be his wish come true.

"Herr Kommandant, everything I've done has been for the benefit of the Reich."

Kloser heaved a breath. "If that's the case, what's going wrong? Why are Jews thriving here?"

"Herr Kommandant, the ledgers will prove—"

"The ledgers, the ledgers..." Kloser shook his head. "You know, I had an unterscharführer in '39 — Mathias Lob. I tell you, you've never seen a sharper eye with a rifle." He winced. "But he just couldn't think straight when it came to the Jewish Question, so I had no choice but to have him reposted. I hear he fell at Stalingrad. And once word spread he was a Jewish sympathizer, his parents suffered an unfortunate accident, too."

Rudi said nothing, his heart racing like a machine gun firing.

"Your parents still alive, Rudi?"

"My mother."

"Well, fingers crossed she sees out the war with you." Kloser patted Rudi on the shoulder. He walked away but turned. "My wife is in Reval till next Tuesday, then she'll be overseeing the refitting of our house after you let your little whore befoul it. In the meantime, have Six scrub it clean. And try not to screw anything else up before we return."

Elena was still struggling. "Six had to have part of her leg amputated and almost died from infection."

"So...?"

"So she's unfit for strenuous labor."

"Unfit? Can you hear yourself, Rudi?" Kloser shook his head. "This is worse than I thought. Look, Six is the only prisoner my wife trusts. Can the woman crawl?"

"I imagine so."

"Then she can clean. See it's done."

"Yes, Herr Kommandant."

Kloser waddled away.

286

Over his shoulder, Kloser said, "If there's any emergency, I'll be at the hotel in town until Tuesday."

Four days. Then Rudi would be back in the general accommodation and Inge would be back in her work detail. Four days. Could he pull everything together in such a short time? If he got the tiniest detail wrong, he'd kill both of them.

However, before telling Inge his plan, he had to test it himself. If he actually had the courage to go through with something so crazy...

74

Cloud shrouding the moon, Rudi gazed into the distance from the bridge. If he screwed this up, he'd drown, be dragged out to sea, and rot in the murky depths. And no one would ever know. But he had to try if he hoped to save Inge.

Below lay the ice, a wall of impenetrable death. Almost.

All that remained of the accident was a jagged hole, its surface a slushy mess in the process of refreezing. Rudi crossed the bridge, a bag slung over his shoulder. In the gloom on the other side, a black rectangle lay opposite the willow on the bank. He shivered. Crazy. So crazy.

He strode to the willow, took a rope from his bag, and stepped onto the ice. Solid.

He walked to the rectangle and peered in. Blackness swirled away into oblivion. "Oh, dear God."

Crazy!

At the far side of the bridge, the other hole was now just a sliver of darkness. His heart pounded and his legs shook. It was only around twenty yards from one hole to the other, yet it would be the longest twenty yards of his life.

He hammered a metal stake into the ice with a claw hammer and secured one end of the rope. Walking down the river, he unspooled the rope, which he'd knotted every foot, until he reached the crash site hole, then he turned around. His gaze followed the rope all the way back to the rectangular hole. He gulped. Twenty yards? It looked twenty miles.

As he'd figured, his rope was around fifteen feet too long. He made five large knots in it, three feet apart — five chances to cling to life if things went wrong.

Coiling the rope, he tottered back to the rectangle, shaking his head. So unbelievably crazy.

But what other choice did he have? He'd already struggled to imagine another plan and failed. Now, Kloser had given him just four days. They had no choice — this was their only chance, no matter how deadly it was.

In the shadows beneath the bridge, he undressed to his underwear and fastened a belt around his waist into which he wedged his hammer. Shaking, more from fear than cold, he scurried back to the rectangle.

Years ago, he'd trained in open water because his coach believed it built muscle and stamina faster than pool training, but Rudi had never swum outdoors in winter. And never under an impenetrable sheet of ice. He snorted. It was just asking to die.

But wasn't that the idea? The only way he and Inge were going to live was if they died.

His hands shaking, he unspooled the rope into the water and pulled on a pair of goggles. Finally, he sat on the rectangle's edge, dangling his legs in. Cold snatched his lower limbs so hard, he gritted his teeth to stop from screaming.

He drew three long, slow breaths to fill his lungs. This was going to hurt. Hurt so much.

"For Inge."

Holding the rope in both hands, he slid into the blackness.

The current dragged him under the ice.

Cold mauled him. Biting so hard, it was how he imagined it felt being electrocuted on the fence.

Rudi panicked as the crushing cold fought to squeeze the life from him, to force him to cry out, to breathe, to die. Every instinct screamed for him to haul himself back to safety, to the rectangle that had been so black but was now filled with a dim light — with life. But instinct didn't rule him.

For Inge.

Forcing his mind to calm, he let the rope slip through his hands.

The current pulled him farther and farther from the safety of the rectangle. Instead of fighting it, he kicked and flowed with the water toward the promise of a future.

He kicked harder. This was working.

He peered through the swirling darkness for the crash hole, but ahead was only murky gloom.

His lungs burned. It was too far. He wasn't going to make it.

Rudi kicked and kicked. He had to reach it. For Inge.

And as if God wanted to play a sick joke, the hole slid past above him.

Rudi lunged for it and snatched a fistful of air. But the current whipped him under the ice beyond the hole.

He was going to die. Die!

Grabbing feverishly, he caught one of the large knots. Saved.

But his frozen fingers couldn't grip. The knot slipped by, and he drifted farther into the blackness.

Another knot. He raked at it. Another slip. Deeper and deeper into oblivion.

He hit the third knot, gripped with all his might, and latched onto it. Fighting, he pulled his legs up to lock his feet around the very last knot.

His lungs screamed for air.

He heaved on the rope, pulling against the current with his hands, pushing with his feet. He reached the first knot. After repositioning his feet on the on the rope, he heaved again, the jagged patch of dim light so tantalizingly close.

Air. Air. Air!

Hauling himself toward the light, he reached out. He hooked a hand over the edge of the ice, kicked against the knots, and...

His face broke through the slush, and he heaved a breath like a baby greeting the world for the first time. Gasping, he pounded the claw hammer into the ice, the closest thing to an ice axe he could find. Inch by inch, he hoisted himself out of the water, then collapsed, gulping air.

On his hands and knees, he dragged himself to the sanctuary of the shadows under the bridge, shaking, lungs devouring air that never filled him.

He trembled as he pulled on his coat, then his trousers and boots. Finally, he grabbed a hot water bottle bound in a towel to keep it warm from his bag and shoved it inside his coat. He staggered to the hole.

He pulled out the rope and threaded the end through a heavy metal cog he'd found in their workshop to tie it on, but he fumbled, his fingers too cold to work. He breathed on them and tried again. The weight secured, he tossed it into the hole. The rope sank out of sight.

Hugging the bottle, he lurched up the bank toward the lonely track on which he'd parked the car. Shivering, exhausted, panting. But alive.

He chuckled. It worked. They were going to escape!

75

The front door of the commandant's house slammed. Inge spun to stare at the living room doorway.

Rudi staggered in, a blanket over his coat, and collapsed against the doorjamb. He shivered violently, face so pale it looked like all the blood had been drained from him.

Inge dashed over. "Oh my God, what's happened?"

Teeth chattering, he said, "I-I di-di-did it."

She helped him toward the fire. "Did what? Where have you been to get so cold?"

He smiled. "I di-did it."

She pushed the armchair to the fire and guided him into it, then ran to the kitchen. What the devil had he done?

She poured coffee, Rudi having asked her to keep a pot warmed, and dashed back. His hands shaking too much to hold the mug, she lifted it to his lips. "Careful, it's hot."

He slurped.

Inge said, "What the devil have you been doing?"

Again, he smiled. "I did i-it. It's going to w-work."

She shook her head and stood up. "Rudi, you're not making sense. I'm fetching Baumann."

"No!" He grabbed her hand, his like ice.

"Rudi, something's wrong. You're freezing cold and talking gibberish. You need a doctor." She yanked her hand, but he held it fast.

"We're g-going to es-escape."

She stopped dead. "What?"

He'd mentioned he had some crazy idea but hadn't expanded. How crazy was it to leave him in this state?

"Rudi, what have you done?" She rested his mug on the coffee table and rubbed his back to warm him.

Holding his palms to the fire, he grinned, the orangey glow bringing color back to his face. His shivering easing and teeth chattering less, he said, "I thought it was a crazy idea — that I'd die — but it works."

"I don't know what your definition of success is, but this isn't it. This looks like you almost killed yourself."

He nodded. "That's how we're going to do it? How we'll get away."

She frowned. "By killing ourselves?"

Suicide wasn't a solution she'd considered, and she was surprised a strong man like Rudi had.

He clasped her hand. "They'll never find us if we're dead."

"I'm fetching Baumann."

He clung on to her to stop her. "I don't mean we really kill ourselves. We just make everyone believe we have."

"You want us to fake our own deaths?"

He nodded.

"How?" She threw her hands up. He'd said it was crazy, not outright stupid.

He squeezed her hand. Tight. "Listen, you can't tell anyone any of this, okay?"

"Okay."

"I mean it, Inge. Promise me."

"Okay, I promise. Now how the devil do you think we can fake our deaths? You might be able to persuade Baumann to declare us dead, but any fool can hear a heartbeat or feel a pulse, so we'll never get away with it."

"We will if they can't find our bodies."

"So how will they know we're dead if they can't examine the bodies?"

He took his mug. "What happened to the guard who ran over the frozen river?"

"He died."

He sipped his coffee. "How do you know?"

"Because I saw him fall through the ice and be swept away."

"But you didn't actually see him die."

"I didn't have to."

"Exactly. Because you know there's no way he could've survived something like that." He smiled and took her hand again. "That's how we're going to do it — we're going to let them see us fall into the ice and drown, with our bodies swept out to sea."

292

She shook her head. "We can't survive being dragged out to sea."

"We won't be. There are two holes joined by a rope under the ice. They see us fall in one and assume we're dragged away, but we'll pull ourselves to the other hole and get out. And that's it — we're dead, so we've escaped."

"Pull ourselves to the other hole?"

He nodded.

"Under the ice?"

He nodded again.

"Seriously? How in the name of God are we supposed to do that?"

"I've done it."

"That's how you ended up in this state?"

Rudi cupped his coffee in both hands. "I had to prove it was possible."

Inge lurched up. "For you, maybe. But you're an Olympic-level swimmer." She patted her chest. "Stick me under a foot of ice, and you don't have to be a genius to work out what's going to happen."

"It's okay. You've got three full days to practice."

She held her head. "Three days? And here I am worrying." She glared at him. "Are you listening to yourself?"

"Inge, it's the only way. If we set foot outside this camp together, they'll have roadblocks across the region within an hour, every soldier from here to Berlin will have our photos, and the Gestapo will establish a division just to hunt us. We'd be lucky to last a day."

She waved her hands. "No, there must be another way."

"If we had more time, maybe. But think about it — a commandant running away with a Jew? It'll be the greatest insult ever to the Reich. They'll never stop looking for us. Never. There'll be nowhere we can hide. So they have to believe we're dead. It's the only way."

Inge held her head. What he was saying seemed reasonable. Except for swimming under a frozen river. The image of the guard being dragged beneath the ice haunted her.

She crouched before him and held both his hands. "Rudi, I want to be with you, but"— tears welled in her eyes —"I can't swim under ice. I'll drown."

He kissed her on the forehead. "Then we'll drown together."

76

As the sun struggled to clear the horizon, Inge shivered behind the commandant's house, wearing just her old dress. This was crazy.

She stared at the frozen surface in the old water butt Rudi had had brought around the previous night and filled through a hose from the kitchen.

Crazy!

Rudi smashed the ice with a hammer and offered his free hand. "Ready when you are."

Accepting his help, she stepped up three boxes to stand at the butt's rim. Chunks of ice bobbed in the dark water.

She pictured the blackness of the river, the imprisoning ice, and the cold that bit so hard it burned.

Her heart pounded at the horror awaiting her.

But Rudi was right — they'd be hunted forever unless everyone thought they were dead. She leaped.

Water splashed and she sank, the icy bitterness devouring her. Instinctively, she gasped, only for the burning cold to scorch her throat. She choked and choked and choked...

Pushing with her legs, she shot through the surface and grabbed the rim, spluttering.

Rudi said, "See, it wasn't that bad, was it?"

Coughing, she glared.

He patted her shoulder. "You'll get used to it, don't worry."

"Get"– cough –"used"– splutter –"to it?"

"You didn't think you were doing this only once, did you?"

"What?"

"Three times a day until we go."

She slapped the water, splashing him. "Three!"

294

He shrugged. "It's the only way you'll be ready."

"Can I get out yet?" She shook as the cold ate into her.

Rudi checked his watch. "Another twenty-eight seconds."

She glowered at him. Everything he was doing was for her, but boy, how she hated him in that moment.

"Time's up." He helped her climb out, draped her in a blanket, and guided her to the living room. She changed into her work dress while he fetched her coffee, then huddled before the fire.

"Three times a day." She shot him a sideways look.

"For a minute each time."

"And after all that, I'll be able to handle the river?"

He winced.

She frowned. "Then what's the point?"

"The butt is a pushover compared to the river, but it's the closest thing we've got for you to practice. You have to learn to resist that initial impulse to gasp when the cold hits you. Once you can, the rest will be easy."

"Easy? Because swimming under ice is a piece of cake."

"That's my job. You'll be tied to me and I'll be pulling us along with a rope. All you have to do is hold your breath."

She blew out her cheeks. "Okay, three times a day." Shivering, she leaned closer to the fire. "What if it doesn't work?"

"You mean if we drown?"

"No, I mean if they don't believe we died."

Rudi grimaced. "Yeah..."

"They'll never stop hunting us, will they?"

"A traitor escaping with a Jew?" He shook his head. "They'll want to make an example of us as a deterrent. Especially me."

"So we'll have to hide forever?"

Rudi stared away, stroking his chin. "You know, even if they don't believe we're dead, it might still work."

"How?"

"They'll know we'll never come out of hiding, so someone might use that to their advantage. For example, they could swear they'd captured and executed us to claim the all glory. That would be one heck of a career boost."

"Wouldn't they need our bodies as evidence?"

He shrugged. "We were burned in a car crash, blown apart in an explosion, lost at sea... take your pick."

"Could they get away with that?"

"If their story was convincing enough. And that would be great for us because the Reich would stop hunting us." He nodded, more to himself than her. "Yes, if we aren't reported dead, it might even be worth starting a rumor like that ourselves. Maybe about how Polish partisans found our frozen corpses shot to pieces in a ditch." He wagged his finger at her. "But you can't mention any of this to anyone."

"I know."

"I mean it."

"*I know.* I'm not stupid."

"Not even Greta."

Inge wouldn't go into detail, but she'd have to say something. She couldn't disappear without saying goodbye to her best friend. "Greta's like a sister. She wouldn't say anything."

"Really? Even when Gruber is flogging her?"

Inge's jaw dropped at the bloodcurdling screams in her mind.

He said, "I'm not saying you can't tell anyone to be mean, I'm saying it because anyone you tell, you're putting in danger. If Gruber gets one sniff that someone knows something, he'll flay them alive to get it out of them."

Rudi was right. Inge would find some pretext to hug Greta on their last day, and that would be it. "I won't say anything. But even if we make it under the ice, what then?"

She'd been so stunned on hearing his crazy plan, she hadn't questioned other parts of it.

He sighed. "Sweden."

Her eyes widened. It was a neutral country, so they could hide there, but it was impossible to reach. "That's hundreds of miles across the sea. How the devil are we going to get there? Or are you going to tell me you've bought a boat?"

"A boat would be no good — the entire Gulf is frozen from here to Finland."

She frowned. "The sea is frozen?"

"Solid."

"But you want to cross it anyway?"

He scratched his head. "I never had you pegged as such a pessimist."

"It's not pessimistic to worry about dying in an arctic wilderness."

"Don't worry, we're not walking."

296

She snorted. "And here I was looking forward to a bracing walk. So we're driving?"

"Nah-huh. There's no ice road, so it would be way too dangerous. If we broke down or a wheel lodged in a crack, we'd freeze within hours."

"So we can't walk, can't sail, and can't drive. Have you got a magic carpet?"

He chuckled. "Better."

"Better than a magic carpet?"

"It is if you love dogs."

"Dogs?"

77

Rudi spent the morning in the office. First, he phoned his mother and convinced her to visit her brother in Bern, Switzerland, the safest place he could get her. Next, as Inge was worried that if she escaped, Kloser might track down her family and punish them, Rudi retrieved her record and changed her surname, home town, the number of the transport on which she'd arrived, and the facility in which she'd first been held. From how Inge had described their arrival in Estonia, it was unlikely that any of her family were still alive, but it was best to play safe.

At lunchtime, he drove into town and posted a letter that would arrive in Bern after his mother did, essentially saying goodbye and apologizing that she could never go home. He then strode toward the bar the men liked.

His plan appeared feasible, but he was no expert. Luckily, he knew someone who was.

Near the bar, he ambled down a track. Huskies barked inside a wire mesh enclosure, luring a balding man from the nearby house, his ruddy cheeks glowing in the cold. The moment he saw Rudi, his face burst with joy. "Herr Oberscharführer, how wonderful to see you."

"Hello, Kaspar."

They shook hands, a genuine warmth in the man's grip.

Kaspar ushered Rudi into a large room with a living area at one side and a kitchen with dining area at the other. His wife stood with her back to them, chopping vegetables and dropping them into a pot.

"Lutsi," said Kaspar, "the vodka and two glasses, quick as you can."

Lutsi didn't look around. "It's barely one o'clock. The vodka stays where it is."

"Women..." Kaspar shrugged and showed Rudi to an armchair beside a log fire. "Lutsi, we have a special guest."

Lutsi said, "I don't care who—" As she turned, her face brightened. "Herr Oberscharführer! Kaspar, why didn't you say?"

She scurried over with glasses and a bottle of clear liquid.

"Please, call me Rudi."

She sat on the sofa beside her husband, smiling, while Kaspar poured the drinks.

Rudi said, "Only a small one, Kaspar. I still have work today."

"And a question, I'm guessing. Yes?"

"There is something, yes." Rudi glanced at Lutsi. "But maybe it would be wiser to talk in private outside."

Anyone who helped him with his plan could be in danger, so the fewer people involved, the better.

Lutsi said, "You talk. I feed dogs." Pulling a coat, she wandered out.

Kaspar said, "Before you say a word, let me to say this — when you saved my Darja, I promised you anything, anytime. This I remember. Today, you arrive unexpected, so I am thinking, '*Kaspar, this friend needs something, so whatever it is, if it is possible to do it, it is already done.*'" He clapped. "Now, you ask, so I can say 'yes' and everyone happy."

"This might sound like a strange question, but is it possible to cross the ice to Finland?"

"You mean me or someone like you?"

"Me."

Kaspar laughed. "No, you freeze to death." He touched Rudi's knee. "No offend."

Rudi smiled. "How about with sled dogs?"

Kaspar squinted at Rudi. "Is this Führer business or Rudi business?"

"My business."

"In that case, yes, is possible. I've done it a few times."

Rudi grinned. "I was hoping you'd say that."

"When you need to go?"

"Monday."

"Just you?"

Rudi held up two fingers.

"The other is heavy like you or...?"

"Smaller than Lutsi."

Kaspar nodded. "Then is good. We go." He raised his drink and they chinked glasses to seal the deal.

The neat vodka slid down Rudi's gullet like hot gravel, but it was the best drink he'd ever tasted because everything was falling into place — he was going to save Inge.

He said, "How long is the journey?"

Kaspar grimaced. "Weather is problem. Is around only forty-five miles but without good trail. My dogs run maybe six miles an hour, so if weather okay"— he wavered his hand —"seven, eight hours."

"Is it possible to cross at night?"

Kaspar sucked through his teeth. "Is dangerous in day because ice move, or maybe there is hole hiding under snow so no one sees ..." He arced his open hand in a diving motion. "Night? Is only for madman."

To fake their deaths, they needed darkness to conceal the subterfuge. So if they had to cross the sea by day, it meant holing up somewhere overnight. Other than finding a hiding spot, that wasn't a huge problem if everyone believed they were dead. Except, each minute they spent in this vicinity, they risked discovery. Not that the problems ended once they reached Finland — the country was aligned with Germany, leaving hundreds of miles of hostile territory to negotiate.

Kaspar must have sensed Rudi's anxiousness and patted Rudi's thigh. "The other who is smaller than Lutsi is woman, yes?"

Rudi nodded.

Kaspar wagged his finger. "Finland is not where you go. Is Sweden."

Rudi heaved a breath, then nodded again.

Kaspar leaned forward. "Me and Lutsi — twenty-nine years. The war took our sons, but you..." He smiled. "You gave us our daughter. I have friend in Finland. Maybe he help to Sweden go."

Rudi clasped Kaspar's shoulder. "You're a good man, Kaspar."

He shrugged. "I good to those who good to me. Now, what supplies you have?"

"What do we need?"

Kaspar waved his hands. "Never mind, I find. You have ice clothes?"

Rudi tugged his army-issue coat. "This is warm."

Kaspar laughed. "Is warm next to fire, yes. I bring reindeer skins."

"Thank you."

They chatted longer, Kaspar insisting Rudi take another bottle of vodka — Tilga '43 — then Rudi returned to camp. That night, after he'd witnessed Inge's third ice bath of the day, he ventured back to the bridge for his second practice session.

Before diving below the ice, he piled snow from the bank to beyond the rectangle hole, like a gently curving drift. He then marched to the crash hole. At river level, the rectangular hole was completely hidden, so anyone looking from here would see nothing that demanded investigation.

Rudi stripped under the bridge, then fished the rope out of the crash hole using a pole with a hook. He jumped in. The cold enveloped him, gnawing like starving rats at a corpse.

Despite being better prepared — both mentally and physically — and having the rope connecting the holes, hauling himself through the water was torturous. Finally, heaving himself out, he collapsed onto the ice, struggling for life like a beached whale.

Gasping, he lurched into the shadows, where he dressed and cuddled his hot water bottle. If it was so difficult to drag himself from one hole to the other, how the devil was he ever going to haul Inge?

78

The next morning, Inge wrung a cloth into a bucket of foamy water as she washed the kitchen windows. She cursed under her breath. She'd hoped physical exertion would be a distraction from Rudi's plan. It wasn't.

As if that wasn't bad enough, her period had come today — for the first time in months. It should have been a joyous event. Children. A family. A future. But how could it be? She'd probably only gotten one again because she was enjoying the luxury of decent meals with Rudi, while hundreds of women, including her best friend, starved only yards away. Joyous? What gave her the right to escape and live her life while everyone here faced slave labor and malnutrition, even death?

She slung the cloth into the bucket and water splashed out. She cried. How could she abandon everyone?

Rudi strolled in, focusing on fastening his tunic. "Have you done the butt yet?"

She bit her lip.

He said, "If you haven't, don't forget."

She snorted. Like he'd let her?

"Is something wrong?" Crouching, he smoothed her tears away with his fingertips. "If it's what you said about Kloser finding your family, it's taken care of. I've falsified the camp records, so no one will have a clue where you're even from, let alone who you're related to."

She cupped her face and whimpered.

"What is it, Inge? What's wrong?" he asked.

"What isn't wrong?"

He stroked her hair. "If it's the butt, I know that thing's horrible, but look on the bright side — we're getting out of here."

"We are. How about everyone else?" She glared at the floor.

"Hey." He squeezed her arm. She ignored him, so he tried again. "Hey."

She flicked her gaze up.

"If I could get everyone out, I would. But it's almost impossible for just the two of us, so..."

Tears streamed Inge's cheeks. "Can't we make room for Greta?"

He shook his head.

Inge said, "Apart from you, she's all I have left."

He took her hand. "I'm sorry."

She wiped her eyes. "How can I leave her in this hell?"

"The plan won't work with three."

"So we change the plan."

"Inge..."

She pulled her hand away. "No. We can't leave her behind."

"The plan only works for two. And if we don't go now, we never go."

She shook her head. "I'm not leaving Greta."

"Is that what she'd want? For you to sacrifice your one chance for her?"

"That's not the point." So what was? How could she argue with him when he was right?

"How would she feel if she discovered you could have escaped but didn't because of her?"

If Greta had a chance to escape, Inge would do all she could to ensure her friend grabbed that chance. She knew Greta would feel the same. But Greta wasn't the one escaping; it was her. And guilt gnawed at her like maggots at a dead dog.

Rudi cupped her cheek. "It's Sunday, so do the butt, then go back to the barracks and spend some time with Greta. Yes?"

Staring at the floor, she nodded.

He said, "Just don't say anything, okay?"

"I know. You've told me a million times."

Scowling, he marched away.

She rubbed her brow. It wasn't fair to take her feelings out on Rudi because he was risking everything to save her.

"Wait." She darted after him and grabbed his arm. "I'm sorry, I just..."

"Just what?"

"I know you're doing this for us, but"— she raked her fingers through her hair —"I'm abandoning everyone to run away and start

303

a new life while they suffer this hellhole." Tears welled again. "Do you know what I mean?"

He nodded. "Sometimes, when a soldier at the front loses a friend, they struggle with how they survived while their friend didn't. The guilt can be overwhelming."

"So how do they cope?"

"Some drink, some close themselves off, some fall apart—"

"All healthy choices, then?"

He cradled her in his arms. "And some get through it with the support of loved ones. Just like you will."

She sobbed against his shoulder. "But I can't bear to think of them here while I'm free."

He stroked her hair. "I know."

Rudi held her for a few minutes, soothing her with his embrace. Finally, she kissed his cheek. "Thank you."

"Look, I'm going to be preparing things in town for most of the day, so go see Greta."

"But I have to do the butt."

"Do it later. You don't only need to be physically prepared for the ice but mentally prepared too. If that means spending time with your friend, that's what you have to do. I'll send an escort to take you to your barracks, okay?"

"Okay."

"Spend as long as you like with her."

"You don't mind?" She'd have a lifetime to spend with him, but this could be her last chance to spend time with her best friend.

"Of course not." He kissed her on the forehead, then left.

Changing her clothes, Inge couldn't shake the image of the suffering that would return to the camp with Rudi gone. If only she could do something. Anything. No matter how small.

She froze. Maybe there was something.

She darted into the pantry and stared at three chocolate bars. She reached for them but pulled back. If she took them and was caught, she'd be flogged. Yes, but if she took them and wasn't caught...

She stuffed them into the remaining pocket in her striped dress, then eyed a pile of unopened packs of cigarettes. She grabbed three, shoved them into her coat pocket, and shot out before she lost her nerve.

The front door banged shut. That would be the escort.

In the kitchen, Inge clutched her mouth, queasiness churning her insides. Could she get away with this? Or should she dash back and return everything?

No, she had to be brave. If the roles were reversed, Greta would do all she could to ease Inge's life.

As meekly as possible, she left the house and was escorted to the compound. In the barracks, the women were washing, cleaning, and tidying — enjoying their usual "rest day" activities. Inge joined in, volunteering to fetch their weekly fuel ration, which was often one of the last jobs to be done as the women liked to complete their chores, then pamper themselves with a few hours of luxury by taking turns relaxing in front of the heat.

Inge retrieved the wheelbarrow outside, a piece of tarpaulin in it to shield any cargo from the elements, and trundled to the gate. She requested an escort to fetch the fuel ration, and a guard whose ears stuck out agreed.

Her heart hammered as they approached the storage room on the side of the SS accommodation block. As her escort would be overseeing proceedings, no one would scrutinize her returning trip, which provided opportunities. However, she didn't know this guard, so if she misjudged the situation, she'd be formally whipped. Especially as the protection Rudi's stature had afforded her had all but vanished with Kloser's impending return. But she had to try. Not just for Greta, but for all the women.

She wiped her palms on her coat as the guard unlocked the door.

The barrow halfway in, Inge gulped and set it down. Her hand shaking, she offered him a chocolate bar and a pack of cigarettes. "Could you wait outside?"

He snatched the bribe and turned his back. "You've got thirty seconds."

Inge shot inside.

Rows of sturdy wooden shelves stocked catering-size cans of food, sacks of vegetables, drums of cooking oil...

She heaved a sack of potatoes into the barrow, threw two sacks of coal on top, and covered everything with the tarpaulin. She scuttled out, stifling a smirk. Baked potatoes would be a wonderful treat for the women. It was a small gesture compared to her escaping to a new life, but even the tiniest boost could tip the balance from perishing in this nightmarish place to getting through another day.

Inge having been under escort, she waltzed through the gate without question. Unable to contain her joy any longer, she grinned.

In her barracks, she tipped the barrow next to their brick stove and the sacks fell onto the floor.

Marta said, "Three bags? What's going on?"

"See everyone gets their share. Burn the evidence." Inge headed for the door.

Marta pulled open the sacks. "Potatoes? We've got potatoes!"

Everyone raced over.

Inge tramped back to the gate. "I'm fetching the ration for Barracks 02 as well."

The big-eared guard eyed her suspiciously, then escorted her again. Her hands no longer sweaty, she repeated the process and hid another sack of potatoes under the ration of coal.

In Barracks 02, Inge upended the barrow beside the stove. "I've got you a present."

"Extra coal?" said a woman.

"Better."

The woman opened the bags. She thrust her hand into the air, clutching a potato. "Look what we've got!"

Prisoners swarmed, Greta among them.

Greta said, "You've done this?"

Inge nodded.

Greta flung her arms around her. Inge clung on. Tight. So tight. She'd never had the chance to say goodbye to her family, so she wasn't going to miss the opportunity this time.

Greta released her, but Inge still clung on, her eyes tearing.

Greta frowned. "What's wrong?"

Inge wiped her eyes. "Nothing. Forget it."

Greta guided her away from the commotion. "What is it?"

Inge ached to tell Greta, but she couldn't put her in danger. "I just wanted you to know how much you mean to me."

Greta gasped. "I knew it." She whispered, "He's getting you out, isn't he?"

"I-I..." If only she could tell the truth.

Greta hugged her again. Far, far tighter. "Whatever you're going to do, just do it. I don't want to know when, I don't want to know how. Just promise me you'll live for both of us."

Inge clung to Greta, tears streaming her cheeks.

Greta jerked Inge. "Promise me."

"I promise." Inge wiped her eyes. "I need to go. Give me ten minutes and I'll be back."

She left with her barrow.

At the gate, Big Ears squinted at her puffy eyes, maybe thinking she was being coerced into this stealing spree, but when she requested an escort for Barracks 01's fuel ration, he again agreed, and again accepted payment to look the other way.

Trundling back with potatoes and coal, Inge sniffled. Rudi had been right — Greta was such a good friend that her first thought hadn't been for the suffering she'd endure but the life Inge would enjoy. Inge smiled. Wherever she ended up, she'd find some way to monitor events at the camp to keep track of Greta, and if Inge could ever come out of hiding, they'd be reunited.

Inge pushed her barrow through the gate. This was her last trip, and once she'd delivered her present, she could enjoy a few hours with Greta.

Behind her, someone shouted, "Halt!"

She froze. Oh God, no.

"Come back here."

Oh dear Lord, she recognized that voice. Of all the people to stop her, it had to be him.

Inge stared at the barrow. Stealing food was a whipping offense. But if they discovered how much she'd stolen...

A gun cocked behind her. "Come back. Now."

Cringing, Inge turned, praying she wouldn't be asked to show the barrow's contents.

"You!" Gruber smirked, then beckoned her.

Inge gulped and trudged to the gate. Shaking before him, she clenched her fists and struggled to appear calm, to shrug this off as a silly mistake. But it was Gruber.

He said, "Why have you taken three barrows of supplies?"

Her gaze lowered, she said, "A fuel ration for each of the barracks, Herr Unterscharführer."

"You don't usually fetch the ration for all three barracks. Why are you today?"

"I finished my duties at the commandant's house, so I was trying to help out."

She flicked her gaze to the camp's vehicles — the car Rudi had been using recently was still missing. Sickness roiled in her stomach.

Gruber swaggered closer. "You've never fetched coal before, have you?"

"No, but I've fetched supplies for the commandant's household."

Gruber nodded. "Okay."

Oh, thank the Lord, he'd bought her excuse. She almost collapsed with relief. But she had to get away before he changed his mind. "Does that mean I'm dismissed, Herr Unterscharführer?"

"Yes—"

"Thank you, Herr—"

"— after you show me what's in the wheelbarrow."

Inge's jaw dropped.

Gruber rested his hand on his pistol's holster. "Now."

"Y-yes, Herr Unterscharführer."

She stumbled back. Oh God, oh God, oh God...

Rudi had said he'd be away most of the day, but she still stared at the road, praying to see him driving into camp. Nothing stirred.

Ahead, faces appeared at the barracks' windows.

Trembling, Inge heaved the barrow back to Gruber. Despite the tarpaulin, any fool could tell it contained way more than two sacks of coal.

Gruber glowered. He kicked the barrow. It toppled sideways, coal and potatoes spilling out.

He smiled. Over his shoulder, he said, "Fetch the Box!"

79

Big Ears didn't move. He stared at Inge. "The Box, Herr Unterscharführer? For *her*? Are you sure?"

Gruber scowled. "Are *you* sure you want to disobey a direct order?"

Big Ears clicked his heels. "I'll get it immediately, Herr Unterscharführer." He dashed away.

Inge gulped. What was the Box that Big Ears was so freaked? She glanced toward the road again. *Rudi, where are you?*

Gruber chuckled. "Look all you want, but he isn't around to save you. And a heinous crime like this will not go unpunished on my watch."

Trembling, Inge panted. Had she just doomed herself and Rudi? What could she do to put things right? She had to do something. Anything. Not for her benefit, but for Rudi. *Anything.* For Rudi.

She dropped to her knees at Gruber's feet. "I'm sorry, Herr Unterscharführer. I only wanted to help my friends, but I was so stupid. Please, forgive me, Unterscharführer Gruber."

She'd witnessed others plead with Nazis — it never ended well. But there was always a first time.

Gruber sneered. "You might have bewitched Oberscharführer Kruse, but your black arts won't work on me."

Big Ears scurried back carrying a wooden chest peppered with tiny holes.

This had brought her to her knees? Had her begging Gruber of all people? *This?* She cringed at the shame welling within her.

"Move." Gruber kicked her. She sprawled in the mucky slush.

Inge clambered up.

Carrying the Box, Big Ears led them to the roll call area.

Faces plastered the barracks' windows and women clustered in doorways, some crying, all horrified. Greta stood in tears. Inge shot her the barest smile. Why was everyone so upset? The Box was a joke. Let them shut her in it — they'd done worse to her. This was nothing. A few hours of discomfort, then she'd be warming herself beside the fire with Rudi again.

Big Ears set the Box down and opened the lid.

Gruber whipped Inge. "Coat off."

Inge glowered, removing her coat. The pathetic little man really thought he'd scored a victory. Really thought he mattered.

"I suppose you want me to get in there." She held his gaze. Defiant, daring, dangerous.

He chuckled again. "Oh, that's right, you weren't here under Kommandant Kloser, so you've never seen the Box."

Gruber was even more cocky than normal. She frowned. Could there more to the Box than there seemed? Like what? It was a box. What *more* could there be?

But she swallowed hard. Something felt off. Like she'd overlooked something obvious.

Smirking, Gruber patted the top of the Box. "This was made for an arrogant whore like you. Get in."

She glanced to the road. No sign of Rudi.

Gruber gestured to the guards. They grabbed her, hauled her to the Box, and stuffed her inside. The lid slammed shut, trapping her.

Her breath sharp rasps, Inge lay on her back, knees pulled up. She twisted to ensure there was nothing inside that could hurt her. Gruber had been too confident for this to be a mere box. Pinpricks of light sliced through the holes peppering each side, but not enough for her to see clearly. Imprisoned in the dark, she conjured all kinds of horrors in her mind — broken glass, rats, snakes, cockroaches...

Gingerly, she drifted her hands over the sides. Nothing cut her, nothing stung her, nothing scurried over her. A box. It was literally just a box. She slumped as relief swept over her.

It was staggering what fear of the unknown could do. Was that the punishment? What made the Box so scary? Now that the worst was over, she relaxed, hugging her arms about her chest. Without her coat, she'd freeze for a few hours, but like that was anything new.

Gruber said, "I'll take those."

Something scratched the top of the Box. An instant later, an almighty bang hit the wood.

Inge jumped. What the devil was that?

Eyes wide, her gaze shot around her prison.

Another bang. And another. Coming from directly above her face. She reached up. Smoothed her hand over the inner wall. Her fingertips brushed a tiny point. Was that new or had it always been there? She felt it again. Another bang and the point lengthened.

Inge gasped. A nail.

The pinpricks all about her — were they holes where nails had been driven in?

So not only was she to freeze, but they were going to pound in nails to make moving without spearing herself difficult. Difficult, but not impossible. Gruber was not going to beat her. Not today. Not ever.

The nail grew longer with each pound of the hammer. She ran her fingertips along its five-inch length.

Gruber pounded in another nail lower down, then one to her left. Each time she felt for the telltale vibrations revealing where the nail was entering. She needed to remember where they were so she didn't accidentally move and cut herself.

Gruber shifted sides and pounded again. Inge squeezed to her left until spikes pressed against her as a nail drove toward her shoulder. She twisted upward, but a point grazed her head. She winced.

Shuffling, she lifted so the new nail penetrated behind her, but then came the next.

Oh Lord, no.

Hammering started a few inches above the last one. Inge arched her back, but something pricked her side. She strained to bend away from the danger but was too restricted, and the next pound stabbed the nail's tip into her flesh. She bit her lip to stop from screaming.

Another pound and the nail drove deeper. Inge shrieked.

Gruber laughed. "Nothing smart to say anymore?"

He hit in another nail, then another, dotting so many around the Box it was impossible for Inge to keep track. She hunched into the smallest ball she could, visions of being skewered and bleeding to death haunting her.

The next nail entered under her right foot. Nails now stabbed through each of the walls imprisoning her and the top. Cringing, she waited for the next to pierce the darkness, but it didn't come.

Pain slicing her side, Inge gulped air. Thank the Lord that was over. The next few hours were going to hurt, but nothing she couldn't handle.

Gruber said, "Okay, stand it up."

Inge frowned. Stand what up?

Her prison tilted. She thrust her hands against the top as it rose onto one end. The repositioning moving her, she squealed as a nail raked her hip.

Gruber said, "You know what to do."

Big Ears said, "How long should we roll it, Herr Unterscharführer?"

Roll it? Inge clutched her mouth. If they rolled it, she'd fall onto the nails. They'd spear her over and over.

Gruber said, "Roll it till it's quiet."

Oh dear God, this was no punishment, it was a death sentence. She'd really thought she and Rudi would get away. Have a life. Have a family. How stupid. So unbelievably stupid.

She braced, hands and feet pressed against safe areas in the vain hope she could avoid falling onto the spikes.

Big Ears said, "Till it's quiet, Herr Unterscharführer?"

"Is there a problem, soldier?"

"No, Herr Unterscharführer."

Something grabbed the Box. It tilted left. Three giant spikes ached to tear her flesh.

Rudi. She was never going to see Rudi again.

The box tilted farther.

She screamed, "Rudi!"

Spikes gleamed in the gloom.

"Gruber!" The shout cut through the stillness, but it wasn't Rudi. "Stand down!"

"You'll get back to your infirmary, if you know what's good for you."

Baumann!

"Stand down, or so help me..."

The sound of Gruber's voice changed, as if he'd turned away from the Box. "So help you what, you tired old quack?"

"Who do you think you're addressing, Gruber?"

"Kommandant Kloser said—"

"Kommandant Kloser doesn't return to active duty for another two days. Until then, Kommandant Kruse is in charge, so when he's available, he'll set a reasonable punishment for any crime that's been committed."

Gruber's voice sounded more animal than human. "You Jew-loving—"

Baumann's voice lowered. "Go ahead, Gruber. See how quickly striking a superior gets you posted to the Front."

Silence.

Gruber grunted, and something slammed into the box. Inge squealed.

"Kick it again, Gruber, and you won't just be reposted, you'll be demoted."

Inge braced, but the box didn't budge.

Baumann said, "Now, open it."

Nothing happened.

"Now, Gruber."

"Okay."

"Okay what?"

"Okay, Herr Scharführer."

The front of the Box opened, light flooded in, and Inge tumbled out.

80

Inge curled up on the infirmary bed. Like a little girl watching her mother telling her father how naughty she'd been, she snuck glances at Baumann talking with Rudi near the entrance. Rudi looked shocked, but worse, he looked angry. So unbelievably angry.

The conversation appeared to end, so Inge smiled at him. She'd apologize, he'd forgive her, and everything would be fine. The darkest of glares made her wither like a flower in a bone-dry vase, then Rudi stormed out. Oh God, what had she done?

A few minutes later, he returned and marched over, face even darker. She cringed. Was he going to beat her? Scream at her? Transfer her?

She braced. After what she'd done, she deserved whatever he deemed fitting.

He stood beside the bed, but instead of looking at her, he glared at the wall. Voice icy calm, he said, "Can you walk?"

"I'm sorry, Rudi. I didn't mean to cause so much trouble."

"Can ... you ... walk?"

"Yes," she said. Baumann had stitched her side and hip, minor wounds considering what could have happened.

"Come with me."

Without looking at her, he stormed away. She scrambled after him.

Trailing in his wake through the compound and out the gate, she apologized over and over, but he ignored her.

At the house, he opened the door and she entered. He stomped in and slammed the door.

His icy calmness exploded. "What the hell were you thinking?"

"I've said I'm sorry. What more do you want me to say?"

"Sorry? You were this close"— he held a thumb and forefinger a fraction of an inch apart —"this close to being dumped in a mass grave."

"I couldn't just abandon everyone. I wanted to help."

"And did you?"

Gazing at the floor, she shrugged. "I think so."

"Really? Barracks 02 and 03 will receive no meals tomorrow because they accepted stolen food. Is that your idea of 'helping?'"

"*You* could give them food."

"No, I can't."

"Of course you can. You're the commandant."

"Not anymore." He stabbed a finger into her chest. "Because of you, I've had to relinquish control of the camp. All decisions now have to go through Kloser."

"Because of me?"

"The only way I could guarantee your safety for the next two days was to agree that Kloser will decide your punishment when he returns." He snorted. "And of course, Gruber loves that because Kloser invented the Box."

"But we'll be away before that." She touched his arm.

He jerked away. "And what if we aren't? What if there's a storm? An air raid? A thaw?"

Inge stared agape. She'd ruined everything. Everything. Even Rudi's feelings for her.

He squinted at her. "Don't you see?"

She sniffled. "See what?"

He gestured to the compound. "If Greta hadn't reached Baumann in time, you'd be dead."

"But I'm not."

He held up his thumb and forefinger again. "This close." His chin quivered and tears welled in his eyes.

She flung herself at him and enveloped him. Clinging, clinging, clinging. "I'm sorry, Rudi. So sorry."

He wrapped his arms around her. And sobbed.

His fingers clawed her back. "I can't lose you."

They stood in the hallway. Holding each other. Tight. So tight it felt like they might never be parted.

81

Rudi bowed his head. "I'm sincerely sorry about this, Elena."
Elena hobbled toward the pantry on crutches, her right leg missing below the knee. "Don't worry, Herr Kommandant, I know it's not your doing. If Inge can help me, we'll manage."

Splashing came from outside the kitchen window and Inge bobbed up in the butt.

Rudi said, "It's punishment. I had to give Gruber something."

Elena nodded and shoved a bucket along the floor to the sink with a crutch.

Rudi bent. "I'll get that for you."

She knocked his hand away. "You'll do nothing of the sort. You're in enough trouble because you've helped us, so I won't have someone catching you helping me."

She was right. He had to exude an authoritative air. For now.

"You're a good man, Herr Kommandant." She sighed. "I hope you know how much we appreciate all you've done."

"I... uh..." He shrugged. He could have done so much more. Maybe. Or if he'd tried, maybe he'd have been replaced already and things would be ten times worse.

Inge clambered out of the butt, shaking.

Elena clicked her tongue. "What are you waiting for? Fetch her a towel."

He chuckled. "Yes, ma'am."

As he helped Inge to the living room fire, he explained how she'd have to help Elena for the day and to remember to use the butt at least once more.

Inge checked over her shoulder, then whispered, "But we're leaving tonight."

"Look, I'm not going to sugarcoat this because you have to

understand — tonight is going to be brutal. Absolutely brutal."

She cupped his face. "But it will be okay because I'll be with you."

He ached to reassure her, to promise he'd keep her safe, but he couldn't. He'd only had time to practice swimming hole to hole three times. Each time, he'd believed he was going to die. *Believed.* And each time he'd swum under the ice alone, not hauling another person behind him.

But he couldn't tell her that.

He squeezed her hand, losing himself in those dark, dark amber eyes.

The morning in his office passed without incident, the highlight being a message from his mother that she'd arrived in Bern. In the afternoon, Rudi unlocked the metal door of the stone armory on the side of the SS accommodation block on the pretext of taking inventory. The camp needed weapons to guard the prisoners, but as Soviet forces were advancing on German-held territory, they now also had a small stock of arms with which to repel a minor incursion.

A rack of machine guns stood nearest the door, rifles hanging above it. Rudi moved to a shelving unit. Taking two extra clips for his pistol, he bypassed a shelf of land mines and opened a metal case on the rear wall — egg grenades. Under four inches long and only two wide, they were far more concealable than stick grenades, so ideal for a stealthy operation.

Rudi unscrewed the blue knob on the top one of the devices. He removed the protective cap and inserted a detonator, screwing in the fuse by hand before tightening it with a key. He armed another two. From the next case, he armed two grenades with red knobs. Blue knobs were ideal for combat, having a four-second delay, whereas reds, with only a one-second delay, were perfect for booby traps.

When initially considering their escape, he'd hoped there'd be no need for weapons, but as he'd pieced the plan together, he'd realized he might have to defend them, or at least cause a distraction. This selection gave him an edge.

He returned to his office, hiding his cache in his desk. The last thing he did before leaving that evening was to pocket the camp's funds from the safe. It wasn't a huge amount of money, but it would see them through a few months until they found work — if they made it.

At 7:45 p.m., leaving Hofmann in charge of the camp, Rudi, Baumann, and Gruber drove into town in the car Rudi had been using the last few days. He parked outside a hotel restaurant behind Kommandant Kloser's car.

As they strode for the entrance, Gruber stopped him. "May I speak, Herr Kommandant?"

Rudi resisted rolling his eyes. "It's a welcome meal for Kommandant Kloser, Gruber. Can't camp matters stay at the camp?"

"This is important."

He gestured for him to continue.

Gruber said, "I know we don't always see eye to eye, but I appreciate the way you dealt with the Box incident and that Jewess."

Rudi nodded. "That woman's been trouble since day one. It just took some of us a little longer than others to see that."

"Exactly. So, I wanted to commend you on letting Kommandant Kloser decide the final punishment. It takes a big man to acknowledge his mistakes."

"Thank you, Gruber." Rudi wanted to punch him but patted him on the shoulder instead.

Baumann raised his eyebrows but nodded approvingly.

Rudi slapped his forehead. "Oh, would you believe it, I've forgotten the vodka you like, Gruber."

"The Tilga?"

"Yes. I got a new bottle especially."

Gruber sucked through his teeth. "Pity. Still, they'll have something drinkable here."

Rudi backed away. "No, a special occasion calls for a special effort. I can be there and back in no time."

Baumann grabbed Rudi's arm. He leaned closer and whispered, "I don't know what's going on, but for God's sake, be careful."

"I will." He'd miss Baumann. If not for the war, they could have been good friends. "Thanks for everything, Klaus. Everything."

He meant over the years but knew Baumann would believe, for now, he was referring to saving Inge.

Baumann nodded.

Rudi eased the car around while watching his comrades enter the building. Once they were inside, he hit the brakes. He leaped out, stabbed his knife into both tires of the Kommandant's car on the side out of view from the hotel, then jumped back into his car. He hammered the gas and shot away.

On the return journey, he made two quick stops — one to sling a final bag of supplies into the hiding place he'd rented, and one to hook the rope out of the river and jam the heavy metal cog into the ice at the far side of the hole so the rope draped across it.

Back in the car, he floored the pedal.

At the house, Inge was biting her fingernails, sitting in her coat on the edge of the sofa like a bird perching on a wire. Teary eyes greeted him.

He rested a hand on her shoulder. "You can do this."

She said nothing. For probably the first time ever, she was lost for words. He hated torturing her like this, but he had no choice — this was their only chance.

"I need to speak with Elena. Give me a minute."

She nodded.

Elena was polishing the dining table, despite it already gleaming. "It's all done, Herr Kommandant, but we'll start first thing tomorrow to make doubly sure." She whispered, "Inge's in pieces. Probably over how Kommandant Kloser might punish her. Isn't there anything you can do?"

He sat. "Elena, I need to ask a favor."

"Anything for you, Herr Kommandant."

Exhaling loudly, he stared at the table. Could he trust Elena? Just because he'd been decent with her didn't mean she'd risk her life for him. And that was what he'd be asking.

She said, "I know something's going on."

"Excuse me?"

"Don't panic, I don't know what it is. But listen, you've been kinder to me — to everyone here — than I would ever have believed possible, so if you need something, just ask."

He shot her a sideways glance.

She patted his hand. "Ask."

"I..." He blew out his cheeks. "I need you to lie for me."

"Okay. And what would you like me to say?"

"I'm taking Inge away from here." He looked at Elena, expecting to see shock.

She gave a firm nod. "Good. So what can I do?"

His eyes widened. If everything went so smoothly, they were as good as in Sweden already. "Fifteen minutes after we leave, I need you to run outside screaming for help."

She patted her right leg and smirked. "Running might be a

problem, but nothing we can't get around. Anything else?"

He took a rope from his pocket. "You'll need rope burns on your wrists so it looks like you were tied up."

She held her arms toward him. "What do I tell the guards?"

"Just say I took Inge. They'll see she's missing and that the car is gone, so Hofmann will do the rest."

"Leave it to me."

"Thank you, Elena." He looped the rope around her wrists. "This will hurt."

She nodded. He yanked the rope from side to side, the fibers rubbing her flesh to leave red marks. Leaving her, he knotted the rope around a water pipe in the kitchen, as if he'd tied her there and she'd escaped. Finally, Rudi synchronized his watch with the carriage clock, which he gave to Elena.

In the living room doorway, he froze. Right this second, he'd done nothing he couldn't right. If he so chose, he could resume his life and have a promising career. But if he left the house with Inge... it was a death sentence for both.

His cap hung on the hook beside him, the silver skull emblem on the front symbolizing that the wearer was loyal to the death. Could he turn his back on his country, his duty, his future?

He ripped the emblem off and threw it on the floor. There was no honor in showing loyalty to a monstrous cause.

Rudi said, "It's time."

He held his hand out to Inge. Her fate was her own, and what he'd planned was unbelievably dangerous, so she had to choose this. No way could he force her, even if it was ultimately for her own benefit.

She tottered to him, face twisted. "I'm scared."

He cradled her in his arms. "I know. But I'll be with you. Ready?"

She nodded.

Elena hobbled in on crutches. Inge hugged her. "Thank you for everything."

"You've a good man, there. Take care of each other."

Rudi said, "Let me check outside."

While the compound lay bathed by security lights, gloom consumed his section of the camp. However, guards with dogs circled the perimeter between the two fences. If one saw Inge getting into the car, their escape would be doomed before it had even started.

Rudi peeked out. Clear.

320

He clicked the hallway light off so they could leave cloaked in darkness, then held the door open. "Remember, be quick, stay low."

Inge nodded.

"Good luck to both of you," said Elena.

Rudi ambled from the house and into the car. He started the engine, then pushed open the passenger door. A dark shape shot through the shadows and jumped in beside him, immediately ducking below the dashboard.

The steering wheel slippery in Rudi's hands, he wiped his palms on his coat one at a time. Rudi desperately wanted to floor the pedal and shoot away, but a roaring engine and tires spitting gravel would draw attention. The car crawled along the track.

Lights burned in the administration block's windows, where the night staff were monitoring the camp. Hofmann would be in there — he was vital to their escape.

Rudi gulped as he eased off the gas. This was the most dangerous part so far. He stopped the car. Leaving the engine running in case they had to run, Rudi got out, eyes fixed on the administration block. If someone saw him now, everything would go to hell.

His heart hammering, he crept over to the remaining camp vehicles and slashed the front and rear driver's-side tires of all the other vehicles. Staying low, he stole back to the car, scanning the administration block's windows and main door, praying no one would run out.

Back behind the wheel, he panted, then eased away again. The car pulled closer and closer to the freedom of the road. And finally, the tires rolled from crunching gravel to the paved surface. He accelerated away.

Inge slid up in her seat and shot him an anxious glance. He exhaled loudly. They'd made it over the first hurdle, but the worst was yet to come. However, as long as Elena played her part and Hofmann followed procedure, the plan had a chance of working. *If* Rudi and Inge could survive the ice.

82

Inge gripped the dash, her knuckles white as the car shot past silhouettes of trees and bushes. "Do we have to go so fast?"

Rudi's gaze drilled into the road. "Sorry, yes."

He could have had Elena wait thirty minutes, not fifteen, allowing them a leisurely drive into town. However, should Inge be discovered missing and the alarm raised early, they had to be in position.

The car's headlights illuminated the bridge ahead. Rudi gulped. This was where things got very, very real.

Inge cupped his hand on the wheel. "Can't we just keep going?"

"There'll be roadblocks across the region within an hour."

"We might beat them."

He shook his head. "After how we've made fools of so many people? They'll never stop until we're dead and strung up for everyone to see."

"So we could drive across the ice. Why wait and risk getting caught?"

"Sea ice isn't like a skating rink — there are cracks, ridges, holes... If a wheel got stuck, we'd die."

They hurtled on.

Rudi's heart pounded in his ears as they raced over the bridge, passing the section with the missing wall where the truck had gone over. Oh Lord... this was it!

Across the bridge, he said, "Hold on."

Inge braced, grimacing.

Clutching the wheel tighter, he hit the gas and swung the car around the bend onto the road to the excavation site. The tires squealed as they fought to maintain grip. But they lost their hold. The car skidded and the rear end swept around toward a drainage ditch running alongside the road.

Inge screamed.

The passenger-side rear wheel slid into the ditch, and the underside of the car thumped into the ground, jolting them. Finally, the car stopped dead.

"Are you okay?" asked Rudi.

"Yes." She reached for the door handle.

"Wait. We have to make it look realistic." He hit the gas, praying the car wouldn't clear the hole.

The engine roared and the vehicle jerked forward, the underside scraping on the ground, then stopping. Stuck solid.

They clambered out, Rudi leaving the engine running to help mask noises later. He also left the lights on so the vehicle was easy to spot.

Using a flashlight, Rudi scanned the ground. Marks from the skid arced across the road, and the area directly behind the vehicle was chewed up where the tires had fought to escape but failed. Excellent. It was obvious such an accident had occurred because the driver was racing away to escape.

He grabbed a coil of rope from the trunk, then snatched Inge's hand. "This way."

They ran toward town.

He'd told Inge the major elements of the plan, but not the fine details — there was no point burdening her with every problem. Nor every danger. Especially that one thing...

He shuddered at what they were going to have to do in only a few minutes. He'd never had the chance to test this element of his plan, though logic said it would work. However, theory and practice could be two terrifyingly different things, as war was only too eager to demonstrate to the naive. Unfortunately, they had no choice now. Whether he'd fully tested everything or not, this was their only path to freedom — a genuine leap of faith.

They raced along the road, passing the track on which he'd saved Darja, the tree from which he'd occasionally snapped off a branch for Bruno to chase, and a hedge in which he'd spied a song thrush building a nest. Passing... his life. All the while, he stared into the distance ahead, hoping Kloser's car wouldn't career toward them. If Kloser got word of the escape too soon, the plan would go to hell.

Small houses gave way to larger buildings, and finally, seventy yards ahead, Kloser's car came into view, still parked outside the hotel. Rudi heaved a sigh — they'd made it in time.

Panting, he pulled her behind a parked van. "You okay?"

She nodded, but fear creased her face.

He peeked around the side of the vehicle. The evening was typically serene, yet any second, chaos would erupt. He tied one end of the rope around his waist, then wrapped the other under Inge's arms and tied it over her chest. No way could she pull herself under the ice, so he'd be hauling them both.

Rudi checked his watch. He swallowed hard. "Thirty seconds."

Inge gripped his hand, her face drawn, eyes screaming panic.

She had to be terrified, never having faced armed conflict.

He squeezed her hand. "It's going to be okay. I promise."

While he didn't want to promise something he couldn't guarantee, he needed to keep her spirits up for her to be able to do all the things they needed to escape. Especially that one thing...

He shook his head. He couldn't think of that now. Couldn't let doubt cloud his mind. Only calmness and narrow-minded determination would see them still breathing in an hour's time.

Checking his watch again, he gulped. Time. He peeped around the van. Any second, the hotel door would fly open and Kloser and his entourage would hare out, Hofmann having phoned from the camp.

He lifted his hand holding hers. "Sorry, I need my hand now, but I'm staying right here beside you."

She nodded and released him. He drew his pistol. And a grenade.

Shouts in German sliced through the stillness. Rudi jerked around the side of the truck. Kloser, his driver Spengler, Baumann, and Gruber raced toward the car.

Rudi blasted four shots at the hotel, aiming high, and Kloser's gang dove for cover. He didn't want to hurt anyone, especially not Baumann, but he had to convince them they were in danger.

Shielding against the rear of the van, he waited, chest heaving, praying one of his primary assumptions was correct. If it wasn't, their plan would end right here, right now.

Shots slammed into the van. Inge clutched his arm and whimpered.

Kloser shouted, "Hold your fire! We want them alive, you darn fool."

Rudi blew out a noisy breath. Thank heaven his assumption was right.

A traitor to the Reich couldn't simply be shot. If possible, they needed to be hauled to Berlin, vilified in public, and executed before the biggest audience possible. A public beheading would boost morale and deter others who harbored sympathies for the Fatherland's enemies. And of course, catching such a traitor would be a huge career boost for the captor.

Rudi said, "We're going to have to run. Ready?"

"Say when."

He held up the grenade. "You'll know when."

Pulling her by the hand, he dodged from behind the truck and into clear view. Kloser's gang broke cover and ran at them.

Rudi unscrewed the grenade's blue knob, which was attached to the device by a cord, and yanked it to ignite the fuse. He hurled the projectile at two cars parked between them and their pursuers.

"Run!"

Inge and Rudi bolted back along the road.

The grenade exploded underneath a car, a gigantic roar tearing through the night. Bursting into flames, the vehicle flipped over in the air and crashed down a blazing wreck.

No longer holding hands, but connected by the rope, Rudi and Inge dashed along the road, arms and legs pumping hard. They raced past the thrush's nest, past Bruno's tree, past Darja's track...

The bridge reared into view smothered in darkness.

Something was wrong.

Rudi peered into the inky murk at the far side of the bridge. Where was Hofmann? Rudi had crippled the vehicles, but why hadn't the man sent out a search party on foot? Surely he wasn't wasting time by changing wheels, or worse, searching in the wrong direction. Whatever the problem, it was ruining the plan. Without Hofmann playing his role, everything fell apart.

At the bridge, they slowed.

"Where are they?" asked Inge.

Rudi stared, but only darkness crawled over the bridge.

Inge gripped his arm. "I thought you said they'd run here."

"I thought they would."

If Hofmann didn't arrive in time, the plan failed — why would he and Inge do what they were about to do when they still had a chance to escape?

From town, a gang of shadows raced toward them.

Rudi unscrewed the blue knob of another grenade. He had to delay Kloser. Had to pray Hofmann was coming.

Heaving his arm back, he hurled the grenade. It flew through the air and crashed down beyond the bridge. A deafening blast erupted and smoke billowed.

That would only delay Kloser for ten or twenty seconds or so. And Rudi only had one more grenade, having left the others in his bag for any later emergency.

Again, he squinted into the distance. No figures stormed out of the darkness.

Where was Hofmann? Where?

Back toward town, Kloser's gang scrambled out of the shadows again.

Inge clutched his arm. "Throw another grenade."

"I've only got one left."

"So throw it!"

He stared at the grenade. At its red knob. This wasn't an offensive weapon. With only a one-second fuse, it could explode even before he'd had the chance to throw it, so it would injure him and Inge.

"I can't. It'll explode in one second."

"One? So what use is it?"

He hadn't wanted to worry her, but he'd needed to plan for every eventuality – every single one. If they were to become trapped, with no escape, one second together was worth more than the rest of their short lives apart.

He said, "It was for us. If there was no way out."

Charging onward, Kloser was almost on the bridge. The other way... only darkness.

Inge gazed into his eyes. "So, is it time?"

He nodded. "I'm sorry, Inge, I thought we—" He gasped. At the far side of the bridge, faint beams of light arced through the night. Hofmann's men.

He grabbed her hand. "Come on."

They darted to the damaged spot on the bridge, then pulled up as Hofmann's men ran from the darkness. The other way, Kloser's gang slowed as they approached the bridge.

They were trapped.

Rudi gazed down at the jagged hole in the ice thirty-odd feet below, a rope resting across the middle and secured by the cog, barely visible in the dark. If he missed grabbing the rope, it was all over – they'd drown beneath the ice and be dragged out to sea.

326

Kloser shouted, "Give up, Rudi. You've nowhere to run."

His heart all but bursting out of his chest, Rudi held Inge's hands in his. "Do you trust me?"

"Of course." The lines on her face had melted away to reveal the face he loved — the face of courage, of kindness, of devotion.

Holding her right hand in his left, he shuffled toward the edge. "Take three big breaths."

He drew in and exhaled as much air as he could twice.

On the far end of the bridge, Kloser shouted, "There's nowhere left for you to run, Rudi, so stop this nonsense. I'll see you receive a fair hearing."

Kloser had treated Rudi well over the years, almost paternally, but with a desperate longing for advancement, he'd see this as an opportunity to further his career by catching a high-value traitor. Nothing else. Not that any of that mattered. Only one thing mattered now.

Toes hanging over the edge, Rudi smiled at Inge. "Ready?"

She nodded.

"Remember to let go of my hand when we hit the water." One last huge breath.

Kloser shouted, "Don't do it, Rudi. She's not worth it."

She was.

They leaped.

83

Inge and Rudi crashed into the water on either side of the rope. Rudi grabbed for it with both hands, latching on as they plummeted into the swirling gloom. Bubbles burst all around him, and the cold bit like a rabid dog savaging every inch of his body.

Before they'd even stopped sinking, Rudi clutched at the next knot in the rope and heaved. They had to be out of sight by the time Kloser reached the middle of the bridge and gazed into the hole.

Rudi hauled and hauled, hand over hand, as he floated up. His head hit the underside of the ice, but still he hauled. Inge was tethered six feet behind him — far enough that he wouldn't kick her — so he had only seconds to get her out of sight too.

Rudi ached to be able to look back to check on Inge, but he couldn't waste the time or the energy. His mind playing tricks, he pictured German boots stomping over the ice, a gun pointing down at them, a muzzle flash...

He heaved on faster. Desperate to get Inge safe.

On and on and on...

Rudi lunged and grabbed another knot. Blackness engulfed them now. Though terrifying, it meant they were under the bridge, where moonlight couldn't reach. If his plan was working, Kloser's gang would be tentatively making their way to the hole and then downstream — the opposite direction. Hofmann's men would be doing the same from the other side. Neither group would dream of investigating upstream. Why would they? The current dragged everything out to sea, and the cog ripped free by their impact would have sunk to submerge the rope. No one in their right mind would imagine he was swimming under the ice. No one would explore in this direction.

His biceps burning from exhaustion, body burning from cold, Rudi snagged the next handhold and heaved, but in the bitter conditions, his extremities were already numbing. He lost his grip and the current snatched them.

He kicked and kicked, struggling to grasp the rope again, but with his waterlogged clothes and Inge dragging him backward, the woven material slipped through his frozen fingers.

Biting blackness engulfed him.

Frantically, he clutched and clutched at the rope. But each time, his grip failed. He couldn't fail Inge. Couldn't. This was all his idea. If she'd never met him, she was strong enough that she'd have had a good chance of surviving the war. *So he'd killed her.* As good as putting a bullet in her head.

The tether around his waist jerked repeatedly. Inge had to know something was wrong and was panicking, flailing like a drowning woman. If only she'd been able to practice here instead of in the water butt. His first practice when he'd struggled to grasp the rope securely flashed into his mind — that was the answer.

He kicked his right leg until the rope wrapped around it. With so much extra weight, he wasn't strong enough to pull them with his arms, even while kicking, but maybe he could "climb" the rope with his hands and feet combined.

His lungs screaming, but all four limbs heaving on the rope, he hauled forward again. Inch by inch, foot by foot, he pulled them upstream, the hungry current relentlessly battling to drag them out to the sea.

But the tether no longer jerked. He daren't think what that might mean. Not for one second. Inge was going to live. Live.

Finally, the darkness devouring them gave way to a murky gloom as the bridge passed overhead and moonlight once more caressed the ice.

The glimmer of hope and how close they were to air energized Rudi, and he heaved and heaved. He could still save Inge. *If* she was still — no, she *was* alive. *Alive!*

Knot after knot, he pulled himself closer to a rectangle of light — the upstream hole. His diaphragm pleading to breathe, lungs on fire, and muscles screeching, he heaved and heaved.

Just a little farther.

Just a couple more feet.

Just one more good pull...

Rudi broke the surface. He gasped a gigantic breath. Though his arms and legs begged for rest, he hauled himself toward the far side of the hole where he'd staked the rope into the ice. Inge had to be alive. Had to be.

His muscles crying out, he couldn't even look back but had to pull ever onward. Was she alive? Please, Lord, let her be alive.

A moment later, splashing arms broke the surface and desperate lungs gulped air.

Rudi ached to shout for joy but instead whispered, "Grab the rope."

One hand holding the metal stake, he swished the rope toward her.

Spluttering, she pawed at it but couldn't grip. "I-I c-c-can't—" She gulped water and coughed.

"Shhh." A car engine revved nearby, and shouts came from the other side of the bridge, but he couldn't see anything for the snowbank he'd molded to hide this hole from downstream. How close were Kloser and Hofmann? If they heard Inge, all this would be for nothing — he and Inge would be in chains within minutes.

As Rudi clambered from the water, the tether automatically pulled Inge to the edge of the hole. She flung her arms onto the ice but didn't have the strength to climb out. He heaved her up. She collapsed, shivering, panting.

Rudi dared to sneak a peek over the snowbank. Silhouetted against the river of ice, men marched away, spread out to cover the whole width, flashlight beams slicing into the darkened banks and murky depths.

"Thank God," said Rudi. He uprooted the stake securing the rope and threw it into the river. It sank, dragging the rope down with it to leave no trace.

"We have to go."

"I c-can't m-move." She shook uncontrollably, just like he had the first time he'd done this.

"We can get warm, but we have to get away from here."

On his stomach, he slithered toward the riverbank, dragging Inge along while the snowbank hid them. With the willow's drooping branches as cover, Rudi dared to stand. He helped Inge to her feet, then supported her as they staggered up the bank and across an expanse of wasteland. They lumbered over the desolate road, through some bushes, and into a field.

Stumbling across the rutted ground, Rudi constantly glanced back at the river. So far, the flashlights were heading away from them, but they had to get away as quickly as possible in case that changed.

Inge lost her footing and fell. Rudi caught her as she crumpled to her knees.

"I've got you." He heaved to help her up, but it was like trying to lift a sack of water.

"R-R-Rudi, I c-can't. I'm so-so c-cold."

"You can. Come on."

"N-no. L-leave me."

"Inge, I'm not leaving you, so if they catch you, they catch me. Is that what you want?"

She shook her head.

"So move." He heaved again. This time, she managed to stand.

Again, he glanced around. Still no flashlights headed their way.

Dragging Inge more than supporting her, Rudi hobbled on. They couldn't be in the open like this. It was too suspicious. If one of the locals saw them, that could cause as many problems as if the Germans did.

His legs shaking with cold and the effort, they gave way and he fell, pulling Inge down.

They both lay, shivering, gasping, frozen.

Rudi said, "We have to"— pant —"have to"— pant —"go." Pushing onto all fours, he grimaced but hauled himself to his feet. He swayed and almost fell again but saved himself, then reached a hand down to Inge. "Come on."

She shook her head.

"Inge, please."

"I"— gasp —"c-can't."

"You can. Please."

"Y-you go." She panted. "Save y-yourself."

"I'm not going without you."

"You"— pant —"must."

"No." He grabbed her. With all his might, he heaved her into his arms. His legs trembled and he almost fell as he took his first step, but he caught his footing and staggered on. They stumbled away into the darkness.

Finally, a glimmer of hope reared out of the shadows — the hideout he'd rented. Carrying Inge, Rudi lumbered toward the barn where he'd rescued Darja. He sat Inge against the wall while he fumbled with the padlock he'd fitted to the door, his hands so frozen he couldn't slot the key into the hole for shaking.

Finally unlocking the door, he eased it open and dragged Inge to a bed of hay he'd created earlier and stripped her to her underwear. He draped a blanket over her, then gave her one of the hot water bottles he'd dropped off on his way back from the restaurant.

Shaking violently, she hugged it.

From one of the other supply bags, he took two stoves that soldiers used in the field. Placing them on a large stone slab so as not to set fire to the barn, he lit them for Inge.

With Inge taken care of, he stripped, grabbed a hot water bottle, and swathed himself in a blanket. He dragged his bag over and poured hot soup from a vacuum flask. He cupped the container to Inge's mouth. She sipped. The bottle, stove, and soup taking effect, she grasped the cup in her shaking hands and drank by herself.

Finally, Rudi huddled over the fire. He smiled, watching Inge gradually coming back to life. Maybe they were going to make it after all.

84

The wind howled over the frozen sea. Inge clawed her coat tighter and trudged on beside Rudi. Despite her fur-lined boots and her two pairs of socks, the cold bit into her feet.

She'd wanted to stay swathed in blankets in the barn longer, but to escape this cruel world, they had a dawn rendezvous to make, so down the frozen river they'd trekked.

Inge glanced back. Darkness shrouded the coastline, all but obscuring the radio mast and the mouth of the river, the two landmarks between which they had to stay to reach the rendezvous point. If they strayed off that line, they'd be lost in the frozen wilderness.

Inge slogged on. Ahead lay only ice and darkness. Miles and miles and miles of it. Beyond, Finland lay hidden, and even farther away, Sweden with its promise of sanctuary. She squinted, straining to see some faint outline, some tiny hint that salvation might be within reach. Blackness.

Could Rudi see something she couldn't? Or were they already lost? She trudged on.

And the wind howled. And the ice bit.

Inge was sure there was a time in her life that she hadn't been shivering, but since the river, she couldn't remember what that felt like. It was as if the cold had burrowed inside her and was eating its way back out.

She hauled herself on. Farther and farther into the ice-strewn wasteland.

Inge stumbled, panting, muscles crying out for rest more than any day at the quarry or trench. Were they even going the right way?

Dragging her feet, she plodded on. But she caught her foot in a crevice. She crashed to the ice.

Rudi dashed over.

"I"— gasp —"I'm done."

"No, you can do it." He hauled her up. She didn't have the strength to protest. Arm around her, he heaved her onward.

They hobbled farther.

Rudi pointed. "There!"

Narrowing her eyes, she peered into the darkness.

Nothing.

"Can you see it?" he asked.

She shook her head.

He jabbed his finger and smiled. "There. We've done it, Inge."

They headed in that direction. Maybe the cold of the river had damaged her eyes because she couldn't see a thing. Or maybe she was seeing what was really there – nothing – and the cold had made Rudi delusional.

But she lumbered on. They had no choice.

She clutched her mouth as a shadow reared up from the ice. "I can see it. Rudi, I can see it!"

"I told you. We've made it, Inge."

"Can you see Kaspar or his dogs?"

If there was a team of huskies preparing for a day's work, wouldn't they be making noise?

"There's a couple of hours till dawn, so he's probably not here yet."

Hope powering weary muscles, they lurched quicker.

The moonlight revealed a large fishing boat with a mast fore and aft, a funnel towering between them. A two-level structure rose from the middle of the deck, probably the bridge, while a one-level block ran to the stern. Trapped in the ice, the vessel was tilted to one side in complete darkness.

Seeing the name on the bow, Inge pointed. "*Estonian Princess*. This is it." She grinned. She quickened her pace but pulled up – Rudi had stopped.

"Come on!" She beckoned. "It's freezing."

He stared at the snow covering the ice. At three or four sets of partially covered footprints. All people; not a single dog.

Oh dear Lord. Please don't say one of the search parties had made it this far out. But surely if they had, they'd have searched the vessel, found it deserted, and so moved on.

He shook his head. "I don't like this. I need to look around."

"For what? No one's here."

"You said you trusted me, so trust me now."

They shuffled around the vessel, Rudi alternating between scouring the ground and scrutinizing the boat. When they reached the place where they'd started, he again shook his head.

He said, "Something's not right. Tracks lead to the boat, but none lead away."

"How fresh are they?"

He shrugged. "I'm not a tracker."

"Maybe the snow's covered them."

"If someone had come and gone, the ones leading away would be the freshest, so why would snow cover those and not the earlier ones?"

Inge gulped. That did make sense. She peered at the shadowy vessel. Had they gone through this hell only for everything to fall apart now? "What now? Go back?"

"We came here because we couldn't risk going into town. There's nowhere to go back to."

Inge said, "Was Kaspar bringing anyone else?"

"Not that I know of."

"Could there have been a problem, so we're meeting the dogs somewhere else?"

Again Rudi shrugged.

"So what are we going to do?"

Rudi rubbed his brow, scrutinizing the prints. "You know, maybe you're right. The wind's blowing this way, so it's possible someone approached the boat from this side, which sheltered their footprints, but then left from the far side, where the full brunt of the wind covered their tracks."

"Really?"

He stared at the boat.

No light came from the windows, no smoke climbed from the funnel, no sound came from inside. Yet, for the first time she could recall, fear lined Rudi's face. He said, "There's nowhere else for us to go."

"So we risk it?" She nodded to the boat.

He drew his pistol. "Stay behind me."

They crept toward the vessel.

A cargo net hung over the side at the bow, probably what the crew had used to escape once the boat had become ice-locked.

They clambered aboard and stood lopsided on the sloping deck. The wind cried and the ice creaked. Shadows drenched the boat and icicles hung from all the edges like macabre festival decorations.

Across the deck, the wind was creating a drift, hiding any footprints that may have been present.

Inge shivered, but not from the cold. There was something not right about this modern-day *Mary Celeste*. They crept along, leaning at an angle, heading for the bridge section.

The ghostly boat groaned in its icy embrace. Inge's heart pounded. It didn't seem like anyone was on board, but if that was the case, why were the hairs bristling on the back of her neck?

Unfortunately, this was their only chance to escape, so they had no option but to go on.

The porthole in the bridge section's door revealed little but a short hallway. Nothing was visible inside the one-level structure because blankets covered the portholes, as if the crew had tried to block out drafts once they'd become stranded.

The hinges squealed as Rudi opened the door to the hallway. They stalked inside. A steep staircase disappeared upward, presumably to the wheelhouse, and a door led to the one-level structure.

Rudi held an index finger to his lips.

Inge gulped. Every ounce of her being screamed to run, to run and never look back. But to run where?

He took out a grenade. He unscrewed the blue knob, ready to activate it, then slowly turned the door handle. He eased the door open with his shoulder and drew his pistol with his other hand.

Blackness greeted them inside. But not only blackness.

"Hello, Rudi. Excuse us crashing your little going-away party."

Kloser.

Inge froze. Fear clawed her spine like a cat clawing drapes.

It was over.

The tiniest of flames in a kerosene lamp flickered brighter as Kloser turned it up, and dim yellow light smeared the sloping room. Hinged bunks lined the walls, all hoisted vertically, transforming sleeping quarters into a mess hall in which stood benches and tables.

"Drop the gun," said Kloser.

The sound of something sliding over wood came from behind Inge. She jumped. Gruber slid down the staircase by holding the rail on either side under his arms. His feet slammed into the floor and he leveled a revolver at her. He gestured for them to enter the room.

She clutched Rudi's side. It really was the end.

They shuffled inside.

336

Emptiness gripped her, and like a person being strangled, she felt her future, her dreams, her life with Rudi drifting into darkness.

Kloser sat in the far right corner of the room near another door, Spengler in the left, his rifle trained on Rudi. The eerie gloom, the slanting interior, the faces drenched in demonic shadows... it was like a horror sideshow in a traveling fair. Except this was not entertainment, this was life or death.

"The gun, Rudi. There's a good fellow."

Gruber cocked his revolver, aiming at Inge's head.

She clutched Rudi tighter. Rudi had found a way out of every situation, no matter how dire, but even he couldn't shoot three men spread out across a room before they shot him. There was no escape.

Rudi dropped his pistol and it clattered to the floor. He raised his hands above his head.

Kloser smirked.

Rudi chuckled.

"Something funny, Oberscharführer? The prospect of being beheaded for treason is entertaining, is it?"

Rudi smiled. "There'll be no beheading."

"Is that so?" Kloser arched an eyebrow.

Over his head, Rudi brought his hands together, to hold the grenade in one and its blue knob in the other. "This is a four-second fuse. Either you toss your weapons over and let us walk out of here or we all enjoy a burial at sea."

Inge pressed against him. Maybe there was hope yet. Or maybe this was their last few seconds on earth together. Either way, she wasn't moving. The Germans had stolen her family, her future, and her life — they weren't separating her from Rudi too.

Standing, Kloser glanced at the open doorway behind him.

Rudi shrugged. "Be my guest. But in only four seconds, can you get far enough away? Because if the blast doesn't kill you, shrapnel wounds this far from help sure as hell will."

Gruber cocked his revolver against Inge's head.

She flinched.

Rudi said, "If you take her, Gruber, I've nothing to lose, so I'll pin you down and ram this grenade in your mouth."

Kloser raised his palms, his cocky tone becoming placatory. "Easy, Rudi. We can all walk away from this."

He gestured to his men to drop their weapons.

Spengler threw his rifle. It skidded across the floor to Rudi's feet. Gruber dropped his and moved over to join Kloser.

Kloser said, "You know there's nowhere the Reich won't find you."

"Your weapon, Kommandant," said Rudi.

Kloser slung a pistol over.

Without taking his eyes off his ex-comrades, Rudi said, "Inge, collect the guns."

Clinging to him, her breath coming in short pants, she didn't want to let go.

"Inge! The guns."

She jolted, as if waking from a dream. Crouching, she picked up the four guns and scurried back behind him.

Rudi said over his shoulder, "The door."

Shuffling backward, they made for the door, Rudi holding the grenade up as if a shield.

The soldiers edged toward the rear door.

"No one move," said Rudi.

Inge didn't know what was beyond that door. Maybe the soldiers would be safe from the blast, even from the shrapnel, but it didn't matter because she had all the guns. Without weapons, they were no threat.

They stepped into the hall. Rudi glared at Kloser. "I've more grenades, so if you try to follow us, there's only one way this is going to end."

Inge whispered, "Can't we keep them hostage and wait for Kaspar?"

"Kaspar's the only person who knew we were meeting here."

"But how did they find him?"

Rudi groaned. "Oh, dear Lord, the vodka."

"What?"

"Doesn't matter. We're on our own." He nodded to the door ot the deck. "Go."

She exited and held the door for him.

Her jaw dropped as Rudi tugged the blue knob and tossed the grenade inside the mess hall. "Run!"

They raced outside and shot for the bow. Rudi grabbed her and dove. They slammed into the deck.

A massive blast rocked the boat, and the portholes burst outward, glass slicing into the night.

Smoke billowed into the darkness as Rudi scrambled up, then hauled Inge to her feet. She bent to pick up the guns that had scattered across the deck, but Rudi pushed her. "Leave them. Run."

338

They bolted for the bow. Gripping the top of the cargo net, she slung one leg over to climb down.

A single shot cracked the silence, and what felt like a hammer slammed pain into Inge's chest.

Rudi screamed, "No!"

She reached for him, but her legs gave. She toppled over the side of the boat, glimpsing Kloser smirking with a tiny smoking pistol — the kind cowards hid in their boots.

Inge crashed onto the ice. Lying on her back, she gazed up at the stars. She gasped the tiniest of gasps, three or four seconds passed, then another tiny gasp and more seconds. Gunfire and flashes came from the boat. She tried to push up, to run to help Rudi, but she couldn't move.

Was she dying?

She'd always imagined death would involve agony and despair and wailing. But this...? This felt like drifting to sleep.

Rudi appeared. He crouched beside her, his cheek smeared with blood. He cupped her face. "Don't worry, I've got you."

Her eyes widened as another bloodied face leaned over the side of the boat. Kloser.

Her voice faint, she said, "R-r-run."

"I'm not leaving you." He shoved his arms under her and lifted. "Rudi, r-run."

"It's going to be okay, I've got you."

Another shot blasted.

Rudi stumbled. Blood spluttered from his mouth. He managed two more steps, then fell. They crunched into the unforgiving ice.

His head on her shoulder, he said, "I'm s-sorry, Inge."

Her hand shaking with the effort, she reached to hug him.

He fumbled in his coat, then raised his hand, but it slumped onto her chest. It held a grenade with a red knob.

She'd seen him throw enough of these to know how they worked. It was time.

Trembling, she unscrewed the red knob.

He said, "One second."

Finding strength she didn't know she possessed, she kissed him on the forehead. "I love you."

"I love you."

She yanked the knob.

Berlin, 1944

The mustachioed man's jaw dropped. He slumped back so sharply in the blue armchair that his cup and saucer rattled in his hand. "Oh, my stars, what a story."

Kloser nodded. "One heck of an adventure, yes."

"And that wonderful Unterscharführer Gruber, please tell me he survived the grenade explosion on the boat, too."

"He did, yes. The bulkhead was metal, so after we dove through the door, the blast was harmless." Kloser snickered. "Well, apart from not being able to hear properly for a week."

His host clutched his chest. "Thank goodness. It really cuts me when our brave warriors are sliced down in their prime." He wagged a finger. "But it's a pity there was nothing left of the bodies. I'd have loved to exhibit those outside the Reichstag as a deterrent for other Jew sympathizers."

Kloser shrugged. "Alas, because of the grenade..."

"Still, justice was done, which is what matters. But how did you know about the boat?"

"Ah, once we discovered the river subterfuge, we dragged all those who could've helped Rudi from their beds — the jeweler, the banker, the vodka brewer, the ice harvester — and with a little, shall we say, 'encouragement,' the third one confessed everything."

The host smirked. "It's funny, isn't it, how it's so often the third time you attempt something that you succeed?"

"It is, yes."

"But I wonder if that's really the case. For example, if my car starts the first time, I think nothing of it, or if it starts the second go, again, nothing. But if it starts the third time, I think, *Third time lucky again,* when in truth, there was nothing unusual at all. The event was made unusual solely by my skewed view of reality."

It was no surprise his host commanded the respect he did — his analytical powers were astounding. "Yes, I'm sure that's probably true."

"Probably? Oh, it is. And anyone who challenges me on it will be in Auschwitz by suppertime." He smirked again, a twinkle in his eye so devilish, Kloser didn't know if he was being serious or joking.

His host stood. "Well, it's been an absolute delight listening to your tale, but I'm afraid duty calls."

Kloser jumped up. "Of course."

The mustachioed man held out his hand. Kloser grasped it and shook.

The man said, "It's thanks to heroes like you that the Fatherland is sure to vanquish its enemies. How could we not when it's proven time and again that we're the superior race? Congratulations again, Obersturmführer Kloser. Wear your medal with pride."

Kloser clicked his heels. "Thank you, mein Führer."

Rural Sweden, 1969

Sitting in her green armchair at her fireside, Annika Magnusson marveled at the black-and-white picture on the front cover of *Sweden Today* — an American in a spacesuit stood in a barren wasteland beneath a black sky, the lunar module reflected in his visor.

Annika flipped the page as crackling logs bathed her room in an orangey glow. The human race had difficulty managing one world, now it was expanding to another? Heaven help the cosmos.

As she paged through, the two missing fingers on her left hand tingled, a visit from ghosts of the past. She flexed the hand a few times until the feeling disappeared. Diving under the ice had been brutal, but it had been nothing compared to the snowstorm that had hit them while crossing the frozen sea on the dog sled. Thank heaven for their expert guide, or it wouldn't have been only a couple of fingers she'd lost to frostbite.

She skimmed the paper: a politician speaking about economic policy; the newly established Swedish Immigration Board; some sportsman who'd been caught with a woman who wasn't his wife... a photograph made her freeze. She stared at beady eyes, chubby jowls, and a barrel chest — Kloser. Annika smirked. A cold prison cell would feel very different from the horse ranch in Argentina from which he'd been dragged.

The article described the culmination of a trial stretching over weeks in the House of the People, Jerusalem, Israel, the building in which Adolf Eichmann had been convicted.

Annika frowned and reread a section aloud. "Iron Cross recipient Franz Kloser garnered fame to rocket up the SS ranks by executing Heinz Rudolf Kruse, his traitorous underling, and Inge Zaleska, a Jewish prisoner. The couple had fallen in love and attempted a daring escape together, only to be betrayed by local man Kaspar Tilga, which led to them being gunned down in a blazing battle aboard an ice-locked ship."

A gunfight on a boat? Annika snorted. "Yeah, right."

If only there had been a boat so they could have sheltered from that nightmare blizzard. She might still have ten fingers.

And Tilga? Wasn't he the guy who'd given Rudi vodka?

What on earth did he have to do with their escape?

She shook her head. What lies Kloser must have told to "rocket" him up the ranks. Rudi had said someone might concoct an elaborate tale for their own gain, and thank heaven Kloser had or the whole world might never have stopped looking for Inge and Rudi.

Annika scanned the names of the survivors who'd given testimony at the trial. Her lips curled upward at one: Greta Rosenberg.

Guilt had gnawed at Annika over letting others do the dirty work while she avoided it at all costs. But she couldn't risk them being drawn into the limelight, couldn't risk anyone learning their secrets, couldn't risk a trial and an overly zealous tribunal taking away the love of her life despite the good he'd done. No, Inge and Rudi had died that night. And they had to stay dead. Forever. It meant they'd each had to sacrifice searching for any surviving family, which was an unthinkable price to pay, but true happiness never came cheap.

She read on. Presiding Judge Yitzhak Halevi gave the verdict of the Jerusalem District Court's special tribunal: the death penalty under the Nazis and Nazi Collaborators Punishment Law of 1950.

Gruber had been convicted at Nuremberg in 1946, but for decades, it had appeared Kloser was going to get away with his crimes. Now, twenty-four years after the war, justice was going to be done.

She smiled, caressed by a warmth that didn't come from the fireplace. Finally.

But should she say anything? Should she allow that nightmare to haunt them one last time?

The front door banged open, and boisterous male voices shattered her solitude.

A teenage boy laughed, his hair as fair as his father's. He jabbed a finger at the man. "Double or quits tomorrow."

Lars Magnusson guffawed. "That works out great for you, but what's in it for me if I win?"

Erik laughed. "The warm glow of believing you're not past it." He ambled over and kissed Annika on the cheek. "Hi, Mama."

343

She stroked his hair. "Go wash up. Dinner's in fifteen minutes."

Lars sniggered. "Past it? I'll show you who's past it." He lunged for Erik, who dodged and scuttled away, giggling.

"Hey." Lars kissed Annika too. "Your son is getting to be quite a handful."

"Oh, *my* son?" Gazing wistfully at him, she caressed the tiny crescent-shaped scar under his left eye. Even after all these years, he was still just as handsome.

He placed a letter with Estonian stamps in her lap. "From Peeter."

"Yes?"

"They've booked tickets for the twenty-second, so they'll be here in time. Great, huh?"

"Fantastic, yes."

A visit from the Erm clan was always an event. But this one would be even more special — Peeter would attend his godson's birthday party. Giving Peeter the honor of being godfather was the least they could do after he'd given them... everything. After all, who better to guide them over treacherous ice than a man who made ice his living?

Lars frowned. "Everything okay?"

"Uh-huh."

"We haven't seen them since February, so I thought you'd be pleased they could make the party."

"I am. It's nothing."

He smirked. "After all these years, don't you think I can tell when '*It's nothing*' means '*It's something*'?"

"It's just me being stupid. Forget it."

"So we're good?"

She tossed the newspaper onto the fire and smiled. "Couldn't be better."

The End.

If you enjoyed *To Dream of Shadows*, you need to read *A Song of Silence*, also inspired by a true story...

War thrust them together. Love will tear them apart.

When the Nazis invade a sleepy Polish town in 1939, Mirek Kozlowski swears to keep everyone in his orphanage safe at all costs.

However, despite his struggles and sacrifices, the war drags him and his children deeper and deeper into its violent nightmare. With 89 children looking to him for hope, Mirek must do whatever it takes to protect them — no matter how criminal, distasteful, or perilous it may be.

And just when he thinks things can't get any worse, the arrival of a sadistic SS captain brings unspeakable atrocities to his town — and surprisingly, a glimmer of hope for Mirek to save all those he cares about if only he has the courage to grasp it...

A story of love, bravery, and compassion, A *Song of Silence* explores how, even in the face of overwhelming evil, one man can become a dazzling beacon of light.

Discover what it means to be human. Discover A *Song of Silence.*

www.stevenleebooks.com/song

Behind the Scenes with Steve

You're known for your heartwarming dog stories and fast-paced thrillers, so Historical Fiction is a huge change of genre. Was it easy to write such a different kind of book?

Yes and no. Inge's journey is an emotional roller coaster, incorporating some genuinely nail-biting scenes. I already had well-developed writing chops for action and suspense from penning my thrillers, but it was my *Books for Dog Lovers Series* that proved to be the key because it let me explore another way of connecting with readers — on a much deeper emotional level by combining heartwarming and heartbreaking storylines simultaneously. Without this contrasting combination of writing styles, I'd never have been able to do this story justice. It's as if those books prepared me for this one.

How did you discover the story?

In 2019, I visited Tallinn in Estonia with my partner, Ania. One of the sights we explored was an old prison called Patarei that the Germans had used during the war. In one room hung a placard with just 404 words on it that described how a German commandant and a Jewish prisoner had fallen in love so deeply that they'd tried to escape together. I pointed it out to Ania and said it would make an incredible movie.

Did you do a lot of research?

Months. Literally. I've visited Auschwitz, explored numerous museums in Poland, communicated with various institutions, and read more books and watched more documentaries and survivor testimonies than I can recall.

Because my book deals with the Holocaust, I wanted to get every detail right, not least to be respectful to those who didn't make it through that horrendous period — including some of Ania's extended family. The research was far harder than I'd figured though because the tiny details of everyday life just aren't easy to find.

Can you give an example of the kind of thing that caused problems?

Roll call. Most stories set in a concentration camp mention roll call, but I've yet to find one that actually describes it instead of simply brushing over it. Clogs is another. Many books say prisoners were forced to wear clogs, but when I think of a clog from that era, I picture a block of wood that's been hollowed out so your foot can slip inside it. That's not what camp clogs were. Again, I've never seen this explained in any novel, so readers simply picture a wooden shoe, which is wrong (a more apt description would be a very basic wooden flip-flop).

A writer who brushes over such things misleads their reader so is doing that reader a great disservice. Yes, it's difficult to uncover the facts, but not doing so is a cop-out. I was determined not to do that, so I pushed and pushed until I found all my answers.

Another problem is that there wasn't an "average" experience for prisoners because different camps instituted different procedures and regulations. Which isn't surprising considering there were nearly one thousand concentration camps and subcamps. Some of the big differences are that not all camps made prisoners wear blue-and-white stripes, food rations were different (though never adequate), not all prisoners were shaved, and security levels could be anything from super high to relatively lax (not that prisoners had anywhere to run away to).

Was telling this true story straightforward?

Yeah, right! There's virtually nothing known about the real commandant/prisoner story. Seriously, nothing. A number of websites mention it, and the odd nonfiction publication has a passage or two, but they all regurgitate the same few facts. I found a number of firsthand survivor testimonies, but even they didn't contain much. The story was simply never properly documented.

It took forever to piece their story together — a snippet from a testimony, a few lines in a text, a hint on a website... forever! I created the most comprehensive biography of them ever produced, but it was nowhere near enough for a novel. (You can get it free — see below.)

*So your *story* isn't their *story*?*

Most of the main elements of the true story are mirrored in some way in my book — Inge arriving in Estonia, separation from her family, incarceration in a prison, suffering slave labor, transfer to a camp, working as a cook for the commandant, falling in love, escaping... it's all there, and more. However, none of those events were properly documented, so I took the bare bones of the true story as an outline and fleshed it out by fictionalizing it. That was the only way to share this incredible tale.

347

All said and done, I'm writing a novel to entertain, not a biography to educate.

"Fleshed it out by fictionalizing it." Did that involve major changes?

Just like in my book, the real-life heroine was compassionate and strove to help her fellow prisoners, but the big difference is that she was beautiful. I didn't want our Inge to be stunning because it seemed too "Hollywood" — a man changes his wicked ways because of a beautiful woman? No, thank you! So I gave Inge dazzling eyes and cheekbones, but nothing else. I wanted Rudi to fall for Inge, not Inge's body. Love not lust. The easiest way was to give her relatively average looks, but to give her a beautiful mind.

However, there was one particular character trait it was crucial to keep — the real-life heroine was a proper smart-mouth! She must have known of the danger that would put her in when dealing with Nazis, but she was simply too courageous and righteous to care. That meant our Inge had to be mouthy too, which made her fun to write.

The biggest difference was Rudi, because he's a real hero in his own right. Yes, he's SS, but he questions the poison he's been fed and fights to change things — crucially, before meeting Inge. This is hugely different from the real commandant, who was typical SS. Falling in love transformed him, but before meeting Inge, he was brutal toward the prisoners and continued to be so for some time after her arrival. He did change significantly in the end, but not enough to fully redeem himself.

How about things like the trench, the quarry, the Box, the frozen sea...? Were they all invented, too?

Good grief, no. All of those were based on documented fact. All I did was to create a fictitious camp and prison and relocate things from their real counterparts.

For example, the prison is based on Patarei, but I wanted to explore things that wouldn't be possible if Inge was held there. For instance, most work in Patarei consisted of the women rebuilding the bombed harbor. I wanted something more interesting than a "building site," so as there were real antitank trenches near the city which prisoners probably worked on, I used them.

Also, prisoners did slave in Estonian quarries, so I created one for my story based on the one in Mauthausen, which had a huge stone staircase known as the "Stairs of Death." I used that one because there's information available about it, but virtually nothing about Estonian quarries.

As for the sea – in some winters, it does freeze between Estonia and Finland. The last time being 2003.

So, yes, everything was based on documented evidence.

Everything? Surely the Box wasn't real?
It wasn't just real but worse than I described. If a prisoner survived the nails and being rolled around, when they were eventually released, dogs were set upon them to finish the job. I didn't include that because even though it's true, it felt gratuitous. Plus, I didn't think readers would believe it because it's so over-the-top. I worried they'd think I'd strayed so far into fiction that I was almost glamorizing the Holocaust.

Did the real couple escape just like Inge and Rudi?
No one knows the truth. The common belief is that they died in one of three ways:
> they were caught and executed
> they were killed in a gunfight
> with the guards closing in, the commandant shot her, then himself.

Literally no one knows. However, some people believe that the couple successfully escaped, which, while improbable, is possible because no bodies were recovered to prove they'd been caught. We're relying solely on the word of a handful of SS monsters.

So, we can only guess at what really happened. Yet even if they did escape, it was probably in a covert way. But again, that's a guess – it could have been a blazing gun battle that would put Hollywood to shame. It's not like the SS would ever have admitted to that happening, is it?

Why is being respectful so important to you?
Firstly, because of the people who suffered that hellish period of our history.

Secondly, because Ania is Polish. Her grandfather survived the camps, as did her stepfather, but some of her relatives didn't. I met her grandfather a few times. It's hard to imagine that such a kind and gentle man had witnessed such unspeakable things.

None of my family fought in WWII, but my paternal grandfather fought the Germans in World War I. He was gassed in the trenches on the Western Front and spent the rest of his life with only one functioning lung.

It's because of Ania's heritage and my granddad that I feel comfortable writing about this period.

What's next?
A *Song of Silence*, which is also inspired by a true story. It follows one man's struggle to protect his children in a small town orphanage when the Germans invade. It's a moving tale of courage, love, and the strength of the human spirit.

Is it just as heartbreaking yet uplifting, with a twist at the end?
Would I give you anything else?

Use this link to lose yourself in A *Song of Silence*:
www.stevenleebooks.com/song

***

Discover the true story in a FREE & EXCLUSIVE ebook.

You will not find a more comprehensive account anywhere. Literally! This ebook has ten times the information available elsewhere. (Wikipedia's entry is only 431 words and does not include vital information such as the prison, Inge's family and what became of them, when and where she was born...)

If you want the true story in full, you need *The Story Behind the Story*. In this book, you will:

> discover the real couple behind Inge and Rudi
> learn how the story started out as something completely different
> see photos from Steve's personal collection of the real prison in which Inge stayed
> enjoy a revealing extended interview with Steve
> find unique artwork to show how the cover evolved
> and uncover much, much more.

Use this link to get your free ebook:
www.stevenleebooks.com/inge

As The Stars Fall

A Desperate Dog. A Scarred Girl. A Bond Nothing Can Break.

An injured, young dog trudges the city streets, trembling from cold, from fear, from lack of food. Battered by the howling wind, he searches desperately for his lost family, yet day after day, week after week, all he ever finds is heartbreaking loneliness. But then, one magical spring morning...

Across town, a little girl sobs into her pillow in the dead of night. Her life devastated by a family tragedy, she can't understand how the world can just carry on. Her days once overflowed with childhood joys, yet now, despair, darkness, and emptiness smother her like a shroud. But then, one magical spring morning...

... the dog and the girl meet.

Read *As The Stars Fall*. Use this link:
www.stevenleebooks.com/stars

Crime Thrillers

⭐☆☆☆☆ Karen Bryan   ⭐☆☆☆☆ J. Alexander   ⭐☆☆☆☆ Stephen Crowe
"Absolutely loved it!"   "Fast-paced and action-packed"   "Bloody fantastic"

If you enjoy dark, fast-paced thrillers laced with gritty realism, you'll love my action-packed *Angel of Darkness Series*.

★★★★★ *"Fast-paced and action-packed, it takes you on a ride you don't want to stop!"* J. Alexander

★★★★★ *"Reacher fans should enjoy this ... a thrill-packed adrenaline rush."* AJ Norton

★★★★★ *"A good fast-paced read with a fabulous female lead."* Julie Elizabeth Powell

★★★★★ *"Fast paced thriller with suspense packed onto every page. Loved it."* Michael Miller

★★★★★ *"Gripping stuff — I couldn't put this one down, read it in one go."* Jan Simmons

Dive into this pulse-pounding action series today with this link:
www.stevenleebooks.com/angel

Book Club Questions

1. At the beginning of the book, Inge has experienced little of the world. What are the main ways in which she changes during the story?

2. Do you appreciate Rudi's internal struggle? Do you believe many Germans struggled like this but were powerless to make meaningful change?

3. Before they meet, Inge and Rudi both suffer horrendous loss. Can discovering love can play a role in the healing process, and if so, how?

4. A turning point in the story is Rudi witnessing Inge feed a bird. What are the other major turning points?

5. How many acts of courage and of kindness can you identify in the story? Which were the most important ones?

6. Explain why you believe Inge was right or wrong to give up Bruno's killers?

7. If the war had never happened, but Inge and Rudi had met, would they have ended up together?

8. Has *To Dream of Shadows* revealed aspects of the Holocaust that you were unaware of and if so, which ones?

9. If you had been deported, would you have survived? Could you have been a kapo who beat people for a better chance of survival?

10. As a starving prisoner, would you have eaten Bruno? Explain your reasoning.

11. If you hadn't known the book was inspired by a true story, would you have believed it, especially about genuine love between a prisoner and a commandant?

12. Do you have a favorite quote, passage, or theme?

13. If this book becomes a movie, who should play Inge and Rudi?

14. What lasting impression has the book left you with? Is it positive or negative, hopeful or despairing, uplifted or saddened?

Made in the USA
Las Vegas, NV
25 October 2023

79684725R10208